WHERE THE DARKNESS FOUND ME

COURTNEY YOUNG

To anyone who's ever felt invisible,
To those who search for themselves in the darkness,
To the brave hearts who rise, even when they can't see the light.
May you find peace in your journey,
and the courage to tell your own story.
To my husband, Rob, and our sons, Axel and Trent
your love and support are my light.

"Once upon a time, I thought monsters lived under my bed. I didn't know they could live in my phone, wearing the words 'I love you' like a mask."

TRIGGER WARNINGS

Your well-being matters. This story explores difficult themes rooted in real-life experiences. Please take a moment to review the content warnings below. If at any time the material becomes too heavy, know that it's okay to pause, skip, or step away. Take care of yourself—your mental and emotional health comes first.

Content Warnings:
- Grooming and predatory behavior involving a minor
- Somewhat graphic depictions of coerced sexual activity (non- consensual due to age and manipulation)
- Emotional, verbal, and physical abuse from a parent
- Narcissistic family dynamics
- Self-harm
- Psychological manipulation and emotional dependency
- Trauma, isolation, and internalized shame
- Substance abuse
- Mentions of depression, suicidal thoughts, and neglect

This book includes emotionally and sexually manipulative dynamics between an adult and a teenager. These scenes are portrayed from the perspective of the victim and are not intended to sexualize or romanticize abuse. They are meant to illuminate the psychological impact and complexity of grooming.

If any of these themes are difficult for you, please take care of yourself. You're not alone, and support is always available.

If you or someone you know is experiencing grooming, abuse, or emotional manipulation, please know: there is help, there is hope, and you are never alone. Below are trusted resources offering support, guidance, and healing. Reaching out is a brave and powerful step.

RAINN (Rape, Abuse & Incest National Network)
- **24/7 Hotline:** 1-800-656-HOPE (4673)
- **Website:** www.rainn.org
- Offers confidential crisis support, survivor stories, and trauma-informed guidance.

Childhelp National Child Abuse Hotline
- **24/7 Hotline:** 1-800-4-A-CHILD (1-800-422-4453)
- **Website:** www.childhelphotline.org
- For children, teens, and adults impacted by abuse—including grooming by a parent or trusted adult.

Love is Respect *(Support for Teens in Unhealthy or Abusive Relationships)*
- **Call:** 1-866-331-9474
- **Text:** Text "LOVEIS" to 22522
- **Website:** www.loveisrespect.org
- Empowers teens to recognize and respond to coercion, emotional abuse, and online grooming.

National Center for Missing & Exploited Children (NCMEC)
- **Report Online Grooming or Exploitation:** report.cybertip.org

• **Website:** www.missingkids.org

• Offers safety tools and survivor support for children and families.

Please take care of yourself. You are worthy of love, safety, and healing.

AUTHOR'S NOTE

This book is a work of fiction, inspired by my emotions and personal experiences. While elements of Melody's story may reflect some feelings I have lived through, all names, characters, locations, and events have been fictionalized. Any resemblance to real people, living or dead, is entirely coincidental.

The story explores themes of grooming, manipulation, and trauma. It is not intended to describe, accuse, or portray any specific person. Writing this book has been a way for me to process my experiences and connect with others who have faced similar struggles.

This book is meant for those who feel lost, abandoned, or misunderstood. May it serve as a reminder that healing is possible, and that your voice is your strength.

With love,
    Courtney

PLAYLIST

"Just Like Heaven" – The Cure
"Silhouettes" – Smile Empty Soul
"Broken" – Seether feat. Amy Lee
"Creep" – Radiohead
"Nobody's Home" – Avril Lavigne
"Love You to Death" — Type O Negative
"Hello" — Evanescence
"Praying" —Kesha
"Dynasty" — MIIA
"Drunk on Shadows" — HIM
"Smallest Man Who Ever Lived" — Taylor Swift
"Don't Cha" — The Pussycat Dolls
"29" — Demi Lovato
"Missing" — Evanescence
"Strings" — Skydxddy

To access the full playlist, scan me!

PROLOGUE

Blackridge, Oregon

They called it a town, but it never felt like one. Not really.

Blackridge sat hunched between the pine-thick hills and the jagged coastline, half-forgotten on most maps, the kind of place people only passed through on their way to somewhere better. Rain lived here like an old tenant— dripping from moss-covered roofs, slinking through cracked sidewalks, staining everything in shades of gray.

In Blackridge, nothing ever seemed to grow quite right. Not the wildflowers. Not the kids.

Especially not the kids.

Melody Rayne had lived here her whole life, tucked into a sagging house at the end of a dead-end street, with peeling paint and a porch that creaked like it had something to confess. Some nights, she dreamed the town was swallowing her whole, the fog seeping through the cracks in her bedroom window, the trees whispering things she didn't understand.

She learned early that survival meant silence. That staying small was safer. That being strange in a place like this was dangerous.

She kept her head down. She counted cracks in the ceiling.

She wrote things she couldn't say out loud. Sometimes, she pressed her ear to the wall and listened to the screaming downstairs and pretended it was the ocean.

Sometimes, that almost worked.

But the truth was, Melody had always known she didn't belong in Blackridge.

The real question was whether she would ever find a way out.

Because sometimes the town felt like a trap laid just for her — a snare of shadows and secrets, waiting. Watching. The kind of place that didn't let girls like her go without a fight.

She could feel it lately, more than ever. In the way her mother's voice sharpened like broken glass. In the way the halls grew colder, quieter, like the house was holding its breath.

In the way her skin itched beneath the weight of her own name.

Something was coming. She didn't know what.

But she knew it would change everything.

The screaming started before the sun even rose.

Melody pulled the blanket tighter over her head, squeezing her eyes shut as her mother's voice tore through the thin walls. The same fight, different day. Something about money. Something about Nick, her half brother. Something about Melody, she was sure, she was always part of the problem.

She rolled onto her side and stared at the peeling posters on her bedroom wall. They hung limp and faded, like even the bands had given up on her. The scent of cigarette smoke and cheap lemon cleaner clung to everything, burning her nose. She hated this house. Hated waking up in it. But where else was there to go?

A soft *meow* rose from the foot of her bed. A small black cat leapt up beside her, her sleek fur shining like ink in the pale morning light. Melody exhaled, letting her hand find the familiar curve of the cat's back.

"Hey, Wednesday," she whispered, her voice hoarse from disuse. The cat responded with a low purr, rubbing her head against Melody's arm before curling up on her chest like a living weighted blanket. "You're the only one who doesn't yell at me."

Wednesday had found her two winters ago, a stray kitten

shivering behind the dumpster at the gas station. Melody had smuggled her home in her jacket and fed her bits of tuna until she trusted her. No one else in the house paid her any mind. Sometimes Melody thought Wednesday was more ghost than cat, slipping silently through the halls, knowing just when to appear.

Downstairs, a door slammed. Nick's heavy boots thudded down the hallway. Wednesday's ears perked up, and she let out a soft hiss before hopping down and vanishing beneath the bed. Melody waited until the front door slammed before she climbed out of bed.

She pulled on a black hoodie, ripped jeans, and laced up her boots with trembling fingers. Her hoodie was too big, swallowing her curvy frame; the sleeves dangled past her wrists, the fabric worn thin at the elbows. The mirror caught her reflection: long black hair, messy from sleep, blue eyes ringed with yesterday's eyeliner, a sadness she couldn't scrub away no matter how hard she tried. Her skin was pale, the kind of pale that spoke more of sleepless nights than any natural complexion, and a faint bruise bloomed under the hem of her jeans where Nick had kicked a laundry basket into her the week before.

She grabbed her backpack, heavier with notebooks than textbooks, and slipped toward the back door. Better to leave before her mom found a reason to scream at her face instead of just her memory.

She turned, her heart fluttering unexpectedly. Her father, Andrew, was standing in the entryway, his boots caked with red dirt, his work duffel slung over one shoulder. He wore the same faded navy work shirt he always did, stretched at the elbows, with tiny burn holes near the cuff from welding sparks. His khaki work pants were stained with grease and time. The air around him carried the sharp tang of oil, rust, and cold metal, the kind of scent that clung to his skin no matter how many showers he took.

Andrew worked out on the pipeline, miles away buried under

fields and forests, in places so remote that cell signals couldn't reach. Sometimes he was gone for weeks, sometimes longer. Melody never knew exactly when he'd come back, or when he'd vanish again. He was a man shaped by distance— quiet, worn, always hovering just outside the edges of her life.

His face was lined in that way that made him look older than he was — windburned skin, a few days' worth of stubble, tired eyes that always seemed to be looking just past her instead of at her. His hard hat was tucked under his arm, and a dent in the side suggested it had seen more than a few close calls.

He didn't say anything right away. He just stood there, shifting his weight like he was already halfway gone. That faraway look settled over his features, the one he always wore before disappearing back to the rigs, but when his eyes landed on Melody, something in them softened. Not much, but enough.

"Hey, kid," he said, voice rough, low. He nodded once. "Didn't think you'd be up."

Melody shrugged. "Couldn't sleep."

He hesitated, like he wanted to say something more — like he knew there was something he should say, but instead he reached up and adjusted the strap on his duffel. His knuckles were scraped, and a smear of black grease ran across the back of his hand.

"You, uh... you need anything before I go?" he asked, but his tone made it clear he didn't expect an answer.

She shook her head.

He nodded again, the kind of gesture that felt like a habit more than anything else. Then he started to turn, pausing just long enough to mutter, "Tell your mom I'll call when I get signal."

He stepped out into the pre-dawn dark, the door closing behind him with a quiet finality.

Melody stood there for a long moment, staring at the spot where he'd been, trying to remember the last time he'd hugged her. She couldn't.

It hurt in that low, dull way she'd gotten used to — like an ache that never healed, just changed shape. He wasn't cruel. He wasn't like her mother. But he was gone more than he was ever here, and even when he was home, it felt like most of him was still out there, buried in some pipeline trench hundreds of miles away.

Sometimes she wondered if she missed him, or just missed the version of him she wished existed.

At school, she walked invisible corridors lined with stares and whispered jokes. Freak. Weirdo. Emo trash. She heard it all, even when they thought they were being subtle. She kept her head down, hiding behind the curtain of her hair, eyes on the cracked floor tiles, counting steps like it might get her somewhere better.

It never did.

The first bell had barely rung when it happened.

Melody rounded the corner by her locker, keeping her eyes down like always, when a shoulder slammed into her. Hard. Her books spilled across the floor with a hollow slap.

"Watch it, freak," sneered a voice, Jamie Parks, one of the girls from her math class. Perfect hair, perfect teeth, perfect life. She tossed her blonde hair over her shoulder and sneered down at Melody like she was something stuck to her shoe.

Melody mumbled an apology, kneeling to gather her books. Her fingers trembled. She hated how they trembled. She hated how she could already feel her face burning, hated how she didn't even bother standing up for herself anymore.

Another voice— Ethan Collins, a football player added, "Maybe if you weren't dressed like you're going to a funeral every day, people would actually see you."

Laughter bubbled around her. It clawed at her ears, at her

throat. Melody swallowed it all down. Shoved the torn notebooks into her bag with shaking hands.

Her boots squeaked against the linoleum as she pushed herself up and fled, leaving one of her pens behind.

No one called after her.

No one cared.

She ducked into the nearest bathroom first, locking herself in a stall. The fluorescent lights buzzed above her, too loud, too bright. Melody pressed her forehead to the cool metal door and tried to breathe. In. Out. In. Out. Like that would fix anything. Like it ever had.

The burning behind her eyes tightened, but no tears came. She didn't even have that anymore— not real tears, not real rage. Just a dull, hollow ache gnawing at the edges of her insides.

After a few minutes, when the hallways were mostly empty, she slipped out and made her way to the library. No one would look for her there. No one ever did.

The library was cold, the kind of cold that settled into your bones. Melody welcomed it. She moved automatically to the back corner, past the worn tables and ancient computer monitors, to the aisles almost no one bothered with.

She ran her fingers along the spines of battered novels until she found one she hadn't read yet, some battered fantasy book with a vampire on the cover. She didn't care what it was. She just needed somewhere else to go.

Curling into the corner by the window, she cracked it open and pretended to read.

Her eyes skimmed the words, but none of them really sank in.

It was enough to be away.

To not have to hear her name like a curse word, to not feel the sharp eyes of people slicing her open, laughing at the guts they left behind.

Through the dusty window, the sky stretched dull and gray, the clouds pressing low like they might crush the world. Melody thought, not for the first time, that maybe she belonged up there, somewhere shapeless and silent, somewhere you couldn't fall any further.

She turned a page without reading it.

A few shelves away, something caught her eye.

A thin, clothbound book leaned precariously between two thick, forgotten encyclopedias. It looked out of place — the cover worn, the title pressed in faded silver: *The Sky Beneath the Floorboards* by Isobel Thorne.

Melody pulled it free, feeling the strange weight of it in her hands.

There was something about it, the way it seemed older than everything else here, like it had been waiting. Like it had survived things, too.

She opened it at random, the pages smelling faintly of dust and something sweeter, like crushed flowers long dead.

Her eyes landed on a passage near the top of the page:

"Some hearts are built from quiet things, unanswered questions, the hum of loneliness, the ache of wanting to be seen. Do not rush to solve them. Let them speak in their own time."

The words hit her chest like a punch and a lullaby all at once.

Her throat tightened. Her fingers brushed over the ink, as if touching it might make it more real, might anchor her.

She read it again. And again.

Let them speak in their own time.

It felt like someone had written it for her — someone who understood the nameless ache, the feeling of being misplaced in every room you entered. The way hope lived like a ghost inside you, stubborn and stupid, refusing to leave even when everything else had.

She closed the book softly, cradling it in her lap like something precious.

Outside the window, the sky hung low and heavy.

Inside, Melody sat still, a tiny flicker of something kindling inside her chest.

Not hope exactly, but something close enough to hurt.

Maybe someday, someone would see her.

Maybe someday, she'd get out.

But she knew better than to believe it.

A soft voice broke through her reverie.

"Mel, hey!" Anna's familiar voice cut through the haze of isolation, and Melody looked up to see her friend weaving through the rows of bookshelves.

Anna was a contrast to everything Melody felt about herself — confident, loud, with fiery red hair that always seemed to be bouncing around, too energetic for the monotony of the school. Where Melody's style was dark and brooding, Anna's was vibrant, colorful, and unapologetic. But even though they were different in so many ways, Anna was one of the few who never judged Melody. She just... understood.

"Hey," Melody muttered, offering her a small, but genuine smile.

Anna dropped into the seat next to her, her eyes scanning the book Melody had been holding. "That looks deep. Poetry again?"

Melody nodded slowly. "*The Sky Beneath the Floorboards*," she said, tapping the cover of the book. "It's... weird. I think it might be for me, but I don't really get it."

Anna raised an eyebrow, leaning in with interest. "What do you mean?"

"Like," Melody started, biting her lip, trying to find the words. "It says stuff like 'let the quiet things in your heart speak in their own time'... like... I'm supposed to be okay with not having answers. I don't know if I can do that."

Anna grinned, nudging her shoulder. "That's totally you, Mel. Always thinking too much."

Melody huffed a laugh, even if it was a little bitter. "Yeah, well, thinking doesn't make the questions go away. And it doesn't make people stop calling me a freak."

Anna's expression softened. "I don't get why they call you

that. I mean, you're unique, but not a freak. And who even cares what those idiots think? They don't get it."

Melody glanced down at her boots, suddenly self-conscious. "It still hurts, though." She paused, biting her lip. "It always hurts."

There was a moment of quiet, the kind that felt comfortable even though the weight of it was heavy. Anna leaned back in her chair, tapping her fingers on the table thoughtfully. "Yeah, I know it does. But, Mel, you can't let them win. You're too awesome for them to make you feel small."

Melody shrugged, looking out the window again, watching the rain begin to trickle down the glass. "I don't feel awesome. I feel... like I'm disappearing, sometimes."

Anna reached across the table, giving Melody's hand a reassuring squeeze. "You're not disappearing. You're just waiting to figure out what's next. You'll get there. And hey," she added with a grin, "when you do, I'll be right here, cheering you on. Always."

Melody looked up, meeting Anna's eyes, feeling something flutter inside her chest. It wasn't hope exactly, not the kind she usually imagined, but it was close. "Thanks, Anna," she whispered, her voice tight.

Anna's smile softened, but there was something in her expression that made Melody feel understood. "You know where to find me if you need someone to kick ass with."

Melody chuckled quietly, a real laugh this time, one that surprised her. "Yeah, I guess so."

They sat there for a while longer, Anna chatting about her latest art project and how her parents were fighting over nothing. Melody listened, her thoughts drifting back to the passage in the book. *Let the quiet things in your heart speak in their own time.* She wondered if Anna could ever really understand how true that felt.

When the bell rang, signaling the end of lunch, Anna stood up with a stretch. "You okay to head back to class? Or you wanna ditch and do something less... school-y?"

Melody hesitated, then nodded. "Yeah, I think I'll just go. I need to be there, even if I don't want to."

Anna smiled, slinging her backpack over her shoulder. "I'll catch up with you later, alright? We'll make it through the rest of the day together."

Melody felt a strange comfort in the promise, something rare and fragile, like a spark in the dark. As they walked out of the library, side by side, Melody couldn't help but feel that maybe, just maybe, there was more to her story than what the world wanted to tell.

The rain had picked up by the time the bell rang, the kind of downpour that soaked through your clothes before you could even think to open an umbrella. The gray sky hung heavy, clouds smothering what little daylight there was left. Melody didn't mind. She loved the rain, it was the one thing in this town that felt like it made sense. Like it could wash everything away, even if just for a little while.

She pulled her hood up and shoved her hands deep into her pockets, the weight of the day pulling at her shoulders. Anna had tried to get her to come hang out after school, but Melody had only half-listened, muttering something about needing some time to herself. The truth was, she just didn't want to face anyone. Not yet. Not when everything inside her felt so... tangled.

Her boots splashed through puddles as she walked through the misty streets of town, the beat of her music thumping in her ears. She wasn't listening to anything particularly special, just some playlist she'd found that afternoon, but it didn't matter. The music was more about drowning out the noise inside her head than anything else.

She made her way toward the cemetery. It wasn't far, just a

short walk down the road from the library, and it was always empty in the afternoons. Sometimes she went there to think, to clear her head, but today it felt like she was walking toward something else. Something she wasn't sure she could explain.

The cemetery was quiet, just the sound of rain tapping on gravestones and the soft rustling of leaves in the trees. Melody made her way through the rows of weathered stones, her boots sinking into the soggy earth. She found a spot by the old oak tree at the back of the cemetery, the one with roots that sprawled out like spider webs, gnarled and tangled. She sat down beneath it, pulling her knees up to her chest, her gaze wandering over the gravestones.

She tried to focus on the music, let the melody carry her away, but that book, *The Sky Beneath the Floorboards*, kept drifting back into her mind. The words from it were still lingering, like smoke in the air, unshakable. *Let the quiet things in your heart speak in their own time.* The thought settled in her chest like a weight, one she couldn't quite shake off. It felt like someone was asking her to be patient— with herself, with the world, with the things she couldn't change.

She closed her eyes, trying to focus on the sound of the rain instead, but her mind wandered again.

Home.

The thought of it made her stomach twist. The house felt like a cage most days, the walls too close, the air too thick. Her mom's voice, always sharp and demanding. Nick's constant presence, his sneering comments that made her skin crawl. And her dad— distant, always gone, never around when she needed him most. He was working again, she knew that. Out on the pipeline, somewhere far away. Every time he left, she felt like a piece of her chipped away. Like there was nothing to hold onto anymore.

She hadn't seen her mom this morning. She had woken up late, sneaking out of the house as quietly as she could. Her mother had been asleep, and Melody hadn't bothered to wake her. The silence between them was something she had grown accustomed to. It wasn't that her mother didn't care, it was that her caring came in the form of control, and Melody was tired of fighting it.

Her mother's love was conditional, based on whether Melody could meet her expectations, whether she could be the perfect daughter, the perfect reflection of what Charlotte wanted to see. And when she failed, when she wasn't enough, Charlotte would lash out, her words as sharp and cutting as knives.

It had been a long time since Melody had tried to talk to her. Her mother never listened, never saw her as anything more than a means to feed her own ego. When Melody needed her the most, Charlotte was always either absent or too wrapped up in herself to notice the strain in Melody's voice, the hollow look in her eyes.

Her throat tightened as she remembered the last time they'd talked. Her mother's sharp words, cutting deeper than she would ever admit. *Always something wrong with you, Mel.* The words had stuck in her throat, even though she hadn't said them out loud. They didn't need to be said; Melody could feel them, heavy like the rain, sinking into her skin.

Her father. He was never there to protect her. Always gone, always working. It was like he didn't even see what was happening. Didn't realize how much she needed him.

Melody felt the weight of it all. The loneliness, the yearning for something she couldn't name. She wanted to scream. To shake it all off, but it stayed, like the rain that wouldn't stop.

She reached up and tugged the headphones off, letting the sound of the rain fill the space between her thoughts. She stared at the gravestones in front of her, wondering if any of the people buried here had ever felt the way she did, as though they were caught somewhere between who they were and who they were supposed to be.

Maybe it didn't matter. Maybe no one ever really understood what it was like to feel this lost.

But then, something inside her stirred, something small, but fierce. A flicker of defiance, as if the words from the book were trying to tell her that it was okay to not have all the answers. That maybe she didn't need to fix everything right now.

Let the quiet things in your heart speak in their own time.

She repeated the words under her breath, letting them settle in her chest, grounding her.

Maybe she couldn't change everything. Maybe she didn't need to. But she could be patient. With herself. With her heart.

And maybe, someday, she'd figure out what came next.

Later that evening, the house was quiet, a dull hum of emptiness that never quite stopped. Wednesday was already there, curled in a tight crescent at the foot of her bed like a shadow that had decided to stay. Her yellow eyes blinked slowly as Melody entered, then she stretched, silent and elegant, before padding up to nuzzle Melody's hand.

Melody collapsed onto her bed, the book still in her hands. *Letters to a Young Poet* — a strange, melancholic collection of Rainer Maria Rilke's letters that had somehow wormed its way into her thoughts and refused to leave. She didn't even know why she had picked it up at the library, but once she did, it clung to her like static in her brain. She flipped the pages, but her mind couldn't rest on the words for long, not when everything else in her life felt like it was unraveling at the edges.

Her room was a reflection of the deeper parts of her soul, organized but purposeful in its darkness. The walls were adorned with black candles, some burning softly, casting flickering shadows, and the space around her altar was carefully arranged. The altar itself was adorned with crystals, jars of herbs, and worn tarot cards, a place where she could quiet her mind and seek comfort in ritual. Posters of gothic figures, dark nature scenes, and mystical symbols lined the walls, carefully placed. The room had an almost sacred atmosphere to it, the darkness infused with intention, not chaos. It was a place she could retreat to, a small sanctuary where she could be herself without judgment.

Wednesday leapt up beside her, circling once before settling near her hip, purring softly— not demanding attention, just there. The steady sound of her breathing was a quiet comfort, an anchor in the storm of Melody's emotions. Melody stroked her cat's fur absentmindedly, letting the rhythmic purring ground her.

She opened one of the journals, its pages worn from years of being carried around and forgotten. She grabbed a pen from the desk, the one she'd almost lost in the hallway earlier that day, and began to write.

In shaky letters, she copied the passage from *The Sky Beneath the Floorboards*:

> "Some hearts are built from quiet things; unanswered questions, the hum of loneliness, the ache of wanting to be seen. Do not rush to solve them. Let them speak in their own time."

Her hand trembled slightly as she wrote, but she didn't stop. Her fingers brushed the paper as if she were tracing the words in an attempt to make them stick, to make them real.

Wednesday shifted closer, resting her head against Melody's thigh, as if grounding her to the present — a quiet, steady presence that asked for nothing but gave everything.

For a moment, Melody paused and looked down at the ink that had bled into the paper, her heart drumming softly in her chest. She pressed the pen down harder, as if the weight of it could hold the ache inside her at bay. Maybe the ache could stay contained, maybe it could be understood, if she could only write it all out, let it breathe on the page. But she didn't know how to make sense of it. She wasn't sure she wanted to.

When she finished, she closed the journal and placed it carefully on her desk. The words still echoed in her mind. *Do not rush to solve them. Let them speak in their own time.* The passage felt like a lifeline and a reminder that maybe the things she was feeling, the things that confused her, the things that hurt, didn't have to be figured out right away. She didn't have to have all the answers, not yet. Not now.

She allowed herself to believe it. That tiny, fragile hope.

She laid back on her bed, staring up at the peeling posters and the faded dreams they once represented. Wednesday climbed up to rest against her chest, her purr a soft, rhythmic lull, a heartbeat for when Melody couldn't trust her own.

Her eyes fluttered closed. Maybe tomorrow she'd wake up and feel something different. Maybe tomorrow, things would change.

But for now, the questions were enough. Just being with them was enough.

CHAPTER TWO

The morning after finding the book, Melody carried it everywhere she went, tucked tight against her ribs like it might slip away if she loosened her grip, like it might vanish if she didn't keep it close enough to feel its weight. The hard corners pressed into her side through the fabric of her hoodie, grounding her in a way nothing else could.

No one noticed. No one ever noticed.

The halls of Willow Creek High buzzed and hummed with the same tired cruelties— laughter too sharp, footsteps too fast, whispers that cut deeper than shouts ever could. Melody moved through it like she was underwater, the voices warping and washing over her, never quite touching her. But the words from the book clung to her like armor, hidden and stubborn, lining the inside of her hoodie like a second skin.

"Some hearts are built from quiet things; unanswered questions, the hum of loneliness, the ache of wanting to be seen. Do not rush to solve them. Let them speak in their own time."

In English class, she sat near the back, head low, tracing the torn edges of her notebook while Mr. Jameson droned on about thesis statements. The chalk squeaked against the board in staccato bursts, sharp and jarring, but Melody barely heard it. Her mind was somewhere else, somewhere quieter. Somewhere dustier and ancient, where the pages whispered to her like secrets from another life.

She wondered if there were more books like it— hidden ones. Books that didn't just tell the truth, but knew it. Words that stitched up the hollow places inside her without demanding anything back. She wondered if maybe, she wasn't completely alone after all.

The bell rang, a metallic clatter, and the classroom emptied around her like water draining from a tub. Melody stayed seated a few seconds longer, cradling the book like a relic, its heartbeat still echoing against hers.

Today, she thought, she might try something different.

Today, she might let herself hope, just a little.

She stood, slung her backpack over one shoulder, and stepped into the crowded hallway. She wasn't seen, but for a flicker of a moment, she felt almost real.

The library was nearly empty during lunch, dim and hushed, as if it too had grown tired of noise. Melody slipped in without a sound, her footsteps muffled by the thick carpet and the heavier hush of solitude. She moved through the rows like a ghost, still clutching the first book, the one that had found her, the one that had cracked something open.

She didn't expect lightning to strike twice.

But something pulled her— not her mind, exactly. Something lower, deeper. Like instinct. Or longing. Or maybe whatever small, stubborn shard of her still believed in magic, even if she'd never admit it out loud. She wandered toward the farthest corner, the forgotten section, where the air smelled older and the shelves sagged with books no one checked out anymore.

That's where she found it.

"Letters to a Phantom", the title etched in fading silver across a cracked black spine. No author. No summary. Just a bare cover, matte and scuffed, like it had been handled by desperate hands. Like it had waited for her.

She opened it slowly. The pages were brittle, delicate— one wrong turn and they'd flake away. Some were smudged, water-marked like someone had cried while reading them. Maybe more than one someone.

"Love, when real, does not save you. It unmakes you. It burns the rot away, even if it has to scorch the bone."

A shiver slipped down her spine, curling beneath her hoodie.

This one wasn't like the other book. It wasn't safe. It wasn't kind. It felt like a warning. Or a promise.

She flipped to a dog-eared page, already worn thin.

"I would've died for him. I almost did. But what he gave me first was something worse and better, he saw me. And I let him."

Melody pressed the book against her chest. Her ribs ached. It was like the words had crawled inside her and settled between her lungs.

She slipped it into her bag without asking, without thinking, her voice still lodged in her throat. No one saw. She walked the rest of the day like she was split open— half here, half... else-where. She didn't know it yet, but the pages she'd just read would echo in her long after the ink had faded. They'd stain her like smoke.

By the time she stepped off the bus, the sky had turned the color of bruises, heavy purple smudged with yellow-grey, like the aftermath of a hit that didn't fade fast enough. The air smelled like rain that never came.

Home loomed ahead— the small, sagging house at the end of Sycamore Lane. The paint peeled in long strips, and the shutters hung crooked like the house was too tired to hold itself up. The windows were dull and smudged, like eyes that had stopped caring what they saw.

Nick was waiting on the porch, slouched in a stained patio

chair like he owned the place. He was tall and wiry, all elbows and resentment, the kind of body that looked like it never stopped pacing, even when still. His hoodie was faded black, sleeves chewed at the cuffs, and his jeans sagged just enough to show the waistband of boxers beneath. Greasy, shoulder-length hair curled around his neck, framing a face that was all sharp edges and smugness. There was a permanent twist to his mouth, like every word he said came with a sneer.

His cigarette burned low between his fingers, more ash than flame, and his eyes gleamed with that cruel boredom Melody knew too well, the kind that made people dangerous when they had nothing better to do.

"Hey, freak," he said, flicking ash at her feet. "Still dressing like you're at a funeral?"

Melody didn't respond. She kept her head down. She knew better. But ignoring him never worked.

He stood as she passed and yanked the strap of her backpack hard enough to pull her back a step.

"You deaf now, too?"

"Let go," she muttered, trying to twist free.

He didn't. He shoved her instead, just enough to make her stumble. Her books spilled from her arms, skidding across the concrete.

"Oops."

"Nick, stop it!" she snapped, the words tearing out of her like glass. For a second, it felt like maybe she'd finally found the edge.

And of course, that's when the screen door slammed open behind them.

Charlotte.

She stood in the doorway like a stormcloud, arms folded tight across her chest like she was trying to hold in all the things she refused to feel. She was thin— not delicate, just dried out, like something pressed too long between heavy pages. Her blonde hair was pulled into a tight, too-high ponytail that tugged her face taut. Her makeup was severe, eyeliner sharp enough to slice, lipstick dark enough to mimic a wound. Her beauty was the brittle kind, desperate and curated, meant for show, not softness. Like if she looked good enough, no one would notice everything else rotting underneath.

Her voice scraped the air— sharp, smoke-stained, soaked in years of bitterness.

"What the hell is going on out here?"

"He started it," Melody said, too fast, too defensive, her heart already jackhammering.

Nick rubbed his arm, the picture of wounded innocence.

"She pushed me."

Charlotte's eyes snapped to Melody— cold, narrowed, unreadable.

"What did I say about lying, Melody?"

"I'm not—"

She didn't see the slap coming. Just the blur of Charlotte's hand, the crack of contact, and the hot sting that bloomed across her cheek.

Silence.

Nick smirked, already turning away, like the scene had played out exactly how he wanted.

Melody stood frozen. Her face burned. Her throat closed.

"Go to your room," Charlotte said flatly, already walking back inside like the moment was finished.

"Maybe you'll learn some respect."

Melody didn't cry until the door was shut behind her. And even then, it wasn't just the pain. It was that no one came after her. No one ever did.

She didn't move for a long time. She sat on the edge of her bed, the room dim with late-afternoon shadows. The curtains were drawn tight, not because she was hiding, she told herself, but because the world outside didn't deserve to look in. The slap still burned on her cheek, a phantom echo of Charlotte's hand. But worse was the ache in her chest— not sharp, not fresh. Just that old, familiar hollow. The kind you learned to live around.

Wednesday leapt onto the bed without a sound, her black fur nearly blending into the dimness of the room. She settled beside Melody, her yellow eyes blinking slowly, knowingly. Melody reached out a trembling hand, brushing her fingers gently over Wednesday's ears. The cat leaned into her touch.

"At least you still like me," Melody whispered, her voice hoarse. Wednesday responded with a soft purr and nuzzled into her side, warm and steady like something tethered to this world when everything else felt like it was floating away.

The stolen book lay on her blanket, spine up like a wounded bird. *Letters to a Phantom*. She reached for it with trembling fingers, flipping it open to the same page that had sliced her open earlier.

"He saw me. And I let him."

She read it again. And again. Until the words bled into something quieter. She didn't know who had written them — or who they were written for. But it didn't matter. They were hers now. They knew her.

A soft knock startled her.

She froze. Waited.

It wasn't Charlotte. She never knocked.

After a moment, she got up and opened the door. No one was there. Just the hallway, empty and humming with the house's usual quiet cruelty. She closed the door behind her and moved back to her bed, sinking into the comfort of its worn sheets. Wednesday had stretched out in the warm spot she left behind and blinked up lazily when Melody returned.

The ache, the empty space inside her, lingered, and so did the urge to tell someone.

She picked up her phone, hesitating for a long moment

before dialing her dad's number. The screen glowed in the dimness, casting a faint light on her face. It rang once. Twice.

"Hey, kiddo," Andrew's voice came through, rough from hours on the job.

"Dad," Melody's voice cracked a little. She didn't know what she wanted to say, only that she needed to hear him. Needed something solid, even if it was distant and disconnected. "Mom... she hit me again."

There was a long pause on the other end. Melody pressed the phone tighter to her ear, waiting for something, anything. A response. An acknowledgment.

"What happened, honey?" His voice was tentative, like he wasn't sure how to react.

"She slapped me," Melody repeated, feeling the words settle in the air like a weight she didn't know how to carry. "She just... slapped me. For no reason."

Andrew let out a long sigh, and Melody could hear the discomfort in his breath. "I'm sorry, kid," he muttered, but there was a distance in his voice, like his words didn't quite reach her.

She clenched her fist around the phone. "I don't know what to do, Dad. She just... she doesn't stop. I don't think she even cares."

"Well... look, just... try not to let it get to you, okay?" He sounded so far away, both in miles and in emotional space. "You know how she is. I'll be home in a few days. Just hold on until then, alright?"

But those words didn't comfort her. They never did. It was always the same— wait. Wait for him. Wait for her. Wait for something that might never come.

"Okay," Melody whispered, even though she didn't feel okay at all. She hung up before he could say anything else.

The house was just as quiet after the call. Just the hum of the fridge, the flickering of a light somewhere down the hall. She stared at the screen of her phone, wishing she could have a real conversation with him, one where he actually heard her. But it wasn't that kind of call. Not ever.

Wednesday curled closer to her side, sensing the tension in Melody's body. She scratched behind the cat's ear again, her voice barely audible.

"I don't even know why I call him anymore," she murmured. "It's like... talking into a void."

Wednesday kneaded softly at her lap in response, a rhythmic reminder that she wasn't entirely alone. That someone, even if it was a small, silent someone, was there.

She felt the weight of the book again. The words that were meant for someone else, someone who understood what it felt like to be lost, to be seen in pieces.

Maybe it was better to hide behind them for now.

Melody lay back on her bed, the book still pressed against her chest, her fingers tracing the edges of its pages. But it wasn't enough. The ache, the hollow space inside her, only seemed to grow the more she tried to fill it. She closed her eyes for a moment, thinking of the words she had just read— and how they, too, seemed to fade like everything else.

It wasn't that she needed someone to fix her. She didn't need a solution. She just needed to feel like she existed somewhere, like someone...something, could see her. Really see her. Not just the surface.

She sat up slowly, the book still resting against her chest, then leaned over the side of the bed to reach underneath. Her fingers found the familiar spine of her old journal— always tucked away, always waiting. Its pages were filled with pieces of her she never dared speak aloud. But tonight felt different. Tonight, the silence was too loud to ignore, and the words inside her needed somewhere to land. Even if she didn't know what they meant yet.

Sitting cross-legged on the floor, she opened the journal to a fresh page, the blankness in front of her almost comforting. Wednesday jumped down beside her, curling into a soft loaf on the rug like a quiet guardian. Melody smiled faintly, glancing over at her.

"Just you and me, huh?" she whispered. Then, without thinking, the words began to spill out, uninvited but welcome.

I'm not sure if I want to be saved. I think I just want to be seen.

There's this ache inside me. Not the kind you can fix, but the kind you can only feed with things that don't matter. Like books that smell like forgotten things. Or silence that fills you up without asking for anything in return.

I keep looking for something to make sense of it all — but maybe there's nothing to make sense of. Maybe I just need to be… noticed. Like the words in those books, where no one has to explain them, and they don't need to be understood to be felt.

I'm not sure what I'm waiting for anymore. Maybe nothing. Maybe something.

But for once, I feel like I'm here. Even if it's just in these pages.

—M

Somewhere downstairs, Nick was laughing at something on the TV. Charlotte shouted at him to turn it down. A door slammed. The sound of the fridge opening. Closing. The world kept moving, without her.

Melody rested her chin on her knees, eyes drifting back to the book. Wednesday lay curled beside her on the bed, a soft, warm weight against her thigh. The steady rise and fall of the cat's breathing was the only thing that felt anchored in the moment.

The words haunted her, not in the way scary stories did, but in the way truth did when you weren't ready for it.

Love, when real, does not save you.

It unmakes you.

Maybe that's what she wanted. To be unmade. Peeled back. Revealed. Like something half-dead that needed burning to finally grow.

Wednesday stirred, stretching out one paw to rest gently on Melody's leg, her claws retracted, as if to say *I'm here.* Melody reached down absently and stroked her fur, grounding herself in the softness, in the simple presence of something that didn't ask anything of her.

A sudden gust of wind rattled her window.

Melody stood and walked to it, pulling the curtain back just enough to peek through. The street was quiet. Empty. But the feeling in her gut stayed, that strange hum, like something was shifting just outside the edges of what she could see.

Wednesday padded softly across the bed to sit at the edge, her eyes tracking Melody's movements with quiet curiosity. She let out a low, almost questioning *mrrp,* and Melody looked over her shoulder, offering a faint smile.

For the first time, she didn't feel like she was waiting to disappear.

She felt like something was coming.

And this time... she wasn't sure if she should run from it, or meet it halfway.

CHAPTER THREE

Melody sat at her desk, the glow of the computer screen casting a soft, blue light across the dimly lit room. The shadows on her walls danced faintly with the occasional flicker from the monitor, like ghosts that came alive only when no one else was watching. She had headphones on, *Drunk on Shadows* by HIM pulsing through them, the haunting melody and Villé Valo's voice drowning out the chaos outside her door.

Wednesday curled in a tight ball on the edge of the bed, her sleek black fur rising and falling with every slow breath. Occasionally, one ear twitched at the distant sound of yelling downstairs, but she didn't move—just stayed there, silent and still, a quiet sentinel to Melody's unrest.

Her fingers moved almost automatically over the keyboard, muscle memory guiding her through a familiar escape route. She scrolled through a moody photography site, the grainy, grayscale images acting like bandages for her fractured thoughts. She wasn't sure what she was looking for—just something, anything, that could take her mind off the ever-tightening noose that was home.

Downstairs, her mother's voice rose again. Sharp. Piercing. Weaponized.

Something about the dishes.

It didn't matter. It was always something. Some fresh injustice to scream about. Nick had thrown another tantrum—slamming doors, breaking another lamp, cursing loud enough that the neighbors probably heard. Her dad was gone, his presence reduced to voicemail messages and receipts.

Melody glanced at Wednesday. The cat blinked slowly back at her, the only soul in the house that didn't demand anything from her. She reached out and ran her fingers gently along the cat's spine. Wednesday leaned into it but made no sound, like she understood this moment was about quiet comfort, not noise.

It felt like the walls of her life were closing in, brick by brick, every scream another stone in the suffocating tomb of her silence. The only way to breathe was through music and art. They were her lifelines. The only places where she felt like she truly belonged. Or at least, the only places that didn't spit her back out.

She paused when she stumbled across a photographer's profile that immediately caught her eye.

Lucian.

The name alone stirred something. It was gothic and old-sounding, like the echo of a bell in an abandoned cathedral. His profile picture was a dark, almost hypnotic image—long black hair that framed a pale face, thick eyeliner smudged beneath intense, heavy-lidded eyes. His expression was unreadable. Stoic. Yet still burning with a quiet intensity. There was something magnetic about him, something that made her stomach twist in a way she didn't fully understand.

It wasn't just his appearance, it was the feeling he gave off. Like he knew something forbidden, something sacred, something secret—something she was desperate to uncover.

Heart pounding, Melody clicked into his gallery.

Photo after photo filled the screen—moody, melancholic shots of abandoned buildings, crumbling gravestones, twisted trees silhouetted against gray skies. The kind of places she dreamed of getting lost in. Each image hummed with the ache of loneliness and the strange beauty that grew out of it. There were portraits too, raw and vulnerable, shadows stretching across lonely faces like bruises. Faces that looked like they knew what it meant to be haunted.

His art mirrored everything she felt inside but could never put into words.

For a few minutes, she just scrolled, the noise of the house blurring into static behind her. In those moments, the photos were a language, and she finally understood it.

Then she noticed it—his profile details.

Age: 32.

Her hand froze on the mouse.

Thirty-two.

A pulse of heat flushed through her, chased quickly by cold doubt. She shouldn't talk to someone that much older. She knew that. Everyone would say it was wrong. Creepy. Dangerous.

But...

Maybe that was why he understood things the way he did. Maybe being older meant he'd seen what she had. Maybe he got it in a way no one her age possibly could. The idiots at school thought heavy metal was just noise. They called eyeliner "slut makeup." They didn't see her, they saw someone weird. Someone disposable.

Her thumb tapped anxiously against her desk.

Still, she hovered over the message button, debating.

Behind her, Wednesday stretched lazily and nestled deeper into the blanket, her soft purring the only sound outside the music.

Almost without thinking, Melody's fingers began to move. Slowly, then faster, as if the words had been waiting all along.

"Your photos... they feel like the world when you're the only one awake."

She stared at the words, heart hammering.

Then, before she could chicken out, she clicked *send*.

The response came faster than she expected.

"Thank you. Most people don't really see. But you do. I could tell the moment I saw you."

The moment I saw you.

Melody's stomach flipped, warmth blooming beneath her skin like a secret sunrise.

She typed quickly, fingers clumsy, heart weightless.

"It's like... everyone's too busy to notice anything real. But I can't unsee it."

"Exactly," he replied. *"People like you and me, we notice the cracks in the world where the light leaks through."*

Her breath caught in her throat.

Something about those words, the cracks where the light leaks through, hit her deep. Like maybe her brokenness had a purpose. Maybe she wasn't just shattered. Maybe she was translucent.

Her fingers hesitated before she added:

"I don't really belong anywhere. Not at home. Not at school. Nowhere."

Lucian's next message made her heart clench.

"You don't need to belong to a place, Melody. You belong to yourself. And maybe... to people who truly see you."

She swallowed hard, her throat thick with something unspoken.

After a minute, she asked, almost shyly:

"How do you know my name?"

There was a longer pause this time. She watched the little "typing..." notification blink on and off, her breath shallow.

Finally, his reply appeared:

"Some things... you just know when you find them."

A chill slid down her spine, but it wasn't cold. It was something heady. Dangerous. Electric.

"You feel like someone I was always supposed to meet," he added.

Melody stared at the screen, her pulse throbbing behind her ears.

She glanced at Wednesday, who lifted her head and blinked at her with sleepy, ancient eyes.

Melody reached out, fingers brushing over the cat's fur, grounding herself in that single act of softness.

He chose me.

The conversation spilled forward, fluid and fast, like a river breaking past a dam. She told him about her love for abandoned places, her sketchbook filled with strange, winged creatures that had no name, about how music felt more like home than any house she'd ever lived in.

Lucian listened.

He really listened.

Wednesday lay curled on the bed behind her, her ears occasionally twitching at the rhythm of Melody's voice as she softly spoke into the mic, half-whispering between laughs and shy confessions. The cat's purring was a steady undercurrent, a soft heartbeat in the room.

Time blurred until the clock blinked 12:37 AM.

And then—

SLAM.

Her bedroom door burst open, smacking against the wall so hard a picture frame tilted.

Melody jumped, yanking her headphones off.

Wednesday shot upright, fur bristling, a low growl escaping her throat as she bolted from the bed to crouch beneath the dresser.

Charlotte stood in the doorway, fury radiating off her in waves, a cigarette clutched between two trembling fingers. The stale stink of smoke poured into the room like a poison fog.

"What the hell are you still doing up?" she hissed. "On that damn computer while the rest of us clean up after your lazy ass?"

Melody's hands scrambled to close the chat window, heart stuttering.

Too late.

Charlotte stormed across the room, yanked the power cord from the wall. The screen went black, and with it, the fragile connection to Lucian snapped, like a wire pulled too tight and finally severing.

"You think you're special? Walking around like some dark little freak? Newsflash—you're nobody!" Charlotte snarled, so close Melody could smell the bitterness on her breath.

Melody bit the inside of her cheek hard enough to taste iron. She wouldn't cry. Not here. Not for her.

Charlotte spun on her heel and slammed the door so violently, the whole frame rattled.

The silence afterward felt cavernous. Crushing.

Melody sat frozen, her chest rising and falling in shallow bursts, like she was trying to hold her entire body together with just breath.

From beneath the dresser, Wednesday crept out slowly and rubbed against her shin, letting out a soft, questioning chirp. Melody reached down with shaking fingers and stroked the cat's back. Her hand trembled, but the warmth of Wednesday's fur helped slow the spiraling in her chest, just a little.

After a while, with shaking fingers, she rebooted the computer.

The screen flickered back to life—and there, waiting like a small light in the dark, was a new message.

"Melody? Are you okay?"

Her breath hitched.

He noticed.

Her fingers trembled as she typed:

"I'm okay. My mom just... lost it."

Another pause. Then:

"What do you mean she lost it? What happened?"

Tears stung her eyes, but she blinked them back.

She hesitated, then added:

"She came in screaming. Pulled the computer plug out. Told me I'm nothing."

There was a longer silence this time. Long enough for dread to start pooling in her chest.

Then:

"You're not nothing. You're rare. You're real. Please don't ever believe her lies."

Something cracked inside her, a fracture she didn't know she'd been holding together.

Lucian sent another message almost immediately:

"Listen... if things ever get too bad, or if you just need someone to talk to... would you want to exchange numbers? Only if you feel comfortable. No pressure. You deserve to have someone who listens."

Melody's heart slammed against her ribs.

It felt dangerous.

It felt real.

Wednesday jumped onto Melody's lap with a quiet thud, Melody didn't look away from the screen, but she let her hand rest gently on the cat's back, grounding herself in the soft, rhythmic rise and fall of her breathing.

For a long time, she just stared at the screen, her soul balancing on a ledge.

A part of her whispered *no*. Be careful. Protect yourself.

But the louder part—the hurting, desperate, aching part, was starving for someone who saw her.

She bit her lip. Typed slowly.

"I don't usually give it out..."

Then, after another long pause:

"But... okay. Just please don't give it to anyone."

She sent her number before she could change her mind.

Almost immediately, a message flashed back:

"Never. Your trust means everything to me."

A second later, her phone buzzed in her hand, an unfamiliar number.

> Hey, it's Lucian. Just making sure this is really you. :)

Melody smiled through the sting behind her eyes. Her fingers tapped out a reply.

> Yeah, it's me. Thanks for checking.

> Good. I'm glad. I didn't want you to think I'd vanish.

Her fingers hovered, her pulse thrumming.

> I'm gonna head to bed... it's getting late.

The reply came instantly:

> Of course. Get some rest, beautiful soul. Sweet dreams.

Her cheeks warmed.

> Goodnight, Lucian.

> Goodnight, Melody. I'll be here when you wake up.

She got up from her computer desk, the low light from the screen flickering softly against the dark walls, and crossed to her bed. The blankets were still tucked in from that morning, and Wednesday had left a warm dent where she'd been curled up earlier. Melody sat down slowly, then eased herself back until she was lying flat, the day still buzzing beneath her skin.

She set her phone down beside her pillow, the screen's faint glow casting a tiny, stubborn light into the dark.

She stared up at the ceiling, heart still thudding with everything he'd said.

"You're rare. You're real. Don't believe her lies."

Her thoughts drifted to the book she hadn't technically checked out from the library, the one she'd slipped into her backpack like a secret. *Letters to a Phantom*. The words still lived inside her.

"I would've died for him. I almost did. But what he gave me first was something worse and better, he saw me. And I let him."

Melody closed her eyes.

He saw me. And I let him.

Was that what this was? Was Lucian seeing her in a way no one else had ever tried?

Maybe it didn't matter that he was older.

Maybe that was *why* he understood.

Maybe she'd finally found the person who could pull her out of the wreckage she called a life.

A part of her whispered warnings, quiet as wind between gravestones.

But louder still was the ache, the desperate longing, for someone to *choose* her.

To *see* her.

To *save* her.

Maybe, she thought, *Lucian is my dark knight.*

Not the kind in shining armor... but the kind who wears the night like a second skin. The kind who doesn't rescue you from the shadows, he teaches you how to live in them.

As her eyes closed, a quiet warmth settled in her chest—delicate, uncertain, but real.

She lay still for a moment, letting the silence stretch, letting herself feel it. Then she sat up, reached for the journal she kept hidden under her bed, and began to write.

I don't know what tonight was.
I've had conversations before online and at school, in passing, but none of them felt like this. It was like

stepping out of my skin and into something softer. Like I was made of glass and someone finally looked close enough to see what was inside instead of just walking past.

Lucian saw me.

Not in the creepy "I'm watching you" way, but in the real way. Like he looked through all the noise and static and sadness and actually found me there, buried under everything I try not to feel. He didn't even ask that much. He just... listened. And he said things that made me feel like maybe I'm not broken. Maybe I'm not nothing.

Mom called me a freak again. Like it's her favorite word. Like it's a curse she's trying to tattoo on my forehead so I never forget who I am to her. But then Lucian told me I'm rare. And I want to believe him so badly it hurts.

Is it stupid that I gave him my number? I keep thinking I'll regret it, but I don't. Not even a little. I don't care that he's older. I care that he gets it. I care that for once, I don't feel like I'm shouting into the void.

He called me a beautiful soul. No one's ever called me that before. Not once.

I wish he could see my drawings. I wish he could hear how loud my heart was beating when I hit send. I wish he knew that his words tonight felt like a hand reaching down into the place I thought no one would ever go.

Maybe he does know.
Maybe that's the scariest part.
—M

She closed the journal slowly, her fingers brushing over the worn edges like she was sealing something sacred inside. The quiet pressed in again, but it didn't feel as heavy this time. Just still.

Sliding the notebook back under her bed, Melody lay down and pulled the blanket up to her chin. Her heart was still beating a little too fast, her mind still echoing with Lucian's voice and the strange, new feeling of being seen.

In the dark, she let herself smile—small, uncertain, but real.

And then, finally, she slept.

CHAPTER FOUR

The next morning, Melody woke to the harsh glare of sunlight streaming through her window. Her eyes felt heavy, the weight of the conversation with Lucian still pressing on her mind. The glow of the computer screen was still fresh in her memory, as were the promises he'd whispered to her in the dark. She wasn't sure how long she'd sat there, clinging to his words, but the loneliness was gone, if only for a brief moment.

She rubbed her eyes, trying to shake off the exhaustion that clung to her like a second skin. As she threw off the covers, the usual silence of the house greeted her, a silence that felt empty, suffocating. Her father was still gone, of course, and Nick was probably still sleeping off whatever mess he'd gotten into the night before. Her mom, though, was always awake. Always waiting for something to erupt.

A soft, familiar weight pressed against her leg. She looked down to see Wednesday curled near her feet, blinking up at her with wide, unbothered eyes. Melody reached down and scratched gently behind Wednesday's ears. The cat purred, a low, vibrating comfort that briefly cut through the heaviness in her chest.

"Wish I could be you for a day," she whispered. "No school. No yelling. Just naps and warm spots."

Wednesday nuzzled her hand in reply.

She pushed open her bedroom door cautiously, trying not to disturb the fragile peace that lingered. She padded down the hallway, the faint scent of stale cigarette smoke still clinging to the walls. As she passed the living room, Charlotte's voice cut through the silence like a blade.

"Melody! Get your ass in here," her mother barked, her tone sharp and already laced with contempt. Melody winced, her chest tightening. She didn't even know what she'd done yet, but that never seemed to matter.

She took a breath and stepped into the room. Charlotte was slouched on the couch, a cigarette burning between her fingers, her eyes narrowed and calculating.

"Oh look," she sneered, "Sleeping Beauty's finally decided to grace us with her presence. What, too tired from doing nothing all night?"

Melody stiffened. "I wasn't—"

Charlotte cut her off with a scoff. "Don't bother. I hear you in there, tapping away like you're too important to lift a damn finger around here. What exactly do you contribute, huh? Besides attitude?"

Melody's throat tightened. "I was just talking to a friend."

Charlotte laughed, cold and sharp. "A 'friend.' Must be nice to live in a fantasy world where nothing's your fault. Meanwhile, I'm the one doing everything—again. But God forbid you get off your high horse for five minutes."

"I'm sorry," Melody whispered.

Charlotte leaned forward, her voice low and dangerous. "You always say that. Like it means something. But nothing changes. You walk around this house like you're some tragic little martyr. Newsflash: you're not special. You're lazy. You're selfish. And honestly, you're starting to act just like your father—disappearing when it matters, pretending you're the victim."

Melody kept her eyes on the floor, gripping the hem of her sleeve to stop her hands from shaking.

Charlotte exhaled smoke through her nose like a dragon about to burn the place down. "You think you have it hard? Try being me. Try holding this entire mess of a family together while your daughter sulks in the shadows and blames everyone else."

"I didn't—"

"Oh shut up, Melody. Just shut up," Charlotte snapped, standing so suddenly that her chair groaned under the shift. She stabbed the cigarette into the ashtray with unnecessary force. "I can't even look at you when you're like this. So go ahead. Hide. Play your little games. But don't think I don't see exactly who you are."

Without waiting for a response, she stormed down the hallway, her presence leaving the air brittle and hard to breathe.

Melody exhaled, her breath shaky, and went to the kitchen, hoping she could disappear into the quiet before the rest of the morning's chaos began.

At school, the day dragged on like it always did. The crowded hallways, the whispers, the disapproving stares—nothing changed. Melody felt like she was wearing a mask, pretending to be just another face in the crowd, even though inside, she was anything but.

She pulled out her phone during lunch, seeking the familiar comfort of Lucian's messages. Her fingers trembled a little as she unlocked the screen.

> How's your day going? Did your mom let you out of your cage yet?

Melody smiled faintly at his playful tone. She couldn't

remember the last time someone had asked her how her day was going, or if she was okay, with such genuine interest.

> It's been... the usual. Mom's pissed because I stayed up too late again.

> She doesn't know you're a night owl? I swear, some people have no sense of timing.

Melody couldn't help but chuckle at his response. It felt good to laugh, even just for a moment.

> Yeah, well, she thinks I'm lazy. That I don't do anything.

> She doesn't get it, does she? I bet if she really saw you, she'd understand how hard you work to keep it all together.

Melody's heart skipped at the kindness in his words. She wasn't used to being seen in that way. Her family never really acknowledged the effort it took for her to stay afloat, to keep quiet in the face of constant criticism.

> You're probably right. I feel like I'm invisible sometimes.

> You're not invisible to me, Melody. You're special. And don't you ever forget that.

The words filled her up, giving her strength. She felt like maybe she wasn't just some background character in her own life. Maybe Lucian could see her, in a way no one else did.

After the final bell, Melody walked slowly through the crowded halls, her thoughts still swirling around Lucian's words. She was already tired of the routine—the same faces, the same whispers behind her back, the same hollow feelings.

Instead of heading home, she found herself walking in the opposite direction, her feet taking her toward the local witch shop. The local witch shop, *Moonlight & Thorn*, was nestled between an antique bookstore and a boarded-up barber shop, its windows filled with dried herbs, crystals, and a crescent moon mirror that always caught her eye. Faded velvet curtains hung just behind the glass, and hand-painted signs advertised hand-made oils, tarot readings, and "charms for the restless heart."

A small brass bell jingled overhead as she pushed open the door. The scent of sage and sandalwood wrapped around her instantly like a cloak.

"Hey, love," called the shop owner, a woman in her thirties with silver-dyed hair, thick winged eyeliner, and rings on every finger. Her name was Rowan, and Melody had only spoken with her a few times, but there was a warmth in the way she said *love* that made Melody feel safe.

At the back of the shop, an altar stood surrounded by offerings of incense and small trinkets. Melody stood before it for a long moment, breathing deeply, feeling the weight of the day slip off her shoulders. Here, in this quiet, magical place, she could breathe without feeling judged or small.

"Looking for something to help you feel grounded?" Rowan asked, her voice soft but knowing.

Melody hesitated, then nodded. "Yeah... I guess I need something to help me focus. Something to protect me."

The woman smiled gently and pointed to a small display of obsidian stones. "Obsidian is a good choice for protection. It can help clear away negative energy and give you a sense of stability."

Melody picked up one of the smooth black stones, examining it closely. She felt its weight in her palm, the cool surface grounding her. Something about it called to her. After a moment, she tucked the obsidian into her bag, deciding it was the right time to take the stone.

Instead of wandering aimlessly through the shop, she made her way to the small book section. Her eyes scanned the titles, and she pulled a worn-looking book from the shelf, its title in gold lettering: *The Craft of the Wise*. She ran her fingers over the cover, feeling the pull of something deeper.

"Is this one any good?" she asked the shopkeeper.

The woman nodded. "That's a great choice. It's full of practical spells, rituals, and ways to connect with the natural world. It might help you with what you're looking for."

Melody smiled and tucked the book into her bag. She wasn't sure what she was hoping to find in it, but she had a feeling it would give her something she needed.

After wandering around a bit longer, she also picked up a bundle of sage for clearing energy and a small vial of lavender oil —something soothing for her nerves.

She made her way to the counter, the woman ringing up her items with a knowing smile.

"That'll be fifty-two dollars," the woman said softly.

Melody counted out the cash, her fingers brushing against the edges of the bills. As she handed the money over, she felt a sense of calm settle over her. It wasn't just the items she had bought—it was the feeling of taking control, of taking a step toward something that made her feel more than just invisible.

With her purchases carefully tucked into her bag, Melody stepped back out into the fading light of the day. The world outside still felt the same, full of noise and expectations. But she felt like she had something that was just hers, a way to begin carving out her own space in a world that had never really understood her.

When she arrived home, Melody wasn't surprised to find her mother's harsh words still echoing in her mind. But the text from Lucian had helped to keep the panic at bay, if only just for a while. As she walked through the door, she steeled herself for whatever Charlotte had in store for her next.

Charlotte was sitting in her usual spot on the couch, cigarette in hand. "Where the hell have you been? You think you're just going to come home and do whatever you want?"

Melody paused in the doorway. "I went to the library. I needed some quiet."

Charlotte scoffed, blowing smoke into the air. "A quiet place? What, you're a scholar now? You think you're better than everyone in this house?"

"I never said that," Melody replied, her voice tight. "I just needed space."

Charlotte's eyes narrowed. "Oh, poor little Melody needs *space*. Cry me a river. You don't pay bills, you don't clean this house, you don't get space. You want something to do? Start acting like a real person."

Melody clenched her fists. Lucian's words echoed through her mind: *"You don't deserve this. You're special."*

"I *am* a real person," she said, her voice firmer now. "And I'm trying. You just don't see it."

Charlotte leaned forward on the couch, jabbing her cigarette in the air. "What I see is a freak playing dress-up in my house, thinking the world owes her something."

"I'm not a freak," Melody snapped. "You just hate anything you can't control."

Charlotte stood abruptly, the couch creaking behind her. "Say that again."

"I said you can't stand that I'm not like you," Melody said, chest heaving. "I want something different. I want peace. And I'm not going to let you make me feel disgusting for that anymore."

Charlotte's face twisted into a sneer. "Different? You think you're something special? You're not special. You're a broken little girl hiding behind eyeliner and excuses."

Melody didn't flinch this time. "Better than hiding behind anger and bitterness."

Charlotte's hand twitched, like she might raise it—but she didn't. She threw her cigarette in the ashtray instead and stormed into the kitchen, muttering curses under her breath.

Melody felt something shift inside her. It wasn't much, but it was enough to keep her standing tall in the face of her mother's relentless criticism.

She took a deep breath. She wouldn't let her mother break her. She'd keep that spark of hope alive.

It didn't make the world any easier, but it made her feel like there was still something worth fighting for.

The evening had fallen heavy and suffocating around Melody. After the blowup with her mom earlier that day—the yelling, the venomous insults, the moment Charlotte lurched forward like she might actually hit her, Melody had barricaded herself in her room, her body buzzing with the residue of rage and fear. She had stood her ground for once, forced the words out through a throat thick with panic, and still, it hadn't mattered. Charlotte had fired back harder, meaner, louder.

"You're a broken little girl hiding behind eyeliner and excuses."

Those words hit harder now, echoing through the silence, embedding themselves in her like splinters. Her brother's laughter had followed, piercing the tense quiet of the house like a blade, his mockery turning her pain into a spectacle.

Her chest was tight, like something was pressing down on it, squeezing until her ribs ached. Her heart thudded with the kind of anxious rhythm she couldn't slow down no matter how many deep breaths she tried to take. She felt dizzy, exposed, humiliated, and worst of all, alone.

The bruises from the day didn't mark her skin, but they

throbbed beneath it, deep in the places no one could see. The tension in the house always bled into her, always landed on her. Charlotte didn't need to leave marks to hurt her. Her words were enough. They always were.

Melody sat on her bed with her knees drawn to her chest, her phone glowing dimly beside her, casting a cold light on the blanket. She felt hollow—emptied out by the fight, the shame, the aftermath. All that was left was the ache.

Wednesday leapt softly onto the bed, curling against Melody's side like she always did when something was wrong. The weight and warmth of her small body grounded Melody, just enough to stop the spiraling. She reached down, stroking behind Wednesday's ears. The cat purred, eyes closing slowly.

Melody sniffled and whispered, "I need to feel safe again."

She got up and pulled a small wooden box from beneath her bed. Inside: a black candle, dried rosemary, a slip of paper scrawled with a protective sigil, and a piece of smoky quartz. She set them out carefully on her windowsill altar, the one she'd pieced together from found bones, thrifted lace, and stolen moments of stillness.

She lit the candle with shaking hands and murmured a protection charm under her breath, the same one she had copied from a tattered book at the library and practiced so many times it had become muscle memory. Wednesday sat nearby, tail curled around her paws, watching silently.

"I cast this circle to keep the pain out," Melody whispered. "I ask for quiet. I ask for strength. I ask for someone who sees me."

The flame flickered, almost in response. She closed her eyes and pressed the quartz to her chest, breathing in the scent of rosemary and wax. For a few moments, the air felt thicker, less sharp. She stayed like that until the candle burned halfway down.

But the ache was still there, simmering beneath the ritual like an unhealed wound.

Her hand moved before her thoughts could catch up, reaching for the hidden drawer. She knew exactly where the blade was. She always did. Her fingers curled around it, trembling.

Just one. One cut to dull it down. One to quiet everything Charlotte had screamed into her. One to feel something she could actually control.

She drew the razor across her skin, exhaling shakily as the sting registered. A single tear slid down her cheek. A part of her recoiled, hating herself for it. But another part, the quieter one that usually won, embraced the relief.

Blood welled in soft, stinging lines. It wasn't enough. She did it again. And again.

But this time, the pain didn't quiet the storm, it amplified it. Her chest tightened further, not with release but with something suffocating and cold. Her hands shook harder. The air felt too thin.

The walls were closing in, and she couldn't breathe.

Her phone buzzed.

Lucian.

She stared at his name for a moment, then quickly wiped the tears from her eyes and the blood from her wrist. She wasn't sure if she should respond, but a part of her felt desperate to reach out. She knew he couldn't fix everything. Hell, she wasn't even sure he could fix anything. But the idea that someone cared, someone actually cared, felt almost as if it could give her a breath of air. Something to hold onto.

> Hey, I just wanted to check in. How are you holding up?

Her heart raced as her fingers hovered over the keyboard. She almost wanted to lie. Tell him everything was fine. That she was fine. But she wasn't. She wasn't fine at all.

After a few moments, Melody typed back, her fingers shaking.

> I'm okay. Just... tired. It's been a rough day.

She bit her lip and waited for his response, the weight of her emotions pressing heavily on her chest. Her hand instinctively reached for the razor blade again, but she stopped herself.

I'm sorry you're going through that. Do you want to talk about it?

Her heart dropped. She wanted to. She really wanted to, but something in her made her hesitate. Her stomach twisted, the words caught in her throat. Her thumb hovered over the keys, but she couldn't bring herself to type them.

I don't know if I can talk about it yet.

Her phone buzzed again.

It's okay. I'm here for you, no matter what. You don't have to talk if you're not ready.

She smiled a little, even as the pain in her wrist continued to throb. He was kind. So kind. But she still felt that overwhelming sense of shame that always followed the self-harm.

I don't deserve your kindness.

The text lingered on the screen before she could even look at it. She hadn't meant to say it, but it was true. She felt like a mess. Like she was a burden.

You deserve kindness, Melody. You really do. And I'm not going anywhere. You don't have to go through this alone.

Her throat tightened. She let the words sink in, feeling a small, fragile warmth at the center of her chest. But the dark pull in her mind was still there. Still lingering, waiting for her to fall back into the numbness.

> I don't know how to stop. I don't know how to
> make the pain go away.

She hit send, then closed her eyes. The weight of it all felt unbearable.

> I don't want you to hurt yourself, Melody. I
> want you to feel better. But hurting yourself
> won't help. I know it feels like it does, but it
> only makes everything worse in the long run.

Her chest ached as she read his words. He was right. She knew that. She had always known it. But it never felt real when she was in the moment, when the ache inside her was so deep, so consuming, that nothing else seemed to matter.

> I don't know what to do. I did something... I
> don't know how to stop.

Her heart raced as she typed the next part, her fingers trembling on the screen.

> I... I hurt myself. I cut. I don't know how to
> make it stop.

The text felt like it might burn a hole in her phone. It was the first time she had ever said it out loud, and the shame overwhelmed her. She immediately regretted sending it, but before she could delete the message, her phone buzzed.

> What? Melody, no. You shouldn't have to do
> that. You don't have to hurt yourself. I'm so
> sorry you're feeling this way. Please, talk to me
> about it. I can't believe you're carrying all of
> this alone.

Melody's breath hitched. She wasn't sure what she had expected, but it wasn't this. This wasn't the angry response she feared. It wasn't judgment. It was concern. Real, raw concern.

She couldn't stop herself from shaking.

> I don't know why I did it. It just... it felt like the only way to get rid of the pain. I hate myself for it.

Her tears came in hot waves now, the dam she had built around her emotions cracking. The blood on her wrist was drying, but the emotional weight of what she'd just confessed felt so much heavier than the pain she had caused herself.

> I'm not mad at you. I'm not angry. I just... I want you to be okay. Please, Melody, don't hurt yourself. I need you to know that you don't have to go through this alone. I'm here. Please, can we talk on the phone?

Melody stared at the screen, feeling the weight of his words pressing into her. The thought of talking to him on the phone felt almost impossible. It felt too intimate, too real. Her chest tightened at the idea of hearing his voice.

> I don't know. I'm scared... of what I'll say, or... or what you'll think of me.

> I won't think less of you, Melody. I promise. But you're carrying all of this by yourself, and I don't want you to feel like that anymore. You deserve help. You deserve someone who's not going to run away just because things get messy. Please, talk to me. Let me help.

She closed her eyes, the shaking in her hands spreading to the rest of her body. He was so kind. So gentle. But it was hard for her to believe that anyone could actually *care* about her like this.

Her fingers hovered over the screen for what felt like forever, and then, finally, her breath shaky, she typed.

Okay... I'll call you.

A few moments passed, and the silence between them felt endless. But then, his reply came through.

I'm here. It's just me, Melody. Take your time.
I'm not going anywhere.

Her palms were sweating, her heart racing in her chest, but she couldn't keep putting it off. This was what she needed. She tapped the call button.

The phone rang, and it felt like the sound filled her entire body. Her breath hitched with every ring. What would he say? Would he be disappointed in her? Would he take back what he said—that he cared?

Then, his voice came through, and it was like a balm to her nerves.

"Hey. I'm here. Take a deep breath, okay? Just talk to me. It's just you and me."

Melody closed her eyes as her tears fell, feeling exposed but somehow safe in his voice. She felt like maybe things could be okay.

"I don't know why it hurts so much. I don't know how to stop."

There was a faint creak on the line, like Lucian settling onto an old mattress or a worn out couch. She heard the rustle of a blanket being pulled up and the soft clink of a mug being set on a nearby table. His voice came through again, low and steady, but something about it now felt different, more vulnerable.

"I know," he said, his words dragging with weight. "I know, and I'm not going to let you hurt yourself anymore. I'm here. And I'm not going anywhere. I'm not letting you go."

Somewhere in the background, a record played—something slow, dark, and rich, the vinyl crackling softly under the melody. The tiny, imperfect sounds of his world made her ache less, grounding her in a moment that felt real, alive.

Melody believed him.

"I'm really proud of you, you know," Lucian's voice softened as if he were speaking to her heart. "It's not easy to open up, especially about something so personal. I know it's hard, but you're not alone in this anymore. You've got me."

Melody held her breath, the weight of his words sinking deep into her heart. No one had ever said anything like that to her before—not her mom, not her dad. Certainly not anyone at school. She had always been the one who kept everything inside, who hid the truth behind a mask. But with Lucian, something about his sincerity made her feel... seen. Like she wasn't as invisible as she'd always felt.

"Thank you... for not leaving," she whispered, her voice trembling, not from pain this time, but from something unfamiliar and fragile. Hope.

Lucian's breath shifted on the other end, a slight hitch as he exhaled, almost as if he were holding something in.

"I'm not going anywhere, Melody," his voice came back strong, but there was a warmth there now, a steady reassurance. "I'll be here, okay? You can reach out whenever you need me. Day or night."

There was a beat of silence between them, soft and intimate. Then, Melody's voice broke the quiet again, small but clear.

"Before... before everything tonight, I actually tried to do something to help myself. I—I did this protection charm. Like a little ritual."

Lucian was quiet for a second, but not in a judging way, more like he was surprised and then deeply interested.

"A ritual? You mean like witchy stuff?"

Melody laughed softly, a tiny crack in the grief. "Yeah. I lit candles, burned rosemary... said this spell I wrote. I know it probably sounds silly but—"

"No," he cut in gently. "No, that's not silly at all. That's actually kind of... badass."

Her cheeks flushed. "You think?"

"I mean, you basically cast a ward spell like a goth witch from some dark fairytale. I love that. I didn't know you were into that kind of thing."

"I don't talk about it much. People already think I'm weird."

Lucian chuckled, the sound warm. "Good. Weird is sacred. I like weird. Especially your kind of weird."

And just then, a soft meow sounded through the phone speaker.

Lucian paused. "Wait. What was that? Was that... a cat?"

Melody smiled despite herself, brushing at the last of her tears. "That was Wednesday."

"As in Addams?"

"Exactly."

"I love that so much," Lucian said, practically grinning through the phone. "What's she like?"

"She's my familiar. Or at least she thinks she is. She follows me everywhere, yells at me when I cry, and knocks over my candles during rituals just for fun."

"Okay, she's definitely a witch cat. Certified. 100%."

Melody giggled softly, and for the first time that day, the sound wasn't forced.

"I think she knew I needed you to call. She started pacing right before you texted."

Lucian's voice dropped to something even softer, something reverent. "She's got good instincts. I'm glad she's there with you."

There was a pause, gentle and full.

Then, Lucian spoke again—quietly, but with gentle seriousness.

"Can you promise me something?"

Melody wiped at her face. "What?"

"That you won't hurt yourself again tonight. I know it's hard, but I need to hear you say it. Just for tonight, okay? Promise me."

Her breath caught. The request wasn't harsh. It wasn't

controlling. It was careful, tender, like he was offering her a life-line, not demanding obedience.

"I... I'll try," she said, her voice small.

"Melody," Lucian said softly, "I'm not asking for perfect. Just a promise. You don't have to carry the pain alone. Let me help you hold it. Please... just promise me for tonight."

She hesitated, her fingers brushing the edge of the night-stand. Then, she pulled her hand away.

"I promise."

Lucian's relief was almost audible. "Thank you. That means everything to me."

She nodded, even though he couldn't see it. It was hard to believe, but in the quiet of her room, it almost felt true.

"I think I need to sleep now... I'm really tired," she murmured, her eyelids fluttering heavy.

"Of course," Lucian said, his voice gentle, as if he were right there beside her. "I don't want to keep you up. You need your rest. But I'm just a text or a call away if you need anything."

"I will. I promise."

She felt exhausted, her body heavy with both the emotional weight of everything she had revealed and the comfort that came with knowing someone cared. It was a strange feeling—like there was a small light flickering inside her, one that she didn't want to extinguish.

Lucian's voice softened, almost like a whisper now, as if he was speaking to her soul rather than just over the phone.

"Sleep well, Melody. You're safe now. I'm here."

His words lingered, wrapping around her like a warm blanket as she took a deep breath, letting them settle in her chest. There was something so real in his voice, like she could hear the care in every syllable.

She ended the call and placed the phone on her nightstand, the silence in the room now soothing instead of suffocating. She turned over onto her side, the soft weight of the blankets surrounding her. It wasn't a perfect ending, but it was something. Something more than she had ever allowed herself to believe.

Wednesday curled beside her, purring softly against her arm. Melody closed her eyes, letting the exhaustion wash over her. She wasn't alone. Not anymore.

Sleep folded over her like a hush, softer than it had been in ages. Deep in her chest, a tender spark of hope glowed—fragile, but unwilling to fade. The world wasn't healed, not yet. But tomorrow would arrive, and with it, the quiet possibility that she didn't have to shoulder everything alone.

CHAPTER FIVE

The sound of her phone vibrating on the nightstand cut through the haze of sleep. Melody's eyes fluttered open, and she reached over, grabbing the device before the noise could wake her mom up.

She blinked, still groggy, but the sight of his message brought a small wave of comfort. She smiled, a slow, tired smile, before typing a response.

She glanced at the clock. It was just after 6:30 AM. Her mom would be awake soon, and Melody needed to get moving if she didn't want to be stuck with her all morning.

I do. Thanks... it means a lot.

She slipped out of bed and padded quietly to the bathroom, her feet cold against the hardwood floor. As the hot water from the shower hit her skin, she let it wash away the tiredness, the heaviness of everything she'd been carrying. It wasn't a cure, but it was a moment of peace.

While the steam fogged up the bathroom mirror, she grabbed her phone and sent a quick message.

I'm in the shower. Just need a few minutes to wake up.

No rush. I'm just glad you're still talking to me.

Melody smiled, the warmth of the water mingling with the warmth of his words. She rinsed her hair and finished her shower, then wrapped herself in a towel before heading back to her room.

She stood in front of the mirror, glancing at the faint marks on her arms, a reminder of the night before. She winced but quickly pushed the thought away. There were things she needed to do. She wouldn't let herself dwell on it.

As she started her routine, she checked her phone again.

How are you this morning? Did you sleep okay?

I didn't sleep much. I keep thinking about everything. But I'm okay. Just really tired.

She opened her closet, pulling out a pair of tight, black jeans, a band tee with an oversized graphic, and a long-sleeve black shirt with slashed sleeves. She dressed quickly, feeling the weight of the day ahead of her. Then, she sat in front of her vanity and started applying her makeup, more eyeliner than usual, thick dark lines accenting her eyes, and a smudge of dark shadow. Her lips were bare, just the pale, cool tone of her skin.

Her phone buzzed again.

> I know it's tough, but you're doing great. Just remember to take it one step at a time, okay?

> Yeah, I'll try. It's just... hard. Every day feels like I'm pretending.

Her fingers trembled slightly as she finished her makeup, but she kept texting.

> You're not pretending to me. You don't have to wear a mask with me. Ever.

Melody paused, looking at herself in the mirror. His words were like a balm on a raw wound. She almost felt... seen.

She quickly finished her makeup—just a bit of mascara, and some dark eyeshadow, and then grabbed her bag. As she moved to the kitchen, she saw her mom sitting at the table, sipping coffee. Charlotte didn't look up as Melody entered, just gave a half-hearted grunt.

"Morning," Melody said quietly, already knowing it would be the extent of their conversation.

Charlotte sniffed and glanced at Melody, raising an eyebrow. "I don't know why you insist on dressing like a freak. You could at least look somewhat presentable for school. Don't you think you'd get along better with people if you didn't dress like that?"

Melody's stomach twisted, and she bit her lip, trying to keep her cool. But before she could reply, her dad stepped into the kitchen, a cup of coffee in hand.

"Leave her alone, Charlotte. She's fine the way she is," Andrew said, his voice low but firm.

"Oh, so now you're defending her?" Charlotte snapped, her voice sharp with irritation. "You've let her get away with everything. She's a mess."

Andrew's eyes narrowed, his frustration growing. "A mess? No. You're the fucking mess, Charlotte. You've let Nick do whatever the hell he wants, and you let him get away with it. It's all about him, isn't it?"

Charlotte's face flushed red with anger. Her hands clenched into fists, and she suddenly shoved Andrew, hard, her shoulder digging into his chest. "Don't talk to me about him, Andrew. You don't know what he's been through. You don't get it!"

Melody froze, her heart pounding in her chest. The sound of her mother's shove echoed in the kitchen like a clap of thunder. Andrew didn't flinch, didn't push back, but his face twisted with a mixture of disbelief and rage. He stepped back slightly, steadying himself, but never raised his hand to her. He just stared at her, his breathing slow and heavy.

"You're the one who doesn't get it, Charlotte," Andrew growled, his voice thick with anger. "Nick's a fucking disaster. He's lazy, selfish, and he gets away with everything because you've built this whole world around him. I'm sick of it. You're blind to it. You've been blind for years."

Charlotte's eyes flashed with fury as she pushed him again, this time more forcefully, her hands digging into his chest as she shoved him back. "Don't talk about my son like that. He's my son, and I will protect him from people like you. You don't know how hard it is to deal with him. You don't know what he's been through."

"I'm not talking about him like that," Andrew snapped, voice steady but full of venom. "I'm talking about how you've made him into some kind of fucking king, when he's really just a lazy, entitled asshole who's never had to work for anything."

Melody's body tensed, every word slicing through her like glass. She didn't know what was worse—the yelling, the pushing, or the sickening feeling that no one was ever going to stand up for her. Her parents were always like this—one-sided, always about Nick, always about Charlotte's blind favoritism.

Charlotte's voice grew shrill, her words coming out in a

biting hiss. "I do everything for Nick! Everything! He's my son, and I will protect him from people like you. You don't know how hard it is to deal with him, to deal with his problems. You never even try!"

Andrew stood there, his chest heaving as he stared at Charlotte, a mix of disbelief and bitterness in his eyes. "You're protecting him from the truth, Charlotte. That's the problem. You've made him think he's untouchable. Well, he's not. He's a fucking loser, and I'm sick of pretending otherwise."

Charlotte shoved him again, so hard this time that he stumbled back a few steps. She was breathing heavily now, her anger almost palpable. "You don't get to talk about him like that. He's my son. I'll deal with him, and I don't need you telling me how to do it!"

Andrew didn't move, his voice low and steady. "Maybe you should start dealing with him, because I'm done. Done with this family, done with this shit."

The words hung in the air, thick with the weight of years of unresolved tension. Charlotte's lip curled into a sneer as she glared at Andrew, but she didn't make another move toward him. The room was silent for a long moment, save for the sound of both of their labored breathing.

"I'm done," Andrew said again, his voice low, his eyes cold.

He stormed out of the kitchen, his steps heavy, leaving the tension in the room like an open wound. Charlotte watched him go, her hands still clenched into fists at her sides, but she didn't say anything more. The anger simmered between them, unresolved.

Melody stood there, feeling the cold air of the kitchen wrap around her like a suffocating blanket. The noise of the argument, the pushing, the anger, it was always like this. She wanted to leave, to run far away, but she knew she couldn't. Her feet felt frozen to the floor, her stomach twisting as she tried to breathe past the knot in her throat.

Charlotte turned away from the door where Andrew had left, muttering to herself. "Fucking coward. You never do anything anyway."

Melody grabbed her bag, feeling the weight of her frustration, her fear, and her hopelessness settle over her like a heavy cloak. She didn't belong here.

How's your morning going so far?

Melody sighed, her fingers hovering over the keys. The fight with her mother was still fresh in her mind, her mom's words echoing painfully.

Same as always. Mom's being... well, mom.
She called me a freak again because of how I
dress. I can't even get through the day without
her saying something hurtful.

There was a brief pause before Lucian's reply came, and she found herself waiting, hoping he'd be there with the right words to make her feel less alone.

I'm sorry she's treating you that way. But let me
tell you something: you are not a freak. You're
unique, and there's beauty in that. I know it's
hard, but you don't have to change for anyone,
especially not her.

Melody stared at the screen, then typed slowly.

> It wasn't just what she said. She and my dad were screaming at each other again. She kept pushing him. He just stood there, didn't touch her back. But I hated it. The yelling, the tension. I was just standing in the kitchen like furniture. No one even looked at me.

She stared at her message before hitting send, her hands shaking slightly. She hadn't told anyone that part before.

Lucian replied quickly this time.

> That sounds terrifying. I hate that you had to stand there and watch all that. You deserve so much better than that kind of chaos.

Another message followed right after.

> You aren't invisible to me, okay? You're not furniture. You matter. And it's so unfair that they treat you like you don't. You should feel safe in your own home, not like a ghost haunting the room.

Melody swallowed hard, eyes stinging.

> I didn't even do anything. I was just there. But somehow I always end up feeling like I'm the problem. Like I'm the reason everything's broken.

> You're not. None of this is your fault. Your parents are responsible for their own choices, and it's not on you to carry the weight of their dysfunction. You being yourself, dressing how you want, feeling deeply, needing love, that's not a flaw. That's what makes you you. And I think that version of you is beautiful.

Melody felt a warmth spread through her chest, the raw emotion of his words wrapping around her like a blanket. She hadn't expected him to be so quick to comfort her, to be so sure of her worth. For the first time, someone saw her. Not the version her mom painted of her, but the real her.

> You're strong, Melody. I'm really proud of you
> for standing strong, even when she tries to tear
> you down. I know it's tough, but just keep
> being yourself. You don't have to put up with
> her cruelty. I'm here for you, okay?

She paused before replying.

> Thank you. I don't know why, but when you say
> those things… it makes me believe it, even if
> just for a second. Like maybe I'm not crazy.
> Maybe I'm not broken.

> You're not broken. You're surviving in a world
> that hasn't given you the care you deserve.
> That doesn't mean there's something wrong
> with you. It means you're resilient. And yeah,
> I'll remind you as many times as you need.
> You're not alone anymore.

Her heart lightened, the weight of her mother's words not so crushing anymore. Lucian's presence, even in a text, felt like a safe haven. She smiled a little, the first genuine smile of the morning.

She tucked her phone into her pocket, grabbed her coat, and slipped out the door. The cold air hit her face, sharp and grounding. She pulled her coat tighter, the weight of her backpack oddly comforting as she walked to the bus stop. The world felt bigger out here, but with the echo of Lucian's words still in her chest, she didn't feel quite as alone.

Between classes, Melody pulled out her phone, her heart giving a tiny lift when she saw his name pop up on the screen.

How's school? You surviving so far?

She smiled to herself, thumbs already moving.

Just about. It's not the worst day, but I'm already counting the minutes until I can go home.

The reply came almost instantly, like he'd been waiting.

Just a few more hours. You've got this.

She laughed under her breath, tucking her hair behind her ear as a few students brushed past her in the hallway. Lucian always knew how to make the worst days feel a little lighter.

I know you're busy, but I'm here if you need to vent or talk about anything. Don't forget.

She clutched the phone a little tighter.

I won't. Promise.

Classes blurred by, each one feeling longer than the last. When lunchtime finally came, she all but collapsed into the farthest corner of the cafeteria, pulling out her phone like it was a lifeline.

Can we talk after school? I just need a little distraction.

She tapped send, nervously bouncing her leg under the table.

Of course. I'll be here. Talk to you soon.

Reluctantly, she started to put her phone away — then hesitated. A question had been itching at the back of her mind. She chewed her lip before typing again.

> Hey, can I ask you something? What do you do
> for a living?

There was a slight pause this time, and she imagined him leaning back somewhere, thinking.

> I'm a welder. I work mostly with metal, building
> and fixing stuff. It's a lot of precision work, but
> I like it. Feels good to make something with my
> hands, you know?

She pictured him— sparks flying, sleeves rolled up, serious and focused, and flushed a little.

> That sounds really cool. I didn't know what to
> picture when I thought about you, but I like
> that. You make stuff.

> Yeah, something like that.

A second message quickly followed.

> What about you? Any idea what you want to
> do when you get older?

Melody stared at the screen, fidgeting with the strap of her backpack. What *did* she want?

> Not really. I just know I don't want to stay stuck
> here. I guess... I just want to feel like I matter,
> you know?

Her heart pounded a little harder after hitting send. What if that sounded stupid?

I get that. And you do matter. To me, you matter.

She bit down on a smile, warmth creeping up her neck.

Thanks. You always know just what to say.

I'm glad I can be here for you.

Her fingers hovered over the keyboard before she added,

I mean... I really love animals. Always have. So maybe something with them, like working at a shelter or even becoming a vet.

She thought for a second longer, her mind flickering to the darker corners of her bookshelf, true crime books stacked under her bed.

But I'm also kinda obsessed with true crime and serial killers. Like, why they do the things they do. Maybe I could be a forensic psychologist or something.

She cringed after sending it. That sounded weird, didn't it?

His reply made her laugh out loud, drawing a few curious looks from nearby students.

That's not weird at all. I actually love true crime too. Always been fascinated by how people think, what makes them snap.

She grinned and leaned back in her chair, feeling a little bolder.

Wait, really? I thought I was the only psycho here.

> Nah, you're not alone. We should start a club:
> Freaks Who Love Serial Killers Anonymous.

She snickered.

> I'm down. We can have secret meetings and
> debate who's the creepiest murderer.

> I'm already prepared to win that debate. Team
> Ted Bundy all the way.

Melody scrunched her nose, tapping a quick reply.

> Ugh, no way. Dahmer's way creepier. Bundy's
> just a boring liar.

> Fair, but you gotta admit Bundy had the whole
> 'charming psycho' thing down. Dahmer was
> just... straight up chilling.

> Exactly why he wins. Straight-up creepy > fake
> charm.

> Tough crowd. Guess I'll have to brush up on
> my serial killer trivia if I'm gonna keep up
> with you.

> Good luck. I'm undefeated.

She hugged the phone to her chest for a second, letting herself bask in the feeling. With Lucian, she didn't feel like some broken girl trapped in a dead-end town. She felt like... herself. And for once, that actually seemed like a good thing.

The front door slammed behind Melody as she trudged into

the house, the sound of her mother's bickering with her father still ringing in her ears. She didn't have the energy to deal with it anymore. She didn't have the energy to deal with anything.

She kicked off her boots and headed straight up to her room, shutting the door behind her with a soft thud. The familiar silence of her sanctuary washed over her, and it felt like a small reprieve.

As she turned to toss her backpack onto the floor, a soft meow caught her attention. Wednesday padded over from the windowsill, her sleek black body weaving through Melody's legs like a comforting shadow. Melody bent down and scooped her up, pressing her cheek into the cat's fur.

"Hey, spooky girl," she whispered, her voice cracking just a little. "You missed me?"

Wednesday purred in response, her tail flicking lazily as Melody carried her to the bed.

She placed the cat gently on her comforter and moved to her nightstand, where a row of mostly-burned candles stood in a crooked line. She chose three—black, white, and deep plum, and struck a match. The scent of sandalwood and patchouli curled into the air as the flames flickered to life, casting soft golden glows that danced across her posters and walls.

She knelt in front of them, closing her eyes for a brief moment.

"For peace," she murmured, lighting the black candle.

"For clarity," she whispered, lighting the white.

"For protection," she added last, touching flame to plum. "From everything that's trying to eat me alive."

It wasn't a full ritual. Just something small. Something to feel like she had even the tiniest bit of control.

She pulled out her phone and checked for messages, Lucian hadn't texted her since school. With a sigh, she plopped down on her bed and grabbed her earbuds, ready to drown out the world.

She slid her phone into the dock and selected Evanescence's *Fallen* album. The opening notes of "Everybody's Fool" filled her ears, the hauntingly emotional lyrics resonating with the dark thoughts swirling in her mind.

Just as the first chorus hit, her phone buzzed with a text notification. Her breath caught in her throat when she saw his name light up on the screen.

> Hey, how did the rest of your day go? You get through school okay?

Melody glanced at the screen, her heart lifting slightly. He was thinking about her. A small comfort in the otherwise heavy air of her room.

> Just another day. But it wasn't too bad, I guess. It's always the same. Get through the day, get home, then hide in my room.

She typed it out quickly, not thinking too much about it. It felt good to be honest, even if it was just a text on a screen.

> I hear you. You're a lot stronger than you think, you know that, right?

She didn't respond right away, letting his words settle into her chest. She closed her eyes for a moment, letting the music continue to play in the background, but her mind wasn't on the album anymore.

Lucian's messages were easy to read, easy to respond to, but there was something that had been nagging at her for a while. She had questions, so many questions. She needed to ask.

She took a deep breath, finally typing out her thoughts.

> Okay, so I've been meaning to ask you something... How do you know my name? And how did you know who I was?

She paused, biting her lip nervously. She had been thinking about this all day, and the need to know the answer had become overwhelming.

> I'm still at work, but I'll call you when I'm off.
> We can talk about it then. I promise.

Melody bit her lip again, chewing on the uncertainty that always clung to her. He was willing to call her, but the wait felt like it would stretch on forever.

"Okay," she typed back quickly, then set her phone down on the bed beside her. She stared at the ceiling for a while, her mind running in circles, but the quiet thrum of her music helped keep her grounded.

The hours seemed to stretch on. She did some of her homework, half-heartedly flipping through pages of a textbook. But her thoughts were still swirling around Lucian. How did he know her name? How did he know who she was?

Finally, her phone buzzed.

> I'm off work now. You still want to talk?

Melody's heart skipped a beat. She quickly grabbed her phone, tapping out a response.

> Yes. Please.

She took a deep breath before answering the call, the phone feeling heavier in her hand than it should. When she swiped to answer, his voice came through immediately, smooth and calm, the kind of voice that made her feel like everything was going to be okay, if only for the moment.

"Hey, Melody," Lucian said, his voice warm and comforting.

"Hey," she replied, trying to keep her voice steady. "I've just... been thinking about everything. About you knowing who I was."

Lucian let out a soft chuckle, though it was more of a sigh. "I know this is probably gonna sound weird, but I've been keeping an eye on you for a while. Not in a creepy way, I promise. I've been looking out for you."

Melody furrowed her brow, unsure of what to say. "But how did you know... my name? My full name?"

"I came across your name through your online profile a while back," Lucian explained, his tone gentle. "And after a bit of research, I found out who you were. I know that sounds weird, but I couldn't stop thinking about you. About how you seemed... lost. And I just wanted to make sure you were okay."

Melody swallowed hard, her stomach flipping at the thought of him researching her. Her mind was racing, but she wanted to understand more.

"So... you've been watching me?" she asked, hesitant.

"Not in a creepy way," Lucian reassured her. "Just... watching over you, making sure you're safe."

There was a long pause. Melody wasn't sure what to feel—relief? Unease? There was something unsettling, yet reassuring, about his words.

"I guess I was just... curious. About you," he continued. "You seem like someone who gets it. Who understands things in a way that others don't. And when I saw you online, I knew I wanted to talk to you."

Melody felt a sense of vulnerability rising in her chest. "I don't know what to think about all of this, Lucian," she admitted quietly. "It's a lot to process."

"I get it," he said softly. "You don't have to figure it all out right away. But I do care about you, Melody. And I want to be here for you."

She closed her eyes, fighting the emotions threatening to spill over. "I'm 15," she said, the words coming out in a rush. "Your profile says you're 32. You're a grown man. I don't know if that's okay."

There was a brief silence on the other end of the line, and Melody's stomach twisted with nervous energy.

Lucian finally spoke, his voice steady and calm. "I understand how that might feel weird, but I'm not bothered by your age, Melody. I'm here because I see you. I see you for who you are—

not just your age, not just the number, but the person you are inside."

Melody felt a strange sense of relief, though the uncertainty didn't fully go away. "I don't know how to deal with all of this," she said softly. "It feels like everything's a mess."

"I know it feels that way," Lucian said gently. "But I'm not going anywhere. You're not alone, Melody. I'm here for you, no matter what."

The comfort in his voice, the reassurance, made something inside her loosen. She didn't know what this was, what they were, but for the first time in what felt like forever, she felt like she had someone who cared, someone who understood.

"Thank you," she whispered, her voice shaky.

"Always," he replied.

After a beat of silence, Melody asked, "Can I ask you something kind of random?"

"Of course," Lucian said, and she could almost hear the smile in his voice.

"Where do you live?" she asked quietly, curious now that they'd been talking so much.

"I'm in northern Idaho. Pretty small place. It's cold and kind of isolated, honestly," he said with a soft laugh. "But I like it. There's peace out here. Mountains, woods... no one breathing down your neck."

Melody smiled faintly. "That sounds kind of nice. I've never been there. I'm in Oregon. It's always raining."

"I knew you had Pacific Northwest vibes," he teased gently. "You feel like someone who lives under gray skies and writes poetry in the margins of her notebooks."

She laughed under her breath, the sound shy but real. "That's... not far off."

"How far are we, you think?" Lucian asked. "Couple hundred miles?"

"I don't know. Maybe more? It's probably like... a ten-hour drive. Maybe more. I've never really been out of Oregon."

"Well, that's not *too* far," he said, his voice soft. "Close enough to feel real. Far enough to still dream about it."

Melody was quiet for a moment, staring at the ceiling. "Do you ever think about meeting the people you connect with online?"

Lucian didn't answer right away. "Sometimes. But only if the connection's real. Only if it's safe, for both people."

She nodded slowly, even though he couldn't see it. "Yeah... yeah, that makes sense."

And the silence between them didn't feel empty. It felt full of something unspoken—dangerous, maybe. But also comforting. Like maybe someone in the world actually saw her.

The phone call stretched on, the connection between Melody and Lucian growing stronger with every word. She had been hesitant at first, but now, there was something comforting about hearing his voice. The way he talked made her feel like he truly cared, like she wasn't just some stranger on the other side of the screen. It was different from anything she'd ever experienced.

"So," Lucian said, his voice playful, "we've talked a lot about deep stuff, but let's lighten things up a bit. What's your favorite band?"

Melody smiled softly, grateful for the change in tone. Music had always been her escape, her constant companion in the darker moments of her life.

"Evanescence," she said without hesitation. "I've been obsessed with their *Fallen* album for years. It's like they get it, you know? That whole... darkness and loss. It's like they've been living my life."

"Evanescence, huh?" Lucian mused. "I can see that. You've definitely got that vibe." He paused, and Melody could almost hear him smiling on the other end of the line. "You remind me of Amy Lee, actually. The way you talk, the way you express yourself... you kind of look like her too."

Melody's heart skipped a beat, a flush creeping up her neck. She'd heard that comparison before, but hearing it from Lucian made it feel different. "Amy Lee?" she asked, her voice a little softer now. "I mean... I guess I can see that. She's beautiful."

Lucian's voice turned sincere, and Melody could tell he wasn't just saying it to flatter her. "You're beautiful, Melody. Just like her. You have this... intensity about you. Like, even though I can't see you, I can tell that your beauty goes beyond just your looks. You have something deep inside that draws people in."

Melody felt a lump form in her throat. She didn't know how to respond to something like that. Nobody had ever spoken to her like that, like she mattered for more than just her appearance.

"Thanks," she whispered, unsure of what else to say. "I don't really think of myself like that, though. But I guess... it's nice to hear."

Lucian chuckled lightly. "Trust me, you'll start believing it soon enough. You've got a lot more to you than you realize."

Melody felt a flutter of warmth in her chest. She couldn't explain why, but she felt safe with him. He saw her in a way that nobody else did. It was a strange, comforting thought.

"So, what about you?" she asked, eager to shift the attention back to him. "What's your favorite band?"

Lucian's response was immediate, almost like he'd been waiting for the question. "Skinny Puppy, Type O Negative, Motley Crue, and Marilyn Manson. I'm all about the dark, industrial stuff... but I also love a little rock 'n' roll, you know?"

Melody laughed softly. "Wow, we've got some overlap. I love Marilyn Manson too. And Nine Inch Nails. But I'm more into HIM, Evanescence... I guess you could say I'm more of the gothic, emotional side of things."

"Gothic and emotional, huh?" Lucian teased. "That suits you.

I bet you've got that whole *romantic darkness* thing down, don't you?"

"Maybe," Melody said with a grin, "I guess I'm just kind of drawn to things that aren't... so happy. I don't know. It just feels real, you know?"

"I get it," Lucian replied. "There's a rawness to it. The darker stuff, whether it's music, or just life in general, feels like it speaks the truth. It doesn't hide anything, and it doesn't pretend to be anything it's not. It just... *is*."

Melody nodded, though she knew he couldn't see her. "Exactly. That's why I love it. It's the only thing that feels honest sometimes."

There was a comfortable silence between them for a moment, the music in the background giving them both space to just exist in the conversation. Melody was starting to feel like they were really getting to know each other, not just the surface-level stuff, but the kind of things that made people who they were. It felt good.

"So, what's your go-to song when you're in your feels?" Melody asked, a bit of curiosity creeping in.

Lucian thought for a moment. "It's hard to pick just one, but probably *Everything Dies* by Type O Negative. That song just hits different. It's got this... melancholy to it that I can't escape, but it's also comforting in a way."

"That's a good one," Melody said with a smile. "For me, it's probably *Missing* by Evanescence. It just... I don't know. It's haunting. It's like the song is written for me, you know?"

"I can hear that," Lucian said softly. "You've got that same kind of weight to you. Like you've been through some stuff, but you still carry yourself with a strength that's hard to ignore."

Melody's chest tightened at his words. She wasn't used to hearing people talk about her like that. Lucian wasn't sugar-coating anything, but his words didn't feel like criticism either. It was like he understood her in a way she didn't even understand herself.

"I guess I'm just trying to survive, you know?" she said, her voice a little quieter now. "Some days, it feels like everything's just too much, and I don't know how to handle it."

Lucian's voice grew more serious. "You don't have to handle it alone, Melody. I'm here, okay? Whatever you need, whenever you need it, I'll be here."

His words made something inside of her relax, just a little. She didn't know where this was going, but she felt like maybe it was okay to need someone. Maybe it was okay to be vulnerable.

"Thanks," she whispered, her voice barely audible. "I really appreciate that."

"Anytime," Lucian replied, his tone soft. "Just remember, you're not as alone as you think you are. I've got your back."

For the first time, Melody felt like she wasn't drowning. She wasn't okay, not by a long shot, but there was hope that she could be.

CHAPTER SIX

The night had grown quiet, and Melody was stretched out on her bed, the soft glow of her bedside lamp casting gentle shadows on the walls. The sound of her breathing was steady, her body finally beginning to relax after a long, emotionally exhausting day. The faint hum of her playlist still lingered in the background, though now it was more like a distant memory of the music she had played earlier.

Lucian's voice had become a soft lullaby to her ears, his words calming and steady, almost like he had been trying to coax her into sleep.

"You still awake?" Lucian asked, his voice quieter than before, as if he knew it was getting late.

Melody yawned, rubbing her eyes with the back of her hand. "Barely," she mumbled, fighting the pull of sleep. "I'm about to pass out, I think."

There was a small chuckle on the other end of the line. "You've got to be one of the toughest people I know, you know that?"

Melody smiled softly, the warmth in his voice making her feel comforted in a way she hadn't expected. "Maybe... or maybe I'm just really good at pretending."

"Well, I'm glad you don't have to pretend with me."

Her pulse fluttered at his words, a sense of sweetness lingering between them, like something unspoken but felt deeply. She let out a soft sigh, her eyelids heavy. "Lucian... I'm really tired."

"Yeah, I can tell." There was a hint of affection in his tone. "I think it's time for me to let you go. You need your rest."

"Mm-hmm..." Melody hummed, barely holding onto the thread of their conversation as the warmth of sleep began to envelope her.

Just then, a soft *meow* sounded beside her. Wednesday had hopped up onto the bed and was curling herself into the crook of Melody's legs, her yellow eyes blinking slowly as if offering her own approval of the night winding down. Melody smiled sleepily and reached down to scratch the cat behind her ears.

Lucian must've heard it through the phone. "Even the cat thinks you should get to bed," he said with a low laugh. "She's probably been trying to cast her own sleep spell on you this whole time."

"She's persistent," Melody murmured, giggling softly as Wednesday settled in with a purr.

But just before she let go, she heard Lucian's voice one more time, low and affectionate.

"Goodnight, baby doll."

Her heart skipped, her breath catching in her throat. The words echoed in her mind, and for a moment, she forgot how to speak. "What... did you just call me?"

Lucian's voice was soft, a teasing undertone mixed with something more sincere. "I called you 'baby doll.' It's just a term of endearment. You remind me of yone... delicate, a little fragile, but strong in your own way."

The words sent a shiver down her spine, and her chest tightened as she processed what he had said. "Baby doll," she repeated quietly, rolling the words around in her mind. "My grandma calls me that."

There was a pause, and then Lucian spoke again, his voice tender. "I think it suits you. You're beautiful, and you've got this kind of... quiet strength. It's like you're both soft and tough at the same time."

Melody's pulse raced, the compliment settling deep within her chest, something unfamiliar and comforting blooming there. "I... I like it," she whispered, her voice barely audible. "Thank you."

"I'm glad. Now, go get some sleep, okay?" Lucian's voice was warm, but it had a finality to it, as if he was reluctant to end the conversation, just as she was.

"Yeah," she said, her voice already trailing off as she snuggled deeper into her blankets. "Goodnight, Lucian."

"Goodnight, Melody. Sweet dreams."

The line went silent, and Melody held the phone to her chest for a moment longer, staring at the screen, feeling the warmth of his words echoing in her mind.

When the phone finally clicked off, she stared up at the ceiling for a few moments, her pulse still quick from the exchange. She smiled softly to herself, closing her eyes. Wednesday purred softly beside her, already half-asleep.

She had never felt so... noticed before. It was an odd feeling, like someone saw more in her than she had ever seen in herself. And it felt safe.

After a few minutes of stillness, Melody grabbed her journal from under her bed and opened it to a fresh page. She grabbed a pen, her hand moving almost instinctively as she started to write:

Lucian called me "baby doll" tonight. It made my heart race, but I don't think I mind. I don't know why, but it felt nice to hear. He said I remind him of a baby doll, and it made me think about how I've always felt so... delicate inside, like I'm holding everything together by just a thread sometimes. I think he might be the first person who actually gets it. I've never really felt like I've belonged, but with him, I feel like I don't have to hide. I don't know what this is yet... but it feels safe, like it's okay to let my guard down. He said I'm strong, but I don't know if I believe that. I just feel like I'm barely holding on most days. But... I think I want to believe him.

I can't wait to talk to him again. I think... maybe he might understand me more than anyone ever has.

–M

Melody finished writing and closed her journal with a soft thud. She felt lighter somehow, like the weight of the day had been lifted just a little bit. The warmth of the conversation still lingered in her chest, and she finally allowed herself to sink into sleep, the comfort of his voice still echoing in her mind.

"Goodnight, baby doll," she whispered to herself before drifting into a peaceful slumber.

The room was still, the soft hum of the lamp now almost inaudible, as the world outside seemed to pause. Melody's breathing deepened, her body fully surrendering to the pull of sleep, but her mind was caught in the space between dreams and wakefulness. The words Lucian had whispered to her, "Goodnight, Baby doll" hung in the air like a faint perfume, something tender, something intimate, something that felt foreign yet comforting.

In the darkness behind her eyelids, memories and emotions

swirled together like a storm, fragments of moments she couldn't quite piece together. The faint smell of the lavender-scented pillow by her side, the soft warmth of her blanket, the echo of Lucian's voice. All of it melded together, pulling her deeper into a dreamscape that felt safe yet unsettling.

She found herself in a place she couldn't quite recognize. The walls around her were an endless gray, almost like the inside of a forgotten dollhouse. It was quiet, almost too quiet, save for a soft rustling noise in the corner.

"Melody..." a voice whispered, gentle and familiar. But it wasn't Lucian.

She turned, and there, standing in the shadows, was a figure. Tall, imposing, their features sharp but somehow distorted, as though they were being seen through a fog.

"Who... who are you?" Melody asked, her voice shaky, though she didn't feel afraid. Not exactly. Just... uncertain.

The figure stepped forward, a face coming into sharper focus, and she felt a shiver run through her. It was her mother.

Charlotte stood before her, her eyes cold and distant. "You always think you're different, don't you? You think you can hide away, pretend you're something special. But you're nothing."

Melody tried to speak, but her throat felt tight, her body frozen in place as the figure of her mother loomed closer. "You're nothing. Just like me. Just like everyone else who tries to escape this family."

Her heart began to race as the figure of Charlotte grew closer, the edges of her vision blurring, the dream fragmenting like shattered glass.

But then, from somewhere distant, Lucian's voice pierced the fog, soft and reassuring.

"Melody... Baby doll, it's okay. You're not alone. I'm here."

The dream twisted, and in an instant, Charlotte's figure vanished, leaving nothing but the echo of Lucian's voice. Melody's pulse slowed, the warmth from his words curling around her like a blanket, pulling her back from the edge of the nightmare.

The darkness of sleep wrapped around her once more, and as the edges of the dream faded into nothingness, she allowed herself to drift deeper into the comfort of his words.

The morning air was damp and heavy with mist, clinging to the edges of Melody's hoodie as she stepped outside. The sky was a pale, gauzy gray, clouds stretched thin like smoke across the horizon. Everything felt hushed, as if the world itself was catching its breath.

She pulled her sleeves over her hands and started walking.

Her boots made soft, wet sounds on the sidewalk as she passed shuttered shops and crooked mailboxes. A crow cawed from a telephone wire above, and she looked up, meeting its black eyes for just a moment. It tilted its head, then flew off, its wings cutting across the clouds like ink on parchment.

Without really planning to, her feet led her to the old cemetery behind the church, the one with mossy stones and half-sunken angels. It was always quiet there, and today it felt like the perfect place to be. A place where the veil between things felt thinner.

She walked between the rows of gravestones, her fingertips grazing the tops of wild yarrow and clover. At a bench tucked beneath a low-hanging cedar tree, she sat down and exhaled, letting her shoulders relax.

From her pocket, she pulled out the small pouch she always kept with her, her "just-in-case" kit. Inside were a few crystals: amethyst for protection, rose quartz for love, and smoky quartz for grounding. She placed them in a triangle on the bench beside her, then closed her eyes.

"I'm safe," she whispered, her breath visible in the cool morning air. "I'm not alone."

The dream from last night still lingered, shadowy around the edges, but it didn't feel as heavy now. Lucian's voice had anchored her. But even more than that, she felt something beginning to grow in her. A quiet knowing. A pull toward something bigger.

She opened her journal and scribbled a few words across a blank page:

I can hold what's heavy without drowning.
I'm not hers to break.
I am mine.

A breeze stirred through the trees, lifting a few dry leaves and spinning them in a slow, lazy dance before they fell again. It almost felt like a nod. Like the earth was listening.

Melody smiled faintly to herself and gently tucked the crystals back into her pocket. She didn't have all the answers—but she didn't need to. There was magic in her bones, quiet and steady, and she could feel it humming beneath her skin.

For now, that was enough.

Just as she began to rise from the bench, her phone buzzed—Lucian's name lighting up the screen. Her heart gave a small, startled flutter.

I miss you.

It was simple, innocent even, but somehow the words hit harder than she expected. The soft buzz of the message lingered in her hand as she walked, boots crunching softly over the gravel just beyond the cemetery gates.

She read it again. And again. The faint glow of her phone lit her face in the growing dusk, casting a pale wash over the shadows beneath her eyes. It was only a few words, yet they felt like a quiet pull, tugging at something tender and uncertain inside her. Part of her wanted to pull back. But part of her wanted to reach for it.

She crossed the street, weaving through the edge of the neighborhood, the amber halo of streetlights flickering above her like fading stars. Her fingers hovered over the keyboard before she typed:

> I miss you too.

She stared at the screen, her chest tightening. A flicker of warmth spread through her ribs like a lit match, even though her thoughts were a swirl of confusion. What was this? What were they?

They barely knew each other beyond the hours they spent in conversation—late nights steeped in vulnerability, confessions wrapped in moonlight. And yet it felt *real*. It felt like *safety*. But it also felt like falling, and she wasn't sure if there was anything at the bottom to catch her.

Lucian's reply came fast:

> Can't stop thinking about you.

She bit her lip. The words stirred something deep in her belly, something tangled in hope and dread. Was she imagining this, or was he beginning to depend on her, too? That scared her. The way someone else's heart could sneak into your chest without permission.

Her phone buzzed again.

> Do you ever feel like you're just... not meant to be here?

Her steps slowed. She reached the corner near the old oak tree and leaned against the trunk, letting the bark steady her. Her breath caught as she read his words again. It was like Lucian had cracked her open, reached into the places no one saw and put them into words.

Her thumbs tapped lightly.

> Yeah. Sometimes.

His answer was almost instant:

> I get it. I feel the same way sometimes. Like
> we're both... lost in different ways.

Melody's heart fluttered. Not in the way that felt light and pretty, but like a bird caught in her chest, flapping against something fragile. It was unhealthy, she knew that. She was still just a girl. He was still just a man. And yet they clung to each other like they were the only two people left on Earth.

She wanted to tell him. About the ache. About the fear. About how she didn't feel at home anywhere—not at school, not at the dinner table, not even in her own skin.

Instead, she typed:

> I'm scared.

It hovered there, hanging in the air between them like a thread pulled too tight.

His response came just as quickly:

> Don't be. I'm not going anywhere. I'm here.
> Always.

As she reached the steps of her house, her phone buzzed again. This time, it was a call.

Lucian.

She hesitated just long enough to feel her heartbeat in her throat before answering. "Hey."

"Hey, baby doll." His voice was soft, low, thick with something that sounded like relief. "I just... I needed to hear your voice."

She slipped inside quietly, heading straight to her room. The house was quiet. Dim. She shut the door behind her and curled beneath her blanket as Wednesday hopped up and nestled at her side.

"You okay?" she asked, her voice nearly a whisper.

"I don't know," he admitted, and there was a rawness there that made her ache. "I guess I just felt like... if I didn't call you, I was gonna go crazy. I've been thinking about you all day."

Her breath hitched. "Me too."

Silence stretched between them. Not awkward...just full. Full of all the things they didn't have words for yet.

"What are you thinking about?" he asked gently.

"Just... how weird it is. How easy it feels when I talk to you. Like everything else fades out. Like... like I'm finally breathing."

Lucian's exhale was slow, almost shaky. "Yeah. That's exactly it. You make the noise in my head stop."

Melody blinked fast, unexpected tears threatening to fall.

"I don't know how you do it," he continued. "But you're under my skin, Melody."

She pressed the phone tighter to her ear. "Lucian..."

"I know," he said softly. "I know it's complicated. I know we're not supposed to feel this way. But I don't care anymore."

She could hear him breathing, slow and uneven.

"I think..." His voice cracked. "I think I'm falling in love with you."

The words hit like a warm wave and a sucker punch all at once. Her throat closed around everything she wanted to say.

"You don't have to say anything," he whispered. "I just needed you to know."

She took a shaky breath. "I... I want to say it."

Another pause. Waiting.

"I've never felt anything like this before. It's scary. You make me feel like I matter. Like I'm not crazy. Like I'm not... too much."

"You're not too much," he said, firm and fierce. "You're not broken. You're *magic*. I see you, Melody."

Her tears came silently now, falling into the folds of her blanket.

"I think..." She choked out the words. "I think I'm falling in love with you too."

Lucian made a soft sound—half sigh, half prayer. "God. You don't know what that does to me."

"I think about you all the time," she whispered. "At school. At dinner. When I'm pretending to be okay. You're the only thing that makes sense."

"You are okay," he said. "You're more than okay. You're everything."

Wednesday stretched and meowed, curling tighter into her side.

Lucian chuckled. "Even your cat agrees. She thinks you should get some rest before you melt my heart completely."

Melody laughed softly. "She's bossy."

"She's smart. Like her girl."

"I don't want to lose this."

"You won't," he said. "Not as long as I'm breathing."

The room was dark now, lit only by the faint glow of her phone screen as it dimmed to black. Lucian's voice still echoed in her ears, like the last note of a song that wouldn't quite fade.

Melody lay motionless under her blanket, her hands folded over her chest, trying to slow the thud of her heartbeat. It wasn't working.

She turned over slowly, reaching under her bed. Her fingers brushed past her headphones and a stick of lip balm before landing on the soft cover of her journal. She pulled it into her lap, dragging her pen from the drawer with the kind of quiet urgency that only came from too many thoughts pressing against her ribs.

But then she paused.

She sat up, gathering the blanket around her shoulders like a cloak, and lit the stub of her lavender candle on the windowsill. The tiny flame flickered against the glass, casting shadows across her posters and stacks of books. The scent of lavender and beeswax slowly melted into the room, soft and ancient. She reached for the small dish beside it, the one shaped like a crescent moon, where she kept the little objects that made her feel grounded: a smooth piece of obsidian, a pressed fern leaf, and a tiny bundle of dried rose petals tied with black thread.

She set the rose bundle gently on her notebook, like it was a talisman.

This was her ritual. When the world felt too loud or too confusing, when her chest felt like it was caving in—she did this. Candle. Crystal. Words.

The pages crinkled faintly as she opened to a fresh one. She stared at the empty space for a long second, the silence around her feeling thick and sacred. Then, slowly, she began to write:

> *Lucian told me he loves me.*
> *I didn't expect it.*
> *But it didn't scare me the way I thought it would.*
> *It felt like something cracked open in my chest, some-*
> *thing that had been locked away for a long time.*
> *I said it back. I don't even know if I was ready.*
> *But it felt real. Honest.*
> *I keep thinking maybe this is what it's supposed to feel*
> *like.*

Safe. Electric.
He sees me.
I think I'm starting to believe that.
—M

She let the pen rest in the fold of the journal and stared at the words, eyes tracing each letter like they were sigils instead of sentences. She whispered them under her breath, as if reading them aloud gave them more power. More truth.

Her fingers drifted to the piece of obsidian, thumb brushing the smooth surface. Protection. Grounding. She remembered reading that somewhere in one of her witchy books—books she didn't let anyone see.

"I'm safe," she murmured, pressing the stone to her chest. "He makes me feel safe."

She wasn't sure if she was talking to the moon, the candle, or herself.

In the distance, an owl called—low and haunting. The wind outside rattled the branches against her windowpane like skeletal fingers scratching for entry, but she didn't flinch. She felt... shielded.

She dipped her pen back into the page and scrawled at the bottom in cramped, looping handwriting:

Let this be real. Let this be mine.
Let no one take it from me.

She leaned forward and blew out the candle, watching the smoke twist into the air like a spirit set free. In the sudden darkness, she clutched her journal to her chest and lay back down, her heart still hammering, but steadier now. Like it had found a rhythm. Like it had somewhere to belong.

her heart still hammering, but steadier now. Like it had found a rhythm. Like it had somewhere to belong.

CHAPTER SEVEN

The days started to feel longer, even though Melody's time wasn't her own anymore. She went to school, came home, went through the motions. But every free moment, every pause between homework, every quiet space between her mother's passive-aggressive jabs or Nick's slamming doors, was Lucian's.

It had been three months since he told her he loved her. He texted her constantly.

What are you doing?

Who are you with?

Are you okay? I miss you.

At first, it made her feel special. Wanted. Like she mattered. Like someone saw her for who she truly was, unlike the people around her who just never seemed to understand. But slowly, something started to shift.

One night, Melody sent a photo of her room—her altar candles glowing softly, a small stack of CDs by her stereo, a black lace choker she'd just gotten in the mail laid out across her pillow. Lucian responded instantly.

You look so beautiful surrounded by all that. It's so you. You're like... ethereal.

She smiled, warmth spreading through her chest. But then, another message followed.

I hope you're not wearing that choker for anyone else.

Her smile faltered, the warmth she had felt slipping away, replaced by a sudden tightness in her chest. She read the message over again, unsure of what to make of it. Was it a joke? Did it even matter? It was probably nothing.

No. Just showing you.

She quickly typed back, not thinking too much about it. It wasn't a big deal, right?

Good. You're mine, you know that, right?

Her heart skipped a beat. *Mine.* The word lingered in the air, pressing on her chest like a weight she couldn't quite shake off. She stared at the text, her thumb hovering over the screen. Was he being serious? Was that normal? He had always been so intense, but this... it felt different. She didn't know why, but it felt wrong.

She shook her head, trying to push the feeling away, but it wouldn't leave her. She typed back, her fingers unsteady on the keys.

What do you mean?

The reply came quickly, as if he'd been waiting for the question.

You know exactly what I mean. You're mine,
Melody. I've told you that.

Melody stared at the words, the unease in her stomach grow-ing. She wanted to ask more, she wanted to say something, but the words didn't come. She had asked the question, but now, the answer felt... unsettling. Did it mean something more than just care? Was it too much?

I'm not sure I get it, Lucian.

The message felt heavy as she typed it out. Was she being too much of a coward? Maybe she was just overthinking this. But then, the thought lingered: she shouldn't have to feel this unsure.

It's not a big deal, right?

she added, trying to sound casual, even though her heart was racing.

Lucian's reply was almost immediate, as always.

It is a big deal. You're mine. Always will be.
Just remember that.

Melody's fingers tightened around the phone. The words echoed in her mind. She didn't know why, but she felt like there was more to it than he was letting on. It didn't feel like just love anymore. It felt like something else... something she couldn't quite name.

She had asked, and now she felt something heavy inside her, but still, she didn't fully understand what was happening. She'd never felt this way with anyone else, why did it feel so confusing?

A moment of doubt rose in her chest, but she shoved it down, telling herself it was just her nerves. She had asked the question. He'd answered. Maybe she was just making it into something it wasn't.

Lucian's reply came quickly, but this time, there was a certain warmth in his words, almost as if to reassure her.

The reassurance should have made her feel better, but the tightness in her chest didn't go away. Instead, she stared at the screen, unsure if she was overthinking things or if something about this relationship was beginning to feel... off. But she pressed down the doubt, still clinging to the idea that Lucian cared more than anyone else did. That he was the only one who truly understood her.

Melody slid into the chair at the back of the school library, the soft creak of old wood beneath her barely registering. She dropped her backpack with a thud and slumped forward, her face pale beneath the heavy eyeliner she'd started wearing thicker lately. Anna looked up from her book and frowned.

"Hey... you made it," Anna said gently, her voice low and careful like she was trying not to scare a wild animal. "You okay? You've kind of been off the grid."

Melody shrugged one shoulder without lifting her head. "Just tired."

Anna watched her for a moment, then closed her book slowly. "This isn't just tired. You barely talked yesterday. I texted you and you left me on read."

Melody straightened up, guilt flashing across her face. "I'm sorry. Things have just been... loud. At home. In my head."

Anna hesitated, then leaned in. "Is it about that guy? Lucian?"

Melody's stomach knotted. She'd mentioned his name once, weeks ago, barely a whisper of a mention, but Anna had remembered. "No. I mean... it's not that. Just... life stuff."

Anna gave her a skeptical look but didn't press. "Okay. Just... don't disappear. You're not alone, Mel. No matter how much it feels like it."

Before Melody could respond, the bell rang—shrill and jarring. They gathered their things and headed into the hallway, a stream of voices and slamming lockers swallowing them. Melody kept her head down, hoping to make it to class without anyone noticing her, but luck wasn't on her side.

"Look who finally crawled out of her cave," a voice rang out, sharp and mocking.

Melody froze. *Brielle.* One of the school's golden girls— blonde, athletic, perfect teeth and razor-blade cruelty under her sugary cheerleader smile.

Melody kept walking, eyes forward, but Brielle stepped directly into her path.

"Did Hot Topic run out of eyeliner, or is that just depression chic?"

There was laughter from behind her, two more cheerleaders egging Brielle on like hyenas.

Melody's hands clenched into fists at her sides. "Get out of the way."

Brielle smirked. "Aww, scary goth girl gonna hex me? Or cry about it in her diary?"

She shoved Melody—not hard, just enough to make her stumble into the lockers. The slam echoed down the hall.

Something cracked.

Melody spun back around, rage boiling over. "Back off, you plastic bitch!" she snapped, and without thinking, shoved Brielle so hard she stumbled backward into a row of lockers with a loud metallic *clang*.

The hallway went silent. Brielle stared at her, stunned. So did everyone else.

Anna was beside her in an instant. "Mel, what are you doing?"

"I've had enough," Melody growled, her voice trembling. Her chest rose and fell rapidly, adrenaline surging through her. "I'm so sick of people like her thinking they can treat everyone like trash and get away with it."

Brielle's mouth opened like she was about to retort, but the teacher on hallway duty was already storming toward them.

"In my office. Now. Both of you!" the teacher barked.

Melody didn't move at first. The buzz in her pocket was going off again, it was Lucian. She could feel it without even looking. The heat in her chest turned cold.

Anna put a hand on her arm. "Come on," she said gently, voice low. "Just breathe, okay?"

Melody let herself be led away, the murmurs of students swirling around them like static. She didn't look at Brielle again. She didn't look at anyone. She just kept walking.

But somewhere, deep inside her, something whispered: *This isn't you.*

And another voice, darker, more familiar, whispered back: *Maybe it is now.*

Melody sat in the hard plastic chair across from the assistant principal's desk, her arms crossed tightly over her chest. The office smelled like stale coffee and cheap cologne, the blinds drawn just enough to cast gray slats of light across the floor.

Brielle, still sniffling, sat off to the side with the school counselor fussing over her like a wounded kitten. She hadn't even fallen that hard—just a stumble, a dramatic gasp, and suddenly *Melody* was the problem.

The assistant principal, Mr. Carter, barely looked up from his computer. "So, Melody... wanna tell me what that was all about?"

"She shoved me first," Melody said flatly, staring at the corner of the desk. "She called me a freak and knocked into me. I just pushed her back."

Mr. Carter sighed, the kind of long, bored exhale that made it clear he didn't care about details. "You're telling me you just reacted? Not buying it. Brielle said she was walking past and you lost it."

Melody's fists clenched in her lap. "Because she's lying. She and her friends have been messing with me all week."

He looked at her finally, his expression hard to read, something between dismissive and annoyed. "Listen, you can't go around putting your hands on people, even if you think they're 'messing with you.' That's not how we handle things here."

Melody opened her mouth to protest, but he raised a hand.

"Look, I'm not suspending you. But you *will* get after-school detention for the rest of the week. And I expect you to stay out of trouble moving forward. Understood?"

"That's it?" Melody snapped before she could stop herself. "She starts it, and I get detention?"

Mr. Carter frowned. "You need to take responsibility for your actions, Melody. Brielle doesn't have a history of behavior issues. You, on the other hand, seem to be... struggling lately."

The implication landed like a punch to the gut.

"So I'm just the angry goth girl acting out?" she asked bitterly.

He didn't answer.

The counselor patted Brielle's back as she handed her a hall pass and told her she was "so brave" for coming forward.

Melody was handed a detention slip like it was a receipt.

As she walked out of the office, the anger burned in her chest, not because she got punished, but because no one even *cared* to ask *why*.

Anna was sitting just outside, wide-eyed. "Mel? What happened?"

Melody shoved the slip into her bag. "Detention. Of course."

Anna stared. "Are you serious? What about Brielle?"

"She's probably getting a sympathy card and a free pass to the vending machines."

They walked down the hall in silence, the weight of injustice pressing down on both of them.

Melody lay on her bed in the dark, her detention slip still crumpled beside her. The house was quiet, too quiet, with her mom gone and her dad still out who knew where. Even the hum of the fridge down the hall sounded distant, like the world was holding its breath.

Her phone lit up, buzzing against the comforter.

Lucian.

She didn't hesitate. She answered.

"Hey," she whispered.

His voice was low, almost sleepy, but laced with something heavier— warmer. "Hey, baby. I was hoping you'd pick up."

"I always do," she said, curling tighter under the covers like the sound of him could shield her.

There was a pause, then, softly: "I think about you all the time, you know that?"

Her chest tightened.

"Even when I'm working. Even when I'm out. I hear a song, I see a candle shop, I watch a crime show, and it's you. You're in my head all the time, Melody."

Her breath caught. "I think about you too."

"I know," he said, voice tender. "That's why I need you to promise me something."

"Okay..." she said cautiously.

His voice dropped, almost a whisper. "Don't let anyone take up that space in your heart but me."

There was a beat of silence so thick it felt like the air itself changed. She blinked into the dark, frozen.

"I..." Her voice came out small. "I won't."

"Say it," he said gently, not demanding, but expectant.

"I promise."

He exhaled like he'd just let go of something clenched deep in his chest. "That's my girl."

They stayed quiet for a moment, the line soft with breath and static. Then, his voice changed— still warm, but sharper, focused.

"How was school?"

Her stomach clenched. "I... got detention."

"What?" His tone sharpened instantly. "Why? What happened?"

"Some cheerleader, Brielle, shoved me and called me a freak. I pushed her back. She acted all innocent and everyone believed her. No one even asked what happened. They just handed me detention. Didn't say a thing to her."

Lucian was silent for a second, then cursed under his breath. "Of course they blamed you. Because you don't kiss their ass like she does. Because you're *real* and they're terrified of that."

Melody's throat tightened. The knot of shame and anger inside her shifted—twisting into something else. Recognition. Belonging.

"They hate girls like you, Mel. Girls who don't shrink themselves to fit in. You scare them. You *should*."

Tears burned at the corners of her eyes. "She didn't even get talked to. Everyone acts like she's some kind of princess. I'm just... disposable."

"Bullshit," Lucian snapped. "You're not disposable. You're *untouchable*. You think that basic ass cheerleader could survive five minutes in your shoes? No way."

Her voice cracked. "Anna waited for me outside the office.

She didn't say much, just looked at me like she was disappointed."

"She doesn't get it. None of them do. Not like I do." He paused. "You don't need them, Melody. You don't need anyone but me."

Something about the way he said it made her blood pulse differently. The words soaked into her like warmth and wet cement.

"They'll never see you the way I do," he murmured. "They're not strong enough to love a girl like you."

"I'm so glad I have you," she whispered.

"And I'm never letting go," he said. "You're mine, Melody."

After they hung up, she stared at the ceiling, heart pounding like she'd just signed something invisible.

And maybe... she didn't want to turn back.

After they hung up, Melody stared at the ceiling, heart pounding like she'd just signed something invisible.

And maybe... she didn't want to turn back.

The silence in her room settled over her shoulders like a velvet cloak. Still buzzing from Lucian's voice, from his words wrapping around her like a chain laced in silk, she pushed herself up and lit the small string of fairy lights around her altar.

It was just a shelf, really. But to her, it was sacred.

She reached for her rose quartz first, the one she always kept tucked under her pillow when she missed him. She pressed it to her chest, breathing in deep. Then came the black tourmaline, grounding her like a tether. Her fingers trembled as she picked up her little jar of salt, sprinkling a circle on the floor, just wide enough to sit in.

The candle flickered to life under the strike of a match. She closed her eyes and whispered under her breath:

"Let what I feel be safe. Let my path be clear. Let what's mine stay mine."

It wasn't from any book. She just said what felt real. What felt necessary.

She pulled a worn tarot card from under her pillow — **The Lovers**. She held it between her hands, staring at the entwined figures, the way they looked at each other like no one else existed. She imagined it was them, her and Lucian, bound by something ancient and powerful.

She whispered his name like a spell. Lit lavender incense. Dabbed a little jasmine oil on her wrists. Wrote his initials in the corner of her notebook and traced a heart around them three times.

It wasn't about control. Not to her.

It was about connection. Devotion. Meaning.

Because if she could feel this much, if someone could love her the way he said he did, then maybe she wasn't invisible. Maybe she wasn't the freak they said she was. Maybe she was something rare. Something magic.

She curled back under the covers with her crystals cradled in her palm, the candle flickering beside her, casting long shadows on the walls.

And somewhere in the smoke and silence, she felt claimed.

Melody came downstairs in her oversized black hoodie, dark circles under her eyes, her headphones wrapped around her neck like armor. The echoes of last night still clung to her— candle smoke, the whisper of a promise, the tight ache in her chest.

Charlotte stood at the stove, stirring oatmeal like it had personally offended her. Her silk robe hung perfectly in place, every hair on her head frozen in lacquered precision. She didn't bother turning around.

"Well, look who decided to show her face," she said coolly. "Got a call from the school. You want to explain why I had to hear from the *principal* that my daughter is shoving people around like a street rat?"

Melody froze.

Charlotte turned slowly, crossing her arms. "What the hell is wrong with you, Melody? Do you *enjoy* humiliating this family?"

"She shoved me first," Melody muttered. "She said—"

"I don't care what she said," Charlotte snapped. "You put your hands on someone. In the middle of a hallway. In front of God knows who. And of *course* it had to be a cheerleader. Do you have *any* idea how bad that looks? They're scholarship-bound, and you're... what? Doodling dead girls in your notebook and skulking around like a corpse?"

The sound of the fridge door slamming made Melody flinch.

Nick sauntered in, shirtless, reeking of weed and Red Bull. "Morning, psychos," he said with a smirk. "What'd Gothzilla do now?"

Charlotte didn't stop him.

"She assaulted a girl at school," she said, almost with pride. "In front of everyone."

Nick cackled. "Seriously? What'd you do, hex her? Scream Latin and throw a dead bird at her?"

"Shut up, Nick," Melody mumbled.

"Aww," he said in a mock pout. "Is the freak gonna cry again? What, did she call you weird? Guess what, Mel? You *are*!"

"Shut up," Melody said louder, her hands tightening at her sides.

Nick leaned in close, grinning like a wolf. "Come on. Shove *me* next. Let's see what happens. Maybe they'll finally ship your ass off to some padded room where you fucking belong."

Charlotte sighed dramatically. "Honestly, if I had a dollar for every time I wished I'd stopped at one kid..."

Melody's voice cracked. "Why do you hate me so much?"

Charlotte walked up to her then, eyes sharp. "I don't *hate* you, Melody. I'm *embarrassed* by you. You walk around like you're so different, like the world's against you, when the truth is, you make people uncomfortable. And now it's not just in this house.

Now it's out there. You're a problem, and sooner or later, problems get dealt with."

Nick snorted. "She's like a feral cat that keeps biting people and pissing on the carpet."

Melody's chest burned. She couldn't breathe. She couldn't speak.

"Get out of my kitchen," Charlotte snapped. "Go walk to school and think about how lucky you are it was only detention."

Melody turned and stormed out, her backpack bouncing against her side, teeth clenched to keep the scream inside.

Behind her, Nick laughed.

Melody's boots hit the pavement in dull, dragging thuds. The wind stung her eyes, but it wasn't the cold that made them glassy. Her hoodie was pulled over her head like a shield, her hands jammed in her pockets. She walked fast, like she could leave the whole damn morning behind her.

She pulled out her phone with shaking fingers and dialed him.

Lucian answered on the second ring, his voice low and rough. "Hey, baby."

The sound of his voice cracked something open in her chest. "Hey..."

"You okay?" he asked immediately, his tone softening. "You sound like hell."

She swallowed hard. "It's nothing. Just... home stuff."

A pause, then the sound of a door creaking. He was stepping away from someone. "What happened?"

Melody's voice was tight. "My mom blew up over what happened at school. And Nick, he just... he tore into me. I didn't even do anything that bad."

"Baby..." Lucian sighed. "I wish I was there right now. I'd tell them to back the fuck off."

Her throat ached. "I just feel like everyone hates me. Like I could disappear and no one would care."

"Don't say that." His voice came fast and firm. "*I* care. You hear me? I care so damn much. You're not invisible to me, Melody. You're the only person I think about."

She let out a shaky breath, blinking back tears.

"I gotta get back in a sec," he said softly. "Boss is on my ass today. But I needed to hear your voice. You're okay, yeah? You're walking to school?"

"Yeah," she whispered.

"You've got me," he said. "Even if the rest of the world is shit, you've got me. And I've got you. Alright?"

She nodded, voice barely audible. "Alright."

"I'll call you later, okay?"

"Okay."

"Good girl. You keep your head down. Text me if you need me."

The line clicked off, and Melody stood still for a moment, phone pressed to her chest like it could keep her warm.

Then she kept walking.

The bell rang, signaling the start of the school day, but Melody didn't move. She lingered by her locker, staring blankly at the rows of students rushing past, their laughter and voices just a dull hum in her ears. The fluorescent lights buzzed above her, the world around her spinning in a haze of noise and confusion.

She opened her locker without thinking, her hands mechanically shifting through the contents— books, papers, her notebook. Everything felt like a blur, like she was floating above it all, detached. Nick's mocking laughter still echoed in her head, his words cutting deep, and her mom's cruel silence had been worse. She felt small. Weak. Nothing but a ghost among the crowd.

I should've been stronger. Why did I let them get to me?

Her fingers brushed over the edge of her notebook, where she had written something earlier, a half-baked thought that had no conclusion. The words seemed to mock her now, almost as if she didn't even understand herself anymore.

"Why do you let them treat you like that?" she whispered to herself, staring at the black ink on the page. "What's wrong with me?"

Her phone buzzed in her pocket. She hesitated before pulling it out, her heart quickening when she saw the screen. It was Lucian.

She opened the message, and his words jumped out at her:

I'm here, baby. Don't forget that. You're mine.
You're not alone.

Her chest tightened at the possessiveness, but it wasn't anger. No, it was... something else. A strange sense of warmth, the comfort of someone who cared. Someone who understood her.

Her fingers hovered over the keyboard as she quickly typed back, needing the connection.

I miss you.

Before she could think much more about it, she shoved her phone back in her pocket, quickly wiping away a tear before anyone saw. She didn't want them to see how weak she felt. She couldn't let anyone see that she was falling apart, even if she already felt like she was.

The bell rang again, but Melody didn't move. She wasn't ready to step back into the chaos of the school day, not yet. She needed a moment. Just a few more seconds where she could be alone with her thoughts, with her phone, with Lucian.

She didn't know how much longer she could keep pretending everything was okay.

The classroom was buzzing with chatter as students settled into their seats. The teacher's voice was a dull murmur in the background, but Melody wasn't really listening. Her gaze was fixed on the desk in front of her, her fingers nervously tapping on the edge of her notebook. Her heart still thudded in her chest from the fight with the cheerleader earlier, the chaos from yesterday. She could feel the bruises, not the ones on her body, but the ones on her soul. They lingered, nagging at her, reminding her of the weight she carried.

"Hey," Anna whispered from beside her, her voice soft but full of concern. She slid into the seat next to Melody, glancing around to make sure no one else was paying attention. "You doing okay?"

Melody flinched slightly, pulling herself out of her thoughts. Her eyes flicked over to Anna, but she didn't know what to say. She didn't want to talk about it. Not here. Not in front of everyone.

"Yeah," she said, forcing a small smile that didn't quite reach her eyes. "Just tired. You know how it is."

Anna raised an eyebrow, clearly unconvinced. She leaned in closer, her voice barely above a whisper. "Look, I'm not stupid, Melody. You were practically shaking when we talked earlier. And after the fight with that cheerleader? What happened?"

Melody's stomach twisted at the mention of the fight. She could still hear the girl's taunting voice in her head, the sneering laughter of her friends. She wasn't sure if the physical pain was worse or the emotional toll. She could still see the disgust on the cheerleader's face when she pushed Melody, the way it made her feel so small, so insignificant.

"I didn't ask for that to happen," Melody muttered, staring at her hands, not trusting herself to look Anna in the eye. "I wasn't looking for a fight."

"I know you weren't," Anna said gently. "But that doesn't

mean you deserved what happened." She paused for a moment, her voice softer now. "Look, I know things at home are crazy. And I know you're dealing with... whatever is going on with Lucian. But this? You can't just keep taking this shit, Melody. You have to stand up for yourself."

Melody's breath caught in her throat. The truth hit her like a ton of bricks, but she wasn't ready to admit it, not even to herself. How could she stand up for herself when she felt so broken? When she felt so controlled?

"I don't know if I can do that," Melody whispered, her voice so quiet that she was almost certain Anna wouldn't hear. "Every time I try, it just gets worse. Nothing changes. And now... now I'm just this freak, right? That's how they see me."

Anna's expression softened, her eyes filled with empathy. "No. You're not a freak. You're different, yeah. But different is not a bad thing. I don't want you to hide, Melody. I just want you to feel like you can be yourself. No matter what."

Melody nodded but didn't speak. She didn't know how to respond to Anna's kindness, to her words that felt so distant from everything that was happening in her life.

The bell rang, cutting the moment short. Anna hesitated for a moment, but she gave Melody a gentle squeeze on the arm before she stood up to head back to her seat. "We'll talk more later, okay? Just... please don't shut me out."

Melody watched her walk away, the words lingering in the air between them. But she couldn't bring herself to answer. She couldn't bring herself to do anything but sit there, the weight of the world pressing down on her chest.

She wasn't sure if she could keep pretending that everything was fine, or if she even wanted to.

The bell rang, and the usual flood of students rushed past

Melody, eager to escape the confines of the school day. But instead of feeling relief, she was hit with an overwhelming sense of dread. She trudged toward the detention room, each step feeling heavier than the last. The hallway, filled with laughter and lighthearted chatter, seemed like a world she didn't belong to anymore. Her heart was still racing from the fight, the encounter with Charlotte, and the suffocating weight of being so unseen in her own life.

The detention room was a suffocating box of fluorescent lights and stale air. Melody slouched into a seat, avoiding the eyes of the others who were either too tired or too indifferent to care. The silence in the room wasn't comforting, it was oppressive. Her thoughts spiraled in the quiet, unable to escape the loop of what had happened earlier. The harshness of Charlotte's words still stung, her mother's voice echoing in her head: *You're just a freak, Melody. You always were.*

Her fingers gripped the edge of the desk, nails digging into the wood as if she could ground herself in something solid, something that wouldn't break apart when she touched it. The room felt too small for her, too suffocating. She couldn't concentrate on the paperwork in front of her. Her mind was a whirlwind of anxiety, anger, and hurt—layers of emotion she wasn't sure how to untangle.

Her phone buzzed in her pocket, a lifeline she had been waiting for. Her heart fluttered in a way that was both comforting and unsettling as she pulled it out. A text waited from Lucian.

> I know you're probably not in the mood for this, but I just wanted to remind you that I'm thinking about you. Don't let them get to you, okay? You're mine, remember? No one can take that from me.

The text hit her like a strange cocktail of relief and possessiveness. She needed this, she realized. She needed him to tell her that she mattered, that someone cared about her, that she wasn't invisible. But at the same time, a nagging voice whispered that she didn't know who she was anymore. Was she becoming something she wasn't? Something darker? Was this what she wanted, to be bound by someone else's control?

Her fingers trembled as she typed back, her heart pounding against her ribs. The words seemed to spill out as if they were the only way to hold onto something real in the storm swirling inside her.

> I'm here. Just getting through the day.

She stared at the message for a moment, her thumb hovering over the send button. What was she even saying? *Just getting through the day*, she wasn't just getting through it; she was suffocating in it. She was drowning in the emotions that she couldn't control, that she didn't understand. She hit send, trying to convince herself that this was enough, that Lucian's words could be enough to hold her together for one more day.

Her phone buzzed again.

> That's all you need to do. I'm proud of you, Melody. Keep your head up.

Pride. The word felt heavy on her chest. Was it really pride he felt for her, or something else? Something possessive? She swallowed hard, pushing the discomfort down. She didn't have the energy to analyze it right now. She needed to feel something other than the emptiness that had settled inside her. She put her phone away and buried her face in her hands for a moment, taking a deep breath, trying to steady the dizzying rush of emotions.

The rest of the detention dragged by in a haze, the clock on the wall ticking like a heartbeat she couldn't escape. By the time the bell rang, Melody felt numb. The bell that should've signified freedom only reminded her that she was trapped in a cycle she couldn't break.

As she stepped out into the rain, the world outside felt strangely distant. The sound of the downpour was deafening, the world reduced to gray and wet, a reflection of her inner turmoil. She barely noticed the chill creeping into her bones as she walked, her head down, eyes unfocused. She didn't care about the rain soaking her hoodie or the way her shoes squelched against the pavement. Nothing mattered except the ache inside her chest—the aching void that seemed to be growing bigger every day.

She pulled her phone from her pocket again, hoping for some distraction, some reassurance from Lucian. Her fingers felt stiff as she unlocked it, and she scrolled through her messages.

> I'll be waiting for you tonight. Don't forget who you belong to, okay? You're everything to me.

Everything to him. The words made her pulse quicken, a surge of warmth spreading through her. She needed to feel needed. She craved the validation, the sense of belonging that he gave her. But deep down, a voice she couldn't ignore whispered: *At what cost?*

She tucked the thought away, buried beneath the flood of longing that followed his words. She typed quickly, almost desperate to reconnect, to hear his voice again, to cling to the certainty he offered.

> I'll be there. I need you, Lucian.

It felt like a lifeline, like something she could hold onto in the storm. But when she hit send, she felt something shift inside her, a coldness that she didn't want to acknowledge. Was she already too far gone?

She shoved the phone back into her pocket, walking aimlessly, the rain blurring her vision. She didn't know where she was going, only that she had to keep moving. She needed to escape from the voices in her head, the ones that told her she was broken, that she was wrong, that she was unworthy of love. But with every step, those voices only grew louder.

Before she knew it, she found herself standing at the gates of the cemetery. The world was silent here, the rain falling in a steady rhythm, like the world was holding its breath. It was the one place she could go to feel something other than the weight of her life pressing in on her.

She walked deeper into the cemetery, her boots sinking into the wet earth as she moved between the graves. She wasn't sure why she came here, maybe because the dead didn't judge her. Maybe because the silence felt like the only thing that understood the noise in her mind. She could hear the rain hitting the gravestones, the soft rustle of leaves, and in the distance, the steady hum of traffic—a world far away from this place.

She stopped beneath an old, twisted tree, its bark slick with rain. She leaned against it, trying to steady her breath. The world felt distant, like she was in a dream. Her chest was tight, and her thoughts were a whirlwind of confusion. Lucian's words were still ringing in her ears, and she clung to them like a lifeline.

But what did it mean? What was she becoming?

The question echoed in her mind as she pulled her phone out again, heart heavy. She opened the messages, hesitating for a moment before typing a new reply.

I'm afraid of what I'm becoming.

Her thumb hovered over the send button for a long time. What if he didn't understand? What if he saw her as weak, or worse, *too much*? But then the fear of not sending it outweighed the fear of his response. She hit send.

The message felt like a confession, like a crack in the dam that was holding back everything she feared. She stared at the screen, waiting for his reply, feeling the storm both outside and inside her.

Later that evening, after the tension of the cemetery had settled, Melody sat on the floor of her bedroom, her knees pulled to her chest. The glow of her phone lit up the shadows under her eyes, casting a faint, unnatural light across the room. She had spent some time alone after detention, thinking about the weight of the day and everything that had happened. Now, as her phone buzzed in her hands, her heart skipped a beat.

Lucian's messages flashed across the screen:

> You said you'd be home soon.

> That was over an hour ago.

> What were you doing?

> I thought you wanted to talk to me.

Melody's fingers trembled as she typed back:

> I'm sorry. I lost track of time. Just... a lot happened today. I walked to the cemetery after detention to clear my head.

There was a long pause. Then his reply came through, a little sharper this time:

> A cemetery? I mean... I get it, but why go there alone? You know how that stuff messes with your head.

Melody felt a sharp pang of guilt. She didn't want to explain it all, but she also didn't want him to feel abandoned.

> I just needed space. I was thinking, sorting
> some stuff out in my head. I didn't mean to
> worry you.

A brief silence, then another message:

> I get it, but I still hate feeling like I'm being left
> out. I don't want to feel distant from you.

Melody's stomach twisted. She couldn't bear the thought of him feeling neglected. She quickly typed:

> I'm not leaving you. I'm just... figuring things
> out. You're not alone in this. I'm still here.

Another pause before his reply, softer this time:

> I just need to know that you're with me, that
> we're still connected. I get anxious when I feel
> like we're slipping apart.

Melody closed her eyes, trying to calm the unease that was rising inside her. She had to say something that would reassure him, but also keep some space for herself to breathe.

> You're not losing me, Lucian. I promise. I care
> about you, I just need time to process
> everything.

His reply came quickly, more tentative now:

> Okay. I just need to hear that from you, you
> know?

> I care about you, too. And I don't want to push
> you away. I just don't want to lose what we
> have.

Her heart ached at the vulnerability in his words. She didn't want to hurt him, but she couldn't ignore the need for clarity within herself. She felt the weight of their connection, and yet there were still so many questions swirling in her mind.

> I don't want to lose this, either. I just... need to take things slow. I'm here. Always.

There was a long pause, the silence stretching between them, before Lucian's message popped up:

> Okay. Just... don't forget I'm here. I need you to know how much I care.

She squeezed her eyes shut, feeling the weight of the moment.

> I won't forget. I'm not going anywhere.

The words lingered between them, soft and fragile, like something precious they were both holding onto.

After the last text from Lucian, Melody felt the silence weigh heavily in her room. She had been holding her breath, waiting for him to respond. The distance between them wasn't gone, not entirely.

Her thumb hovered over her phone screen, then, without thinking, she pressed his name and hit call. She needed to hear his voice, to ground herself in the familiarity of it.

The phone rang twice before Lucian answered. His voice, soft and hesitant, came through. "Hey, baby. I just needed to hear you. You know how messed up I get when I feel far from you."

"I'm here," she whispered, her voice barely a breath.

"That's better," he sighed, his relief clear in the sound. "Just stay close. That's all I want."

Melody sank deeper into the warmth of her blanket, her phone pressed tightly to her ear. Lucian's voice had a way of softening the jagged edges inside her, even when those edges were caused by him.

At her feet, Wednesday curled tighter against her legs, purring faintly like he knew she needed the comfort. She reached down and scratched behind his ear, grounding herself in the soft rhythm of his presence.

"I hate the thought of you slipping away," Lucian said after a pause. "Of someone else getting to see your smile in person when I can't."

"I'm not slipping away," she said, her voice fragile. "I wish you could be here."

"I wish that too." He paused, and his voice lowered into something more intimate. "If I was, I'd hold you so close. I'd never let you go. I'd make sure you felt safe. Like no one else ever made you feel before."

Melody's eyes fluttered shut. Her room, usually a place of shadows and silence, felt full of his presence now. It wrapped around her like the scent of her candles—warm, heady, consuming.

"You do make me feel safe," she murmured. "Even when... even when things get hard."

"Things get hard because we care," he said quickly. "Real love isn't easy, Melody. It's not some shallow thing you feel for a school crush. What we have, it's deep. It's soul deep. That's why it hurts when I think of you with people who don't understand you the way I do."

She didn't know what to say to that. Her fingers twisted in the edge of her comforter.

"You're right," she whispered.

Lucian exhaled softly, the sound crackling slightly through the phone. "You're so good, baby. So loyal. Not like the others."

Melody frowned slightly. "Others?"

There was a beat of silence. "Forget it. Doesn't matter. None of them mattered, not once I found you. You're the only one who ever really got under my skin. The only one I couldn't stop thinking about."

Something about that should've made her feel special. It did. And it didn't.

"Do you ever think I'm too much?" she asked, her voice barely audible.

"What? No," he said, and the intensity in his voice returned like a flare. "Never. You're exactly what I need. If anything, I'm afraid I'm too much. I know I get a little... possessive. But it's only because I care so much it scares me sometimes."

Melody's throat tightened again, her thoughts darting between Anna's worried face and Lucian's impassioned voice. She wanted someone to just tell her what was right. What was real.

"You're not too much," she said quietly. "You just feel everything. I get that."

"I know you do. That's why you're mine." A smile crept into his voice. "God, I wish I could kiss you right now."

She flushed. "Me too."

Lucian let the silence stretch for a moment, like he was savoring the fantasy. Then, softer: "Will you do something for me tonight?"

"What is it?"

"Sleep in my shirt again. The one I sent you. And light one of your candles. The patchouli one. I want you to feel me there."

Her heart beat a little faster. "Okay."

"And no talking to Anna tomorrow, okay? Just for one day. I just... I want to feel like it's just us again."

Melody hesitated.

Just one day.

"Okay," she said. "Just one day."

"Good girl."

A pause. Then his voice dropped, gentle and full of something that clung to her ribs.

"I love you, Melody."

She closed her eyes, clutching the phone a little tighter.

"I love you too."

Another quiet beat passed between them, tender and heavy.

"Oh," she added suddenly, her voice a little brighter, "I was thinking of going to the witch shop downtown tomorrow. They just restocked their crystal shelf and I kinda want to pick up something new for my altar."

Lucian chuckled—low and fond. "Of course you are. My little witch. What are you looking for this time? Something to hex your enemies?"

She laughed softly, petting Wednesday again. "Maybe something to protect my peace. Or a black obsidian tower. You'd like that one, it's sharp and intense."

"Sounds like you," he said. "Beautiful and dangerous."

She rolled her eyes, smiling. "You're so dramatic."

"I mean it. Get something for us, yeah? Maybe a love spell, just for fun."

"I already cast one," she teased. "Why do you think you're so obsessed with me?"

He groaned playfully. "Too late now. You've already got me under your spell, baby doll."

She grinned, the warmth of it blooming in her chest.

"You should get some sleep," he murmured. "Dream of me."

"I always do."

They lingered a moment longer, neither wanting to be the first to hang up.

"Goodnight, baby," he said at last.

"Goodnight."

CHAPTER EIGHT

The morning sun filtered weakly through the slats of Melody's blackout curtains, casting pale lines across her cluttered bedroom. She stirred beneath her blanket, one arm stretching out to where her phone buzzed softly on the nightstand.

Morning, baby. Did you sleep in my shirt?

She smiled sleepily, thumbs tapping quickly.

Of course. Still wearing it.

Good girl. I needed to feel close to you.

Melody pressed the shirt, his shirt, closer against her body before reluctantly crawling out of bed. Wednesday blinked up at her from the foot of the bed and let out a long, complaining meow.

"Yeah, yeah," she muttered affectionately. "You want breakfast too."

She padded down the hall in fuzzy socks to scoop food into Wednesday's bowl before heading to the bathroom. The warm rush of water from the shower felt like a reset, at least physically. She let it run longer than she should, steam curling around her like a fog. The events of the week swirled in her chest—Anna's worry, the fight, Lucian's late night voice in her ear.

Wrapped in a towel, she wiped the condensation from the mirror and leaned in to do her eyeliner. Sharp wings, smoky shadow—like armor. Her lip gloss gleamed faintly in the dim bathroom light. She slipped into a black skater skirt, ripped tights, and a hoodie with an occult design. Her silver moon necklace sat perfectly just above the hollow of her throat.

Wednesday wove around her ankles as she stepped into her boots.

You up to anything today?

Just thinking about you. Woke up missing you
more than usual.

Her stomach fluttered.

I'll text you from the library later. I need your
voice tonight.

You'll have it. All of me. Just stay close today,
yeah?

Downstairs, her father sat at the small kitchen table nursing a cup of gas station coffee. His plaid shirt was wrinkled like he'd slept in it. He glanced up when she entered, eyes tired but watchful.

"Hey," he said. "You got a second?"

Melody paused near the counter, arms folded across her chest. "Yeah?"

"I heard about what happened at school. The fight."

She stiffened.

"I'm not mad," he added quickly. "I just... I wanted to check in. Make sure you're okay."

She shrugged, eyes on a crack in the linoleum. "I'm fine."

"You don't look fine," he said gently. "I know things have been rough lately, with your mom, with—everything."

She didn't answer. Wednesday jumped onto a chair and started grooming himself noisily. The silence stretched awkwardly between them.

"I'm just trying here," her dad said finally, his voice low. "I know I'm not great at this stuff, but I want to be better. I want you to talk to me."

Melody's lips pressed into a thin line. Part of her wanted to spill everything, how hollow she felt, how Lucian was the only person who ever made her feel truly seen. But that part was quickly smothered by the louder instinct to shut down.

"I gotta go," she said, grabbing her bag.

"Melody..."

"Bye, Dad."

She didn't look back.

The air outside was crisp, the kind of early fall chill that hinted at winter. Melody tugged her hoodie tighter around her body as she walked the familiar path to school, her boots crunching against fallen leaves. Wednesday had tried to follow her out the door again, mewling dramatically until she shut it gently behind her.

She slid her phone into her sleeve, keeping one hand wrapped around it like a secret.

Her dad's voice still echoed faintly in her ears.

"I'm trying here... I want to be better."

He always said that. Quiet, clumsy words that hung in the air and never quite reached her. Maybe if he'd tried years ago, before her mother had hardened everything between them, before she learned how to build walls faster than bridges. Now, his efforts felt too late, like showing up to a fire with a garden hose and wondering why nothing changed.

Still... there had been something in his voice this morning. Not just tired, but worn. Frayed at the edges. Maybe he really was trying. Maybe he really didn't know how to reach her. But that wasn't her job, was it? She was tired of parenting her parents. Tired of being the emotional interpreter in a house where everyone spoke in silence and slammed doors.

She exhaled, watching her breath fog in the cool air.

Lucian would understand.

He *did* understand.

With him, she didn't have to explain the weight in her chest or why she sometimes wanted to disappear. With him, it was okay to just *feel*. To be angry, sad, intense. Too much for everyone else, but not for him.

She passed by the cemetery on the way, her little shortcut to school. The iron gate creaked open just a little, as if inviting her in. She hesitated for a moment, her fingers brushing the cold metal, before moving on. Not today.

Today, she needed to be near him, even if it was just through a screen.

The school library was nearly empty. It always was this time of day— last period, just before the final bell, when most students were half-checked out already. The air held that sleepy, stagnant stillness that Melody had come to crave. While the rest of the school buzzed with anticipation for release, the library exhaled.

Melody liked the quiet. Needed it.

She wandered past the rows of outdated encyclopedias and dusty language dictionaries until she reached her usual hiding place, a sliver of space tucked between the tall fiction shelves and the back wall where the light from the high window fell in a golden diagonal on the carpet. It was cramped, barely enough room for one person, but that was what made it perfect. No one else came here. No one else fit.

She dropped her backpack silently to the floor and slid down beside it, pulling her knees up to her chest. Her black hoodie enveloped her like a shell, the sleeves hanging past her fingertips. She tugged her hood further down until only her eyes peeked out from behind her curtain of black hair. The familiar weight of it grounded her, like armor.

A thick true crime book sat open across her lap, *Disappearances That Shook the Nation*. She'd been "reading" it for the last twenty minutes, but the words refused to sink in. Her eyes skimmed paragraph after paragraph about missing women, about timelines and police failures and families left behind, but it all felt distant. Pale. Nothing compared to the electric pulse of the phone resting in her palm.

She kept one ear tilted toward the librarian's desk, just in case Mrs. Waller decided to come patrolling. Every time she heard the soft rumble of the rolling cart, she flipped a page or leaned forward like she was engrossed in the story. But really, she was in another world entirely.

Her fingers moved under the folds of her hoodie sleeve as she tapped out another message.

> I've been thinking about you all day.

The reply came almost instantly. Lucian was always quick to respond, like he'd been waiting for her too.

> Same. It's like the whole day doesn't even feel real until I hear from you.

Her breath hitched, and she stared at the glowing screen as warmth bloomed beneath her ribs. God, he *got* it. That feeling she carried around like a weight— the fog, the numbness, the way everything felt dull and disconnected until he reached through it. When Lucian messaged her, it was like someone turned the lights on inside her.

She traced the edge of her phone case with her thumb,

cheeks flushing, lips curling into a soft smile she'd never show anyone else. It was a quiet kind of joy, the kind that made her feel like crying if she looked at it too directly.

> Counting the minutes until I can talk to you tonight.

> I hate that I can't be there with you right now.

> I'd sit next to you, hold your hand, read over your shoulder. I'd tell everyone else to go fuck themselves.

Her smile widened, then faltered slightly. A lump formed in her throat.

> You really would, wouldn't you?

> Of course I would. You're not like them. You're real. They don't see it, but I do.

Melody swallowed hard. Her vision blurred slightly at the edges, and she wiped at her eyes quickly with her sleeve, pretending it was just dust in the air. But she knew it wasn't. It was the way his words wrapped around the raw places in her, the parts no one else bothered to look at, let alone touch.

> I wish I could disappear with you. Just... go somewhere far away.

Her fingers trembled slightly after she sent it. It was too much. She was probably being dramatic. But she meant it. She'd been thinking about it all day, especially after that half-hearted conversation with her dad that morning, the awkward "I heard about the fight at school" and the way he looked at her like she was slipping through his fingers and he didn't know how to catch her. And maybe she didn't want to be caught. Not by him, not by anyone.

Except Lucian.

Her phone buzzed again.

> One day, maybe we will. Just you and me.
> Somewhere quiet. Somewhere no one can hurt
> you again.

A single tear slipped down her cheek, but she didn't wipe it away this time. The idea of it— of escape, of being chosen, protected, it was almost too much to carry. Her heart ached with how badly she wanted it to be real.

She paused before typing again, hesitating for just a second.

> Don't forget! I'm going to the witch shop after
> school today. That little one downtown with the
> purple windows.

> God, I wish I could go with you. I'd love that
> place.

> Text me if you see anything cool. Especially
> anything that reminds you of us.

She smiled again, a little more wistfully this time.

> I will. Maybe I'll get something that ties us
> together. A charm or a candle. Something
> small but real.

> Everything about you is real to me.

> You're the only real thing in my whole damn
> life.

A muffled cough echoed from the front of the library, pulling her back slightly. Melody curled deeper into her hoodie, drawing her knees closer to her chest. She could hear students shifting in their seats, a chair scraping against tile. But all of it felt far away.

In this dusty, hidden corner of the school, Melody wasn't the strange girl with the haunted eyes. She wasn't the disappointment her mom rolled her eyes at or the ghost her dad tried too late to reach. She wasn't the freak who sat alone at lunch or the girl who flinched when her name was called.

She was *his*.

And in this sliver of time, surrounded by rows of forgotten books and the hush of filtered afternoon light, that was enough.

The final bell rang. Melody closed her notebook and slipped out the side entrance, avoiding the crowd of students pouring into the main hallway. She didn't want to deal with anyone today.

Her boots scuffed against the pavement, the rhythm steady and grounding. She kept her headphones in, drowning out the world with a playlist of droning guitars and haunting synths.

She pushed open the door to Moonlight & Thorn, the small brass bell above jingling overhead. The familiar scent of sage and sandalwood wrapped around her like a cloak.

"Hey, love," called Rowan from behind the counter, her silver-dyed hair catching the light. Her winged eyeliner was perfect, as always, and her fingers glittered with a dozen rings. Melody didn't know much about her, but Rowan's voice always made her feel seen—warm and effortless.

"Back for more magic?"

Melody gave a soft smile and a wave. "Just browsing."

"Take your time," Rowan said, waving a smudge bundle gently over a bowl of smoky quartz.

Melody wandered through the shop, letting her fingers graze crystal towers and bundles of dried herbs. She picked up a rose quartz heart and turned it over in her palm, watching it catch the antique light. Without thinking too much about it, she snapped a quick photo and sent it to Lucian.

> Look what I found. It reminds me of you.

A moment later, her phone buzzed.

> You found my heart in a witch shop? Damn, I knew I was mystical.

Melody smiled down at the screen, cheeks flushing. She wandered further, pausing at a display of black salt jars and candle bundles wrapped in twine. She took another picture, this time of a deep burgundy candle labeled "Devotion" with a wax-dripped rose stamped on the tag, and sent it without a message. He'd get it.

Her phone lit up again.

> That one's perfect. I'd burn it for you if you were mine tonight.

You kind of already are, she typed, then hesitated. She deleted it and sent:

> I'm gonna light this one when we talk later.

Another reply came quickly:

> I'll feel it. I always do with you.

> It's like you're a string tied to my ribs or something. Tug the right way and I swear I feel it in my chest.

She held the phone to her chest for a moment, heart racing.

She picked up a small patchouli votive, the scent instantly pulling Lucian's voice into her head:

Light the patchouli one. I want you to feel me there.

Melody added it to her growing collection, then tucked a tiny black cat charm into her palm. At the counter, her eyes landed on a jar of loose mugwort.

"Thinking of dream work?" Rowan asked, her voice softer now.

"Something like that," Melody said. "Or maybe I just want to sleep better."

Rowan nodded, sliding the mugwort into the paper bag with the rest of her items. But just before folding the top, she paused, her fingers resting lightly on the edge. Her eyes met Melody's—serious now, thoughtful.

"You're walking with shadows lately," she said quietly. "I don't need to know why. But... be careful who you let into your inner circle. Especially now. The veil's thinner than usual, things get tangled."

Melody blinked. "What do you mean?"

Rowan gave her a faint smile, not unkind. "Let's just say... not everything that feels powerful is safe. And not every soul that claims to love you knows how."

A chill crept up Melody's spine. She swallowed and gave a small nod, fingers tightening on the paper bag.

"Thank you," she murmured.

"Trust your gut, love," Rowan said, handing her the bag fully now. "You've got good instincts, you just need to listen to them."

Outside, twilight had begun to bruise the sky. Melody walked slowly, the black cat charm clinking in her pocket with each step. Her thoughts were already drifting back to her messages.

As she reached the corner, her phone buzzed again.

> Don't forget, tell me everything you picked out tonight.

> I want to feel like I was there with you.

She smiled down at the screen, but something Rowan said stirred faintly in the back of her mind.

Not every soul that claims to love you knows how.

Melody slipped the phone into her pocket.

She'd tell him. Of course she would.

The walk home from the witch shop had left Melody with a strange ache in her chest. Something about the air felt thicker now, more electric, like the herbs in her pocket were whispering, like her heart had soaked in all the strange warmth from the candles and crystals. The shopkeeper's words echoed faintly in her mind: *"You're more powerful than you know."*

When she got home, the house was quiet— weirdly quiet. No music blaring from Nick's room. No yelling. She toed off her boots by the door and started toward the stairs when—

"Mel."

Her stomach dropped.

Andrew was still home.

He was never around this long. Usually out working long shifts on the pipeline, or keeping himself busy until Charlotte barked at him to come back. She hadn't even realized he was here earlier.

She turned, surprised. "You're still home?"

Andrew stood in the kitchen, a can of Coke in his hand. His plaid shirt was unbuttoned, his boots dusty, face worn. He looked like someone who hadn't slept well in years.

"Job got rained out," he said, not quite meeting her eyes. "Figured I'd stick around for once."

Melody nodded, the strap of her backpack cutting into her shoulder. The air between them felt awkward, like walking into a conversation that never really started.

Andrew hesitated, fingers drumming on the can. "You good?"

He didn't say it like he really expected an answer, more like he hoped she'd say "yeah" so he wouldn't have to figure out what to do if she said "no."

She shrugged. "Just tired."

He nodded like that was enough, like that was something he could carry. There was so much unsaid between them, so many moments where he might have spoken up but didn't. Melody didn't hold it against him. Not really. She knew he was surviving, same as her, just in a different way. His silence wasn't cruelty. It was habit. Fear. Exhaustion.

She looked at him for a second longer, the man who stayed out of the way to keep the peace, who tried to fix things with paychecks and long work days. Who had once picked her up from school when Charlotte forgot, and didn't say a word the whole ride home except to hand her a pack of gum from the dashboard.

"I'll be upstairs," she said quietly.

"If you need anything..." he started, but it trailed off. He didn't finish the sentence.

She nodded, already heading for the stairs.

Melody closed her bedroom door with a soft *click* and leaned her forehead against the wood for a breath.

She hated how heavy everything felt.

Her backpack slid off her shoulder and landed on the floor with a quiet *thud*. The house still echoed with silence— no yelling, no footsteps, just that stale hush that settled in the corners like dust. She could still hear the way Andrew had said *"You good?"* like it was a question wrapped in fear, like he already knew she wasn't and just didn't want to know how deep the not-okayness ran.

A soft *mrrrp* broke through her fog.

Wednesday was curled on the window ledge, eyes half-lidded, tail twitching lazily. She stretched and padded across the room, hopping onto the bed like she'd been summoned by the weight in Melody's chest.

Melody crouched by her nightstand and pulled the small paper bag from her coat pocket, the one from the witch shop. Inside, nestled between tissue paper and the faint scent of sage, was the candle.

It was small and deep purple, waxy and smooth under her

fingers. Tied around it was a slip of parchment with a hand-written word: *Devotion*.

She lit it with a match from the drawer. The flame flickered to life, casting soft, golden shadows across her walls. Something about it felt sacred, like she'd created a crack in the world that no one else could touch. Like this space, this moment, belonged entirely to her.

The scent was sweet and smoky, with something dark underneath. The kind of smell that made her feel like maybe she was in control of something. Like maybe she could carve out a corner of her life where she wasn't being watched or judged or yelled at.

She sat cross-legged on her bed, and Wednesday settled beside her, her small body pressing against Melody's thigh, warm and certain. The candle flame danced gently, like it was breathing with her.

She whispered, just to herself, "I don't want to disappear."

It wasn't something she'd ever said out loud before. But the candle didn't flinch. It didn't try to fix her. It didn't shrug her off with a "you'll be fine" or ask what her problem was. It just burned, steady and warm.

Her fingers brushed the crystal the shopkeeper had given her, a chunk of amethyst that she didn't really believe could *do* anything, but felt nice in her palm anyway. Lucian's voice came to her memory, something he'd said a few nights ago on the phone:

"You're not crazy, you know. You just feel too much for people who don't feel enough. That's a kind of magic, Mel."

And in that moment, she believed him. Or at least, wanted to.

She leaned back against the pillows, letting the candlelight wash over her, one hand resting on Wednesday's back, feeling her soft, steady purr. She felt just a little less invisible.

Just as her eyes started to flutter closed in the warm flicker of candlelight, her phone buzzed beside her pillow.

You lit it, didn't you?

Melody sat up a little, her heart skipping. The candle flame wavered as if it knew it had been caught.

She stared at the screen, thumbs hovering. A chill curled down her spine, not a cold one, but the kind that came when someone saw you too clearly.

> ...how did you know?

Three dots appeared. Paused. Vanished. Then appeared again.

> I felt it. Like something opened.

> That kind of energy doesn't go unnoticed, Mel.
> Especially not by me.

She swallowed hard, glancing at the candle. The word *Devotion* was glowing faintly in the low light, like it had become part of the flame.

> What are you thinking about right now?

> Tell me the truth.

Melody hesitated. Wednesday rubbed her head against Melody's arm, a soft nudge of grounding comfort. The air smelled like something old and important. She typed slowly.

> That I wish someone could really see me. All of
> me. Even the parts that feel ugly.

> Like... not just tolerate it, but want it.

There was a long pause.

> I do.

Her breath caught.

> I see every part of you, even the ones you hide.

> And none of them are ugly. Not to me.

She stared at his words until they blurred. She hadn't realized how much she needed them, or how fast he always seemed to know *exactly* what to say.

Beneath the covers, with the candle still burning and Wednesday purring quietly against her side, Melody let herself believe it, just for tonight.

That someone, somewhere, wanted all of her.

Later that night, Melody lay in bed with Wednesday curled up at her side, purring softly as the weight of the evening pressed down on her. The dried flowers from the witch shop were still tucked in her jacket pocket, but she hadn't yet had the courage to look at them. The ache in her chest felt bigger now, more unbearable with each passing moment. Her phone buzzed on the nightstand, its soft glow casting a light over her face like a secret doorway waiting to be opened. When Lucian's name flashed on the screen, a rush of warmth flooded her chest.

She picked up the phone, a smile tugging at her lips. Her fingers hovered over the screen for a second, a sudden burst of nervous energy in her fingertips before she tapped the screen, feeling her heart pick up its pace.

"Hello?" Her voice was soft, unsure, but filled with anticipation.

Lucian's voice came through the phone, low and smooth, the kind of voice that felt like it was meant for whispered secrets. "You know you drive me crazy, right?"

Melody curled up into her blanket, feeling warmth spread through her body as his words sank in. She bit her lip, trying to steady the racing in her chest.

She couldn't help but laugh lightly, the sound of it a little nervous. "Why?"

"Because you don't even know how beautiful you are," he replied quickly. "How badly I want you."

The words hit her in a way that made her heart stumble. She stared at the ceiling, her fingers twisting the edge of her blanket, feeling the heat creep up her neck.

"I'm just me..." she murmured, unsure if she even believed the words.

"Exactly," Lucian responded, his tone deeper now. "You, just being you... it's enough to mess with my head. No one else makes me feel like this."

Her breath caught in her throat, a flutter of warmth rushing to her cheeks. She hadn't expected him to say that, not in the way he did. Her heart skipped.

"You're not like the girls my age," Lucian continued, his voice more intense now, as if the words were spilling out without him even thinking. "They're fake. They only care about money and parties and pretending to be something they're not."

A soft smile tugged at her lips, though it was mixed with a tinge of sadness. She couldn't help but wonder if he really saw her, all of her.

"You're real," he went on, and Melody could hear the sincerity in his voice. "Sweet. Pure."

That one word—pure, sent a shock to her chest. It left her feeling exposed and vulnerable, like something precious. Her stomach twisted, her pulse quickening at the thought.

"I wish I could hold you right now," Lucian's voice was slower, quieter now, almost like he was trying to soothe her. "You don't even know the things I'd do just to make you smile."

Her breath hitched, and she gripped the phone tighter, almost instinctively. She pulled the blanket higher around her shoulders, as if it could shield her from the emotions swirling inside.

"Like what?" she asked, her voice trembling a little, the words slipping out before she could second-guess herself.

There was a brief silence on the other end, a slight pause before he answered, the tone in his voice deepening.

"I'd tuck you against my chest," he said softly, almost reverently. "Play with your hair. Kiss your forehead. Make you feel safe."

Melody's heart raced at the softness in his voice. She bit her lip, uncertain of what to say, the words hanging heavy in the air between them.

"No one's ever made you feel safe before, have they?" Lucian's question came, quieter, almost like he was already anticipating her answer.

Her chest tightened, and for a split second, the tears welled up before she even realized they were there. She wiped them away quickly, trying to keep her voice steady.

"No," she whispered, barely audible.

"I would," he said, his voice low, gentle. "I'd take care of you. I'd never hurt you."

His words wrapped around her, soft yet overwhelming, filling the space between them. She held her breath, the heaviness in her chest almost suffocating. The phone seemed to feel like it was the only thing anchoring her to the moment.

"I'd be gentle with you, baby," Lucian murmured, as if to reassure her. "Always. I know you're young. I know you're... innocent. That's what makes you so perfect."

Melody's pulse quickened, her thumb hovering over the phone screen. She didn't know if she was ready for any of this, if she understood it. The thoughts crashed together in her head, making it hard to think clearly.

"I've never... done anything like that before," she said, her voice barely above a whisper.

"I know, baby," Lucian's voice was soft, like he was speaking directly to her heart. "That's why it would be so perfect. I'd be your first. The only one who really deserves you."

Melody's chest tightened, and the phone felt warm in her hand, like a lifeline, even though she wasn't sure where it would lead. She didn't know if she was ready for any of this, yet it felt impossible to pull away.

"I would never, ever let anyone hurt you," Lucian's voice was full of conviction now, like a promise. "You're mine. Always will be."

Her hand trembled slightly as she gripped the phone tighter, biting her lip to stop herself from saying more, but she had no words. Only a growing ache in her chest.

Her fingers hovered over the screen, unsure of what to say next. "Isn't it wrong?" she asked, almost hesitantly, the words feeling small compared to everything else she was feeling.

There was a pause, long enough for her to almost second-guess herself. Then his voice came through, steady and calm.

"No," Lucian answered firmly. "Not when it's real."

"Not when it's love," he added, the words carrying weight.

Melody felt the tension ease just slightly, like the warmth of his words was melting the doubts. She closed her eyes, taking in a shaky breath.

"You trust me, don't you?" Lucian's voice softened again, coaxing her, but not forcing her.

"Yes," she said, without thinking. "I trust you."

There was another pause, this one more tender. Then, softly:

"What were you up to today, little witch?"

Melody smiled, the nickname curling warm around her ribs. "You already know. I sent you those pictures, remember?"

Lucian chuckled softly. "I know, but I wanted to hear you say it. That place looked like it was pulled straight out of a dream."

"It kinda felt that way," she admitted. "Rowan, the owner, she gave me these dried flowers. Said they were for devotion spells. Told me to light a candle and focus on someone I trust."

There was a pause. Then, his voice, low and deliberate:

"Did you think of me when she said that?"

Her cheeks flushed. "Yeah... I did."

Lucian exhaled slowly, and for a moment, she could almost feel the heat of it against her neck. "You have no idea what that does to me."

Her fingers curled around the edge of her blanket. "I lit the candle earlier. Before we talked."

"I knew it," he said, a touch of awe in his voice. "I could feel it. I was in the middle of everything and I just... stopped. Like something reached out and grabbed me."

Melody closed her eyes, her heart fluttering. "Do you think it worked?"

"I don't have to think, baby. I know. I felt you." His voice dropped to a whisper. "Light it again for me tomorrow. I'll do the same. We'll stay connected, no matter how far apart."

A shiver threaded down her spine. "Okay. I will."

"My little witch," he breathed.

They lingered in that hush, the silence full of something potent and unseen, until he spoke again, his voice dark.

"One day soon, baby doll. One day soon, you'll be all mine for real."

Her breath caught. "I'll wait for you," she whispered.

And just like that, it all felt inevitable.

When the call ended, Melody stared at the screen, her chest tight with something between yearning and magic. Her cat pressed close, purring like a spell of its own, and she slid her hand into her pocket, feeling the small bundle of dried flowers still wrapped in tissue. Rowan's words echoed in her mind— quiet, careful, warning.

She hadn't told Lucian everything.

And a part of her wasn't sure if she ever would.

But the candle had been lit.

And something had begun.

Melody sat cross-legged on her bed, the house dark except for the soft string of fairy lights tacked along her ceiling. Her journal sat in her lap, the corners worn from years of half-finished entries.

Tonight, though, her pen moved fast, like her heart was pulling the words straight out of her.

I don't even know how to explain what I'm feeling.

It's like... my chest is too small for it all.

Like there's this huge, glowing thing inside me that only he can see.

Lucian gets me.

No one ever has. Not like this.

He says he thinks about me all the time.

He says I'm different... special. That I'm not fake like everyone else.

And I believe him. I really do.

When he talks to me, I feel real.

Not invisible, not stupid, not a burden.

I feel like I matter.

He says I'm his.

HIS.

I can't even write that without smiling so hard my face hurts.

And tonight... he said things I never thought anyone would say to me.

He said he'd take care of me.

He said he'd be gentle with me, that he'd make sure I felt good, that he'd teach me everything.

(Just writing that makes me feel like I'm floating.)

I know some people would say it's weird, because he's older.

But they don't understand.

They don't know what it's like to finally have someone who sees you when everyone else looks right through you.

I trust him.

I love him.

I don't care what anyone thinks.

I belong with him.

I just know it.

Maybe it's crazy.

But it feels real.

It feels more real than anything in my whole life.

One day soon, we'll be together for real.

And I won't have to hide how much I love him anymore.

I can't wait.

—M

Her hand ached a little from how fast she'd written, but it didn't matter.

Melody hugged the journal to her chest, closed her eyes, and smiled into the dark.

In her mind, she could almost feel Lucian's arms around her, whispering all the things she wanted so badly to believe were true.

She didn't know that what she felt wasn't safety at all.

It was the soft, sweet first tightening of the trap.

Melody sent a couple more text messages to Lucian, and then tucked the phone under her pillow, curling herself around it like it was a lifeline. Her eyes fluttered closed, and she imagined Lucian's arms around her— safe, warm, loving.

Lucian's POV after the messages:

Lucian leaned back in his chair, the soft hum of industrial music playing from the old speakers at his desk.

His phone glowed in the dark, Melody's messages lighting up the screen one after another.

> Goodnight, baby. I'm yours forever. I mean it.
> 

> Thank you for loving me when nobody else
> does.

> You're the best thing that's ever happened
> to me.

He smirked, running his thumb slowly across the screen like he was touching her.

Fifteen.

Fifteen and already so sweet. So desperate to be loved. So easy to mold.

He opened her messages again, rereading them, savoring each word.

She was falling harder by the hour. Exactly how he wanted it.

Exactly how he *needed* it.

He typed slowly, deliberately, letting the words bleed power.

> Mine. You hear me, baby?

> No one will ever touch you but me.

> You're perfect. Exactly the way you are. You were made for me.

> You belong to me. Always.

He watched the "Delivered" note pop up but no "Read."

She must have fallen asleep clutching her phone like she usually did.

The thought made him chuckle darkly.

So easy. So trusting.

He leaned forward, typing again— this time slower, more deliberate.

> One day soon, I'm going to show you how much you mean to me.

> You won't ever doubt it again.

> I'll make you feel things you've never even dreamed of, baby doll.

> You'll beg for it. You'll beg for me.

He paused, feeling a twisted satisfaction coil in his gut.

Melody didn't even realize it yet, but he was already inside her head, inside her heart, weaving himself into every empty crack she had.

By the time he was finished, there wouldn't be a single piece of her that didn't belong to him.

And she would think it was love.

Lucian leaned back again, lit a cigarette with a flick of his silver lighter, and stared at the ceiling.

All he had to do now was be patient.

She was already his.

It was only a matter of time before she'd be begging to prove it.

CHAPTER NINE

Melody blinked awake to the soft vibration of her phone against her pillow.

Morning light leaked through her bedroom curtains, casting a sleepy haze over everything.

She rubbed her eyes and grabbed her phone, heart fluttering the moment she saw his name lighting up the lock screen.

Lucian (8 Messages)

Sleep still clouded her mind, but excitement cut through it.

She sat up, clutching the blanket to her chest, and opened the texts with trembling fingers.

> Mine. You hear me, baby?

> No one will ever touch you but me.

> You're perfect. Exactly the way you are. You were made for me.

> You belong to me. Always

Her chest squeezed tight, her heart pounding so loud she could hear it in her ears.

No one had ever said things like that to her before.

No one had ever made her feel like she was *wanted* like that.

She hugged her knees to her chest, rereading the messages over and over, a giddy, breathless feeling rising in her belly.

It almost scared her, how much she *liked* it. How much she *needed* it.

And then she saw them, the last messages he had sent while she was asleep.

> One day soon, I'm going to show you how much you mean to me.

> You won't ever doubt it again.

> I'll make you feel things you've never even dreamed of, baby doll.

> You'll beg for it. You'll beg for me.

Her cheeks flushed deep red.

Her stomach flipped over and twisted itself into nervous, excited knots.

She didn't totally understand what he meant, but it filled her with a strange, heady kind of anticipation.

It felt secretive and grown-up and thrilling, like stepping into some hidden world that only Lucian knew how to show her.

She typed back quickly, her hands trembling just a little:

> Good morning my love 🖤 I'm sorry I fell asleep. I dreamed about you. I can't stop thinking about you. I want to be yours forever.

She hesitated, then added another message, heart pounding:

> I want you to show me everything…

Her thumb hovered over the send button for half a second, but then she hit it before she could lose her nerve.

Almost instantly, the typing bubble popped up.

Lucian was awake.

> Good girl.

> You're already mine, baby. I'm just going to make sure you feel it everywhere.

> You're so perfect. I don't deserve you... but I'm never letting you go.

Melody pressed the phone to her chest, closing her eyes, trying to hold in the overwhelming rush of feeling.

She belonged to someone.

Someone who saw her.

Someone who wanted every piece of her, even the broken ones she tried to hide.

Wednesday pawed at the edge of her blanket before hopping gracefully onto the bed. She circled once, then curled against Melody's hip, purring softly.

She didn't understand the full weight of his words.

She didn't realize how tangled she was already getting.

All she knew was that Lucian made her feel wanted. Needed.

And that feeling was worth everything.

Even if it meant giving him her whole heart.

She couldn't wait.

Before her thoughts could spiral or her nerves could catch up, she hit his contact and pressed call.

Lucian answered on the first ring.

"There's my girl," he said, voice thick with warmth.

"You miss me already, huh?"

Melody tucked herself under her covers, grinning hard enough it hurt.

Wednesday nosed her hand gently, as if sensing her excitement. Melody gave her a quick scratch behind the ears.

"Maybe," she teased shyly.

Lucian laughed low in his throat. "Don't tease, baby doll. You know it drives me crazy when you're cute."

That flutter bloomed in her chest again, the one that made her feel like she mattered.

Then, his tone softened, turned quieter.

"Hey... are you alone?"

She blinked, surprised by the question.

"Yeah. It's Saturday, so my dad took some overtime. My brother's at a friend's house. And my mom is... who cares where."

Lucian chuckled softly. "Good. I like when I get you all to myself."

They talked about silly things for a while— what music they liked, what she had for dinner last night, how boring her classes were.

Lucian asked a lot of questions, about everything:

What color socks she was wearing, what shampoo she used, what stuffed animals were on her bed.

She looked over at the small collection arranged near her pillow— a faded bear, a plush bat, a tiny crocheted frog. Wednesday blinked lazily beside her, one paw stretched across Melody's arm.

Every little detail, like he was building a map of her.

After a long, comfortable silence, Lucian spoke again, quieter this time.

"Can I tell you a secret?"

Melody's heart skipped. "Yeah."

"I think about you all the time," he whispered.

"When I wake up. When I'm at work. When I'm lying in bed at night."

He paused, and she heard him exhale slowly.

"Especially when I'm lying in bed."

Melody swallowed, nerves dancing in her stomach.

"I think about your sweet little smile," he murmured. "Your pretty eyes. Your soft little body."

She blushed so hard her face burned, hiding her face in the pillow even though he couldn't see her.

Wednesday meowed gently, shifting with a faint sigh and pressing her body closer to Melody's warmth.

"I bet you're laying there right now, looking all cute and cuddly, huh?"

His voice dipped even lower, almost a growl.

"Wish I could see you."

Melody giggled, nervous but giddy.

"Maybe you will someday."

Lucian groaned softly.

"You're such a tease, baby. Making me imagine it. It's not fair."

There was a beat of silence before he said, even softer:

"Can I ask you something, baby doll?"

She nodded, then remembered he can't see her: "Yeah."

Lucian's voice was velvet-wrapped steel now.

"Will you do something for me?"

Melody clutched the pillow tighter.

"Okay," she said, barely breathing.

"Nothing bad," he promised instantly.

"Nothing that would scare you. Just something little. Just for me."

Her heart pounded so hard she thought he might hear it.

"Touch your tummy," he said.

"Right under your hoodie. Just there."

Melody hesitated, confused—but it didn't sound bad.

It didn't sound scary.

It was her tummy, after all.

"Okay," she whispered, sliding her hand under the soft fabric.

"Good girl," he murmured, voice full of molten approval.

"Just your tummy. Tell me how it feels."

Melody bit her lip, feeling the warmth of her own skin under her fingertips.

"Warm," she whispered.

Lucian let out a shaky breath.

"God, I wish I was there to feel it too. You're so soft, baby. So perfect."

A deep, aching warmth spread through her chest.

She didn't know why his words made her feel so glowing, so special.

"You're doing so good," he praised.

"I'm so proud of you. You're so brave."

Melody closed her eyes, soaking it in like sunlight.

Brave.

Good.

Special.

All the things she had never felt at home.

Wednesday stretched again, her purring a soft backdrop to the praise Melody clung to like a lifeline.

Lucian didn't push further.

After a few more minutes of soft talking, he made her promise to spend some time for herself today.

"Light a candle," he murmured. "Put on something soft. Do something that makes you feel good. You deserve that, baby."

And Melody, warm and dreamy from the sound of his voice, agreed.

As the call ended, she lay still in the quiet, one hand still tucked beneath her hoodie, the other gently petting Wednesday's back.

The cat purred on, grounding her in the moment, the only witness to how deeply Melody was falling.

When the call ended, she lay in bed for a while, hugging her pillow, her skin still tingling from the things he'd said— the praise, the promises, the way he made her feel like the most precious thing in the world. She stayed like that for a long time, letting the weight of his words settle into her bones. The air felt thick and golden, humming with a strange kind of electricity. She traced patterns into the pillowcase with her fingertips, little loops and hearts and the letter L. Her lips still carried the ghost of a smile, the kind that lingers after being seen by someone.

Eventually, she got up, moving slowly, like she didn't want to break the spell. Her legs felt heavy, but not in a bad way, more like she was still carrying some of his warmth, some of that floating feeling he gave her. She crossed the room and opened her nightstand drawer, pulling out her favorite candle, lavender and sandalwood. She cupped her hands around the match as she struck it, shielding it from an invisible breeze. The small flame caught, flaring bright before softening. She held it to the wick and watched it bloom to life.

She placed the candle on her windowsill and crouched beside it, watching the flickering flame sway in the late afternoon haze. Outside, the sky had turned a dusky rose, the color of quiet endings and secret hopes. For a moment, she imagined Lucian sitting beside her, his fingers laced with hers, his voice low in her ear: *You're magic, Melody. No one's ever seen it, but I do.*

Music buzzed through her headphones— a mix of moody industrial, heavy riffs, and soft melancholy. She scrolled to the track Lucian had sent her the night before: "Broken" by Seether and Amy Lee. "This reminds me of us," he'd said. "The way you've been hurt, the way I just want to hold you together." She'd listened to it three times before bed, curled in her blankets with her eyes shut tight, letting Amy Lee's voice wash over her like a lullaby made of grief and devotion. Now, as the haunting chorus wrapped around her again, she felt it all over— the ache, the need, the tenderness she didn't have words for.

She moved through her room with slow, absent rhythm, straightening piles of clothes and stacking books with careful precision. Her body moved on autopilot, but her mind was far away, half in the song, half in the memory of his voice. She lined up her bracelets on the desk edge, adjusting each one until they were perfectly spaced. They clinked softly, bits of color and metal and cheap plastic, small tokens of who she was trying to be. A girl worth seeing. A girl worth saving.

When she crouched to look under the bed, her fingers brushed something soft, her old teddy bear. The one she hadn't touched in years. The one she told Lucian about late one night, embarrassed and laughing, and he'd said, "Don't ever be ashamed of what kept you safe." She pulled it out gently, brushing the dust from its ears, and pressed it to her chest. The bear still smelled faintly of vanilla, or maybe that was just memory playing tricks on her. She sat down on the edge of the bed, cradling it, and smiled softly.

Not everything in her world was good. But this moment— warm candlelight, music in her ears, his voice still echoing in her heart, felt like something close to okay.

Suddenly, she heard the familiar soft padding of paws on the floor, and before she could react, Wednesday jumped up onto the bed beside her. The cat purred, curling up beside her, a comforting presence. Melody smiled, absent-mindedly running her fingers through Wednesday's fur.

Her thoughts drifted back to the small witch shop she'd visited earlier in the week. The dimly lit shelves, the heavy scent of incense in the air, and the strange, almost magnetic energy she'd felt there. She had bought a small bundle of dried herbs and crystals, just a little something to add to her collection. Lucian knew about the shop, of course. He'd always been inter- ested in the witchy things she did, sometimes even playfully teasing her about it. She hadn't hidden that part of herself from him. He just didn't know about the conversation with Rowan, or the unease that had lingered after their discussion.

She felt a strange tug in her chest, wondering if she should tell Lucian about what Rowan had said. Part of her wanted to —

to share every part of herself with him. But then there was the warning Rowan had given her, the part of her that felt the weight of his words. *Be careful who you trust, Melody. Some things aren't what they seem.*

She swallowed hard, the words echoing in her mind. Would telling Lucian about the conversation make things more complicated? Was Rowan right to be so wary? She wasn't sure.

With Wednesday curled up beside her and the candle flickering softly in the quiet room, Melody closed her eyes for a moment, the feeling of warmth and possibility settling over her.

Later, she curled up on her bed with her notebook, pen in hand, heart still tangled in his voice.

The room had settled into twilight, shadows pooling in the corners, the last light of the day barely grazing the floor. A single candle flickered on the windowsill, lavender and something faintly smoky, like firewood left smoldering, the scent curling through the air and wrapping around her shoulders like a whispered promise.

The comforter was bundled high around her legs, soft and familiar, and her old stuffed bear, the one she'd had since she was six, sat at her side, half-hidden beneath a fold of fabric like a secret too precious to be seen.

Perched at the edge of her bed, her cat Wednesday had draped herself across Melody's ankles, a warm weight grounding her in the moment. Her purr rumbled softly, a steady vibration against the quiet hum of "Broken" playing in Melody's headphones. Always "Broken." It felt like the song was stitched into her ribs now. Every lyric cracked open something raw and tender in her chest, like the song had been written for her. For them.

On a fresh page, she began writing the lyrics from memory, her pen pressing into the paper with intent.

Every word poured out like confession.

She paused, her fingers curling tighter around the pen as something shifted inside her— not sadness, it was sharper than that. Lonelier. But sweet, too, in a way that made her eyes sting. The dizzying ache of being noticed. The quiet thrill of being claimed.

She let out a breath and rested her cheek against her bent knee. Then, in smaller, careful handwriting, she added a tiny black heart beneath the chorus, shading it in until the ink bled slightly.

In the corner of the page, barely larger than a whisper, she wrote it:

$$\mathcal{L} + \mathcal{M}$$
$$\textit{Together Forever}$$

The letters curled together like something sacred, as if writing it could make it real. As if maybe it already was. As if they were written into each other now.

Wednesday stirred at her feet, stretching one paw toward the edge of the notebook and then curling back up, as if to say, *stay.* Melody gave her a soft smile and ran her fingertips gently along the cat's spine, grateful for the quiet companionship.

She held the notebook to her chest and closed her eyes.

In her mind, she saw Lucian lying in bed, thinking of her. She imagined the soft rasp of his voice saying her name, imagined his hand brushing her hair back behind her ear, calling her brave. Calling her his.

And even though she was alone in her room, with only her candle, her cat, and the static hush of headphones wrapped around her ears, she didn't *feel* alone.

The sun finally dipped below the horizon, casting the room in bruised purples and faded gold. Light softened into shadows. The world outside blurred and disappeared.

Melody felt something loosen inside her, like an exhale she hadn't realized she'd been holding. The knot in her chest eased. The sharp edges of her day dulled. Even the sounds of her house, her mother clattering in the kitchen, the echo of old arguments lingering in the walls, faded behind the music and candlelight.

She felt calm.

Steady.

Almost... happy.

That night, it started again— gentle, slow, so easy it barely registered as anything at all.

Lucian's voice was soft through the phone, syrup-thick and warm. He asked about her day, about her candle, about what she wrote. Then, like a breeze slipping under a door, his voice dropped.

He asked her to touch her hair.

Then trace her collarbone.

Then say, just once, "I'm yours."

Each request wrapped in velvet— gentle, careful, laced in praise and sweetness. Nothing sharp. Nothing that felt wrong.

It didn't feel like a command.

It felt like closeness. Like trust. Like love.

And Melody, with her whole heart already leaning in, already folded into his words, didn't think to hesitate.

Didn't see how far she was already being led.

He made it feel like belonging.

Like being wanted.

Like being *enough*.

And that, for a girl who had always felt like too much and never enough all at once, was everything.

CHAPTER TEN

The next morning arrived slowly, with soft gray light filtering through Melody's curtains. She stirred beneath her blankets, stretching into the quiet hush of her room, the warmth of last night's call still clinging to her skin like a second layer. Her phone was tucked under her pillow, where she'd fallen asleep with it cradled in her hand.

She unlocked the screen and blinked at the soft glow. A message from Lucian waited at the top of her notifications.

Good morning, my girl. Dream of me?

A tiny smile tugged at her lips. She tapped out a reply with still-sleepy fingers.

Always. Morning 

Then she added, hesitantly:

Shower and coffee calling me. I'll text you after?

His reply came almost instantly.

> I'll be thinking of you. Wish I was there to help rinse that pretty hair of yours. ;)

Heat flushed across her cheeks. She hugged the phone to her chest for a moment, letting the warmth of his words linger, before slipping out of bed.

The shower was quiet, steamy, and unhurried. She lathered her hair slowly, closing her eyes and imagining his hands instead of her own, like he said he wished. The water poured over her shoulders like soft fingers. Her mind played back the sound of his voice, how he'd murmured *I'm yours* like a vow.

Wrapped in her towel afterward, she stood at the mirror and traced the faint line of her collarbone, remembering.

Back in her room, as she slipped into soft leggings and a hoodie, her phone buzzed again, but this time it was a call.

Anna.

Melody hesitated for a second, thumb hovering. Then she answered.

"Hey," she said softly, settling onto the edge of her bed.

"Hey, Mel!" Anna's voice was bright and familiar, grounding. "I was just thinking about you. You doing okay?"

Melody hesitated, curling a piece of hair around her finger. "Yeah. I'm... fine. Just tired."

Anna didn't push, at least not right away. "Well, I was calling to ask if you wanted to come with me and Jace to that concert next Saturday. Local show, nothing huge, but it's supposed to be super fun. Emo night kinda vibe. Thought it'd be good to get out of the house."

Melody's stomach fluttered at the name *Jace*. She glanced at her phone screen like Lucian might be watching through it. "I don't know..."

Anna picked up on it instantly. "Mel," she said gently, "you haven't been out in forever. You deserve a night to breathe. And it's not like it's a date, Jace is going because he knows the drummer or something. You'll be with me the whole time."

Melody chewed on her lip. "It's just... complicated," she murmured.

There was a pause. "Lucian?"

Melody's silence answered for her.

Anna softened her voice. "You don't need permission to have fun, babe. Seriously. One night out with your best friend isn't a betrayal. It's normal."

Melody stared at the floor, her bare toes curling into the carpet. A small part of her wanted to say no. To avoid the argument, the guilt, the quiet tension in Lucian's voice when he found out Jace was going.

But a deeper part of her, wanted to feel the bass under her skin. Wanted to scream lyrics into a crowd. Wanted to laugh without checking her phone every five minutes.

She exhaled. "Okay. I'll go."

Anna whooped. "Yesss! I'm buying your ticket before you change your mind. Black eyeliner, big boots— the whole thing. It's happening."

Melody smiled despite herself. "Alright, alright."

When they hung up, she stared at her phone, already imagining how Lucian might react when she told him. Her heart tightened.

But maybe she wouldn't tell him just yet.

Maybe for now, she could hold onto the good, the idea of laughing in the dark next to her best friend, music pulsing through her chest like a heartbeat that belonged only to her.

That night, Melody stayed up late waiting for Lucian's call.

When her phone finally buzzed after ten o clock, she answered so fast she almost dropped it.

"Hey, pretty girl," Lucian said, his voice like velvet.

"Miss me?"

"So much," Melody whispered, curling up tighter in bed.

He chuckled, warm and low. "God, you're cute. Makes my chest hurt thinking about you."

They talked for a while— soft, dreamy conversations about favorite colors, dreams, the stars outside their windows.

Lucian painted futures with his words: trips they'd take, secret places they'd hide away together, songs that would be *theirs*.

"You feel it too, don't you?" he murmured.

"This thing between us. It's not just normal. It's... bigger."

Melody's heart beat so hard it almost hurt.

"Yeah. I do."

Lucian was quiet for a moment, then said, even softer, "I've never felt this way before. Not with anyone."

She smiled so big it hurt.

She didn't notice the sharp edge tucked behind his tenderness.

"Can I tell you something?" he whispered.

"Yeah," she breathed.

"I think about you when I'm lying in bed."

A small pause.

"About how sweet you must look in your pajamas. About how soft your skin must feel."

Melody buried her face in the pillow, too flustered to answer.

Lucian's voice coaxed her gently.

"Are you wearing your pajamas now, baby doll?"

"Uh-huh," she mumbled.

"Tell me what they look like."

She hesitated, giggling nervously.

"It's just a tank top and shorts. Black ones."

He groaned quietly. "You're killing me, baby doll. You have no idea."

Lucian let the silence stretch, heavy and warm. Then, softly:

"Can I ask you something else? You can say no."

"Okay," Melody whispered.

"I want you to touch your shoulder," he said.

"Just with your fingertips. Like you're tracing little circles. Nice and slow."

It was such a small thing.

Harmless.

Safe.

Melody obeyed, brushing her shoulder lightly.

"You're doing so good," Lucian praised, his voice thick.

"God, you're such a good girl for me."

A rush of heat and pride filled her. She wanted to keep making him happy.

Wanted to be his good girl.

"Do you trust me, baby?" he whispered.

"Yeah," she breathed without hesitation.

"I trust you too," he murmured. "You're so special. You're the only one I want."

The words melted into her.

"You know," Lucian said after a moment, his voice turning softer again, "there are ways we can feel close even from far away."

Melody's breath caught.

She didn't fully understand what he meant, but she trusted him.

She *wanted* to feel close to him.

"What kind of ways?" she asked, innocent.

Lucian chuckled, but it was a kind sound, not mean.

"You're too pure for your own good, baby."

Another pause.

Then, tenderly:

"Maybe sometime... if you want... we could do something special together. Something just for us."

Her heart fluttered.

"I'd like that."

"You're everything to me," Lucian said, voice almost breaking with emotion.

"I'll be patient. I promise. I'll take care of you."

Melody clutched the phone tighter against her ear, feeling like she was holding onto the only real thing in her world.

She didn't hear the trap closing.

She only heard *love*.

After they hung up, Melody didn't move.

The silence felt strange. Not empty, but *humming*. Like Lucian's voice had left a residue in the air, soft and clinging, like smoke from a candle that had just been snuffed out.

She lay there for a while, her phone still warm against her cheek, her heart still racing.

He said I'm the only one he wants.

She rolled onto her back and stared up at the ceiling, her eyes tracing the faint shifting shadows from the glow of her string lights. Everything felt slower now. Drenched in honey. Her skin still tingled where she'd touched her shoulder, and she didn't know why something so small felt so *big*.

He made it feel like something sacred.

Melody reached for her notebook, the one she kept hidden behind the loose panel in her nightstand. The one with the torn edges and bent cover, where her real thoughts lived.

She flipped to a clean page and began to write in slow, curling letters:

He said I'm special. He said he's never felt this way before. I feel like I'm floating.
I know it's wrong that I want this so much. But it doesn't feel wrong. Not with him.
He sees me. Like, really sees me. Not like everyone else. Not like Mom. Not like Nick.
With him, I'm not too much. I'm just enough.

She paused, chewing on the end of her pen, her brows

furrowed in thought. Her chest ached in a way that felt both good and scary. She didn't understand all of what had just happened. But she knew she wanted more.

More of his voice.

More of the way he made her feel wanted.

More of the warmth that bloomed in her belly when he called her *baby doll*.

He said we could feel close in other ways...
I think he means stuff I'm not ready for.
But I don't want to lose him.
What if he stops wanting me if I say no?

The thought made her throat tighten.

She turned the page and started sketching instead. Something soft, like the curve of a shoulder, a hand reaching toward another. Lines that didn't quite connect.

Her fingers smudged the pencil as she shaded in the shadows around them. She liked the way it looked— reaching, wanting, but never fully touching.

That was what it felt like with him.

So close it almost burned.

But still just out of reach.

She pressed her palm flat against her chest, trying to steady her breath.

"I trust you," he'd said.

She closed the notebook gently and slid it back into its hiding spot. Then she turned off her light, curling up in the dark with her phone clutched to her chest like a secret.

It had been a couple of nights since their last late call, and

Melody had felt the space between them like an ache. She checked her phone constantly, waiting for the vibration, the flash of his name. When it finally came, her heart fluttered like it always did—but tonight, something was different.

Lucian's voice came through the phone, soft and slow, as if savoring the moment.

"Hey, baby doll," he said, his tone different tonight. Not playful, not the usual teasing, but something more serious. Intimate. "I've been thinking about you all day. And I can't stop imagining how amazing it would feel to be with you."

Melody's stomach twisted, but she didn't pull away. She never wanted to pull away. She wanted him close. She wanted him in her life more than anything.

"How would it feel?" she whispered, a question she didn't even fully understand herself, but she felt a tug in her chest, like she was meant to ask.

He sighed, a sound so full of longing it made her heart ache.

"You have no idea, Mel. I've never met someone like you. Someone who... I don't know. You make me feel things I haven't felt before."

His voice grew lower, pulling her closer, until his words almost brushed her skin.

"I think about you when I'm alone, in my bed. I think about you in ways that aren't just normal. It's not just about loving you, baby... it's more than that."

He let the silence settle for a moment, thick and intimate.

"It's about desire."

Melody's heart raced, but she couldn't stop herself from feeling a rush of excitement. He was talking to her like no one ever had. Like she was the center of his world.

"What do you mean?" she asked, her voice small but hungry for his approval.

Lucian's laugh was soft and full of quiet hunger.

"I mean... when I say I think about you, I mean I think about you all the time. About the way your skin must feel under your clothes. How soft your hair is. The way your lips must taste when I finally get close enough."

The words sent a hot shiver down her spine. She knew what he was implying—knew, but didn't yet understand the full weight of what she was being led into.

"I just... I want to be close to you in a way that's different from all the other guys," he continued, voice smooth, coaxing. "And I know you want that too. Don't you?"

"Yes," she whispered, breath caught between fear and longing. The idea of being close to him in a way that belonged only to them was too tempting.

Lucian's breath seemed to quicken on the other end of the line. Melody's pulse raced with it.

"You don't know how much that means to me, Mel. You're everything to me. I just want to take care of you, protect you... and show you how special you are."

His voice softened again, wrapping around her like a warm blanket.

"You know, there's something we could do... something private, just for us. You can say no, I'll never be mad. But I think you'll like it."

Her stomach fluttered.

"I don't... I don't know what you mean," she murmured, but the question was already pulling her in.

Lucian's tone became even more patient, even more gentle.

"It's just something simple, baby. You don't have to do anything you're not ready for. But... I want you to do something for me, and I'll help you. I'll explain everything. Okay?"

Melody bit her lip, torn between hesitation and the aching desire to keep his love, to be what he wanted.

"Okay," she breathed.

"I want you to touch yourself," he said, his voice slow and deliberate, testing her. "Just gently. Like I would, if I were there."

Melody froze, heart hammering.

She didn't fully understand why this felt so confusing, so

heavy—wrong and right all at once. But the thought of making him happy was stronger than anything else.

"You don't have to know what to do yet," Lucian reassured her, voice like honey. "That's what I'm here for. I'll teach you. Just close your eyes. Breathe. Imagine my hands—soft and slow, brushing your hair behind your ear, kissing your neck... my fingers trailing down your arms, your stomach... lower, only if you want me to."

His tone turned reverent, like he was guiding her into something sacred.

"You're beautiful, Melody. Let yourself feel it. Let yourself be it."

Melody's breath came faster. She did as he said, letting her hand drift hesitantly across her skin.

"You're safe," Lucian whispered. "You're mine. Let go, baby. I've got you."

There was a long and trembling moment when everything inside her felt too much. Too much heat, too much need, too much of him in her head.

And then it happened. Her breath caught. Her whole body went tight, and then soft, like waves breaking against the shore. A sharp, unfamiliar rush washed over her, her legs trembling as she gasped softly into the phone.

Lucian was silent for a second, then spoke with quiet awe.

"That's it... That's my girl."

Melody lay still, dazed and flushed, her heart still pounding in her chest. Her hand trembled as she pulled it back, breath shallow.

"I... I didn't know it would feel like that," she said, stunned, not even sure what she'd just experienced, but knowing she'd never forget it.

Lucian's voice was heavy with satisfaction.

"You just had your first release, baby. Your first real moment. And you let me give it to you."

Melody closed her eyes, a dizzy smile on her lips, a single tear sliding down her cheek.

"I just wanted to make you happy."

"You did," he murmured. "More than you'll ever know."

A pause stretched, quiet and thick.

"I should let you sleep now," he said at last. "But don't forget what you felt tonight. That was just the beginning. You're mine, now."

"I love you," she whispered, already tangled in something deeper than she understood.

"I love you too, my brave, beautiful girl. Sleep tight."

The moment the call ended, Wednesday stirred from the foot of the bed, where she had been silently watching, her eyes glowing faintly in the dim light. She padded over to Melody, her movements almost too silent for the soft plush carpet, curling up beside her with a gentle, knowing purr.

Melody glanced down, feeling the weight of the cat's presence as though it was more than just a comforting familiar. Wednesday pressed her head against Melody's hand, eyes bright and full of understanding, as if she had felt all the tangled emotions that had passed through her that night. Melody couldn't help but reach down, her hand trembling, and stroke the soft fur of the cat's back. There was something in the way Wednesday seemed to sense her every shift, the way she nestled closer, as if to reassure her.

Melody closed her eyes, her chest still tight with the rawness of the emotions that had flooded her, and she let herself breathe, the cat's warmth against her side grounding her as the quiet of the room settled in around them.

Melody lay there in the dark, her breath still shallow, rising and falling against the silence like a secret. Her skin buzzed with the memory of Lucian's voice, still vivid and alive in her ears. The way he had guided her, praised her, told her she was his. The room felt too small, like the air had thickened around her. Her fingers trembled at her sides, uncertain of their own touch.

She didn't know what to do with herself now. There was no one to talk to about this, no frame of reference for what she had just felt. Her heart pounded like she'd done something terrible, or maybe something protected. Or both.

Was this what love felt like? It had to be. He said he loved her. He called her beautiful. He made her feel... chosen.

But then the thought hit her: he was thirty-two. She was fifteen.

The number clawed at her brain like a sharp edge. She tried to push it down, but he didn't *feel* thirty-two. He didn't treat her like a kid. He said she was mature, said she understood him in a way no one else did. That had to mean something, didn't it?

But her body still felt strange. Like it had been opened too fast, like someone had read a page in her diary she hadn't written yet.

She rolled over, curling into herself, hugging her pillow tight against her chest. Her phone was still warm where it had rested beside her. She stared at the blank screen, wanting him to message her again, to tell her she did good, that he loved her, that she hadn't ruined anything.

A sudden rush of shame bloomed under her skin. Not because of what she'd done exactly, she didn't even fully understand what she'd done, but because of how badly she wanted his approval. How much of herself she was willing to give just to hear his voice say she mattered.

Is this who I am now?

Her eyes stung. She blinked hard, refusing to cry. Crying felt childish, and Lucian always said she was so grown-up, so strong. She couldn't break now. Not when she was finally someone's whole world.

Still, the truth lingered beneath her thoughts like a shadow:

if he really cared, why did this feel like a secret that could ruin her?

"Maybe I'm just overthinking this," she whispered into the silence, hoping the words would anchor her. But they felt weightless, floating away the moment they left her lips.

She thought of her friends, the way they giggled about boys at school, about awkward kisses and crushes. What had happened tonight didn't feel like that. It felt heavier, older, more real. But also wrong.

Lucian had told her this was love. That he wanted to protect her. That she was safe with him.

So why did she suddenly feel so alone?

The ceiling above her blurred as her eyes welled up. Her chest ached—not just from confusion, but from wanting. Wanting him to say it again. Wanting to feel that powerful, that desired, even if a tiny voice in the back of her mind whispered that something wasn't right.

That voice was quiet, but it didn't go away.

She pressed her hand to her stomach, where the trembling still hadn't stopped, and let out a long, shaky breath.

I just wanted to be loved.

And for one terrifying, beautiful moment, she thought maybe she finally was.

Lucian's POV:

Lucian stared at the screen, watching the last message Melody had sent light up his cellphone.

Goodnight... I love you.

Three dots had hovered for a moment, like she wanted to say more. But then they disappeared. Silence.

He leaned back on his bed, the dim light of his phone screen casting a bluish glow across the clutter around him. The silence was satisfying. It was the kind that followed a successful performance, a curtain dropping after a perfect final act. She had followed his lead. Trusted him. Given herself over to him in the way he'd been carefully guiding her toward for weeks.

A slow smile tugged at the corner of his mouth.

She was his now.

He lit a cigarette with shaking fingers, the adrenaline still prickling through his veins. He exhaled slowly, imagining her curled up in bed, flushed and confused, thinking only of him. The thought made something in his chest tighten—not guilt, never guilt. But a kind of possessive pride.

She'd been so open with him lately. All it took was the right words, the right pauses. A little reassurance. A little praise. He'd seen it in the way she texted him—the speed of her replies, the little things she confessed late at night. The desperation, that ache to be loved. It made her pliable. Devoted.

He had studied girls like her. Lonely. Smart. Isolated. Just the right mix of innocent and broken. He had known from the beginning how to listen, how to mirror her feelings, how to say exactly what she needed to hear. And she needed him. He'd made sure of that.

No one else understands you like I do, Melody.

He had said that so many times it was practically scripture now.

He took another drag from the cigarette and looked around his room. Posters of old metal bands lined the walls, faded and curling at the corners. A few clothes lay crumpled on the floor. His world hadn't changed, but hers had. He could feel it. Something irreversible had happened tonight.

He imagined her fingers, trembling. Her voice, small and unsure if she spoke aloud to the dark. Her trust in him... complete.

His smile faltered slightly, just for a second. A flicker of something colder passed through him. She was only fifteen.

Fifteen. A kid. His mind snapped toward the edge of that thought, hovered, and recoiled.

But she wanted it.

She came to me.

She's not like the others. She's special.

He needed to believe that. He chose to believe that.

He had been careful. Always let her take the lead. Always asked, *"Are you okay?"* Always reminded her she could stop. It wasn't like he forced her. It was a connection. A rare, pure connection in a world full of liars and fakes.

Besides, the world didn't see girls like Melody. They mocked girls like her. Her family didn't protect her. Her friends didn't really know her. But *he* did.

She told him things no one else knew. And tonight, she gave him a piece of herself that no one else had.

That meant something.

Still, as he stubbed out the cigarette and stared back at the glowing screen in his hand, a whisper of unease curled at the edges of his thoughts. He pushed it away, hard.

He had to stay focused now. Keep her close. Keep her dependent. She was still young—emotional. Unpredictable. She could panic. Confess. Pull away.

No. He couldn't let that happen.

He needed to be careful. Gentle. Reassuring.

He typed:

> You're everything to me, Melody. You make me feel alive again. Sleep well, my dark angel. I'm proud of you. I'll always protect you.

He paused, then added a heart emoji. The kind she liked. A small, calculated touch.

He hit send and let the phone rest on his chest, the screen slowly dimming.

She was his.

And he would do whatever it took to keep her that way.

As the days passed after that first time, the moment her body reacted in ways she didn't fully understand, Lucian's messages kept coming. They were drenched in sweetness, soaked in devotion, filled with the kind of tenderness that Melody had always longed for. She clung to his words like they were lifelines, each one a balm to wounds she didn't even realize were still bleeding.

He checked on her constantly. Told her she was beautiful. Told her how proud he was of her. That she made him feel alive. That she was everything he had ever wanted.

"You gave me something no one else ever could," he wrote one night. "You're mine now, Mel. You always will be."

And it felt good. So good.

But somewhere beneath the warmth of his affection, a quiet unease began to grow, like a shadow stretching longer at dusk.

She would lie in bed, staring at the soft glow of her screen in the dark, rereading his words. Lucian told her she was special. That she was the only one who truly understood him. That he couldn't stop thinking about her.

"When I'm not with you, I feel like I'm missing a piece of myself," he said.

"You belong to me now, baby. I'll never let anyone hurt you again."

Melody told herself it was love. Of course it was. He had been so gentle, so patient with her, even when she hadn't known what to do. Even when she had hesitated. He had told her how proud he was of her afterward, and that meant something, didn't it?

She had felt... something. A tremble, a burst of heat, a moment of floating. He had said she was amazing, perfect, everything he'd ever wanted.

So why did her chest feel tight now? Why did it sometimes feel like she had crossed a line she didn't even know existed?

Still, she couldn't talk to anyone about it. Her friends wouldn't get it. They didn't know what it felt like to be invisible, to be treated like a freak, like a burden. But Lucian saw her. He *chose* her. That had to mean something real.

The next time they spoke, his voice melted over her like honey.

"I'm so proud of you, Mel," he said, slow and warm. "You're incredible. Stronger than you think. No one's ever made me feel the way you do."

Her throat tightened. "I just want to make you proud," she whispered. "I never want to mess this up."

"You won't," he replied with a soft chuckle. "You already make me so happy. You just have to trust me, baby. Let me lead you. I'll never let anything happen to you."

Her stomach fluttered at his praise. It felt like safety. Like love.

But beneath it all, another feeling simmered. Like she was being pulled along, gently but firmly, into something she couldn't slow down. Like each step they took together was just a little farther from the person she used to be.

Sometimes, when she caught her reflection or lay awake at night, she wondered why her chest felt heavy. Why the warmth from Lucian's affection came with a chill she couldn't shake. Why she felt like she needed his approval more than her own comfort.

But then her phone would buzz, and it would be *him*. Another nickname. Another heart. Another message reminding her she was wanted.

And she'd smile. Because being wanted felt better than being alone.

"Everything will be okay," she whispered to herself, her fingers trembling as she typed out her reply. "I just need to give him more. Then he'll really see how much I love him."

CHAPTER ELEVEN

The morning light bled through the cracks in her blinds far too soon. Melody had barely slept. Her body felt like stone, her limbs leaden beneath the covers. Her thoughts drifted in and out of fragments—Lucian's voice, her mother's glare, the silence of her father's absence.

She rolled onto her back and stared at the ceiling, numb. Her skin was clammy under the blanket, and the room smelled faintly of old incense and anxiety.

Another day to survive. That's all it ever was.

A crash from downstairs made her flinch.

"I swear to God, she's still in bed," Nick's voice barked, already laced with contempt. "It's almost eight. She's late for school. She's so fucking pathetic."

Melody sat up, adrenaline replacing exhaustion. Her hoodie was draped over the end of the bed; she grabbed it, shoved her arms through the sleeves, yanking them down past her wrists. She opened the bedroom door just as Nick stormed up the hall toward her.

He didn't even pretend it was an accident when his shoulder slammed into hers. Hard.

"Get the fuck outta the way, freak," he sneered.

"Nick!" Charlotte snapped from the kitchen.

Melody paused. Maybe her mother had finally had enough.

But then Charlotte added, sharp as glass, "Don't shove her. You'll bruise her and then she'll milk it for attention like she always does."

Melody's gut twisted.

"She's not even dressed," Nick called over his shoulder. "Still playing dead like some roadkill raccoon."

Charlotte laughed. "Raccoon's too generous. At least raccoons are resourceful. She's more like one of those sad little opossums that just lays there and drools."

Melody gritted her teeth and started to walk away.

"Don't turn your back on me," Charlotte snapped. "We're talking to you."

Melody turned slowly, her hands clenched in her sleeves. "I didn't ask for your commentary."

Charlotte's lips curled into something smug and venomous. "And I didn't ask to raise a lazy, ungrateful little parasite who hides in her room all day feeling sorry for herself and acting like the world owes her something."

Melody felt her breath catch.

Charlotte stepped closer, eyes narrowing. "You think you're the only person with problems? You think this house revolves around your little depressive episodes and attention stunts?"

"I'm not pretending," Melody whispered, voice cracking.

"Oh, please," Charlotte scoffed. "You don't even try anymore. You just rot in that room, wallowing. Maybe if you got off your lazy fucking ass, someone would actually give a damn."

Nick grabbed his keys off the counter and chimed in with a laugh. "That's rich, Mom. She thinks someone's gonna give a damn."

He turned to Melody, all malice. "Dad stopped calling for a reason, you know. He saw what you are. A mopey, useless, high-maintenance little freak. Everyone does."

Melody's face went hot. Her throat closed up. Her chest heaved but no words came.

"And wipe that look off your face," Charlotte added, stepping closer. "The fake 'hurt little girl' act doesn't work on me. I see straight through it. You've been a disappointment since day one."

Melody couldn't take it. She bolted up the stairs, two at a time, nearly tripping as she reached the top. Her eyes blurred with furious, humiliated tears.

She slammed the bedroom door and collapsed onto the floor. The silence afterward was deafening. Her heart pounded like it wanted out of her chest.

Wednesday, her cat, darted from under the bed, ears back. She crept forward and rubbed against Melody's leg, sensing the tension, the spiral.

Melody let out a shaky breath and scooped the cat into her lap. "They hate me," she whispered, voice barely audible. "They actually hate me."

Wednesday didn't move. Just pressed close.

Melody rocked slightly, hugging her knees around the trembling cat, but it wasn't enough. The words, the venom, it all echoed too loudly.

She reached for the drawer.

Her fingers found the blade easily. Smooth. Cold. Familiar.

There was no hesitation this time.

The sting bit sharp and fast. A red line bloomed under her sleeve. She exhaled through her teeth, not in relief but in release, like unclenching a fist that had been held too long.

Wednesday pawed gently at her arm. Melody dropped the blade and pulled her sleeve back down.

It didn't fix anything.

But for a moment, it silenced the screaming in her chest.

Somehow, she still made it to school before second period.

She drifted through the hallways like a ghost, hood up, earbuds in, keeping her eyes low as she slid into her seat before the bell rang. The sleeves of her hoodie clung to the fresh wounds underneath, but she didn't flinch. She was too practiced at this.

The world moved around her in fast forward—slamming lockers, laughing voices, the distant screech of a teacher trying to maintain order. It all passed over her like wind against glass. She stayed quiet, unreadable, unreachable.

"Hey," Anna said brightly, dropping into the seat beside her and nudging her with an elbow. "You okay? You look... I dunno. Extra tired."

Melody forced a small nod. "Didn't sleep much."

Anna gave her a sympathetic smile. "Same. I stayed up way too late making a playlist for tomorrow night."

Melody blinked. "What's tomorrow?"

Anna's jaw dropped, scandalized. "The concert! Echo Funeral and Violets in Black at The Orbit Room? I've been talking about it for *weeks!*"

"Oh... right. Sorry. I forgot."

Anna tilted her head, studying her. "You sure you're okay? You've been kinda out of it lately."

Melody gave a weak shrug, tugging her sleeves further over her hands until her fingers disappeared. "Just... rough morning."

Anna nodded knowingly. "I get it. My mom flipped out because I used all the conditioner again. Parents are the worst."

Melody smiled faintly, a pale ghost of amusement flickering across her lips, but it didn't reach her eyes. Her mind flashed back to the shouting, the accusations, the slammed door. The sharp edge of her mother's voice slicing her open before school even began.

If only it were about conditioner.

She turned her gaze toward the window, willing her eyes not to water. The sky outside was grey, the kind of sky that pressed down on your chest. A pressure she couldn't shake, no matter how many layers she wore or how low she pulled her hood.

Anna had already moved on, scrolling through her phone. "I made you a playlist too," she added. "It's kind of like a pre-show vibe. Some darkwave, some post-punk. I thought you'd like it."

Melody's lips parted like she might say thank you, but nothing came out. She nodded instead.

It was easier not to speak.

It was easier not to let anything real slip through.

In the library, she sat tucked in the farthest corner, hidden between tall shelves and the soft whir of the HVAC system. A heavy math textbook lay open in front of her, untouched. The equations blurred into meaningless shapes. The teacher's voice from earlier in the day still echoed in her mind like background static, long since drowned out.

Her notebook remained blank, pen idle between her fingers as she stared at the window. Outside, the wind teased the branches of the leafless trees. Her reflection ghosted faintly in the glass—hood up, eyes sunken, sleeves tugged over her palms like armor.

She thought of Lucian.

Of the way his words had wrapped around her the night before like a lifeline... and a chain.

He cared about her. He needed her.

And she—she needed someone to need her.

But deep inside, that quiet voice she always tried to smother stirred again:

Is this what love truly is? Should it be this possessive?

She shoved it down, hard.

Lucian made her feel *seen.* Even when everything else in her life made her want to disappear.

Across the room, the faint tapping of keyboards and the rustle of pages barely registered. A few kids from her grade were studying in pairs. A librarian wheeled a cart slowly past, nodding at her in quiet acknowledgement. Melody lowered her gaze and adjusted her hoodie.

Her stomach turned, and the granola bar in her bag stayed untouched. Anna had invited her to eat lunch outside today, to "soak up the weird sun while it lasted," but Melody had made an excuse—headache, too much homework, didn't feel like talking.

She hadn't told Anna the real reason: she needed silence. Space. Somewhere to disappear.

Her phone buzzed quietly in her hoodie pocket.

She fished it out with numb fingers.

Thinking about you. You okay?

Her thumb hovered above the keyboard for a long moment, debating how honest to be. Then:

I'm at school. Had a rough morning.

The reply came almost instantly.

What happened? Who hurt you? I swear to
god, if it was your mom or that asshole brother
of yours…

Her stomach twisted. She could feel the heat behind his words — the *protectiveness*.

But also the *possessiveness*.

She didn't know where one ended and the other began.

Her thumbs hovered again.

It's fine. It's always like this.

A pause. Then she typed something else. Slower this time.

> I... I cut this morning.

The typing bubble blinked to life right away.

> Jesus, baby. Are you bleeding? Where? Are
> you safe?

Her eyes stung. She blinked hard and looked down at the faint red spots on her sleeve where the fabric had stuck. It wasn't deep. She knew how to make it look worse than it was. But still —she had.

> It's not bad. I just... needed to feel something
> else.

Another pause. Then:

> I hate that they make you feel like this. I hate
> that I'm not there. You should be with me. I'd
> never let you hurt like this again.

She stared at the message until her vision blurred.

She clutched the phone tighter in her palm, like it might vanish if she let go.

Was this safety? Or was it something else wearing the same mask?

Her breath caught in her throat.

Maybe he was right.

Maybe the only way out of this was him.

That night, Melody sat cross-legged on her bed, the glow of her lamp casting shadows on the walls. Her fingers trembled as she held her phone, the hum of anticipation vibrating in her chest. She pressed it to her ear, heart thudding in her throat.

The line crackled, and then came his voice—low, warm, and wrapped in static.

"How's my girl? You okay?"

The sound of him hit her like a wave. She didn't answer right away, eyes fixed on the faint red lines on her thigh, the ones that still stung. She pressed her lips together, fighting the shame clawing up her throat.

"I..." Her voice cracked. "I don't know. I cut again. I didn't want to, I just... I couldn't stop it."

There was silence— long enough that she worried he'd left, or worse, that he was disappointed. She pulled the phone slightly away, already bracing for rejection. But then she heard it: a soft, trembling inhale.

"Baby..." His voice was softer now, heavier. "No. No, I'm not mad. God, no. I just... it kills me to hear you hurting like this. You don't deserve that kind of pain. You don't have to carry it by yourself."

Tears pricked the corners of her eyes. His words wrapped around her like a blanket, but something in her chest still ached, still throbbed with self-loathing.

"I don't know how to make it stop," she whispered. "It's like... everything gets too loud in my head. I feel like I'm drowning, and hurting myself is the only thing that makes it quiet."

"I get it," he said quickly, too quickly. "More than you know. I've been there, Melody. But listen to me, you don't have to bleed to be seen. I see you. I hear you. All of you. The pain, the confusion, the fear... I'm not going anywhere."

Her shoulders shook as she cried, the sound of his voice the only thing anchoring her in the moment.

"But it's like... if I don't do it, I can't breathe. And my mom —she just keeps screaming at me like I'm nothing. And Nick... he's worse. He calls me a freak. He laughs when I cry."

Lucian's tone shifted. She could hear it—tightening, turning sharp.

"I swear to God, Melody. If they ever touch you again, if they ever say one more thing to hurt you...I'll lose it. No one treats you like that. No one. You hear me?"

His words sent a jolt through her—part terror, part thrill. He sounded dangerous. But he was angry for *her*. No one had ever done that. No one had ever been this mad on her behalf.

"I feel so broken," she said, her voice barely audible. "I keep trying to be better, but it never works. I think something's wrong with me."

"There's *nothing* wrong with you," he said, firm now, urgent. "You're not broken. You're not crazy. You're just hurt. And you don't need to fix yourself. You just need someone who won't let you fall apart. That's me. I'm here. Always."

She closed her eyes, letting those words soak in. *Always.* The way he said it felt like a fated promise.

"But what if I mess up again?" she asked, almost afraid to hear the answer. "What if I ruin everything?"

"You won't," he said, voice hushed now. "Even if you do, I'll still be here. I'm not like the others. I don't scare easy. You're mine, Melody. You belong to me, and I take care of what's mine."

Her breath caught at that word again—*mine*. It should've scared her. But instead, it curled around something hollow inside her and made it feel full. He *wanted* her. Claimed her. Maybe that meant she mattered.

"I just wish I could disappear sometimes," she said. "Like, just vanish into nothing so I wouldn't have to feel this anymore."

There was silence again, and then a shaky breath from him.

"Don't say that," he whispered. "Don't ever say that. If you disappear, I disappear. Do you understand me? I *need* you. You're not allowed to leave me. Not like that."

Her chest tightened, and for a moment, all she could hear was the beating of her heart and the way his voice trembled like it might shatter.

"I'm not going anywhere," she whispered. "I promise. I can't."

"Good," he said, and there was relief in his voice. "Because I can't survive without you, baby. You're the only thing in my life that makes sense. Don't let go. Please."

She nodded, even though he couldn't see. "I won't. I swear."

And in the quiet that followed, her pain didn't vanish. But it was muted. Not gone, but less sharp. For now, his voice was enough to keep her afloat.

She rested her cheek against her pillow, letting the silence between them stretch in a way that felt safe for once. Her breathing had slowed, and her body, still tense, began to settle as his presence filled the emptiness.

After a long pause, his voice came through again, quieter now, almost shy.

"You know what I was doing before you called?"

"What?" she asked, her voice fragile but curious.

"I was listening to 'Just Like Heaven' by The Cure. And I couldn't stop thinking about you."

A small, involuntary smile tugged at the corner of her lips. "Really?"

"Yeah," he said, and she could hear the smile in his voice too. "That part where Robert Smith goes on about some magical trick that drives him wild—I swear, I heard it and all I could picture was you—jumping around your room, that big laugh of yours, singing along like you didn't care who was listening."

She laughed softly, the sound catching in her throat. "You've never even heard me sing."

"I've imagined it. A thousand times," he said gently. "And I know you'd sound like magic to me."

Her cheeks flushed hot. "You're such a liar."

"I'm not. I mean it. You're... I don't know. You've got this way of making everything feel like it matters. Even when you're sad. Even when you're breaking. You're still the most alive person I know."

She curled her fingers around the edge of her blanket, his words wrapping around her like a quiet embrace.

"I was thinking," he continued, "if I ever got to see you in person—like really be with you, not just on the phone, I'd take you out somewhere weird and beautiful. Like, some abandoned carnival or a broken down museum no one's touched in years. Just us, wandering around, making up stories about the ghosts that live there."

Melody giggled. "That sounds so creepy."

"Exactly," he said, proud. "Perfect for us."

A beat passed. She imagined them like that—her in some tattered black dress, eyeliner smudged, hand in his, laughter echoing through dust covered halls. For a second, it didn't feel like a fantasy. It felt possible.

"I wish you were here right now," she whispered.

"I know," he said, voice tight. "Me too."

Then, after a pause, softer still:

"I'd hold you so close, Melody. I'd kiss your scars, all of them. I'd tell you every day that you're beautiful until you believed it."

She closed her eyes again, her body trembling with emotion. Her heart ached in a thousand different ways, and still... she clung to the sound of his voice like a lifeline.

"Will you sing it for me?" she asked suddenly, a little embarrassed. "That song. Just a little."

He chuckled. "You really want me to?"

"Yeah," she said, tucking the phone closer. "Please."

There was a rustle on the other end, then a moment of silence, and then—his voice, low and imperfect, began to hum the melody before slipping into soft words. The ones about aching loneliness, ocean-deep love, and the kind of beauty that felt otherworldly.

Melody's breath hitched, her throat tightening with emotion. For once, she didn't feel alone in the dark.

As he sang, something deep in her chest loosened.

Maybe she was broken. Maybe he was too. But for now, in this sliver of night with a song between them, they felt whole.

CHAPTER TWELVE

Saturday morning sunlight streamed through the slats of Melody's blinds, casting thin lines across the floor. The house was quieter than usual—no thudding footsteps, no slamming doors. Nick was gone. That alone made it feel like she could breathe a little easier.

Wednesday was curled at the foot of the bed, her small black body a shadow against the pale comforter. She stretched lazily as Melody sat up, giving a soft chirp before hopping down and padding silently toward the door. Melody followed her out, her bare feet cool on the hardwood.

She padded into the kitchen, the hem of her hoodie brushing her legs, Wednesday tailing just behind like a quiet sentinel. Charlotte was at the stove, clattering a spatula against the frying pan a little too loudly, while Andrew stood nearby sipping his coffee.

Wednesday leapt silently onto a dining chair and perched there, watching the scene unfold with slow blinks.

Melody hesitated before speaking. "I'm going to a concert tonight."

Charlotte didn't even turn around. "No, you're not."

Melody's stomach tightened. "What? Why not?"

"Because I said so," Charlotte snapped, flipping a pancake with more force than necessary. "You don't need to be out all night with God knows who. It's not safe."

"You're always telling me I need to get out of my room," Melody said, voice rising. "To go do something, to stop being so depressing. Now I finally make plans and you shoot it down?"

"That's not the same and you know it," Charlotte said, turning now with her arms crossed. "A concert? At night? You don't even know those people."

"I do know them," Melody snapped. "And even if I didn't, why do you care? You don't even want me here half the time."

"That's enough," Charlotte said sharply. "You're not going."

Before Melody could respond, Andrew set his mug down with a loud clink. "She's going."

Charlotte's head whipped toward him. "Excuse me?"

Andrew straightened his back. "I said she's going. She made plans, she's being responsible, and she deserves to go."

Charlotte stared at him like he'd grown two heads. "You're undermining me now?"

"I'm standing up for my daughter," Andrew said, calm but firm. "She's not doing anything wrong, and I'm not going to keep watching you control every part of her life."

Melody blinked, surprised. It was the first time he'd said anything like that—out loud, to Charlotte's face.

From her chair, Wednesday let out a low meow, like she could feel the tension crackling in the air.

Charlotte's lips curled. "Fine. Let her go. But don't come crying to me when something happens."

Andrew turned to Melody, his voice softening. "You're allowed to go. Just be safe, okay?"

She nodded, her chest tight with a mix of relief and disbelief.

Andrew picked up his keys from the counter. "We're gonna be out most of the day, errands and your mother's dragging me to the mall or something. You've got the house to yourself for a while."

Charlotte muttered something under her breath, grabbing her purse. Melody didn't catch it, but she saw the way Andrew looked at her, she knew it was something bad.

She felt seen. And, for once, not just by Lucian.

Wednesday jumped down and brushed against her legs as they left, her small body warm and grounding. Melody bent to scratch between her ears.

"Guess it's just us for a while," she whispered.

Wednesday purred in response.

The front door clicked shut behind her parents, and the house fell into a hush.

Melody stood in the hallway for a moment, blinking in disbelief. Quiet. No shouting. No slamming. No Nick. Just silence.

A slow smile crept onto her face.

Wednesday slinked around the corner from the living room, tail high, her green eyes blinking up at Melody with curiosity. Melody scooped her up without thinking, burying her face into the cat's soft black fur for a brief second.

She padded down the hall to her bedroom, the soft slap of her socks on the hardwood floor the only sound, Wednesday nestled against her chest. Once inside, she closed the door and locked it—an unnecessary precaution, maybe, but one that felt like a small act of control. A small act of peace.

Her room was dim, but sunlight filtered through the black lace curtains, casting soft patterns on the walls. She set Wednesday gently down on the bed, where the cat immediately curled into a small circle, purring.

Melody crossed to her dresser, lit a candle, a dark cherry and smoke scent that reminded her of Halloween, and placed it on the windowsill. The flame flickered, catching the amber in her eyes.

Then she walked over to her speaker, scrolling through her playlist until she found it.

Type O Negative – "Love You to Death".

As the slow, haunting guitar chords filled the room, she turned the volume up louder than she ever dared when someone else was home. The sound vibrated through the floorboards, the walls, her bones.

For the first time she felt okay. Not just okay. Good. Like herself. The real her, not the hollow, anxious shadow she'd been lately. She grabbed her hairbrush and used it like a microphone, mouthing along to Peter Steele's low growl as she twirled in the middle of the room, the hem of Lucian's oversized black shirt fluttering around her thighs.

On the bed, Wednesday flicked her tail to the rhythm, her eyes half-lidded, utterly content.

Her phone buzzed from the bed. She flopped down onto her mattress, breathless and grinning, and picked it up.

Hey, baby. What are you up to?

Blasting Type O and dancing like a freak. I'm alone for once. It's amazing.

God, I wish I could see that. You in my shirt, jumping around, hair a mess...

Lol. It's a whole scene. I even lit a candle like some dramatic goth witch.

You are a dramatic goth witch. And you're mine.

She smiled, her cheeks warming.

You're such a dork.

A sexy dork, though.

Mmhm. Sure. Anyway... I'm gonna jump in the
shower before I start getting ready.

Oh? Want company? I promise I'm real good at
helping wash behind ears... and other places.

She snorted, rolling her eyes even as her stomach fluttered. She typed back slowly.

You're bad.

Only for you, baby.

She bit her lip, the smirk lingering on her face as she set the phone aside and grabbed her towel. The music still throbbed through the walls, echoing like a heartbeat. Tonight was hers. For once, she didn't feel trapped. She didn't feel worthless.

She felt like Melody again.

The bathroom filled with steam, curling around the edges of the mirror and softening her reflection into a ghost. Melody stepped under the hot stream of water, letting it cascade over her shoulders, down her back. She closed her eyes, tilting her face toward the spray, the music still faintly echoing through her bedroom door.

For a little while, it was easy to pretend everything was normal.

She lathered her hair, fingers scrubbing through the thick black strands. As the suds slid down her neck, her thoughts drifted.

Should I tell him?

The question landed hard in her chest, heavier than the steam in the air.

Lucian hadn't asked if she was doing anything tonight. Not directly. But she also hadn't brought it up. She was supposed to go to the concert with Anna and Jace. Just a local show—nothing wild. Cheap tickets, loud music, a chance to feel like a person instead of a prisoner.

But she already knew how it would sound in his head: *You didn't tell me.*

Who's Jace again?

Why didn't you ask me first?

He'd get quiet. Or worse, sarcastic. He'd say he understood and then text her nonstop all night. She'd feel her phone vibrate in her pocket while the band played. She'd feel his presence like a shadow. She'd feel guilty.

Even if she hadn't done anything wrong.

She leaned her head against the tile, letting the water run down her back.

It's not like I'm going on a date. It's a show. My friends. That's all.

But that never seemed to be enough for him.

He'd tell her it was because he cared. That he worried about her. That he didn't trust other people. She was his special girl. His only safe place. His angel.

But even angels needed air.

She picked up the vanilla body wash and squeezed a little into her palm, massaging it into her skin. The smell reminded her of warm nights and of feeling pretty. Normal. Fifteen.

And she was. Fifteen.

Fifteen.

Not thirty-two.

Her lips pressed into a thin line.

Maybe I just won't tell him until after. Or maybe I'll say I'm going somewhere else. Or maybe I'll just—

She cut off the thought with a frustrated sigh and turned the water off. The decision hung in the humid air, suspended, sticky.

She wrapped herself in her towel and stood in the mirror, wiping a streak through the condensation. Her blue eyes looked back at her, shadowed at the edges again.

She's not going to let this ruin her day.

She deserves to have at least one good day.

Melody tugged on a clean pair of tights and slipped into her favorite black skater dress—simple, soft, the neckline just wide enough to show her collarbones. She twisted her damp hair into a messy bun, then leaned close to the mirror, applying a smudge of black eyeliner with a practiced hand.

The music still played faintly in the background, something moody and industrial now, pulsing low through her speaker. Her candle had burned low, scenting the room like cherry smoke and burnt sugar.

Her phone buzzed again on the bed.

She glanced at it.

> Still in the shower, pretty girl? Or did you melt
> into steam?

She hesitated before picking it up. Her fingers hovered over the keyboard.

She took a deep breath. Just... be cool. Keep it light. He didn't ask if you were going anywhere. You're not lying. Not *really*.

> Out now. Smelling like a goth cupcake. You'd
> love it.

A moment passed.

Mmm. I'd lick the frosting off you.

What are you doing now?

Her stomach tensed.

Just say you're getting ready. Not for what, just... getting ready.

Just picking an outfit and finishing my makeup.
Felt like actually looking cute today.

There. Not a lie. Not really.

She waited. The screen stayed blank. No typing bubble.

She opened her drawer, pulling out her favorite spiked choker and fastening it around her neck. Then her fishnet gloves. She looked at herself in the mirror—eyes rimmed in black, cheeks flushed, lips pale. For the first time in what felt like forever, she looked like *her* again.

Her phone buzzed.

Looking cute for me? Or someone else I should know about?

She froze.

God. Why did he *do* that?

She stared at the message for a moment, her fingers tightening around the phone. The fear crept in again—quiet, insidious. A voice whispering, *You messed up. He knows. He's mad.*

But then she shook her head, trying to push it away.

He's joking. He's just teasing. That's all.

She typed slowly.

For me. Just wanted to feel good today.
Nothing wrong with that, right?

A pause.

Of course not. You should always feel good.
Especially when I'm the reason.

She let out a quiet breath. Relief and something else, something heavy, settled in her chest

Seconds later, her phone lit up:

Incoming Call: Lucian.

She answered with a quiet smile. "Hi."

"*There's my girl,*" Lucian's voice came through the line, smooth and soft like smoke curling around her. "God, I missed you."

Melody's cheeks went pink. "We were *just* texting…"

"Texting's not enough," he said. "I wanted to hear your voice. What are you doing, baby doll?"

She glanced toward her speaker, where music still thumped at full volume.

"Just… hanging out in my room," she said, crossing to the speaker and turning the volume down a notch. "Music's probably too loud. Didn't even hear the phone ring."

"Sounded like *Ministry* or something in the background. You trying to shake the walls down, baby?"

She giggled. "Maybe."

"I'd give anything to be there right now," he said, voice dipping into that familiar velvet edge. "You, looking all cute. Dressed up. Spinning around your room like a little witch… I can *see* it."

She twirled once in place just because.

"You're so dramatic," she teased, biting her lip. "You're gonna make me blush."

"I *want* to make you blush," he murmured. "Wish I could see your face right now."

Before she could respond, the next song hit.

A spark of recognition lit her up like a firecracker.

"*Oh my God!*" she squealed. "I love this song!"

Lucian chuckled. "What is it?"

"'Don't Cha' by the Pussycat Dolls," she said, already reaching to crank the volume. "It's so dumb, but I *love* it!"

"Of course you do," he said, laughing softly. "You're such a little brat sometimes."

"Shut up," she shot back with a grin, leaping onto her bed and bouncing in rhythm as the beat dropped. That bold, bratty anthem filled the room, and she jumped into her own full-blown concert, flipping her hair and lip-syncing like she owned the place.

He groaned, "You're gonna *kill* me, Melody."

She tossed her head, her long black hair flying wildly as she danced and sang into her imaginary microphone a line that had driven club crowds wild in the early 2000s, something about being hotter and freakier than the other girl.

"I *know* you're a freak," he said, voice darker now, but still playful.

She laughed breathlessly, falling back onto the bed. "You're so bad."

"I'm just picturing it," he said, voice honey-thick. "You, bouncing on that bed, in my t-shirt... hair everywhere..."

She giggled, grinning wide. "You're such a dork," she said, feeling warm and bubbly.

"Send me a pic," he added, light but loaded. "Just one. You said you looked cute, and now I can't stop thinking about it."

Melody rolled onto her side, twirling a strand of damp hair around her finger. "Okayyy," she said with a little eye-roll in her voice, clearly flattered. "But only 'cause you asked so nice."

"Good girl," he murmured, low and smooth.

She opened the camera, still grinning, and struck a playful pose on her pillow. Her music thumped in the background, but her focus was only on him, on how wanted he made her feel.

She sent the picture, a little thrill rising in her chest as she hit "send."

There was a pause.

Then—

"Fuck," Lucian breathed, voice dark and reverent. "You're perfect, baby. You don't even know."

Melody laughed softly, flushed and fluttery. "It's not even that good. My hair's still wet."

"I don't care," he said, low. "I'd frame this shit if I could."

She kicked her feet behind her on the bed, biting her lip. "You're such a weirdo."

"I'm obsessed," he replied. "Sue me."

They stayed quiet a second, just the low pulse of her music in the background.

Lucian broke the silence first. "So... what are you doing the rest of the day?"

Melody sat up a little straighter. "I don't know. Probably just hanging out. Might touch up my makeup. My eyeliner looks dumb."

"That's it?" he asked, a little too quick. "You're not going out or anything, right?"

Her stomach tightened, just slightly. "No," she said, keeping her voice light. "Just... here."

He made a small sound—half-sigh, half hum. "Good. I like knowing you're safe. With how pretty you looked in that picture... I'd lose my mind if some guy saw you like that."

She giggled, a little nervous. "No one's gonna see me."

"You're mine, baby doll," he murmured, low and possessive. "Only mine."

She didn't know how to respond to that exactly, but it made something flutter in her chest anyway.

"I should finish getting ready," she said softly, fingers brushing down her skirt. "I still haven't even brushed my hair."

"Alright," Lucian said, reluctantly. "But text me when you're done. I want to see the final product."

"I will," she promised. "Talk soon?"

"Don't make me wait too long."

She smiled. "Okay. Bye, baby."

"Later, pretty girl."

She ended the call, her phone screen going black as the music filled the silence again.

The mirror waited...so did the night ahead.

CHAPTER THIRTEEN

The screen dimmed, and silence settled in the room, wrapping around Melody like a weighted blanket. Her phone rested against her chest, her heart still fluttering from Lucian's voice.

Wednesday leapt lightly onto the bed beside her, curling up without ceremony near her hip. Melody reached down and stroked the cat's back absently, comforted by the steady purr that vibrated against her fingers.

She stayed there a moment longer, then pushed herself up and crossed to the bathroom. Wednesday followed, her paws making the faintest sound as she trailed after Melody and perched in the doorway like a tiny sentinel.

The mirror was slightly fogged from her earlier shower, softening the edges of her reflection. Her hair hung damp around her shoulders, clinging to the neckline of the black skater dress she'd put on earlier. The hem twirled a little when she moved. She liked how it made her feel—soft and pretty, a little grown-up.

Still, she paused, tugging at it gently.

Is this right for a concert? Is it too much? Too babyish?

Her fingers brushed over the skirt again.

Lucian liked it.

She decided not to change.

She flicked on the blow dryer and leaned into the mirror, fluffing her hair dry in sections. It took a little effort to smooth out the waves, her bangs curled in awkward directions from air-drying, but she wrestled them into place with a round brush and some stubborn patience.

Wednesday sat just behind her, tail curled neatly around her paws, watching with lazy interest.

Once her hair was dry, she grabbed her eyeliner and touched up the wings with quick, practiced flicks. A little shimmer on her lids, a dab of highlighter at her cheeks, and lip gloss. Just enough to feel like someone else for the night. Someone braver.

Melody gave herself one final look.

She looked fine.

Actually—she looked good.

On impulse, she grabbed her phone, angled it just right in the mirror, and snapped a photo. She hesitated for half a second, then sent it to Lucian with a quick message:

> Do I pass the vibe check?

She tossed the phone onto the counter and reached for her bag, her stomach doing a little flip. A moment later, the screen lit up again with Lucian's reply.

> You look stunning tonight. I can feel the energy already. I hope the night brings you something unexpected.

A smile tugged at her lips. There it was again—that pull. Her chest warmed in a way that was both comforting and disconcerting. She'd almost forgotten how powerful his words could be, how they seemed to curl into her mind, making everything else feel smaller.

But then another message popped up, this one from Anna.

> We're on our way to pick you up now. Don't
> make us wait too long, you know Jace can't
> stand it!

Melody chuckled softly at the message, her nerves shifting slightly. The night was becoming real now, no more hesitation.

She stayed there for a moment, feeling the gentle thrum of excitement mingling with a bit of uncertainty. She wasn't sure if she should reply to Lucian just yet. Maybe he didn't need to know where she was going. Not tonight. She wanted to keep this moment to herself, let it be her own, without his watchful eyes on it.

But something about his message stuck with her, lingering in the air like the warmth of his voice. She took a breath, then typed quickly.

> You always know how to make a girl feel
> special. Maybe tonight will be unexpected.
> Maybe I'll make some trouble of my own.

She hit send before overthinking it, and then went back to finishing her look, her heart doing a quick skip as she waited for his reply.

A moment passed, then her phone buzzed again. Lucian's reply was quick.

> You're already trouble, Melody. I hope you find
> what you're looking for tonight. Just don't
> forget who you belong to.

Her fingers froze for a moment on the screen, the weight of his words settling deep in her chest. The possessiveness in his tone was always there, unspoken, like an invisible thread that connected them.

Melody let out a soft breath, a little smile creeping across her face. She wasn't sure how she felt about that part of him, but she liked how it made her feel seen, in a way she hadn't been before.

> Guess we'll see if that's true. Don't worry, I'll be fine. I'm just... figuring things out.

She tossed her phone back on the counter and finished fixing her hair. The thought of Lucian still hung there, but the sharp beep of Anna's text reminded her to get moving.

> Don't make us wait too long!

Melody grabbed her bag, taking one last look at her reflection. She wasn't sure where the night would take her, but she felt like she was exactly where she needed to be.

Wednesday sat on the edge of the bed, her yellow eyes half-lidded, tail flicking lazily. Melody crossed the room and knelt beside her, gently scratching behind her ears.

"I won't be gone long, baby," she whispered. "Try not to miss me too much."

Wednesday bumped her head against Melody's hand, purring loud and steady. Melody smiled and kissed the top of her cat's head.

"You're the best girl," she murmured, standing and smoothing out her dress. "Hold down the fort."

She stepped out of her room and checked her phone one more time. Lucian's message was still there. She smiled to herself before putting it in her bag.

Lucian didn't need to know where she was going. Not tonight.

The sharp honk of a car horn snapped Melody out of her head. She startled, grabbed her bag, and rushed downstairs. Her parents had turned in early, and Nick was over at a friends house. The house felt hushed and hollow, just the TV murmuring behind a door and the faint creak of the stairs under her feet. Another honk. She opened the front door to see Jace's Chevy S10 idling at the curb, headlights catching on the edges of the overgrown grass. The truck gleamed under the streetlight, midnight black with chrome trim and just enough rumble in the engine to sound cocky. Anna leaned out the window, waving both arms like a maniac.

"Melooooody! Get your cute ass out here!"

Melody laughed softly and stepped outside, letting the door fall shut behind her.

As she approached the truck, Jace shifted into park and got out of the driver's seat, coming around to open the passenger door for her.

His presence hit her all at once. He had that brooding kind of vibe that lingered in the air like smoke after a fire—quiet, intense, a little dangerous. His hazel eyes held a flicker of something unreadable, like a storm always threatening to break just beneath the surface. The full weight of his stare hit hard—direct, piercing, like he saw more than he let on.

His dark hair brushed the tops of his cheekbones, falling in jagged strands that framed his angular face. The chain around his neck caught the dim light with every subtle movement, giving him the look of someone who didn't mind being noticed but never asked to be seen. He wore a black tank that clung to his lean frame, hinting at defiance, maybe rebellion, maybe just survival. He didn't smile. He didn't have to.

Melody's heart skipped a beat as her gaze followed his movements. There was an unspoken pull to him—magnetic, subtle, but undeniable.

"Hey, thanks," she murmured, her voice softer than she intended as she climbed into the truck.

Jace leaned against the door, a half-grin forming on his lips. "Anytime."

He shut the door behind her, and she let her fingers linger on the cool handle as she settled into the seat, suddenly aware of the tightness in her chest. The inside of the truck smelled like vanilla and weed, warm and sweet and just a little hazy. It hit her like a hug she hadn't realized she needed—familiar, soft around the edges, and oddly comforting.

Jace gave a low whistle. "Damn, Melody," he said, eyebrows raised, "you trying to get us in trouble tonight or what?"

She rolled her eyes, cheeks warming as she climbed in.

"I'm serious," Jace said, glancing over at her again with a grin. "You look... really good. Like, goth goddess levels of hot."

"Okay, Romeo," Anna snorted, tossing a piece of gum at him.

Jace caught it one-handed and smirked, but his eyes were still on Melody for a second too long before he turned his attention back to the road.

Melody buckled her seatbelt, tugging her dress down a bit. "It's just a skater dress."

"Yeah, and it's doing you all kinds of favors," he said, drumming his fingers on the wheel. "Trust me. That guy of yours is an idiot for not tagging along."

Anna twisted around in her seat, half-laughing. "Careful, Jace. You're gonna make her blush."

Melody smiled despite herself. The compliments felt different coming from Jace—light, but warm. No pressure, no hunger behind them. Just... flirty fun.

He tapped the wheel again. "Alright, spooky babes, let's make some trouble."

The truck pulled away from the curb, bass already thumping, and the warm pulse of the night opened up in front of them.

The night air whipped softly through the cracked windows as Jace's Chevy S10 rolled down the quiet streets, its low rumble humming under Melody's feet. The stereo thudded with a playlist Anna had thrown together—industrial, a little darkwave, a few unexpected throwbacks. Jace drummed his fingers against the steering wheel, nodding along.

Melody sat back against the seat, letting herself relax into the scent of vanilla and weed, the flickering streetlights, the rhythm of their laughter. Lucian felt far away now—like a different version of her, in a different room, under a different moon.

"So," Jace said, glancing at her sideways, "how come your boyfriend didn't wanna come out tonight? Too scared of the goth kids?"

Melody smirked, gaze on the window. "He's not really into crowds."

"Lame," Anna declared from the passenger seat. She twisted around to look at Melody. "You look like fire tonight. Seriously. That dress? The boots? The eyeliner? Iconic."

"Don't forget the fishnets," Jace added, stealing another glance. "Those are what we in the business call devastating."

Melody laughed, covering her face for a second. "Oh my God, shut up."

"I'm just saying," Jace shrugged. "If he's dumb enough to let you go out looking like that alone, someone else might snatch you up."

Anna rolled her eyes. "Okay, smooth."

Jace grinned. "What? I'm just being honest. Goth girls in little black dresses? Top-tier. Untouchable."

Melody bit her lip, heat creeping up her neck, but it wasn't the uncomfortable kind. Jace's attention didn't coil around her like Lucian's did, it didn't push or pull. It just existed. Light and teasing, like a flashlight beam instead of a spotlight.

She looked out the window at the blur of small-town neon, heart still fluttering but for entirely different reasons now.

"You nervous?" Anna asked, popping a piece of gum in her mouth.

"A little," Melody admitted. "I've never been to a real show before. Not like this."

"You're gonna love it," Jace promised. "Nothing better than feeling the bass in your bones and the crowd moving like one giant monster. Trust me, it's church for freaks like us."

Melody smiled, fingers resting against her knee. Something inside her felt light.

She leaned her head back against the seat, letting the music wash over her. Outside, the town blurred by, sleepy and golden under the streetlights. Inside, in this warm little bubble of vanilla, weed, and bass, she felt like she was finally exactly where she belonged.

Jace reached into the console between the seats and pulled out a joint, and lit it. He took a slow drag, exhaling the smoke in a smooth stream.

"You want some?" he asked casually, offering it to her. The smell was heavy but comforting.

Melody hesitated, her fingers twitching. She had never smoked weed before, what if she didn't do it right? But there was something about the moment, something about how comfortable she felt with Jace and Anna, that made her second guess her usual resistance.

Jace looked over at her, giving her a lazy grin. "No pressure, just something to take the edge off."

Melody bit her lip, looking at the joint, then back at Jace's easy expression. She'd never been much for rebellion, but maybe tonight could be different.

She took a breath, then nodded, extending her hand. "Okay. Just a little."

Jace grinned, passing it to her with a wink. "You're a cool chick, Melody."

She took a tentative hit, the smoke filling her lungs before she coughed lightly, a surprised laugh escaping her lips. The taste was sharper than she'd expected, but the warmth it left behind was strangely soothing.

"There you go," Jace said, laughing as he reached for the joint again. "Told ya it'd help you chill."

Melody smiled, feeling a little lighter, a little less tethered to the weight of everything that had been lingering in her mind. She leaned back, closing her eyes for a moment, just letting herself drift.

CHAPTER FOURTEEN

As the music roared, the heavy beats vibrating through the floor, Melody couldn't shake the sense that Anna was watching her a little too closely. Maybe it was just the overwhelming noise of the night, but she couldn't help feeling like Anna was waiting for her to open up, to tell her about the darker parts of her life that no one else knew. Melody had always kept her family life locked away from others, hidden in the corners of her mind, because it was too hard to explain. Too painful.

"Is everything okay?" Anna asked, leaning closer, her voice barely audible over the heavy music. "You've been kind of quiet tonight."

Melody shrugged, the loud thrum of the concert almost drowning out her thoughts. "I'm fine. Just... tired, I guess."

Anna raised an eyebrow, clearly unconvinced. She glanced at Melody, then back at the stage, where the band was playing their hardest, the crowd pushing and pulling in a frenzied rhythm. "You sure? It's been a while since we hung out just the two of us," she said, a little too gently. "You don't have to tell me anything, but if you ever need to talk, I'm here."

Melody's heart squeezed a little in her chest. She didn't know how to explain the mess of her life, or the deep well of sadness that had been building for so long. She didn't know how to tell Anna that there was so much more to her than what anyone could see, that she was pretending to be okay when she wasn't.

Before Melody could respond, a familiar face appeared next to her. Jace grinned wide, his eyes scanning the crowd before landing on her and Anna. "Hey, mind if I join you two?" His voice was cheerful, cutting through the intensity of the concert's sound. "The mosh pit's getting a little too intense for me, but this spot looks perfect for rocking out."

Melody's heart fluttered, grateful for the distraction. Jace had always been someone she could talk to without the pressure of too many questions. He was carefree and easy to be around, unlike Anna, who had a way of reading her like an open book.

"Of course!" Anna said, her smile lighting up. "The more, the merrier."

Melody smiled back at Jace, her chest lightening a little. It was nice to have someone she didn't have to hide behind. "You sure you can handle the crowd?" she teased, nodding toward the thrashing, chaotic crowd around them.

Jace chuckled, pulling his jacket sleeves up as if preparing for battle. "I've got this," he said confidently, offering his hand to Melody. "Come on, let's show Anna how it's done."

Without thinking, Melody placed her hand in his, feeling the warm rush of excitement mix with the pulsing beat of the music. For a moment, she allowed herself to forget about everything else—the weight of her family life, the constant pull of Lucian's messages, the secrets she kept hidden. She was here, in this moment, with friends who cared, and that felt like enough.

The three of them made their way toward the center of the crowd, where the music blared even louder, and the energy of the fans seemed to push them into the rhythm. The crowd surged around them, people bouncing and shouting along to the lyrics of their favorite songs. Melody found herself laughing, momentarily swept up in the joy of it, her hands raised in the air as she sang along with the crowd.

Jace's enthusiasm was infectious, and Anna, who had initially been quiet, began to loosen up, jumping in time with the music. Melody let herself enjoy the moment, laughing when Jace accidentally bumped into someone in the crowd and nearly knocked him over. The whole situation was ridiculous, but it was also freeing, and for once, it was nice to feel like a normal teenager, without the weight of all her secrets.

Still, even as she danced and sang along, Melody couldn't fully escape. The quiet voice in her head reminded her that she was still pretending. Pretending to be someone she wasn't. Pretending that everything was okay when she knew it wasn't.

But for just a few minutes, the music and the noise and the laughter made her feel like she could let go.

The bass rattled through Melody's chest as she stood pressed between two of her friends in the crowded concert hall. The stage lights cut through the darkness like lightning bolts, pulsing reds and purples against the smoke in the air. For a few brief moments, she forgot— she forgot Charlotte's screaming, forgot Nick's cruel sneers, forgot the weight of loneliness that usually dragged behind her like a shadow.

She laughed, genuinely, as she bumped shoulders with Anna. It felt foreign but good, like breathing real air for the first time in years. Jace grinned down at her and tossed an arm casually around her shoulders when the crowd surged. Melody stiffened for a second but let it happen. *It was innocent. He's just a friend. Lucian would understand*, she told herself. He'd want her to have fun.

But when she looked up at Jace, something flickered between them, just for a heartbeat. His smile softened, less playful now, and his eyes lingered on hers longer than they should have. The air between them felt charged, like static waiting to spark.

"You okay?" he asked, his voice low, not quite a shout, but just loud enough to cut through the sound.

Melody nodded, but her voice caught in her throat. "Yeah,"

she said, but the word didn't quite capture the strange warmth rising in her chest.

Jace didn't pull his arm away. Instead, he let it rest there a beat longer, and Melody didn't move. Her shoulder tucked against him, and she was surprised by how safe it felt— how grounding. Not like Lucian's intensity, not like the chaos of home. Jace was just... here. Present.

When the crowd jumped again, he instinctively pulled her a little closer to steady her. "Sorry," he laughed. "Didn't mean to crush you."

She laughed too, lightheaded. "It's okay. I've survived worse."

His gaze settled on her, quiet and unflinching, as if he could see every scar her silence never spoke of. "Yeah... I bet you have."

Something in the way he said it made her chest tighten. She wanted to look away, but she didn't. And neither did he.

They stood like that for a while, the music raging around them, bodies moving in every direction, and yet, for a few seconds, it felt like the world had narrowed down to just them.

Then Anna leaned in, breaking the spell. "This band is seriously killing it tonight!"

Melody turned her head, nodding, and when she glanced back at Jace, his arm was gone, but the warmth lingered. So did that look.

And when their hands brushed again, by accident or not, neither of them pulled away.

Her phone buzzed violently in her hoodie pocket.

She ignored it at first, swaying to the music, the adrenaline buzzing under her skin. But it buzzed again. And again. And again.

Melody stepped away from the crowd, weaving through the bodies until she found a quieter corner by the bar.

When she pulled out her phone, her heart dropped.

Lucian (11 missed calls)

Lucian (4 new texts)

Where are you??

Why aren't you answering me?

Who's with you?

I swear to God if you're with some guy...

Panic coiled tight in her stomach. She called him back, chewing her bottom lip raw.

He answered immediately. "Melody, what the fuck?!"

His voice, usually smooth and low, now lashed like a whip across the line.

"I'm at the concert" she said quickly, turning her face toward the wall for privacy. "I'm just with Anna and Jace. It's nothing, I swear."

"Jace?" Lucian spat the name like poison. "You're letting some dude put his hands all over you while I'm sitting here thinking about you, worrying about you? Do you even fucking care about me?"

Melody felt her throat tighten. "I—I do care. Please, I do. It's not like that. He's just a friend. I swear, Lucian."

She could hear his breathing— heavy and furious, on the other end.

She pressed a hand over her ear, trying to block out the crowd noise. "Lucian, please, I just needed one night. Just one night to feel normal. I'm sorry."

There was a long pause. Then, in a quieter, deadlier voice: "I knew it. You're just like the rest of them."

The words stabbed deep, and before she could stop herself, tears blurred her vision.

"I love you," she choked. "Please don't say that. Please, please don't hate me."

Another pause.

Then a soft, cold, "Have fun with your little boyfriend, Baby Doll."

The line went dead.

Melody's hands were still shaking as she slipped the phone back into her pocket, the cold weight of Lucian's words echoing in her ears. For a moment, she just stood there, staring at the darkened walls of the venue, trying to calm the storm inside her chest. The pulsating lights, the thrumming music, the noise—it all felt so far away now, like it was happening to someone else.

She didn't know how long she stood there, lost in the static, but eventually, she felt a tap on her shoulder.

"Everything okay?" Jace's voice was soft, almost concerned, and when she turned, he was standing there, eyes searching hers.

Melody tried to force a smile, though it felt brittle. "Yeah. Just needed a minute to breathe. Sorry."

Anna was close behind, her brow furrowed in worry. "You've been kind of off since the call," she said quietly. "What happened?"

Melody swallowed, the words trapped in her throat. She didn't know how to explain the weight of it all—the guilt, the shame, the fear that Lucian's control was getting tighter with every passing day. "Nothing... It's just... Lucian," she finally said, the name feeling like a bitter pill. "He's just... you know. Getting upset that I'm out with you guys."

Jace gave her a knowing look, his smile fading just a little. "You should be able to have fun, Mel. You deserve it." His hand found hers again, a steady anchor in the chaos, and Melody squeezed it back, grateful for the warmth.

Anna, always the more perceptive one, frowned. "It's not just that, is it?"

Melody turned away for a moment, not trusting herself to look Anna in the eye. She didn't want to talk about Lucian's constant need to dominate her life, to question her every move. The pull of his jealousy felt suffocating, but how could she explain that to Anna without it sounding like an excuse? How could she explain how tangled she had become in his web?

"I just... I don't know how to explain it," Melody muttered, looking down at her shoes. "It's just... he's not like you guys. I don't think he gets how important nights like this are to me. He just... he says stuff, and it makes me feel like I'm doing something wrong, even though I'm not."

Anna's expression softened, but she didn't push, sensing Melody's need for space. Instead, she gave a small smile. "Well, if you need to talk about it later, we're here, okay?"

Melody nodded, but she could feel the familiar ache in her chest again. She wasn't sure what to say to them anymore, wasn't sure if anyone could understand. Her friends were great, but they didn't know the real her, not the broken parts that Lucian always seemed to see. The parts of her that he twisted to fit his needs.

She turned to go back to the crowd, but Jace gently tugged her hand. "Hey," he said, voice low. "Hold up a sec."

Melody looked at him, surprised.

"You don't have to say anything if you don't want to," he continued, his brows pinched with concern. "But you don't look okay. You've got that look like you're trying not to fall apart."

That nearly undid her.

Her lip trembled, and she looked away quickly, blinking fast. "I'm fine. Really."

Jace stepped in a little closer, lowering his voice further. "You don't have to be fine around me, Mel. I mean it."

She let out a shaky breath. "He just... he said some stuff that really messed with my head. That's all."

Jace hesitated, then gently pulled her into a hug. She stiffened for a second, uncertain, but then let herself relax against him. There was a current between them, soft but steady, and the way his arms held her made her feel like she wouldn't break this time. She didn't understand it, how something could be this gentle and still shake her.

"He shouldn't talk to you like that," Jace murmured near her ear. "You're too good to be treated that way."

Melody didn't respond, but her grip on his jacket tightened.

"You're not crazy for wanting to feel normal. Or safe. Or happy," he added softly. "I know I'm just the dumb guy friend, but... I care about you, Mel. And I'm really glad you came tonight. Even if he made you feel like shit for it."

That pulled a soft laugh from her, and she wiped at her face, trying to regain composure. "You're not dumb."

"Debatable," he said with a smirk. "But I know a shitty situation when I see one. Believe me. I used to date someone who made me feel that small too. Thought it was love for the longest time... turned out it was just control."

Melody blinked. "Really?"

Jace nodded. "Yeah. It took me forever to realize it. She'd blow up every time I did something without her. Even being here tonight, she would've hated it."

Melody looked at him differently now, like someone who got it, even if he hadn't said much. "What happened?"

"She didn't like the fact I had friends who cared about me," he said simply. "Especially not girls. She always thought they were a threat. Even you. Back when we first met, she told me to stop talking to you."

Melody's eyebrows lifted. "And you didn't?"

He gave a crooked smile. "Nope. That was kind of the beginning of the end."

She didn't know what to say, so she just nodded. But her chest felt a little less heavy now.

"C'mon," he said gently, "we'll just stick by the edge. No pressure. But I'm not letting you go through the rest of this night feeling like garbage."

He held out his hand again, and this time, when she took it, it felt like something solid to hold onto in the middle of a storm.

As they made their way back into the crowd, Anna glanced at her, quietly reassured by the tiny spark of color that had returned to Melody's face. The noise swallowed them whole, but this time, she wasn't drowning in it.

Even with Lucian's voice lingering in the back of her mind, Jace's warmth beside her cut through the chill. Just enough to breathe.

The car ride was mostly quiet. The hum of the engine and the faint sound of music playing through the speakers, something soft and unfamiliar, was all that filled the silence. Melody sat in the passenger seat, her head leaning against the window, watching the blur of streetlights pass like glowing ghosts. Anna sat in the back, scrolling her phone, eyes heavy with sleep.

The adrenaline from the concert had long since worn off, and now there was only the crash, the stillness that came after too much emotion. Melody felt hollowed out, like she'd been scooped from the inside.

When Jace pulled into Anna's driveway, she roused just enough to mumble, "Thanks, guys," then climbed out with a tired wave.

Melody gave her a weak smile. "Call or text me tomorrow."

Anna nodded, then disappeared behind the closing front door. And just like that, it was quiet again. Just the two of them.

Jace pulled back onto the road, one hand on the steering wheel, the other draped over the gearshift. Melody could feel the weight of the words building between them like pressure in her chest.

"I didn't mean to ruin the night," she said finally, her voice barely louder than the engine.

"You didn't," he replied quickly, glancing at her. "You just... had a rough moment. That's not the same thing."

She stared down at her lap. "He called me selfish. Said I didn't care about him."

Jace's jaw tightened. "He said that because you went out with your friends?"

She nodded. "And because you were there."

There was a beat of silence. Then he let out a quiet breath, the kind that said he was holding back stronger feelings.

"Mel... I don't know what he's got going on in his head, but none of that is okay. You're not selfish for needing a break. And you sure as hell don't deserve to feel guilty for being around someone who actually gives a damn about you."

She looked at him then. His face was lit softly by the dashboard glow—sharp angles, gentle eyes. There was a sadness there, but not pity. Something deeper. Understanding.

"I keep telling myself I'll say something next time," she whispered. "That I'll hang up or stand up for myself or...something. But I freeze. It's like... my whole body goes cold."

He nodded slowly, eyes on the road. "Yeah. I know that feeling."

Melody blinked. "From your ex?"

"Yeah," he said. "I'd tell myself I'd walk away the next time she lost it on me. But then she'd cry or twist it around or remind me how no one else ever really 'got' me like she did. And for a while... I believed her."

Melody swallowed. "That sounds a lot like him."

He glanced at her again. "You ever feel like... if you left, you'd be proving them right? Like all the things they accused you of— being cold, being a liar, being disloyal, it'd all come true?"

Tears pricked at the back of her eyes. "Yes. Exactly that."

He didn't say anything right away. Just reached over and gently turned the volume down on the music. The silence between them grew heavier, but it wasn't uncomfortable. It was intimate.

"You're not any of those things," he said after a moment. "You're not cold. You're not a liar. You're one of the most honest people I've met. Sometimes too honest, probably," he added with a faint smirk.

Melody let out a small, watery laugh.

"And you're loyal to a fault," he went on. "Even to someone who doesn't deserve it."

That quieted her again. Not in a bad way, but in the way where her thoughts felt a little clearer.

She turned her face back toward the window. "I hate that I still love him."

"I don't," he said softly.

She looked at him, startled.

"I don't hate that you love him," he clarified. "It means you still have your heart. That he hasn't destroyed that yet. And that's... kind of amazing, Mel."

They were almost to her house now. The streets grew more familiar, her neighborhood slowly unfolding around them like a story she wasn't sure she was ready to return to. The porch light was on, casting a lonely yellow glow on the driveway.

When he pulled up to the curb, he didn't put the car in park. Just kept it idling, his fingers still resting on the gearshift.

"You okay to go in?" he asked gently.

Melody nodded, but didn't move to open the door.

Jace's voice was quiet when he spoke. "You can always call me. Dumb or not. I'll show up. No questions asked."

She turned to look at him, the shadows softening his features. "Why?"

He gave her a small, tired smile. "Because I see you, Melody. And I want you to know there's someone in your life who doesn't want to take anything from you. Who just wants you to feel... safe."

Something in her chest cracked open.

"Thank you," she whispered.

He nodded once. "Go inside before I keep you here all night."

She smiled and reached for the door handle. But before she got out, she turned back.

"Hey, Jace?"

"Yeah?"

"I'm really glad I have you."

He smiled. "Me too, Mel."

She stepped out into the cool night air and closed the door behind her.

Jace waited until she reached the front door and gave him a little wave before he pulled away, headlights vanishing down the quiet street.

Inside, Melody leaned against the front door for a long moment before heading upstairs. Lucian hadn't texted again. For once, she didn't feel the need to check.

She peeled off her coat, tossing it over the desk chair, revealing the black skater dress beneath— and the thin, angry marks already faded to pale scars along the inside of her forearm. She traced them absently with her fingertips, as if searching for answers in old wounds.

The rain had started outside, a soft drumming against the window. It should have been comforting. But tonight, it only deepened the ache.

Wednesday was curled up at the foot of her bed, blinking slowly at Melody as she walked into the room. Melody moved toward her and sat down beside her, letting her fingers trail through the cat's soft black fur. The steady rhythm of Wednesday's purring filled the quiet, grounding her.

"I missed you," Melody murmured, leaning down to press her

face gently against Wednesday's side. "You're the only one who doesn't make everything feel so complicated."

Wednesday let out a small meow in response, pressing her head against Melody's hand.

Melody sat at the edge of her bed, her chest tight with shame and loneliness. She wanted to call Lucian. She wanted to hear his voice, even if it was angry, even if it hurt. Anything was better than the silence swallowing her whole. Her thumb slid over the phone screen, dialing the familiar number.

Lucian picked up on the third ring, his voice as calm as ever, but it had a coldness to it that made Melody's stomach tighten. "Melody," he said, the way he said her name both intimate and distant, like he was already pulling away even as he spoke.

"I'm sorry," she said quickly, the words tumbling out before she could stop them. "I didn't mean to upset you earlier. I just... I was with my friends, and it got loud, and then you hung up before I could explain. I didn't want you to think I was ignoring you."

There was a silence on the other end for a moment before Lucian spoke again, his tone more measured now, as though he were collecting himself. "You know, I get it. I understand why you're out there, having fun. But you have to know something, Melody." His voice was soft, too soft, and it made her nervous.

She bit her lip. "What's that?"

"You're young," he said, his words deliberate. "You don't realize it yet, but you're too young to be dealing with someone like him."

She frowned. "What do you mean? Jace is just a friend. He's—"

"Just a friend," Lucian interrupted, his voice taking on a sharper edge. "I'm not talking about him, I'm talking about you, Melody. You're still figuring things out, but you're not ready for someone like him. Someone your age. Someone who can't even comprehend what you're really going through. What *we* have is different, you know that, don't you?"

Melody's chest tightened. She hadn't expected this kind of response. "I don't need anyone else, Lucian. I told you, Jace is just a friend. I'm not interested in him like that."

Lucian didn't answer right away. Instead, there was a long, heavy pause. When he did speak, his voice was lower, almost as if he were trying to steady himself. "I'm not just talking about him," he repeated. "I'm talking about the age difference. You're too young for him, Melody. You don't see it now, but you're just a kid, and he's not what you need. I'm not trying to control you, but you can't keep pretending like someone your age can be the one to understand you, to take care of you the way I can. He's just a kid too."

Her stomach flipped. She didn't like the way he was framing it, the way he was making Jace seem so insignificant compared to him. "I don't know what you're talking about," she said, her voice quiet, but there was a new defensiveness in it now. "He's just my friend, Lucian. Nothing more."

"Don't lie to me, Melody," Lucian said, his tone calm but sharp enough to cut. "I know you better than you think. You say he's just a friend, but I can hear it, the way your voice changes when you talk about him. You're different lately. Distant. You can pretend it's nothing, but I feel it... and so do you."

The words stung, but Melody swallowed hard. She didn't want to admit it, not even to herself. "I don't—" she started to say, but Lucian cut her off again, his tone softer now, more coaxing, as if he could sense her resistance and was pushing against it.

"Look, baby, I'm not saying he's a bad guy, but he's not you. He's not like me. I know what it's like to be where you are, Melody. I know how to take care of you. He doesn't even understand how broken you are. How broken I am."

Melody's breath caught in her throat, her hands gripping the phone tighter. There was a quiet venom in his voice now, a possessiveness that made her uneasy.

"Lucian, I don't want to talk about Jace anymore," she said, the words trembling at the edges. "I just wanted to talk to you. I'm sorry about the concert. I didn't mean to hurt you."

Lucian exhaled slowly, and for a moment, she thought he might say something comforting. Instead, his words came out slow and deliberate, cutting through her like a sharp blade. "I'm not the one you're hurting, Melody. You're only hurting yourself by thinking someone like him can give you what I can."

Her throat tightened, her eyes stinging with the threat of tears. She didn't want to hear it. She didn't want him to keep saying these things, but something about his calmness, his calculated words, made her want to listen.

"You don't need anyone but me," Lucian said softly. "You never have. And you'll see that eventually. You just have to trust me."

Melody felt a wave of confusion wash over her, and for a brief moment, she almost agreed with him. *Almost.* But a small voice inside her resisted.

"I'll always be here for you, baby doll," Lucian continued, his voice now a whisper. "I won't let you fall."

She didn't respond right away. The silence between them was deafening.

"I'll call you tomorrow," Lucian added, as if it was a given, as if there was no question in his mind that he would always be there, hovering, watching.

"Okay," she whispered, the word escaping before she could stop herself.

Lucian's voice softened even more, and it was almost gentle now, but the manipulation was still there. "I'll be waiting, Melody."

The call ended, and she lowered the phone, her hand trembling slightly. She sat there in the dim light of her room, feeling the weight of his words settle over her like a thick, suffocating blanket. She couldn't shake the feeling that, somehow, he was right. He always seemed so sure. So calm in his conviction.

But deep down, she wasn't so sure anymore. She just didn't know how to break free from the pull of his words.

Wednesday, sensing the shift in her energy, climbed into her lap without hesitation. Melody looked down, her fingers instinctively sinking into the warm fluff of her fur. The tears she'd been holding back slid down her cheeks, silent and slow.

"You're the only one who sees me," she whispered, voice cracking. "And you don't ask me to be anything else."

Her hands trembled as she reached for her journal. By the dim glow of her bedside lamp, she wrote:

I'm sorry I'm not enough. I'm sorry I ruin everything. I just wanted one night. I just wanted to feel real. But I'm nothing without him. I'm nothing.

The pen shook in her hand, smearing the ink with small drops of tears.

For a moment, her gaze flicked toward the drawer of her nightstand — where old, dangerous comforts hid.

Her fingers hovered there, trembling.

But tonight, something inside her whispered, *Not tonight. Please not tonight.*

Instead, she grabbed her pillow and hugged it to her chest so tightly it hurt, muffling her sobs against the fabric.

From her small stereo, almost too soft to hear, the haunting strains of *"Broken"* by Seether featuring Amy Lee filled the room. The song wrapped around her like a ghost, every lyric carving deeper into her heart.

Melody curled in tighter on herself, mouthing the words into the darkness, a silent promise to the broken girl inside her that she was still here.

Wednesday padded quietly across the bedspread and nestled against her side. The warmth of her tiny body and the soft rumble of her purring grounded Melody in the moment, a small island of comfort in a sea of ache.

Melody's fingers found Wednesday's fur, and she stroked her absently, grateful for the weight and presence of something that didn't ask questions, didn't make demands, didn't judge.

The tears kept falling, but she was no longer alone in the dark.

Still fighting.

Even if no one else saw it.

Eventually, exhaustion dragged her under.

She fell asleep crying, the pillow damp beneath her cheek, the rain still whispering against the glass, a lullaby only the lonely would recognize.

In her dreams, the world softened.

The rain outside her window became a soft mist, curling into silver tendrils around her bed.

And there he was.

Lucian.

Standing by the edge of her mattress, cloaked in shadow and eyeliner and the leather jacket he always wore in the photos he sent her.

But his face...his face was different tonight.

Softer.

No anger.

No bitterness.

Just that sad, broken smile that always made her feel seen.

He crouched down beside her, brushing a strand of hair from her tear-streaked cheek with a touch so feather-light it almost didn't feel real.

His voice was barely a whisper:

"Baby... I'm sorry."

Melody swallowed hard in her sleep, heart fluttering like a dying bird.

"*I miss you.*"

"*I love you.*"

"*You're all I have.*"

He opened his arms, and without hesitation, Melody crawled into them.

Here tucked against his chest, she felt small and protected, like all the sharp edges inside her dulled for just a moment.

Like she could breathe again.

The rain in the dream faded into a low hum, like the beat of a distant drum.

Lucian rocked her gently, murmuring promises into her hair, promises he would never keep.

But here, in the fragile safety of sleep, Melody believed every word.

And for a few fleeting heartbeats, she wasn't broken anymore.

She was just a girl who was loved.

But dreams were liars.

When Melody blinked awake in the gray light of morning, the warmth of his arms was gone— only the cold, heavy ache in her chest remained.

Melody lay still for a moment, staring at the ceiling, trying to hold onto the last remnants of the dream.

The echo of Lucian's voice, *"I miss you. I love you."* clung to her like a phantom, but it faded quickly, replaced by the heavy silence of her room. She could almost hear her heartbeat in the stillness, a reminder that the dream was just that: a dream.

With a sigh, she slowly sat up, the weight of the night still clinging to her like a second skin. Her body felt too heavy, as though her limbs were made of stone. She swung her legs over the edge of the bed, feet barely touching the floor, and just sat there for a moment, feeling the chill of the morning air seep through her thin pajamas.

The rain had stopped, but the world outside her window was still gray and muted. She could hear her mom's voice in the distance, arguing with her dad, probably. Her brother Nick's laughter cutting through the tension. Melody didn't care anymore. It was the same noise, the same routine.

Dragging herself to the bathroom, she looked into the mirror, barely recognizing the girl who stared back at her. Her eyes were puffy, the remnants of last night's tears still clinging to her lashes. The emptiness inside her seemed to stretch farther and farther, as though she was slipping through a crack in the universe, falling into a place where no one could reach her.

With a deep breath, she turned on the faucet and splashed cold water onto her face, the chill snapping her back to reality, but only for a second.

She couldn't escape the ache inside. The ache that had never gone away. The ache that came from loving someone who wasn't really hers.

Not yet.

CHAPTER SIXTEEN

After the concert, Melody drifted through her days like a ghost —present, but disconnected.

Melody kept replaying everything—what she said, what he said, how fast it all escalated. Lucian had called afterward, soft-spoken and apologetic, telling her how much he hated fighting with her, how it tore him up inside. She listened. She always listened. She even said she was sorry, even though she wasn't sure what for.

They talked. They messaged. But something had shifted.

Each conversation felt heavier, like walking through molasses. She couldn't explain it, even to herself. It wasn't that he'd stopped saying the right things, he still called her special, still told her she was the only one who truly understood him. But underneath it, there was a pressure. A tension. A feeling like she was being squeezed into a shape that didn't quite fit.

And no matter how much she tried to pretend everything was normal, that gnawing sense of guilt and confusion lingered— quiet, persistent, and impossible to silence.

Her phone sat on the desk in front of her, buzzing every few minutes. Each vibration felt like a cruel reminder of how trapped she was, how she couldn't seem to escape him. She kept her ringer off, kept her messages unread, hoping that maybe, just maybe, he would give her the space she needed. But Lucian didn't do space. Not with her.

It wasn't that she didn't care about him. It was just... she couldn't breathe with him suffocating her like this. Every time he reached out, the panic in her chest grew tighter. She wanted to pull away, but it felt like something was pulling her back in—like his gravity was too strong for her to resist.

Her phone buzzed again. This time, she glanced at the screen, expecting to see Lucian's name.

But it was Jace.

> Hey, just checking in. You okay?

Her heart stuttered. The simplicity of the message felt like a lifeline. No pressure. No guilt. Just... care. Before she could respond, another buzz. **Lucian.**

> Where are you? I've called you like a hundred times. What's going on? Why are you ignoring me?

She winced without meaning to. The contrast between the two messages couldn't have been clearer.

She hesitated, then replied to Jace first.

> Kinda hanging in there. Things are just heavy right now.

A pause. Then she typed to Lucian.

> I need some time, Lucian. I just can't deal with everything right now.

Her heart raced as both messages sent out into the void. She felt like she was holding her breath, waiting for both of them to react.

Lucian was the first.

Time? What are you talking about? We're supposed to be in this together. I don't understand what's happening. Why are you doing this?

Almost at the same time, Jace replied too. Melody opened Jace's message.

I get that. You don't have to talk about it if you don't want to. Just wanted you to know I care.

Tears pricked at her eyes. It was strange—how much tenderness could exist in just a few words.

She chewed her lip, then typed to Jace.

Thank you. I really needed to hear that.

Then to Lucian, her fingers trembling.

I don't know what I'm doing anymore. Everything is just... too much. My family, you... I don't know how to handle it.

Lucian's response came quickly.

Don't say that. Don't talk like this. You know I care about you. I care about us. Please, you have to understand, this isn't just about your family. I don't want to see you hurting. If I could, I would take it all away.

Melody's stomach twisted. The sincerity in his words was there, but so was something else. Something heavy and unrelenting.

Another text came through. Jace again.

If you ever just wanna hang out or sit in silence or whatever... no pressure. I'm here.

She smiled faintly, the corners of her mouth twitching despite the ache in her chest. She sends a message back to Jace first.

> That means a lot, Jace. Really. You always
> make me feel like I can breathe.

Next she sends a reply to Lucian.

> I just can't do this anymore. It's too much. My
> family... everything's falling apart, and I don't
> know how to keep going.

> I hate them for doing this to you. I hate your
> family for making you feel like this. They don't
> understand you, Melody. They don't get how
> special you are, how much you deserve. If I
> could, I would take you away from all of them.
> You wouldn't have to deal with any of it
> anymore.

The flutter of unease returned. Lucian's earlier words still echoed in her chest like the aftershock of a slammed door. And now, even in this moment of calm, they wrapped around her like chains.

Then her phone buzzed. Another text from Jace. She opened it.

> You deserve to feel safe. And to be with people
> who respect your space. You ever wanna talk
> about anything, even random stuff, I'm here.

Her heart stung. It was such a simple thing to say. But no one said things like that to her.

She typed slowly, carefully, as if the wrong words might scare him away.

> You're like the only person who makes me feel
> like I'm not a problem.

There was a pause. A single tear slid down her cheek before the next message from Jace lit up her screen.

> That's because you're not.

The lump in her throat tightened. Her hands trembled just slightly as she held the phone. She wanted to believe him. She really did.

Another message, to Lucian, hovered unsent in her other chat. Her thumb moved to it, hesitating.

She switched screens.

> I don't want to be hurt anymore. I just want to feel okay.

She hit send. Her pulse raced.

Minutes passed in silence, stretching thin. Her breath hitched. Maybe he wouldn't answer at all. Maybe she'd pushed too far this time.

But then, the screen lit up again.

Lucian's name.

His reply came slowly, like someone trying to patch together something already unraveling.

> I can't bear the thought of losing you. Please, just talk to me. We'll figure this out, okay? I just want to help you. We're in this together, I promise.

Her eyes flicked between the two conversations.

One was steady. Warm. Real.

The other was a storm that knew how to whisper just before the thunder cracked.

She didn't respond again. Not to either of them.

She just sat in the quiet and let the silence hold her, unsure of where to turn next.

The phone slipped from Melody's hands and landed beside her on the bed. Her eyes were red, but she didn't cry. She just stared at the ceiling, arms crossed over her chest like she was trying to hold herself together.

Wednesday leapt softly onto the bed, circling once before settling beside her hip. The cat's warmth was subtle but grounding, her purrs faint and steady like a heartbeat Melody couldn't find in herself.

The late afternoon sun filtered through the curtains in thin golden slits, catching the floating dust in the air. Everything felt still and heavy. Her thoughts were loud, but the room was silent.

Then her phone buzzed again.

She hesitated before looking. It was Jace.

> Hey... you wanna come outside for a bit? The air feels good. It's kinda breezy, not too cold.
> Thought maybe it'd help clear your head.

Melody blinked.

Just a few words. No expectations. No guilt. No pressure.

She could practically hear his voice in the text—calm, thoughtful, like he was standing outside somewhere nearby, maybe leaning against a tree, waiting but not rushing her.

She got up slowly, legs shaky from sitting so long in one place. Her fingers hovered over her screen.

> Yeah... I think I'd like that.

She hesitated. Then added:

> Thanks for asking. Really.

> Of course. I'm just a few steps away. No rush.

She slipped on her hoodie and quietly pushed open her bedroom door. The air in the house felt too thick. Charlotte was on the phone in the kitchen, her voice sharp and clipped. Melody didn't stop to listen.

She stepped outside and was immediately greeted by a soft breeze that kissed her cheeks and tangled through her hair. The sky was streaked with lavender and rose as the sun dipped low.

Jace was leaning against the porch railing, his hands in his hoodie pockets. He looked up as she came out, offering a gentle smile.

"Hey," he said, like he wasn't sure how much noise she could handle.

Melody just nodded. "Hey."

He didn't push. He didn't ask questions. He just stood there beside her, silent, facing the same direction she was. Out toward the empty street and the whispering trees.

After a while, he said, "Wanna walk a little? Just around the block?"

She looked at him, the ghost of a smile pulling at the corner of her lips. "Yeah. I'd like that."

And for a little while, they just walked. No talking. No pressure. Just the sound of their footsteps, the breeze in the leaves, and the small, quiet comfort of someone who didn't ask her to be anything other than what she was in that moment.

They walked in step, their shoes crunching softly on the gravel that lined the edge of the street. The wind tugged at the hem of Melody's hoodie, and she hugged it tighter around her. Jace didn't say anything at first, just walked beside her like he'd done this a thousand times before, like he'd always known how to give her space without making her feel alone.

Melody stared down at the sidewalk cracks, watching her feet trace the lines.

"I don't want to feel like this anymore." The words she'd texted Lucian echoed in her head. She felt raw, like her emotions had been skinned and left open to the air. Being outside helped a

little, the wind in her face, the wide open sky— but inside, she still felt tangled up and tight.

She glanced sideways at Jace. He looked ahead, calm and steady, the way mountains feel from a distance.

"Do you ever feel like…" she began, then stopped. Her voice came out small, unused.

He glanced over at her, encouraging but still quiet.

Melody tried again. "Like you're just… tired of having to explain yourself all the time? Like no matter what you say, it never comes out right?"

He nodded slowly. "Yeah," he said. "Yeah, I've felt that."

She let out a breath. "I don't even know how to explain what I'm feeling right now. Everything's just… tangled. It's like I'm trying to be okay, but it never sticks. Not really."

Jace let that sit for a few steps. Then, "You don't have to explain it all right now. Or at all, if you don't want to."

Melody blinked. She wasn't used to that kind of grace. Most people in her life either pushed for answers or ignored the signs altogether. But Jace was just… here.

"I was with someone," she said suddenly, voice shaky. "Someone older. He… he made me feel like I mattered. Like he saw me when no one else did. But now it's like… I don't know if he actually saw me. Or if he just saw someone he could shape into what he wanted."

His face didn't change, but his hands tucked deeper into his hoodie pockets. He didn't interrupt.

"I keep thinking I'm the one who's messed up," Melody said. "Like maybe I wanted too much. Or needed too much. Like it's my fault for falling into it."

"You're not messed up," he said gently. "Wanting to be seen doesn't make you weak. Wanting to feel safe doesn't make you wrong."

A tight breath slipped out of her. Her eyes burned, but she didn't cry.

They turned the corner. The wind carried the scent of some-one's laundry vent— warm, clean cotton.

She didn't speak for the next few minutes, and Jace didn't try to fill the silence. Instead, Melody retreated into her thoughts again.

Lucian's words were so full of need. So full of pain. But they wrapped around her like barbed wire. Soft and dangerous all at once.

And then there was Jace. Walking beside her. No barbs. No pressure. Just presence.

Her heart was a storm, but something in Jace's quiet made her feel like she could ride it out.

They reached the edge of the block and paused.

"Thanks," she said quietly, not looking at him.

"For what?"

"For not trying to fix it. For not being like everyone else."

He smiled faintly, the corners of his mouth barely turning up. "You don't need fixing, Melody. You just need space to breathe."

She nodded, her throat tight.

They turned back toward home. The sky was deeper now, the first stars blinking through.

The silence between them didn't feel like loneliness. It felt like peace.

The walk with Jace had settled something in her— not entirely, but enough. Enough to remember what it felt like to breathe without fear taking up all the space in her chest. When they got back to the house, she thanked him again with a quiet smile and slipped into her room, closing the door softly behind her.

She kicked off her shoes, climbed onto the bed, and sank into the blanket like it might hold her together. Her phone buzzed almost instantly.

Baby doll, where did you go earlier?

Another buzz.

You just disappeared mid-convo. Are you
okay?

Melody hesitated, her fingers hovering over the screen. She stared at the last message Jace had sent her earlier, just a simple *"You're stronger than you think."*

She swallowed hard and replied to Lucian.

I was outside for a bit. Went for a walk with
Jace.

The typing dots appeared immediately.

With Jace?? Seriously??

What the fuck. Melody! Are you kidding me
right now?

Her stomach flipped. Her thumbs trembled over the keyboard.

It wasn't like that. I just needed some air. He's
my friend.

You said you LOVED me. Now you're running
around with some dude??

I'm not running around. He's not "some dude."
He's my friend. I needed to clear my head.

A moment of silence.

Then her phone lit up with an incoming call: **Lucian**.

She froze.

It rang again.

She answered.

"Are you out of your mind?" His voice was sharp, venomous. "You went walking around with *him*? While I'm here falling apart and waiting to hear from you?"

Melody's breath hitched. "Lucian, I didn't mean to upset you. I just—"

"Do you even *care* what that looks like? Do you have any idea what that *feels* like for me? Knowing you're out there with someone else while I'm—"

"I'm allowed to take a walk," she said, quieter now. "I just needed space. Jace isn't—he's not anything like that. You know that."

"I thought I *meant something* to you," he snapped. "But you don't even care. You leave me hanging, you talk to other guys... what am I even supposed to think, Melody?"

Her throat tightened. "You mean something to me. You do. I just—please, I'm just trying to think clearly right now."

"Oh, you're *thinking clearly* now?" Lucian's voice shifted, cold and biting. "Since when? Since when do you *need time* to decide if I matter to you?"

"That's not what I'm saying," she whispered.

A pause. He exhaled loudly. Then, a quieter voice, but still edged with control. "I just don't want to lose you. But if this is how it's going to be... maybe I already have."

The line went dead.

Melody stared at the screen, the silence afterward louder than his yelling.

She lay back on the bed, heart pounding, her eyes burning, not just from the confrontation, but from how quickly love had turned into guilt. How fast comfort became control.

She curled onto her side, holding the phone to her chest, torn in two. One half aching for the warmth Lucian once gave her, the other reeling from the storm he now became.

The lights in her room stayed off.

The soft blue glow of her computer screen lit the corners of her desk, barely reaching her bed. The faint hum of the fan circled the silence like a ghost. On her headphones, "Hello" by Evanescence played. Amy Lee's voice filled the room.

Melody lay on her side, knees drawn to her chest, her chest rising in shallow, quiet breaths. The song pulled her under like a tide she didn't resist anymore.

Wednesday was curled behind her knees, nestled into the crook of her legs. The little cat's presence was silent and warm, a subtle pressure grounding her to the moment, even as everything else felt like it was unraveling.

She reached for her journal, the worn spine cracking softly as she flipped past pages of restless ink—frantic thoughts, fragmented dreams, moments she didn't dare say out loud. And then her eyes caught it. A passage she had copied months ago from the book she wasn't supposed to have, the one she slipped from the library shelf like a secret: *Letters to a Phantom*.

"Love, when real, does not save you. It unmakes you. It burns the rot away, even if it has to scorch the bone."

She stared at the words, her heart thudding in her chest. Back then, she hadn't really understood what it meant. She thought it was beautiful, maybe even romantic—tragic in a way that made her feel seen.

But now...

Now the words felt different. Heavier. Like a warning she hadn't realized was meant for her. Was this what love was supposed to feel like? Like being torn open and hollowed out? Was that what Lucian was doing? Burning away her rot? Or was he just burning her?

Her phone sat beside her on the bed. She hadn't heard from Lucian in hours.

She texted anyway.

> I'm sorry I upset you.

> Please just say something. Please… I'm really not okay.

No reply.

The song swelled.

She pressed her face into her pillow, trying not to cry. She didn't want to cry again. She was so tired of crying.

Wednesday moved closer, gently placing her small head against Melody's calf like she knew something was wrong. Her purring rose, steady and soft, vibrating through Melody's bones like a thread holding her together.

The silence from Lucian weighed heavier than his words had earlier. The way he flipped between furious and loving, she couldn't tell which version was real anymore. But either way, she needed him to say something. Anything.

She opened their message thread and stared at it until the lines blurred.

Then, a notification. From Lucian.

> You're being dramatic.

> I need space.

That was it.

That was all.

The floor inside her gave out.

She got up slowly, like she wasn't really moving herself. Her body felt like a puppet. She walked to her dresser, opened the top drawer, and pulled out the razor she'd hidden under socks.

She didn't even hesitate.

Not this time.

Her hands trembled.

Wednesday meowed softly behind her. A fragile, pleading sound. But Melody didn't look back.

She sat on the floor, legs crossed, and pulled her sleeve back.

It wasn't about dying.

It was about silencing the noise. The guilt. The shame. The feeling of being too much and not enough all at once.

One shallow line.

Then another.

The sharpness bit through the numbness. Red beaded along her skin.

The music kept playing.

She breathed out slowly.

A tear slid down her cheek— not from the pain, but from the release.

She wasn't trying to make a statement.

She just didn't know what else to do.

She picked up her phone and dialed Lucian.

No answer.

Her phone buzzed again. A message from Lucian.

> I said I needed space. Why can't you respect
> that?

Her fingers hovered over the keyboard, slick with guilt and a little blood.

> I'm bleeding.

> I didn't know what else to do.

> Please… I just needed to hear your voice.

The typing dots appeared.

Then disappeared.

She waited.

Nothing came.

The next morning, Melody's arms were a mess of raw, red lines—some fresh, others fading, layered over one another like secrets she couldn't hide fast enough. Her skin stung beneath her hoodie, every brush of fabric a bitter reminder of the night before: the fight with Lucian, his voice morphing from sweet to venom in a heartbeat, the way her phone screen had gone dark like he'd disappeared with it. The silence afterward had been the loudest part.

She sat on the edge of her bed, legs pulled up to her chest, sleeves tugged down past her knuckles. Her head throbbed from lack of sleep. Her chest felt hollow, like it had been scooped clean with a rusty spoon.

She had done it again.

It wasn't the first time, and deep down, she knew it wouldn't be the last. The pain wasn't just in her head anymore—it lived in her skin now, buzzing, bleeding, breathing.

She didn't want to die. She just wanted everything to stop. To go quiet. To feel anything other than the heavy, howling ache that clawed at her ribs.

Just as she blinked into a foggy daydream, the door creaked open.

Charlotte stepped in without knocking, still wearing her robe, coffee cup in hand. Her eyes scanned the room like she was already looking for something to criticize. Melody's hands moved instinctively, tugging the sleeves down tighter.

Too late.

Charlotte's gaze narrowed, her voice slicing the air like a blade.

"Melody," she snapped, sharp as broken glass. "What did you do to yourself?"

Melody froze. Her breath caught in her throat like it didn't want to leave. She looked at the floor.

There was no point in answering. She already knew how this would go.

Charlotte's voice rose immediately, turning shrill. "Andrew! Get in here!"

Footsteps pounded down the hall. Andrew appeared in the doorway, still in his work pants from the night shift, eyes bleary with sleep and worry. His face shifted when he saw the panic in Charlotte's expression.

"What's going on?" he asked, his tone rough but grounded.

Charlotte didn't answer. She stormed over, grabbing Melody's wrist and yanking her sleeve up with force. The cuts were angry and red against her pale skin.

"Look at this," Charlotte shouted. "Look at what she's doing to herself!"

Andrew's eyes widened. His body tensed like someone had punched him in the stomach.

He stepped closer, more gently than Charlotte had. His hand landed on Melody's shoulder with a softness that surprised her.

"Melody," he said, voice hushed, breaking. "Why?"

Her mouth opened, but her voice cracked before the words could find form.

"I—I don't know," she finally whispered.

She wanted to say more. She wanted to tell him that her chest felt like it was caving in, that Lucian's love came with knives, that she felt like she was vanishing from the inside out, but the words stayed trapped behind her teeth.

Charlotte scoffed, arms folded, her expression twisted with disgust.

"This is just another way to get attention. You've always been a drama queen, haven't you?"

The comment landed like a slap.

Andrew's face turned pale. His lips pressed into a hard line, the way they always did when he was trying not to yell. But this time, something broke.

"No, Charlotte," he said, voice rising. "This isn't a joke. She needs *help*."

Charlotte rounded on him like a storm.

"You don't understand! You're always gone. When you are here, you're not really here. You think showing up for two minutes means anything?"

"I'm trying," Andrew said, his voice tight. "I've been trying. But maybe if you stopped acting like you're the only one who knows everything—"

"You think you're helping?" she spat. "By undermining me? By taking her side when she's pulling this kind of crap?"

Andrew's fists clenched at his sides.

"You know what, Charlotte? Maybe it's time you stopped pretending like everything's fine. You've been messing with her head for *years*."

Charlotte's expression turned ice cold.

"What are you implying?"

"You know damn well what I'm implying," Andrew said, his voice cracking under the weight of years swallowed and silenced. "She doesn't need to be scolded. She needs someone to listen. She's drowning, and you're standing on her shoulders."

The air went still, like the house itself was holding its breath.

Then Charlotte lunged, her hand swinging toward his face.

Andrew caught her wrist mid-slap.

Everything shattered.

Voices exploded. Shouting. Accusations. Years of buried resentment rose like floodwater, crashing into walls, ricocheting off furniture. Melody backed up, her spine pressing against the farthest corner of her room. Her breath came fast and shallow, her heart galloping like it wanted out of her chest.

She clutched her sleeves tighter.

Under the bed, Wednesday let out a low, distressed yowl.

This was it.

This was the last straw.

She couldn't take it anymore.

Melody ran.

She didn't know where she was going, only that she had to get out. Her breath came in ragged gasps, lungs burning as her sneakers pounded the pavement. The streets blurred around her, the cold morning air sharp in her throat, her heartbeat roaring in her ears like a siren she couldn't outrun.

She didn't look back. Couldn't.

The last words her mother had thrown at her still rang in her head, cruel and venom-laced. *"You're a freak, no wonder no one wants you."*

And Nick looming in the hallway like a shadow with fists. Laughing when he cornered her. Sneering when she cried. There was never a safe room in that house. Not even her own.

She ran until her legs gave out.

By the time she reached the school, she was shaking, her arms wrapped tight around her body like they were the only things keeping her from shattering into pieces. She moved through the halls like a ghost, her eyes red-rimmed and glassy, her hair clinging to her face from the cold sweat on her skin. No one stopped her. No one saw her. That was the worst part.

When the call to the guidance office came over the intercom,

Melody didn't flinch. She stood and walked to the office as if pulled by something beyond her control, her feet moving through a fog. A part of her thought maybe this would be a safe place, but the louder part of her, the one that screamed inside her head, wanted to bolt. Don't tell. Don't say anything. It'll only make things worse.

Mrs. Thompson looked up from her desk as Melody entered, offering a forced smile. "Take a seat, Melody," she said, her voice lacking the warmth that Melody had been hoping for.

Melody slumped into the chair, her bones feeling heavier with every second. She couldn't meet Mrs. Thompson's gaze. She stared down at her shoes, the silence stretching between them like a chasm.

"I'm glad you came down," Mrs. Thompson said, her tone flat. "What's going on?"

Melody wanted to say something, but her mouth wouldn't cooperate. She swallowed hard, fingers twisting the cuffs of her hoodie.

"I'm not sure," Melody said, her voice barely above a whisper. "It's like... I'm stuck between two worlds. One where everything's suffocating, and one where, for a moment, I feel like I can breathe, but... it doesn't feel right. It's all wrong."

Mrs. Thompson didn't react at first, only narrowing her eyes, as if processing the words. Then, after a long pause, she said, "Wrong how?"

Melody's heart thudded in her chest. She had already said too much.

"It's just... home's a nightmare," she muttered, quickly covering up her words with a half-truth. Her hands trembled, and her insides screamed to tell someone the real reason she was falling apart. But the fear that clenched around her kept her mouth shut. If they found out about Lucian, everything would unravel.

Mrs. Thompson didn't seem to understand the weight of

what Melody wasn't saying. She raised an eyebrow. "What's going on at home? Tell me."

Melody's pulse raced. She didn't know how to explain that there was more to it than her brother and her mom. She didn't know how to say that Lucian, someone outside all of this, had become her anchor. Even if everything about it was wrong.

"My brother... Nick, he is emotionally and sometimes physically abusive to me," Melody said, her voice small. "Pushes me around. Calls me names. And my mom just... lets it happen. She doesn't care. She's always on his side."

Mrs. Thompson's lips tightened, but her eyes held no sympathy. She leaned back in her chair, arms folded. "Has he ever hurt you badly? You know, we can't ignore that if he has."

Melody shook her head quickly, her throat tightening. "No. Not really. Just... it's the way they look at me. Like I don't matter. Like I'm just in the way."

A silence hung in the air. Mrs. Thompson's eyes scanned her face, trying to piece it together, but there was no softness in her expression.

Melody could feel the unspoken judgment. Maybe it was just the way she was looking at her, but it was there.

"I can't keep pretending everything's okay," Melody whispered, finally letting it spill out. "It's not just at home. It's everything. There's someone... someone who's made me feel like I matter. Even if it's messed up. But I can't..." She stopped herself, realizing she had said too much.

Mrs. Thompson leaned forward now, her eyes narrowing. "Someone? What do you mean, Melody?"

Melody tensed, unsure of how much to reveal. She could feel the urge to protect Lucian, even if it meant staying silent.

Instead, she just muttered, "Nothing. It's... nothing."

Mrs. Thompson's gaze didn't soften. She sighed, pressing her lips together in something close to frustration. "You need to deal with your home situation first. And we need to talk about what's really going on. If you're not going to be honest with me, I can't help you."

Melody felt a sinking feeling in her chest. The weight of her secrets, of Lucian, seemed too much for the cold indifference in Mrs. Thompson's voice.

When Melody didn't respond, Mrs. Thompson's voice turned firm. "You don't get to pick and choose what parts of this we address. If there's something you're not telling me, it'll only make things worse. I need to hear everything...now."

Melody looked down, her hands trembling harder now. The silence pressed in, louder than anything she could say.

Finally, with a whisper, she said, "Can I show you something?"

Mrs. Thompson nodded curtly, but her expression remained impassive as Melody pulled up the sleeve of her hoodie, revealing the fading red lines etched into her skin.

There was no gasp. No comforting words. Mrs. Thompson only glanced at the marks, eyes hardening.

"You need help, Melody. You can't keep doing this to yourself."

"I don't know how to stop," Melody whispered, the tears she hadn't allowed to fall until now threatening to spill over.

Mrs. Thompson didn't move. She simply reached for the phone, her fingers tapping the numbers with mechanical precision. "I'm calling your parents. We need to address this. You can't ignore what's happening."

Melody's chest tightened as she sat there, the walls closing in around her. She felt more alone than ever.

When the door finally creaked open, Andrew and Charlotte emerged from the guidance counselors office, their faces hollow, as if drained by something heavy. They didn't speak to her, and the silence between them all was deafening.

"Time to go, Melody," Charlotte snapped, her voice sharp enough to cut.

Melody barely nodded, swallowing the lump in her throat as she stood and followed them out into the parking lot. Her legs felt like lead, each step heavier than the last as they made their way to the car. The sunlight, harsh and unforgiving, felt like it was pressing down on her, suffocating her.

She slid into the back seat, the door closing with a soft thud that felt far too final. The car rumbled to life, but the only sound was the engine. Nobody spoke. The tension in the air was thick and oppressive.

Melody leaned her forehead against the cool glass of the window, her eyes tracing the blurred landscape outside. The world moved by in flashes—rusted fences, abandoned buildings, streets she didn't recognize. Her stomach twisted in knots. There was a feeling of being pulled further away from everything familiar, slipping into something darker, something she couldn't name.

"Where are we going?" she finally whispered, her voice barely audible.

Andrew didn't look at her, his eyes focused straight ahead, the muscles in his jaw working like he was trying to keep something hidden. "Out for pizza," he said flatly.

Her stomach dropped. Something about it didn't sit right. She glanced out the window again, the passing scenery a blur of unfamiliar streets. Her skin prickled, and she couldn't shake the sense that they weren't headed anywhere normal. The air outside felt thick, suffocating. It was wrong.

The trees began to close in around them, the road narrowing, winding through unfamiliar, isolated areas. Everything looked older, worn out. Melody's chest tightened with each turn, her breath coming in shallow gasps.

They turned down a road that felt like it went on forever, a stretch of nothingness. The air was dense with the scent of damp earth, and the trees grew closer, their bare branches swaying like skeletal hands. She felt trapped in the car, the walls of it closing in around her.

Then, through the windshield, she saw it.

A faded sign, swinging loosely above a rusted gate: *Forestwood*.

Her heart froze. The panic bubbling up her throat.

This wasn't a pizza place.

"Dad?" she choked out, her voice trembling.

Andrew didn't answer. His hands gripped the steering wheel so tight his knuckles were white. The muscles in his face twitched, but he kept his gaze fixed straight ahead.

Charlotte's head turned slowly toward Melody, and her smile was cold, too wide, like it had been stretched too far. There was no warmth in it, no care. Just a flat, emotionless expression that made Melody's stomach churn.

"Get out of the car, Melody," Charlotte ordered, her voice hard and final.

Melody didn't move immediately. Her hand hovered above the door handle, the feeling of dread creeping over her. The words didn't make sense. *Forestwood*. The name sounded foreign, sickening. She was frozen, unable to process the reality of it, her thoughts spinning in circles.

For a moment, the world outside the window went silent, as if everything was holding its breath. Melody wanted to speak, *this isn't right, please, take me home*, but the words stuck in her throat.

Charlotte's patience snapped.

"Get out of the car, Melody!" she barked, her voice now sharp and biting, echoing off the walls of the car. "I don't have time for this."

The force of Charlotte's command struck like a whip, making Melody flinch. Her chest tightened, and the panic hit her in full force. The door clicked open, but Melody didn't move. She just sat there, staring out at the bleak, ominous entrance of Forest-wood. She couldn't make her body move. Every part of her screamed to run, to fight, to do something, but her legs wouldn't obey.

Charlotte's gaze darkened, her jaw clenched as she leaned over, grabbed the door handle, and pulled it open with a violent yank.

"Get. Out," she hissed.

Melody hesitated, her breath coming fast, the air thick and suffocating. She could feel the weight of Charlotte's anger pressing on her like a physical force, suffocating her. Melody stumbled out of the car, legs shaky, her feet dragging on the cracked pavement. The air outside was cold, the wind biting at her skin.

As the car door slammed behind her, the sound reverberated like a final judgment.

She stood there, frozen, the ground beneath her feet feeling like it was shifting. The heavy iron gates of Forestwood loomed in front of her, the name mocking her as it seemed to pulse in her mind.

She couldn't move. Every instinct screamed for her to run, but her body betrayed her. The world around her felt suffocating.

This was it. This was the moment she couldn't escape from.

CHAPTER EIGHTEEN

The cold, sterile atmosphere of the intake room only made the tightness in Melody's chest worse. Fluorescent lights flickered overhead, casting a harsh glow that only made everything feel more unsettling. The nurse behind the desk, a middle-aged woman with glasses perched on the end of her nose, shuffled through papers as Melody, Andrew, and Charlotte stood in silence.

"Please, I don't belong here," Melody whispered, her voice barely audible, the words tumbling out as she tried to make herself understood. "I'm fine. I'll get better, I promise. Just don't leave me here."

Her heart raced as she looked from one face to the other. Andrew's was etched with concern, but there was something else. Something heavy and hopeless that made her stomach drop. Charlotte's expression was cold, her arms crossed over her chest, distant as ever.

The nurse didn't respond immediately. She continued flipping through papers, her voice even and neutral as she finally broke the silence. "We're going to need you both to sign these forms," she said, handing over a clipboard and pen to Andrew.

"It's standard procedure. Once the paperwork is done, we'll go over what to expect during the next week."

Andrew looked down at the forms, his brow furrowed, his jaw tight. Melody could see the strain in his shoulders, the uncertainty in his eyes. She tried again, her voice trembling as she reached out to him.

"Dad, please... don't leave me here. Please, I'll stop. I won't cut myself anymore. I swear. I'll do whatever it takes. Just don't leave me."

But Andrew's face remained unchanged. He glanced at Charlotte, who was watching Melody with that same cold indifference, then back at the forms in his hands.

"I don't have a choice, Melody," he said quietly, his voice thick with emotion. "I'm concerned about you. I'm afraid you're going to hurt yourself. Whether on purpose or by accident. This is what's best."

Melody's heart shattered at his words, the finality of them cutting through her like a blade. She shook her head, tears welling up in her eyes as she turned her gaze to the nurse, then back to Andrew.

"No... No, I won't do it anymore! Please!" She could feel the panic rising in her chest, her voice cracking as she spoke. "I'll stop! I promise. Please don't leave me here, please..."

But Andrew was already signing the paperwork. Melody's stomach twisted, her hands trembling at her sides as she watched him. The weight of his decision hit her like a punch to the gut, and she could barely breathe.

Charlotte, who had been standing off to the side with her arms crossed, finally spoke, her voice as cold and final as ever. "That's enough, Melody. You're staying here. End of story."

Melody's heart felt like it stopped beating. Her entire world seemed to fall apart at that moment. The rage that had been building inside her for weeks, months, finally exploded.

"You did this to me!" Melody shouted, her voice raw and frantic. "You've always wanted me out of the picture! You've always wanted me gone, and now you finally got your way! I'm nothing to you! You don't care!"

The words tumbled out in a torrent, fury and grief mixing into an uncontrollable force. Charlotte stood there, unmoved, while Andrew's face twisted in pain, but he said nothing. It was like he couldn't even look at her.

The room felt like it was closing in around her, her vision swimming as her emotions surged. The helplessness, the betrayal, the deep, gnawing pain of it all became too much to bear.

Without thinking, Melody shoved one of the chairs across the room. It crashed against the wall with a deafening noise. Then, she grabbed another, hurling it with all the force she could muster. It tipped over and slammed to the ground with a violent clatter.

"Stop! Stop it!" the nurse yelled, her voice high-pitched and frantic as she backed away. She quickly grabbed the phone on her desk, her fingers trembling as she called for help.

"Get security in here, now!" she shouted.

But Melody was beyond hearing her. The fury inside her was all-consuming. She threw another chair, then swiped at the desk, knocking over a stack of papers. She didn't care anymore. She didn't care about anything but the white-hot rage that coursed through her veins.

"I'll never forgive you!" she screamed, her voice wild with fury. "You're monsters! You did this to me!"

Security burst through the door, two large men who quickly grabbed hold of Melody, their grips tight and unyielding. She fought against them, kicking and thrashing, but they were too strong. She screamed again, but it was lost in the chaos as they dragged her out of the room, one of them holding her arms behind her, the other walking in front of her to keep her from thrashing too violently.

"Let me go! Let me go!" Melody yelled, her voice breaking

with desperation. She kicked her legs, trying to break free, but it was hopeless.

As they hauled her down the hallway, her mind spun. She couldn't stop thinking about what she had just said. She was right. They had done this to her. They had always made her feel like she didn't belong, like she was a problem to be fixed, and now she was paying the price.

She twisted her head to look back at them one last time.

"I'll never forgive you!" she screamed again, her voice raw and hoarse. "I hate you!"

Andrew was standing there, frozen, his face pale. Charlotte stood next to him, her arms still crossed, as cold and unfeeling as ever. Melody's chest tightened as she met Charlotte's eyes one last time, expecting to see nothing but that same indifferent, emotionless mask.

But instead, something in Charlotte's expression shifted— just for a moment. A slow, deliberate smile spread across her face, one that felt as cold and calculating as the rest of her.

The shock hit Melody like a physical blow, her throat closing up as she stared at her mother. That smile, it wasn't a smile of comfort or reassurance. It was the smile of someone who had won. Someone who had finally gotten what they wanted.

Melody's heart pounded in her chest, and for a split second, it was as if the ground beneath her was shaking.

And as the door slammed shut behind her, as the sounds of her screams faded into the distance, Melody's heart shattered. She had never felt so alone in her life.

The hallway felt like it was a mile long. The linoleum floors echoed with the shuffle of her sneakers as the guards led her forward, their grip still firm on her arms. Melody's breath hitched with each step, her chest burning from the screaming, her throat raw. The walls were painted a dull, sterile blue that made her feel like she was fading into nothing.

They turned a corner and led her through a heavy door that locked behind them with a mechanical *click*. A new room—smaller, quieter, but no less cold—waited for her. An examination table stood in the center, and a plastic chair sat in the corner beside a large plastic bin. A different nurse stood waiting for her now. She was younger than the last, maybe in her thirties, her brown hair pulled tightly into a bun. She didn't smile. Her face was serious, but not unkind.

"We need to do a quick intake check," the nurse said. "Please stand over there."

Melody stood stiffly in the center of the room, arms shaking slightly, her eyes darting between the nurse and the door. The two men let go of her and stepped back but didn't leave.

"I'm going to need you to remove your belt, your shoelaces, and any straps on your pants," the nurse said, reaching for a clear bag with a clipboard attached. "We'll also take any jewelry or other items that could be used to hurt yourself."

Melody blinked. "Why?" she croaked.

"It's policy," the nurse replied gently. "We have to remove anything that could be used for self-harm. Even if you say you're not going to hurt yourself right now... our job is to make sure you stay safe."

Melody's hands hovered at her belt, but she didn't move. "But I don't... I don't have any other clothes."

"I spoke with your parents before you got here," the nurse said, making a quick note on the clipboard. "They're going to bring you what you need. For now, we'll get you set up with something clean and temporary."

The word *parents* made Melody's stomach twist violently. She turned her head away as she slowly slipped the belt from the loops of her pants, her fingers clumsy and trembling. It felt like giving away the last bit of control she had.

When she looked back up, the nurse was watching her closely.

"I need to ask you something," she said, her tone measured but gentle. "What happened back there, in the intake room? That was a big outburst."

Melody's eyes dropped to the floor. Her jaw clenched. She didn't want to talk. She didn't trust this place. She didn't trust *anyone*.

"I don't know," she muttered.

"You seemed really upset," the nurse said, her voice calm, her eyes not leaving Melody's face. "Angry. Hurt. Like something's been building for a long time."

Melody didn't respond. The nurse gave her a moment, then continued.

"I know this probably feels like a punishment. But it's not. You're here because someone's worried about you... and because something's clearly not okay."

Melody's eyes flickered upward, filled with silent rage and confusion. "What's the point of talking?" she mumbled. "No one ever listens."

The nurse crouched a bit so they were eye level.

"I'm listening," she said. "And I mean it when I say this: it'll be a lot easier for you in here if you talk about what's going on. You don't have to say everything right now. But shutting down, holding it all in... that's only going to make things harder."

Melody swallowed hard. Her arms folded over her stomach like a shield, her body closing in on itself. For a moment, she looked so much younger than she was—scared, heartbroken, and drowning in silence.

"I just..." she whispered, her voice barely audible. "I don't think I can trust anybody anymore."

The nurse nodded, as if she expected that.

"Then let's start with something small," she said. "You don't have to trust me yet. But let me prove that I'll be here when you're ready."

She handed Melody a plain, folded set of gray sweatpants and a white t-shirt—hospital clothes.

"You can change in here. I'll give you a minute."

The nurse stepped out and shut the door gently behind her. Melody stood there alone, holding the clothes in her arms, feeling like they weighed a thousand pounds. She stared at the wall, her eyes burning.

In that moment, she didn't know how she was supposed to survive a week in this place.

But somewhere, beneath the numbness and the fear, a tiny voice inside her whispered: *Maybe this is where you finally start to fight back.*

The silence in the room was loud.

After the chaos of intake, after the yelling, the restraints, the cold fluorescent lights that hummed overhead like they were alive—now, it was just Melody, a duffel bag, and four walls that felt far too close.

The nurse had walked her in with a few final instructions, a clipboard to sign, and a pat phrase about "adjustment taking time." Then she left her alone.

Melody sat stiffly on the edge of the twin bed, the mattress too firm, the corners tightly tucked in with military precision. The bedding smelled like bleach and plastic—nothing soft, nothing comforting. Just clean, cold sterility.

She finally unzipped the duffel bag.

Her stomach dropped.

Pink.

Everything was pink.

Shirts, sweatpants, underwear, socks, even the stupid cropped hoodie. All in various shades of blush and baby pink and bubblegum. Not a single black tank top. No band tees. No ripped jeans. Not even a hoodie she could hide in.

Melody swallowed hard, her hands balling into fists as she pulled out the folded clothes one by one, each item a slap in the face. She could see Charlotte's smug satisfaction all over this. This wasn't just carelessness. It was calculated.

A knock on the open door made her jolt. She quickly shoved the clothes back in the bag, her body tense like a cornered animal.

A girl about her age stood just outside the doorway, arms crossed, chewing on the corner of her sleeve. Her hair was bleached to hell and cut short in uneven choppy layers, and her hoodie sleeves had been cut off at the elbows. Her eyes flicked from Melody's face to the pink clothes in her lap.

"Let me guess," the girl said, her voice dry. "Mom's a piece of shit?"

Melody didn't answer. She looked down, focusing on smoothing the crumpled hoodie in her lap.

The girl shrugged and leaned against the doorframe. "Cool. I'm Ivy. You don't have to talk or whatever. Just figured you might wanna know the bathrooms are rank after nine p.m., and don't drink the orange juice at breakfast. It's, like, not real orange juice. It's... glue."

Melody gave a tiny nod but didn't look up.

Ivy stared a second longer, then pushed herself off the frame and started to leave.

"Thanks," Melody said softly, surprising herself.

Ivy paused and glanced over her shoulder. "You'll get used to it. Or you won't. Either way, nobody here's watching to see if you cry."

She was gone a second later.

That night, Melody lay on top of the blanket in the ridiculous pink hoodie.

Sleep didn't come.

She stared at the ceiling, trying to keep her thoughts from sinking too deep, but they kept circling the drain.

What had she done to end up here? What had she done wrong? She thought of Andrew. The guilt on his face. The way his hand shook as he signed the paperwork. She thought of Charlotte's smile—cold and satisfied.

She felt like a prisoner, not just in this facility, but in her life.

And then, Lucian.

His voice was softer in her memory now, like a song played through a closed door. The way he talked to her, listened to her. Told her she wasn't broken, even when she felt completely shattered. She didn't know what to think about him anymore. She just knew she missed him. The sound of his voice, the way he made her feel like she mattered.

But did she still matter to him?

Her phone was gone. They took it from her at intake and gave it to her parents. She didn't even get a chance to text him, to explain where she was going, or why. Not that she could've. There wasn't even time to think.

Was he wondering where she was? Had he called her, messaged her? Did he think she was ignoring him? Pulling away?

Or did he not care at all?

They hadn't exactly left things on the best note. He was angry at her the last time they talked. He was jealous, accusing her of spending too much time with Jace. He said she'd been distant, like she was pulling away, and he didn't know where he stood with her anymore. He said he needed space.

She couldn't remember if she'd told him she loved him. Maybe he thought she didn't. Maybe he was already moving on. She pictured him on his couch, scrolling through his phone, maybe seeing her name and choosing not to open the message.

The thought stung.

A part of her still wanted him to come rescue her, to break through the doors and drag her out of this place like the hero in a movie. But that was just a fantasy. Real life didn't work like that. People didn't come for you. They left. Or worse...they forgot.

Melody turned onto her side and clutched the pillow tight against her chest.

It was hours before she finally drifted off.

Screaming.

The sound tore through the stillness like a blade.

Melody sat bolt upright in bed, her heart racing, confusion clouding her vision. The scream was close—*too* close.

Before she could make sense of what was happening, her door burst open with a loud bang.

A small boy, no older than eight or nine, rushed into the room, shrieking at the top of his lungs. His eyes were wide, unfocused, and brimming with panic. He threw himself against the far wall of her room, slamming his head into the cinderblock with a sickening crack.

Thud. Thud. Thud.

Melody froze, her mouth open but no sound coming out. The boy screamed again, a raw, primal noise that cut through her. He began pounding his fists against the floor, then turned and rammed his head against the wall over and over.

The door flew open again, and a heavyset guard rushed in behind him. "Jayden! Stop! That's enough!"

The boy didn't stop. He didn't even seem to hear.

Another guard came in moments later. It took both of them to wrestle the child off the floor. His arms flailed, his face a twisted mask of rage and terror. He kicked and screamed as they dragged him from the room, his voice echoing down the hall, childlike and cracked, and somehow already echoing like a memory.

Melody sat frozen on the bed, her knees drawn up to her chest, staring at the scuff marks on the wall where his head had struck.

When the door finally shut, she leaned forward and locked it with trembling fingers. Then she pressed her back against it, as if that might somehow keep the world out.

This place wasn't just a hospital.

It was a cage full of ghosts that screamed at night.

And for the first time since being admitted, she realized: they didn't put people here to get better.

They put them here to forget them.

CHAPTER NINETEEN

Morning came like a punishment.

The overhead light buzzed to life before the sun even had a chance to rise, and Melody blinked against the sterile glare. Her limbs felt heavy, her thoughts fogged by broken sleep and the memory of screams still echoing faintly in her ears. She wasn't sure if it had really happened or if it had been some fever dream stitched together by her exhausted mind.

But when she pressed her ear against the door, the silence was too still. Too clean. It happened.

She changed into the least pink outfit she could find—a white tee and grey sweats, and padded down the hall with the other girls, quiet as ghosts.

The showers were down another corridor, sectioned off from the rest of the unit. Cold tile, buzzing fluorescents, and the faint smell of mildew met her as she stepped inside. She clutched her towel tighter.

"Hey," said a woman in light blue scrubs, an aide Melody hadn't seen before. She looked about thirty, with a clipboard and tired eyes. "You'll need to leave the door open during your shower."

Melody stopped in her tracks. "What?"

"It's just policy. Safety precaution."

Her stomach twisted. "Can I at least close it partway? Just a little?"

The woman shook her head. "Sorry, no. Has to stay fully open. We can't risk anyone hurting themselves."

Melody didn't move. She could feel the burn rising in her chest, the sting of humiliation waiting just beneath her skin. "I'm not going to hurt myself."

The aide's voice softened, but her stance didn't budge. "I hear you. But that's not up to me. It's the rule."

For a second, Melody thought about turning around and just walking out. But the grime of the last day clung to her skin, and all she wanted was ten minutes under the water to pretend that she was somewhere else.

Her hand hovered on the doorframe, knuckles white. A fresh pang bloomed in her chest, not just from the humiliation, but from something gentler and more aching.

She wondered if Wednesday was okay.

Her sweet, skittish cat, probably curled up on her unmade bed, waiting. Or hiding beneath it, scared by the shouting, confused by her absence.

Melody pictured those round, yellow eyes peering out at the door every time it creaked open, hoping it would be her. Missing her.

The thought pierced deeper than she expected.

She blinked fast, swallowing the lump in her throat.

She hesitated, her grip tightening around the towel, then finally gave a small, bitter nod.

"Fine."

She stepped inside, placed the towel on the hook, and pulled the thin curtain shut, knowing it wouldn't really hide her. The cool air kissed her bare skin, and she stood under the lukewarm stream, arms wrapped tightly around herself.

Even here, there was no privacy. No peace. Just walls and

watchers and the sense that someone, somewhere, was always waiting for her to slip.

The cafeteria was loud in a way that didn't make sense. The kind of loud where nobody was really talking, but trays clattered, chairs scraped, and somewhere off to the side, someone was humming tunelessly under their breath.

Melody stepped in hesitantly, scanning the room.

Ivy spotted her and waved her over.

"Word of advice?" Ivy said as Melody joined her. "Don't eat the hot food unless you want your insides to die a slow, tragic death."

Melody glanced at the trays. Rubber eggs, grayish sausage links. Her stomach twisted.

"What do you eat then?" she asked.

"Cereal. If you're lucky, they have the good stuff."

Melody stepped into the line and, miraculously, there it was —Lucky Charms.

She grabbed a bowl and poured some of the cereal into it.

"I love the marshmallows," she mumbled, almost to herself.

Ivy grinned. "Same. Only reason to eat it."

They sat down at a corner table. Melody stirred her spoon through the floating bits of color, the milk slowly turning pastel. For the first time since arriving, something felt... not okay, but manageable.

Then came the voice.

"No, I won't do it. I won't do it. No, no, no..."

Melody turned toward the sound. A girl at a nearby table, maybe sixteen, was rocking in her seat, her eyes wide and distant. She was speaking to no one, or maybe to someone Melody couldn't see.

"No, I *won't* do it!"

Then she stood. Her tray clattered to the ground. Her hands shook.

"I won't hurt them! I *won't!*"

In one sharp motion, she grabbed her tray and flung it at the wall. It hit with a metallic crash, food splattering across the linoleum.

A guard was there within seconds.

The girl screamed again as he approached—not in anger, but in pure, raw panic.

They spoke softly to her at first. The girl pressed her hands over her ears, eyes squeezed shut, her whole body trembling. Finally, the guard reached out and gently guided her away, her voice trailing off in broken fragments.

Melody sat frozen.

"What... what was that?" she asked quietly.

Ivy's face was calm, but sad.

"That's Dani," she said. "She has schizophrenia. Sometimes the voices get too loud. They scare her."

Melody glanced toward the spot where Dani had stood, now just a smear of eggs and cereal on the floor.

"She thought she might hurt someone?"

Ivy nodded. "She wouldn't, though. She's kind. But when your brain is screaming at you... it's hard to know what's real."

"Where are they taking her?"

"The quiet room," Ivy said. "It's supposed to help people calm down. But mostly... it just makes them feel alone."

Melody watched the hallway where Dani had disappeared, the silence that followed feeling heavier than the outburst, like the walls themselves were holding their breath.

Later that morning, a staff member appeared in the doorway with a clipboard pressed to her chest.

"Melody Rayne?" she asked.

Melody stood slowly. Her legs still felt heavy, like the silence after Dani's outburst had settled into her bones.

She followed the aide down a corridor that seemed trapped in time. Its beige walls scuffed and dented, the flickering overhead lights casting an anemic glow. It smelled like stale air and industrial soap, mixed with the faint, lingering trace of something metallic, like pennies on a radiator. The kind of hallway where time moved sluggishly and whispers felt too loud.

They stopped outside a plain door with a small plaque: *Dr. R. Halvorsen, M.D.*

Inside, the office was surprisingly warm. Not cozy, but lived-in. There were books crammed into mismatched shelves, a coffee mug with a chip in the rim, and a half-dead plant on the windowsill that looked like it was trying its best. A single ticking clock provided the only sound.

The man behind the desk stood as she entered. He looked to be in his early fifties, with soft gray hair and eyes that saw more than they said.

"Dr. Halvorsen," he said, extending a hand. "You can call me Rick, if that's easier."

Melody didn't take his hand. She just sat.

He didn't seem offended. Just nodded and lowered himself into his chair.

"You don't have to talk today," he said. "But if you're going to be here for a while, I figured we might as well meet."

She said nothing. Her arms folded tightly across her chest.

He reached for a manila folder, opened it briefly, then closed it again. "So. Melody. Why do you think you're here?"

She stared at the plant on the windowsill. "Because my mom doesn't want to deal with me."

His eyebrows lifted slightly. "That sounds like a story."

"It's not," she said flatly. "She thinks I'm being dramatic. She said I was trying to embarrass her."

He leaned back slightly, elbows resting on the arms of his chair. "Is that something you do often? Embarrass her?"

Melody gave a short, bitter laugh. "Apparently. Existing does the trick."

He didn't interrupt, didn't rush her. The silence between them was open, not empty.

"She's always been like that," Melody said eventually. "Everything's about her. If I cry, I'm doing it *at* her. If I get upset, I'm punishing *her*."

"And your dad?" Dr. Halvorsen asked gently.

Melody's expression shuttered. "He's... gone a lot. He works on the pipe-line. Sometimes he's gone for days at a time."

"Does he check in?"

She hesitated. "Sometimes."

"Do you feel like he sees you?"

She looked at him sharply, then dropped her gaze to the floor. "I don't know."

"Or hears you?"

She shrugged, but her voice cracked just slightly. "I guess I stopped trying to make him."

Halvorsen waited a moment before speaking again.

"I'm not here to force anything out of you, Melody. But you don't have to protect people who have hurt you. Not in here."

That made her eyes flash, just for a second. Not with anger— but with something messier. Wounded. Uncertain.

"I'm not protecting anyone," she muttered. "Some things just... aren't anybody else's business."

He nodded like that was a fair answer.

"I get that," he said. "I do. But I'll still be here. Every morning. Same chair. Same plant that refuses to die."

That coaxed the faintest twitch of a smile from her lips. It didn't reach her eyes, but it tried.

She stood, wrapping her arms tighter around herself. "Are we done?"

"For today, yeah," he said. "Thanks for showing up."

She opened the door without another word, but before she stepped out, he added, "Melody?"

She paused in the doorway.

"Just because you've learned to carry the weight doesn't mean you're meant to."

The common room buzzed with quiet movement as the nurse's cart rolled in. A few patients shuffled over without being called, like they'd done this routine a hundred times before.

Melody hung back, unsure. Ivy nudged her lightly with an elbow.

"That's med time," Ivy said. "They come around a couple times a day. Don't worry, you'll get used to it."

"I'm supposed to take something?" Melody asked, furrowing her brow.

"If your parents signed off, yeah," Ivy said. "Most people here are on something. Helps take the edge off."

The nurse called her name, and Melody stepped forward, unsure whether to trust the outstretched paper cup and tiny pill inside.

"What is it?" she asked.

The nurse checked her chart. "Prozac. Antidepressant. Your parents approved it."

Melody stared at the pill like it might bite her. "They didn't tell me."

"They don't have to," the nurse said matter-of-factly. "But you have the right to know what you're taking. It's up to you."

Melody hesitated, the cup trembling slightly in her hand. A silence stretched.

Then Ivy's voice cut through. "We're gonna be late to group."

Melody glanced at her, then back at the nurse—and with a resigned breath, she tipped the pill into her mouth and took the offered water.

It left a chalky aftertaste that clung to her tongue.

As they walked down the hall together, Ivy kept her voice low. "First time's always weird. Just don't psych yourself out about it. If it helps, great. If it doesn't, they'll try something else."

Melody nodded absently, her thoughts already spiraling inward. But she followed anyway, toward the echo of voices down the hall.

Group therapy was about to begin.

The room for group therapy wasn't what Melody expected. No sterile white walls or metal folding chairs. It was warmer— soft yellow paint, a circle of cushioned seats, a fake ficus plant in one corner doing its best to seem real. A dry-erase board stood off to the side, yesterday's affirmations still faintly visible beneath the eraser smudges.

A man stood at the center, mid-50s, dressed in a sweater vest and slacks. His name tag read *Dr. Carson*. He had a kind face but eyes that missed nothing.

"Find a seat anywhere," Ivy whispered, nudging her toward the circle.

Melody picked a chair near the edge. Not directly beside Ivy, not too far either. Just close enough to make a quiet exit if she needed one.

Dr. Carson looked around the circle, nodding at each of them like he already knew who they were and why they'd come.

"Morning, everyone," he said. "For those who are new, I'm Dr. Carson, one of the psychiatrists here. This space is for talking, listening, and hopefully learning how to sit with what's hard. No pressure to share if you're not ready."

Melody sank lower in her chair.

"Why don't we check in?" he continued. "You can share your name, how you're feeling today, and if you want, something that's been on your mind."

A few kids went ahead—some awkward, some overly rehearsed. When it came to Ivy, she said, "Tired. A little anxious. But I'm glad Melody's here." She shot her a quick grin.

Melody gave a weak smile back, unsure how to respond.

Then Dr. Carson's gaze landed on her.

"You don't have to talk if you'd rather not," he said. "But you're welcome to."

Melody hesitated. Every part of her screamed *no*.

But the room was quiet, waiting—not demanding, just open.

"I'm Melody," she said, eyes locked on the floor. "I'm... I don't know how I'm feeling. Tired, I guess."

Dr. Carson nodded. "Thank you, Melody."

The conversation moved on, but her pulse still thudded in her ears. Names, emotions, fragments of pain passed around like secrets being folded into origami.

When the focus returned to her, it wasn't planned. Dr. Carson was asking about stress, and someone brought up family.

He glanced her way.

"Family can be complicated," he said gently. "Especially when we don't feel seen by them. Is that something you relate to?"

Melody froze. The room felt smaller.

"Sometimes," she admitted. "My mom... she doesn't really understand me."

Dr. Carson nodded slowly, giving her space.

"Want to tell us more?"

Melody shook her head. "Not right now."

"That's okay," he said. "That's enough for today."

And somehow, it felt like it was.

Evening settled over the unit in a hush.

Dinner trays had been cleared, and most of the residents had drifted off to their rooms or small huddles around board games and puzzles. Melody and Ivy claimed the worn brown couch in the common room, legs tucked under them, a muted sitcom flickering on the mounted TV. The laugh track felt distant, hollow, but not as sharp-edged as it usually did. Just... dull and quiet.

Melody sat with her arms wrapped around a throw pillow, fingers tracing the fabric absently. Her thoughts still swirled, but they felt slightly slower, like the volume had been turned down just enough to notice.

"You ever actually *like* this show?" Ivy asked, nudging her gently with her knee.

Melody gave a small shrug. "It's... okay. My brother used to watch it a lot. Before he got too cool for it."

She was surprised by the steadiness in her voice. It felt strange, almost like she was watching herself from just outside her own skin, but not in a scary way. Just... different.

Ivy smirked. "I used to love shows like this. They made life look easy. Even when people messed up, it was funny. Forgivable." Her smile faded a little. "Real life's not like that though. You mess up in real life and people treat you like you're a problem."

Melody looked at her. "You're not a problem."

Ivy was quiet for a beat. "I have borderline personality disorder," she said softly. "It means I feel everything like... times a thousand. I get scared people are going to leave, or that they hate me. Sometimes I hate myself first so they don't get the chance."

Melody's eyes stayed on the screen, but she was listening.

Ivy leaned back against the couch cushion, eyes drifting to the muted television.

"It took me a while to even know what was going on," she said. "I thought I was just broken. One of the nurses gave me this worksheet once, about emotions and impulse control. I thought it was dumb. But I tried it. Started tracking what set me off. What helped. I still suck at it sometimes, but... now I write stuff down when I feel like I'm spinning out. Just to see it. Make it real and not a monster in my head."

She glanced sideways at Melody. "I'm not saying it fixes everything. But it gives me space to pause. I need that pause."

"You don't have to tell me anything," Ivy added. "But... if you wanted to, I'd get it. Probably more than most."

Melody's voice came out low, like it wasn't meant to be said out loud.

"I was still cutting. Like... up until a couple days ago. I thought I could hide it. Just wear long sleeves and pretend every-thing was fine. But it wasn't."

Ivy didn't flinch. She just nodded slowly, her face open and soft.

"I know what that's like," she said. "For a long time, it was the only thing that made the pressure go away. Even if just for a second."

Melody swallowed hard. Her thoughts, usually jagged and relentless, seemed quieter tonight. Not gone, but padded some-how. Less violent.

"I didn't want to die. I just wanted... everything to stop for a while. The noise, the guilt, my mom's voice in my head..."

"Yeah," Ivy murmured. "I've been there. Too many times."

They sat in silence for a minute. Not uncomfortable—just still. Melody's heart didn't feel like it was about to explode from her chest for once. That alone was unsettling in its own way.

Then Ivy said, "It's visiting day tomorrow."

Melody blinked. "What?"

"Yeah. Tuesdays. Parents, guardians, whoever's listed." Ivy gave her a look. "You don't seem thrilled."

"I'm not ready," Melody admitted. "I don't want to see them. Not yet. I don't know what I'd say."

"You don't have to say anything you don't want to," Ivy said. "You can set boundaries. Or ask for staff to sit in. Or even skip it. You've got choices, Mel. Even here."

Melody let out a breath she hadn't realized she was holding. Her chest didn't feel quite so tight anymore.

"I don't feel like I have any choices. Not with them."

Ivy bumped her shoulder gently. "Then maybe that's what we figure out. Together."

The laugh track on the TV played again, but neither of them laughed. Still, for the first time that day, Melody didn't feel like crying either.

The lights in the common room dimmed as Melody stood up, feeling oddly lightheaded as the room settled into a quiet hum. The medication, still new in her system, made everything feel a little slower. A little less sharp. Her thoughts weren't racing like they usually did, there was a dullness to them, a sluggishness that made her feel both empty and... relieved.

Ivy was already heading toward her room, and Melody followed, not quite sure if she wanted the company or the solitude. The hall felt longer than usual, the overhead lights casting shadows that seemed to stretch further with each step.

When they reached their rooms, Ivy gave her a small smile and a quiet "Night," before disappearing into hers. Melody stood in front of her door, her fingers tracing the cold metal handle, her mind still swimming in the haze of the pill. Everything felt quieter. She felt quieter.

Inside, she pulled off her shoes and sat down on the edge of the bed. The room was small and plain—no extra touches, just a bed, a small nightstand, and a chair by the window. Melody swung her legs up onto the bed, the sheets soft but still unfamiliar, and pulled the blanket up, curling into the fetal position.

The quiet was almost too much. She was used to noise, the constant hum of anxiety, the crash of thoughts racing through her mind. Now, it was almost... peaceful. She didn't know if she liked it or if it scared her. She wasn't used to feeling this still.

Her chest felt heavy, thoughts of the visit with her parents tomorrow flooding in. She wasn't ready for it. She didn't know how to face them, how to tell them what she needed. What she felt. She still wasn't sure they'd even understand.

But then her mind wandered, slipping into thoughts of Lucian.

She imagined him sitting on his couch, scrolling through his phone, waiting for her messages. Was he worried? Was he thinking about her too? She hadn't heard from him in days, but what if he was still out there, looking for a way to reach her, wondering why she hadn't called? She imagined him pacing, the way he did when he was upset, but she quickly shook the thought away. She couldn't let herself think about him too much. It wasn't safe. Not right now.

Her heart ached as she wondered what he was doing. What was his life like without her in it? Did he miss her the way she missed him? Or had he moved on?

She closed her eyes tightly, trying to push the thoughts of him away, but it was hard. He was always there, lurking just beneath the surface. The pull to him, to the way he made her feel seen, heard, loved—it was something she couldn't shake. It was like a drug, and no matter how much she tried to distance herself from it, it always crept back.

He wasn't here, but the absence of him felt almost as heavy as his presence.

Melody hugged the blanket tighter around her, squeezing her eyes shut again. She just needed to sleep, to get through tonight, to make it to tomorrow. Tomorrow with her parents. Tomorrow with whatever the future held. She didn't know how to handle it, but maybe, just maybe, things would get a little clearer once she was awake again.

With a slow, shaky breath, she let herself drift off, the faint echoes of Lucian's absence still lingering at the edges of her mind.

CHAPTER TWENTY

Melody stirred beneath the blanket, her body slow to move, limbs heavy with a fog that hadn't quite lifted since yesterday. The Prozac still tugged at her mind like static, softening everything around the edges but not in a comforting way.

She didn't want to get up.

But Ivy's voice floated in from the hallway. Something about the showers being free, and that was enough to push Melody into motion. She slid out of bed, pulling her hoodie around her like armor before stepping out of her room.

The showers weren't bad, at least. Warm water. Weak pressure. But for a few minutes, she stood under the stream and let it wash over her, her thoughts swirling in the mist. She tried not to think about what the day would bring. Tried not to imagine the look on her mom's face. Or worse—no emotion at all.

Afterward, she got dressed quietly, brushing through her tangled hair with her fingers. No makeup. No accessories. No mirror.

In the cafeteria, the smell of scrambled eggs and instant oatmeal drifted through the air, but Melody barely picked at her food. Ivy talked about a funny dream she had, trying to lighten the mood, but Melody could only manage a distracted smile. Everything felt tight and distant.

By the time she was called in for her morning session with Dr. Halvorsen, she was already feeling the swirl of emotions under her skin like a pot just about to boil.

He greeted her with a nod and gestured to the seat across from him. His office had soft lighting, a rug that muffled footsteps, and a small shelf of colorful stones and calming trinkets— things that were supposed to make it easier to talk. She sank into the chair, wrapping her arms around herself.

"So, Melody," he began, his voice calm and even. "How are you feeling today?"

Melody shrugged. "Fine, I guess."

He gave her a patient look. "It's visiting day. That can bring up a lot. Especially if it's your first time seeing your parents since arriving here."

She didn't answer right away. Her eyes dropped to the corner of the desk, where a small, smooth worry stone rested, worn from use.

"I'm not excited about it," she said flatly.

"Can you tell me more about that?"

She let out a slow breath. "They're the ones who put me here. My mom... she didn't even ask how I felt about it. Just signed the papers and dropped me off like I was a broken appliance that needed fixing."

Dr. Halvorsen nodded, not interrupting.

"I know I needed help," she added quickly, before he could say it. "But it doesn't mean I'm ready to look them in the face. I'm still... angry."

"That's okay," he said gently. "It's okay to feel angry. Especially when you feel like your voice wasn't heard. Maybe today isn't about pretending everything's okay. Maybe it's just about showing up and seeing where you are."

Melody didn't respond. She wasn't sure she agreed, but she

didn't want to argue either. The idea of sitting across from her parents felt like walking into a fire.

After the session, she was guided down the hallway to the medication window. The nurse was already waiting, holding out a small paper cup with a pill inside. The same pill as yesterday.

Melody stared at it.

Her stomach turned. The dullness, the strange haze, it wasn't what she expected. It made her feel off, disconnected. Like she was walking through a dream but never quite awake.

"Something wrong?" the nurse asked.

She blinked. "No. Just tired."

She looked at the pill again.

Part of her wanted to refuse it. To say no. To take control back.

But another part, the part dreading the visitation, the confrontation, the fake smiles and tight words—wondered if it might be easier with the edges taken off.

Just one more day, she told herself. Just for this.

She tossed it back, the water lukewarm as it slid down her throat.

Then, quietly, she made her way to the common room, where chairs were already being arranged for visiting hours. She sat down in the far corner, the hum in her head returning like a fog rolling in off the sea.

And she waited.

She picked a corner seat, close enough to the door to see who came in, but far enough from the center to stay invisible. Ivy had gone off to her own visit, giving Melody a quick squeeze on the arm before disappearing through the hallway. Now, the room was slowly filling with the quiet buzz of nerves and polished shoes on linoleum.

Melody tucked her hands beneath her thighs to keep from picking at the skin around her nails.

The first to arrive was a boy she didn't know well—Tim, maybe? His mother swept in like a gust of overcompensation, carrying a bag of snacks and talking too loud, too fast. She kissed his head like he was still a child, like he hadn't tried to die two weeks ago.

Melody looked away.

Across the room, a girl with tear-streaked cheeks clung to her grandmother. There was something soft in the way they held each other, something that made Melody's chest tighten. Not jealousy, exactly, but something close.

She wondered if her own grandmother knew she was here. What had her parents told her? That she needed help? That she was being dramatic again? Maybe nothing at all. They hated involving her. Hated how she always saw through them.

Grandma never liked Charlotte. She used to say Melody's father should have left her years ago. Melody had heard it more than once, whispered in the kitchen when she thought she was asleep. That woman is poison. You'd be better off without her.

She was the only one who ever said it out loud.

Her grandmother had always felt more like a mother than the one who gave birth to her. She remembered things. She listened. She didn't need everything to be a performance.

She stared at the clock.

Ten minutes.

Another boy met with his dad, a man with calloused hands and a crumpled baseball cap he kept twisting in his lap. They didn't talk much. Just sat beside each other in silence, sipping from paper cups of vending machine coffee like it was the most normal thing in the world.

Melody wondered if Lucian was thinking about her right now.

Did he know where she was? Did he care? Had he tried to call? Had he been angry?

The thought twisted in her stomach.

He always said he could tell when something was wrong. That he just knew when she was off. Was he pacing his apartment, imagining the worst? Or was he doing what he always did when he got overwhelmed? Shutting off and disappearing into music, his phone lighting up with texts he wouldn't answer?

Would he still want her, after this?

Her foot tapped quietly beneath the chair. The Prozac made her feel like she was underwater, and even her thoughts seemed slower to form. But they still hurt.

More voices filtered in from the hallway. Mothers and fathers and siblings holding flowers, or books, or uncomfortable smiles.

And still, her parents hadn't arrived.

She pulled her hoodie tighter, feeling the tension coil around her spine.

The clock ticked.

And the air kept thickening.

She was just about to stand—maybe to leave, maybe to pace, maybe just to escape the itch crawling beneath her skin, when she heard her mother's voice.

Sharp. Controlled. Trying too hard to sound calm.

"There she is."

Melody froze before turning her head.

Charlotte stood in the doorway like she owned the place, one hand clutched around a small, designer purse, the other adjusting the strap of her fitted coat. Her blond hair was too neat, not a strand out of place. Her makeup was done, even at this hour. And next to her stood Andrew, hands shoved in his jacket pockets, shoulders slightly hunched like he wished he could shrink into the floor.

They looked exactly the same.

And nothing like parents visiting their suicidal daughter in a mental hospital.

Melody's stomach flipped.

Charlotte's eyes swept the room like she was judging the

wallpaper, before landing on Melody with a smile that didn't reach her eyes. "Hi, sweetheart."

Andrew gave a small nod. "Hey, kid."

Melody didn't move. Her legs felt like they were bolted to the floor.

Charlotte walked toward her with that tight-lipped expression she wore when she wanted the world to think everything was fine.

She leaned in for a hug that Melody didn't return.

"You look pale," Charlotte said, her voice a little too loud. "Are they feeding you enough here?"

"They're fine," Melody mumbled, pulling back.

Andrew took the chair beside her. Charlotte sat across, crossing her legs like this was brunch at a café and not a psych ward visitation room.

For a moment, none of them spoke.

Then Charlotte clapped her hands softly, like trying to lighten the mood. "Well. We're here."

Melody stared at a spot on the wall just over her mother's shoulder, her heart thudding too loudly in her chest.

She wished she could melt into the seat. Disappear. Be anywhere else.

Even Lucian's angry silence would've felt better than this.

Charlotte smoothed the hem of her coat over her knees, eyes flicking around the room like she was afraid to make contact too long with anyone who might be "too disturbed."

"So," she said, voice light and too high-pitched, "how are things here? Are you... settling in?"

Melody shrugged. "It's fine."

Andrew cleared his throat. "You look tired."

"She always looks tired," Charlotte muttered, just loud enough to sting.

Melody blinked slowly, pressing her tongue against the roof of her mouth. *Don't react.*

Charlotte leaned in slightly, adjusting a nonexistent speck on her purse. "Ivy...that's the girl you've been with, right? You've mentioned her on the phone."

Melody nodded once, guarded.

"She seems... intense," Charlotte said carefully. "I just hope you're being smart. About who you let get close to you."

Melody frowned. "What's that supposed to mean?"

"Oh, nothing," Charlotte said with a tight smile. "I just mean... it's easy to let the wrong people in. Especially when you're feeling vulnerable."

Andrew shifted in his seat. "Your mom's just worried."

Melody folded her arms. "Since when?"

Andrew looked away.

Charlotte's tone sharpened. "We wouldn't be here if we didn't care."

"You're here because you signed me away," Melody said, her voice low. "You didn't ask. You just dumped me here."

Charlotte's eyes flared. "What were we supposed to do, Melody? Pretend everything was normal? Ignore the cutting? The secrets?"

Melody's stomach twisted.

Charlotte smoothed her coat again. "You've been different. Distant. Like someone else is putting ideas in your head."

Melody's chest tightened. "What does that mean?"

Charlotte's gaze flicked toward Andrew, then back to Melody. "It means you're not the only one who notices when something feels... off."

There was a beat of silence. Melody didn't breathe.

Andrew opened his mouth like he wanted to speak, but closed it again.

Charlotte cleared her throat, her expression softening artificially. "I know you think we've been hard on you. But I'm just trying to keep you safe. Even if you can't see that right now."

Melody's voice came out flat. "You don't know anything about me."

Charlotte flinched, but didn't argue.

"I tried," she said instead. "But you never made it easy."

Melody laughed, bitter and low. "You never made it possible."

"How's Wednesday?" she asked suddenly, the question slipping out before she could stop it. Her voice cracked just slightly. "Is she okay?"

Charlotte gave a dismissive wave. "That cat? Still hiding under the couch, probably. You know how dramatic she is."

Melody's heart twisted. "She's not dramatic. She's scared. She doesn't know where I am."

Andrew cleared his throat again. "She's alright, kid. She's been sticking to your room mostly. I think she misses you."

Melody swallowed hard and nodded, her eyes burning. "I miss her too."

The silence that followed was brutal.

Charlotte's lips pressed together. "This isn't how I wanted this visit to go."

"No," Melody said quietly. "It's exactly how it always goes."

She stood up.

"Where are you going?" Charlotte asked, her voice rising just slightly.

"I don't know. Anywhere but here."

She walked out of the room, the walls closing in around her, her pulse pounding loud enough to drown everything out.

She didn't hear Andrew sigh. Didn't see Charlotte glance toward the exit like she might follow. Didn't notice the counselor watching from the hallway, eyes narrowed thoughtfully.

She just kept walking— needing air, needing distance, needing to not feel like a mistake someone was trying to erase.

Charlotte waited until Melody was out of sight before letting out a breath she'd been holding.

"Well, that went well," she muttered, picking at a loose thread on her coat sleeve.

Andrew sat heavily on the bench beside her, staring at the doorway where Melody had disappeared.

"You pushed her," he said. "You always push."

Charlotte rolled her eyes. "She's not a child anymore. She needs to start taking responsibility."

"She's fifteen."

"She's *acting* like she's thirty," Charlotte snapped. "Do you think I *wanted* to find those messages? Do you think I *wanted* to know that some man...some *creep*, is in her head?"

Andrew flinched, eyes darting around to make sure no one was close enough to overhear.

"You think she's just going to tell us the truth?" Charlotte continued, lowering her voice. "He's probably filled her head with all kinds of things. Made her feel like he's the only one who understands her."

Andrew rubbed a hand over his jaw. "She's not stupid. She has to know it's wrong."

"No," Charlotte said tightly. "She's lonely. That's worse. She'll justify anything if it feels like love."

There was a long silence.

"She looked at me like I was the villain," Andrew said, voice hollow. "Like I threw her away."

Charlotte's expression softened for a flicker of a second, but then she shook her head. "We're doing what we have to. Maybe one day she'll understand that."

Andrew stared at the floor.

Charlotte's voice dipped lower. "We can't say anything yet. Not until we know what they've documented. What she's told them. If we bring it up now, she'll just shut down—or worse, defend him."

Andrew didn't reply.

"She's going to hate us either way," he finally said.

Charlotte folded her arms. "Better she hates us and lives than loves someone who'll destroy her."

Another silence fell between them, heavier this time.

Charlotte glanced toward the hallway again.

"She'll come around," she said. "Eventually."

But the way her mouth tightened said she wasn't sure.

And the way Andrew didn't answer said he didn't believe her.

Melody pressed her back against the cool hallway wall outside the visitation room, her breath shallow, fingers trembling where they gripped the edge of her sleeve. Her skin felt too tight, her thoughts loud and echoing inside her head like footsteps in an empty tunnel.

Ground yourself, she reminded herself. *Five things you can see...*

She looked around: the flickering exit sign, a crooked "Feelings Chart" taped to the wall, the chipped corner of a picture frame, the scratch on the toe of her sock, the faint stain on the tile floor.

Four things you can touch...

Her sleeve. The rubbery seam of her wristband. The textured stitching of her pants. The cool, smooth laminate of the wall.

It wasn't magic, but it helped.

The storm inside her slowed from a scream to a hum.

She didn't cry. Not because she didn't want to, but because she couldn't. The tears had frozen somewhere in her chest, thick and heavy like tar.

She drifted back to the common room, quiet as a ghost.

She sat cross-legged on the faded common room couch, pretending to read a book she wasn't actually processing. The soft hum of fluorescent lights and the occasional squeak of shoes on the waxed floor filled the space with a strange kind of stillness.

She looked up when the door opened.

Dani walked in slowly, arms wrapped tight around herself like she was trying to hold her pieces together. Her hair was mussed, but her expression was different now—blank, maybe, or just tired in a way that went deeper than sleep.

Ivy nudged Melody gently. "That's Dani," she whispered. "They let her out."

Melody watched as Dani crossed the room and sat on the floor near the window, her gaze trained on a dust mote drifting through a sunbeam like it was something holy.

"She seems... different," Melody said.

"She always does after," Ivy replied. "The voices aren't always loud. Sometimes it's quiet. But that quiet can be just as scary."

Melody hesitated, then stood and walked a little closer. Not too close—just enough that she could speak without shouting.

"Hi," she said softly.

Dani looked up, blinking like she wasn't sure if Melody was real.

"I'm Melody," she added. "I'm... new."

Dani tilted her head slightly. "Are you scared?"

Melody was surprised by the question, and even more surprised by how easily the answer came.

"Yeah," she said. "A little."

Dani nodded like that made perfect sense. "Me too."

They sat in silence for a moment. Then Dani said, very quietly, "The marshmallows are the best part."

Melody blinked. "Of the cereal?"

Dani gave the tiniest smile. "Yeah. Lucky Charms. The colors make my brain feel soft."

Melody smiled back. "Mine too."

That night, Melody lay in her narrow bed staring at the ceiling, the rough hospital-grade sheets tucked too tightly around her legs. She hadn't said much after the visitation. No one asked her to.

The lights were dimmed, the halls quiet except for the occasional footsteps of a tech doing rounds. Ivy was already asleep across the room, her soft breaths rhythmic and comforting.

But Melody's thoughts refused to settle.

She thought about her mother's sharp voice, all sugar and poison. The way her father wouldn't meet her eyes. The questions they didn't ask. The ones she couldn't answer.

They had signed the papers. They had put her in here. They said it was for her safety, but it didn't feel like safety. It felt like abandonment with a medical wristband.

And underneath all of that—something deeper. A tug she couldn't quite name.

Do they know?

That flicker in her mother's expression, that subtle pause when she mentioned someone "putting ideas" in her head. Her dad's jaw tightening when he glanced at her folded hands.

Did they go through my phone?

The thought made her stomach twist. She turned onto her side, pressing her cheek into the pillow. The Prozac still made her feel fuzzy around the edges, like her thoughts were trying to surface through murky water.

Eventually, the haze pulled her under.

In her dream, Melody stood barefoot in the middle of a street soaked with rain, the world around her cast in violet dusk. Streetlights buzzed overhead, flickering like dying stars.

Lucian was there.

He stepped out from a doorway, dressed in black as always, his boots echoing against the wet pavement. His eyes found hers immediately.

"I've missed you," he said softly.

His voice didn't echo in the dream world—it landed heavy and slow.

Melody didn't say anything. She just stepped closer.

"You've been somewhere dark," he murmured. "I could feel it."

She nodded, her throat tight.

Lucian reached out, his fingers brushing her hair behind her ear. The touch was tender, almost reverent.

"They don't understand you like I do," he said. "They never did."

Rain started to fall again—soft at first, then harder. But neither of them moved.

"I just want to come home," she whispered, not sure what she meant by home anymore.

Lucian leaned in, pressing his forehead to hers.

"You already are."

Melody woke with a start, her pillow damp with sweat, the dream clinging to her like a second skin.

For a long time, she just lay there, the phantom weight of his hand still lingering at the curve of her jaw.

She wasn't sure if it comforted her or terrified her.

CHAPTER TWENTY-ONE

Three days had passed since the visitation with her parents, but the memory clung to her like cigarette smoke in her lungs—faint, but persistent. It lingered in her chest, in her jaw, in the hollow ache behind her eyes.

Time didn't blur here; it stretched. Long, thin hours unspooling across fluorescent-lit hallways and the low murmur of distant conversations. There were rhythms to follow—groups, meals, meds, but they felt like scaffolding around something broken.

Melody had stopped taking her meds on the third day.

She didn't like how they made her feel—slow and cotton-brained, like her thoughts were stuck underwater. So when the nurse handed her the little paper cup, she'd press the pill under her tongue, sip the water, nod politely, and walk calmly back to the bathroom.

Flush.

It was the one small rebellion she allowed herself. Quiet. Invisible. Hers.

Now she sat in her usual spot in the therapy circle, arms tucked close to her sides as Dr. Carson paced slowly in front of the group.

Dr. Carson gave a small smile, then looked around the room.

"Let's talk about something that affects most of us, whether we realize it or not—self-worth."

A few heads nodded. Others stayed still, guarded.

"Sometimes we learn who we are based on how others treat us. Parents, friends, partners. Sometimes those people lift us up. Other times…" He let the sentence trail off. "We start to believe the worst things they say about us."

Melody's stomach clenched.

"What's one thing someone told you about yourself that stuck with you?" he asked. "And do you think it was true?"

There was a long pause.

A boy across the circle muttered, "That I'm a screw-up."

Dr. Carson nodded. "Who told you that?"

"My dad."

"Do you believe it?"

The boy shrugged. "Sometimes."

Another kid said, "My mom told me I was too emotional. That I make things worse just by reacting."

"Is that how you see yourself now?"

"I don't know," she whispered.

Dr. Carson turned toward Melody, but not directly. His voice softened.

"Sometimes the people closest to us are the ones who confuse us the most about who we are. Especially if they're dealing with pain of their own."

Melody felt a lump rise in her throat.

"My mom…" Her voice cracked slightly, but she pushed through it. "She said I was a freak. Because of the way I dress. The music I like."

Ivy leaned in slightly, offering a silent kind of support.

Dr. Carson didn't interrupt.

"She makes me feel like… like I'm hard to love."

The words came out in a whisper, but they felt loud inside her chest.

Dr. Carson nodded slowly.

"Thank you for sharing that. That's incredibly brave."

He looked around the group.

"Here's something I want everyone to hear. What other people say about you doesn't define you. Especially when it's said through fear, anger, or ignorance. But those words still hurt. They stick. And part of our work here is learning how to peel them off. One belief at a time."

He stood and walked to the dry-erase board.

"I want you to write one thing you've believed about yourself that you think might not be true anymore."

As the group slowly got up, Melody stayed seated, unsure.

Ivy whispered, "You can just make something up if it helps. That's what I did the first time."

Melody stood. Walked to the board. Picked up the marker with a shaky hand.

She wrote:

"Hard to love."

Then she stepped back and stared at it.

Dr. Carson met her eyes and nodded once, like he saw her— even the parts she didn't want anyone else to see.

The group session broke apart slowly. Chairs scraped against the tile floor, a few kids muttered goodbyes, and Dr. Carson offered small nods as everyone filtered out in pairs or silence.

Melody lingered, unsure where to go or who she wanted to be around. She glanced toward the corner by the wide window and found Dani there, legs drawn up to her chest, chin resting on her knees, staring out at the gray sky.

Melody approached quietly.

"Hey," she said softly.

Dani looked over but didn't speak right away. Her eyes were distant, like she was still halfway inside whatever memory Dr. Carson had stirred up.

Melody sat on the floor beside her, not too close.

After a beat, Dani said, "You wrote something real."

Melody swallowed. "Yeah. I wasn't going to. But it just... came out."

Dani gave a tiny nod. "Mine used to be 'worthless.' I wrote that every time. Over and over. I still think it some days."

Melody picked at a loose thread on her sleeve. "Do you still believe it?"

"Depends," Dani said. "On how loud the voices are. On how quiet the world is."

Melody nodded slowly. "Yeah. I get that."

A silence settled between them, not heavy, but present. The kind that invited truth if either of them was ready for it.

"I liked what you said," Dani added after a moment. "About feeling hard to love. I think a lot of us feel that. Even if we don't say it."

"I wish I didn't," Melody said. "But... when someone says it enough, you start to wonder if they're right."

Dani leaned her head against the wall, letting her eyes close for a second. "That's what they count on. That you'll believe them instead of yourself."

Melody stared at her. The words settled in her chest like something sacred. Or maybe just honest.

"Thanks," she said quietly.

Dani opened one eye and gave her a faint, tired smile. "You don't have to thank me. Just... don't disappear in here, okay?"

Melody nodded. "Okay."

They sat in silence after that, the two of them side by side beneath a buzzing light, both pretending they weren't trying to keep the cracks from spreading.

That night, Melody lay in bed staring at the water-stained ceiling, the soft creak of the old building settling around her like a lullaby gone wrong.

Dani's words echoed faintly in her mind, *don't disappear in here.*

She didn't want to. But she didn't know how to stay, either. Not when her thoughts kept drifting back to everything she'd left behind.

Not when the edges of her reality kept blurring with the quiet ache that came from missing someone she wasn't supposed to miss.

Her eyes fluttered shut.

And in that half-conscious breath between awareness and dreaming, Lucian found her.

The world around her shifted. The white cinderblock walls of the facility gave way to something deeper. A dim room washed in red lamplight. Incense curling from a ceramic holder. Heavy curtains drawn against the outside world.

Lucian was there, sitting on the floor, back against a wall, legs stretched out. He looked up at her and smiled like she was the only thing that ever made sense.

"There you are," he said, voice smooth.

Melody moved to him, knees hitting the carpet with a soft *thud.* "I missed you," she whispered.

He reached for her hand—warm, familiar, safe. "I've been thinking about you every night."

She leaned her head against his shoulder, breathing in the scent of clove and something darker. "It's so quiet here," she said. "Like I'm screaming but no one hears it."

"I hear you," he murmured, brushing her hair back gently. "I always hear you."

Tears welled in her eyes, but they didn't fall. "Do you think I'm a freak?"

Lucian pulled back just enough to meet her gaze, eyes burning with that strange, devoted intensity. "You're the only real one, Melody. Everyone else is just scared of what they don't understand."

She closed her eyes, letting the weight of his words wrap around her. In the dream, she wasn't a patient. She wasn't broken or misunderstood.

She was wanted.

Safe.

Loved.

And then the world began to flicker, like a candle running out of wax. His face dimmed. The warmth cooled. She tried to hold on, but the dream was already slipping—

She woke up with a jolt, breath caught in her throat.

The dorm was dark and still. No red light, no incense. Just the low hum of a distant exit sign and the rustle of another girl shifting in her sleep.

Melody rolled over, the ghost of his voice still tangled in her ears.

You're the only real one.

She lay still, heart thudding slow and strange in her chest.

It had felt so real.

Lucian's touch. His voice. The way he looked at her like she wasn't just another broken girl in a locked building. Like she was whole to him—sacred, even.

She turned onto her side, clutching the edge of her blanket, trying to hold onto the last trace of that warmth. But it was already fading, leaving behind the cold shape of longing.

It wasn't just missing him. It was missing the way she felt when she was with him, like she mattered. Like her weirdness wasn't something to be ashamed of, but something to be adored.

Here, she was just another chart. Another dosage. Another diagnosis.

But with him...

Melody exhaled slowly. Her throat ached.

She knew what Dr. Halvorsen would say. That the mind clings to what feels comforting in times of uncertainty. That dreams sometimes mask what we're not ready to face.

But she didn't *want* to face it. Not the silence. Not the pills she wasn't taking. Not the eyes watching her through observation glass.

In the dream, Lucian hadn't judged her. He hadn't asked her to explain why she was falling apart.

He'd just held her.

And that—that made it harder.

Because she wasn't stupid. She knew she wasn't supposed to miss someone like him. She knew it didn't make sense that the only place she felt safe anymore was in a memory that wasn't even fully real.

But the feeling stayed with her, curling around her ribs like smoke.

She blinked against the sting behind her eyes, then pulled the covers over her head.

She didn't want to think. Didn't want to feel.

Not now.

Not when morning was only a few hours away, and the real world was waiting on the other side of the sunrise.

A dull clatter in the hallway stirred Melody from sleep.

Light filtered through the narrow window, striping the wall in fractured beams. Somewhere outside her door, a janitor's cart squeaked along the floor. Plastic wheels turning over waxed tile, a soft swish of mop water sloshing in its bucket.

She lay there for a moment, the thin blanket bunched at her waist, her body still heavy with the residue of the dream.

Lucian.

His voice still echoed somewhere in the back of her mind—gentle, low, too vivid for comfort. She could almost feel the warmth of his hand on hers, even now. The way he'd looked at her. Like he saw straight through her armor.

She swallowed hard and pushed the thought away.

It was morning. It was real. And she had two days left in here.

Two more days of group sessions and pill cups. Of bland food and stares and trying to remember which parts of herself were safe to show.

She swung her legs over the edge of the bed, toes curling against the cold tile. The silence of the room pressed in, familiar but no less hollow.

She hadn't taken her medication again yesterday. She'd smiled at the tech, nodded, tucked the pill under her tongue, and spit it out into a tissue in the bathroom. Flushed it like she had the past three mornings. She didn't like the fog it wrapped around her brain. It felt like someone else was living in her skin.

Still, she knew she couldn't keep this up forever. Not once she left.

But that was two days from now.

Today, she had to keep moving. Pretend it was okay. Pretend *she* was okay.

Melody dressed in the usual: the softest pants they'd let her keep and a worn pink t-shirt. Her cropped pink hoodie— no drawstrings. Too dangerous. She tied her hair back with the elastic Ivy had smuggled in for her. Small acts of rebellion. Tiny islands of control.

The common room was half-full by the time she got there. Dani sat by the window again, tracing the glass with her fingertip like she was drawing invisible maps.

Melody grabbed a bowl of oatmeal, took a seat by the wall, and let herself sink into the rhythm of the morning. Two days. She could do this.

She had to.

Melody sat curled into the corner of the couch, knees hugged to her chest, her socked feet barely brushing the carpet. The morning light spilled in through the blinds in quiet slats, washing the room in a soft, almost unreal stillness.

Dr. Halvorsen sat across from her in his usual chair, legs crossed, a yellow notepad resting in his lap though he rarely wrote anything unless it mattered.

"So," he said after a moment, his voice gentle. "Two more days."

Melody nodded, eyes flicking toward the clock before dropping again. "Yeah."

"You've been here almost a week now." He studied her face carefully, not prying, but seeing. "You've done some really hard work in that time. Group, individual. I've noticed you've been sharing more. Letting people in. That's not easy."

Melody shrugged, but her throat tightened. "I guess."

"I know it's uncomfortable," he said, his voice a little softer. "But I also think you're starting to realize that your story matters. That *you* matter."

She blinked quickly, willing the sting in her eyes to go away. "Sometimes it feels like I'm just... saying stuff. Like I open my mouth and the words come out but they don't stick to anything."

Dr. Halvorsen tilted his head. "What do you wish they'd stick to?"

Melody stared down at her hands, twisting the edge of her sleeve. "I don't know. Maybe something real. Something that doesn't vanish when I leave here."

He nodded slowly. "That's what I want to talk about today. Coping. What you take with you when the doors open. Because this place—it's a bubble. Safe, in a way. But real life doesn't stop just because you're doing better."

She looked up at him. "What if I'm not doing better?"

His voice didn't waver. "Then we plan for that, too. Coping isn't about pretending everything's fine. It's about making space for the hard parts. Having tools. Support."

Melody looked away, her voice low. "What if I go home and it all feels the same? My mom... she's not gonna change. And my dad barely looks at me anymore. It's like I'm this... ghost in their house."

"That's why we start with what *you* can control," he said gently. "Small things. Breath work. Journaling. Calling someone you trust. Taking a break from your phone when it gets too loud. You don't have to do it all alone."

"I don't really trust anyone," Melody said after a moment. "Not really. Not like that."

Dr. Halvorsen nodded. "Then maybe you start with you. With building that trust back into yourself."

Melody sat with that. The idea that she might one day feel steady enough to hold herself up. It felt impossible. And yet... she wanted to believe it could be true.

"What if I mess up?" she whispered.

"You will," he said simply. "We all do. The point isn't perfection, Melody. It's choosing to keep trying. To be curious about yourself, even when it's messy."

She swallowed hard. "I don't want to go back and forget everything I felt here."

"Then don't," he said. "Write it down. Say it out loud. Keep the parts of yourself you found here, and let them grow."

She didn't respond right away. But something loosened inside her chest.

Melody didn't feel like she had to disappear to survive

Later that afternoon, Melody found herself sitting in the quiet corner of the common room, her legs crossed, the worn fabric of the couch beneath her a comfort. The sun had shifted, casting a new, softer light across the room, and the usual hum of activity had died down a little.

Ivy appeared first, her quiet presence like a shadow in the doorway. Dani followed, her head low, eyes distant as always, but there was a different weight to her step today—softer somehow, like the pieces of her had clicked back into place after a long, jagged stretch.

"I'm not interrupting, am I?" Ivy asked softly, leaning against the arm of the couch.

Melody shook her head, offering them a small smile. "No, I'm just—thinking."

Dani sat down next to Melody, pulling her knees up to her chest and hugging them tightly. She didn't say anything at first, but the stillness between them wasn't awkward, just... quiet.

"You're leaving in two days, right?" Ivy asked, her eyes flicking to Melody, noting the change in her posture.

"Yeah," Melody murmured, her fingers tracing the edge of the couch. "Two more days."

Ivy's voice softened. "How do you feel about it?"

Melody hesitated. "I don't know. Part of me is... scared? But I guess part of me is ready to leave too. It's just, everything still feels so... *unreal*. I don't know if I can keep it all together once I'm home."

Dani gave a small, understanding nod. "It's hard," she said, her voice quiet but steady. "Leaving here, I mean. You think you're ready, and then you realize how much you're carrying."

"I thought it would feel better. I thought... I'd be different by now," Melody confessed, her voice cracking slightly. "But I'm still me. And I'm still scared. I still feel like I'm going back to the same things that made me fall apart in the first place."

Ivy met her gaze, her expression soft. "You've already made more progress than you realize, Mel. Just being able to say that out loud… that's huge. You don't have to have it all figured out. No one does."

Dani shifted next to her, giving Melody a sideways glance. "I used to think I had to leave this place fixed," she said, her words slow, deliberate. "Like if I left and everything wasn't perfect, then I failed. But that's not how it works. It's more about making the decision to keep showing up for yourself."

"I don't know if I can do that," Melody whispered, her words slipping out before she could catch them. "What if I go back and everything falls apart again? What if I don't know how to be okay?"

Ivy's eyes softened, and she reached over, her fingers finding Melody's hand. "You don't have to be perfect, Mel. Just take it one step at a time. You've been doing it. Even when it's hard."

Dani nodded, her expression serious. "None of us are perfect. But you're strong, and you're learning. That's what matters."

Melody blinked rapidly, a tightness in her chest easing for the first time all day. It wasn't perfect, but she wasn't alone in this. She wasn't expected to do it all herself. The weight she carried didn't have to be hers alone.

"Thanks," Melody whispered, her voice catching slightly. "I— I don't know what I'd do without you two."

Ivy smiled, her fingers gently squeezing Melody's hand. "You'll figure it out, Mel. And no matter what happens, you're not alone here. You've got this."

Dani gave her a quiet but genuine smile. "Yeah. We're all just trying to figure it out together."

Melody managed a shaky smile in return, a warmth spreading through her chest. Maybe the road ahead would be difficult, but at least she knew she wasn't the only one walking it.

CHAPTER TWENTY-TWO

The morning light felt different today. It wasn't just the warm streaks filtering through the room, or the way the air seemed a little fresher than usual, it was something in the way Melody's chest tightened with each passing moment.

Two days had passed since her last therapy session, and now the day she'd been both dreading and waiting for was finally here. It was the day she left the inpatient facility.

The clock on the wall ticked louder today, the sound sharper, like it was counting down to something inevitable. Melody had barely slept, tossing and turning in the quiet hours of the night. Even as the morning unfolded, she felt more restless than calm.

The janitor's cart rolled down the hall outside her room, its wheels squeaking softly on the polished floor. Melody could hear it, but it didn't soothe her the way it usually did. Instead, it just reminded her that her life was about to shift again.

She sat on the edge of her bed, hands wrapped around the edge of her blanket, twisting the fabric between her fingers. The room felt too still. Was she ready for what came next?

Ivy had given her a small smile when they spoke earlier, telling her that she was proud of Melody for making it this far. Dani had only nodded, her usual quiet presence as grounding as ever. Both of them would stay here, where things felt somehow more predictable, even if unpredictable was the last thing any of them wanted to deal with.

Melody wasn't sure if they'd ever fully understand how much harder it was to leave than to stay. But they tried. They understood her in a way, at least.

A soft knock on the door made her jump. It was Dr. Halvorsen, standing there with his usual calm expression, but today, there was something different in his eyes—a quiet sense of finality.

"Good morning, Melody," he said. "You ready?"

The question caught her off guard. She wanted to say no, to tell him she wasn't ready for any of this, but she didn't. She just nodded, the tightness in her throat keeping the words lodged somewhere deep inside.

"I've been thinking about our last session," he said as he stepped inside, holding a small notepad in his hand. "About everything you've shared and the progress you've made. I think you're more prepared than you realize."

Melody glanced up at him, trying not to fidget. His words felt hollow in her ears, because what if she wasn't prepared? What if the world outside was just as hard, if not harder?

"I don't feel prepared," she admitted quietly, her voice wavering just slightly. She quickly wiped her hand over her face as if to push the feeling away.

Dr. Halvorsen nodded, setting his notepad aside. "It's okay to feel that way. It's normal. Leaving here doesn't mean you have to be perfect, or that you'll have everything figured out. But it's a step. And that's all we can do right now, take it one step at a time. You've already started that journey."

His words held weight, but Melody still didn't feel reassured. What if that journey was too heavy? What if she couldn't carry it anymore?

He paused, then added, "I'd like us to talk more about your coping mechanisms. I know we've worked on grounding techniques and mindfulness, and I think it's important to keep practicing those. And if you feel yourself slipping, remember, it's okay to reach out for help. You've got a good foundation here."

Melody stared at her hands, trying to steady the tremor that seemed to be overtaking her. She wasn't sure how to react, how to respond. It was easy to say she'd reach out, but her world felt too big and too uncertain to trust in those promises.

"And," Dr. Halvorsen added, his voice softening, "if you ever feel the urge to hurt yourself again—if those thoughts come back, even just for a moment, use the rubber band trick. Put a rubber band around your wrist, and snap it when you feel the urge. The pain won't be the same, but it can redirect your focus."

Melody blinked, caught off guard by the suggestion. She frowned, unconsciously rubbing her wrist, as though the sensation of it still lingered from the old wounds. *Snap a rubber band?* The idea felt...odd. She didn't want to hurt herself, not anymore, but the thought of inflicting even a small amount of pain, just for the sake of distraction—seemed counterproductive.

"Isn't that just... more pain?" she asked, her voice quiet but curious. "I mean, doesn't it just... hurt in a different way?"

Dr. Halvorsen's gaze softened, and he took a deep breath before speaking. "It's not the same, Melody. The goal is to interrupt the pattern, not to cause harm. It's a way to refocus your mind, to break the cycle of self-destructive thoughts, even if it's only for a moment."

She didn't quite understand, but nodded anyway. It seemed like a strange solution, but if it helped, maybe it was worth trying.

"I'll keep it in mind," she said, though she wasn't entirely convinced.

Dr. Halvorsen's smile was warm, almost encouraging. "I know it's not easy. But remember, you don't have to do it alone. You're not alone, okay?"

Melody nodded again, a quiet storm of uncertainty swirling inside her.

As Dr. Halvorsen left the room, Melody was left alone with the question that seemed to linger in the air: Was she truly ready for the world outside?

The goodbye was quiet.

Melody didn't cry when she hugged Ivy and Dani goodbye, but her chest ached like she was leaving something important behind. Dr. Halvorsen offered her one final nod of encouragement, and then she was walking through the front doors of the facility, the weight of sunlight and freedom both comforting and crushing at once.

Charlotte stood by her car in the parking lot, arms crossed, sunglasses shielding her eyes. Her blonde hair was pulled back tight, not a strand out of place. She didn't step forward, didn't open her arms. Just looked at her daughter like she was someone she had to deal with, not someone she missed.

"Ready?" she asked, as if Melody had any choice.

Melody nodded stiffly and slid into the passenger seat. The familiar scent of her mother's perfume hit her instantly—sharp, floral, suffocating. The car door shut with a heavy thunk. Charlotte didn't say anything as she put the car in gear.

They drove for a while in silence. The road stretched out in front of them, gray and endless. Melody stared out the window, arms tight across her chest. It felt too bright outside. Too fast. She could still hear the hum of the fluorescent lights from the facility in her head.

Charlotte cleared her throat, voice clipped. "We need to stop by your school."

Melody turned sharply. "Why?"

"To pick up your assignments. Your teachers sent down some things for you to work on. I told them you'd be back next week."

"No," Melody said instantly. Her voice came out sharper than she meant, but she didn't care. "I don't want to go there."

Charlotte's jaw tightened. "You have to. It won't take long."

"That's where everything happened. The last time I was there, I—" She cut herself off. She didn't want to revisit the memory of collapsing in the hallway, crying in front of the school nurse, being ushered into a counselor's office she barely remembered. "Can't you just go in without me?"

Charlotte hesitated. For a split second, Melody caught something in her expression—something twitchy, almost guilty. She didn't look at Melody when she replied.

"No. You need to come in. They want to see that you're doing better."

Melody narrowed her eyes. "Why are you acting weird?"

"I'm not," Charlotte snapped too quickly. Her fingers tightened around the steering wheel. "Stop being dramatic."

Melody sat back in her seat, heart pounding. There was something wrong. Her mother's voice was too tight, her posture too rigid. She kept adjusting her sunglasses even though they hadn't moved. Melody couldn't explain it, but a cold knot started forming in her gut.

The school loomed into view, and her stomach flipped. The brick building felt like a monument to everything she was trying to forget.

Charlotte turned into the parking lot without another word.

Melody closed her eyes. Her pulse throbbed in her ears. She had a bad feeling, like something was waiting for her, just beyond the edge of this moment.

She didn't know yet that it was waiting at home.

The car slowed to a stop in the almost-empty parking lot. A few teachers' cars were scattered here and there, but the rest of the lot was quiet, deserted. Melody's eyes traced the familiar shapes of the building, the windows, the entrance she had walked through so many times. She hadn't realized how much she'd been avoiding it until now.

Charlotte killed the engine and got out without waiting for Melody. She walked around the car and opened the passenger door, expecting Melody to follow.

"I'm not going inside," Melody said firmly, staying seated.

Charlotte turned to face her, her face unreadable. "You are. Now come on, we'll be quick."

Melody shook her head. "No. I'm not going in there. Not today."

Charlotte's expression didn't change, but there was a small flicker in her eyes, something that might have been frustration or impatience, but it wasn't really aimed at Melody. It was something else. Something Melody couldn't place.

"Melody," Charlotte said, her voice low and steady, like she was trying to be patient. "You're going in. This is what's expected of you, alright?"

The words hit her like a slap, the tone so cold, so matter-of-fact. Melody's throat tightened, and she turned her gaze away from her mother, staring at the school in front of her, the place that had felt like a prison for weeks now. A place that had swallowed her whole, chewed her up, and spit her back out.

The place where everything fell apart.

"I don't want to," Melody whispered, but Charlotte wasn't listening. She was already halfway to the entrance.

Reluctantly, Melody climbed out of the car and followed her mother, feeling every step drag her closer to something she wasn't ready to face.

The school's doorbell chimed as they entered. A couple of teachers passed by them, nodding curtly, but no one stopped to say anything. Melody felt the weight of their glances, but she didn't meet their eyes.

They made their way down the familiar hallway, and Melody's

heart raced. She kept her head down, not daring to look at the doors, the walls, the lockers. The fluorescent lights buzzed above, filling the space with a low hum that made her feel dizzy.

At the end of the hallway, the school counselor's office loomed. The last time she'd been here, she'd been ushered in for a meeting after the episode. It felt like a lifetime ago.

Charlotte knocked on the door before entering without waiting for a response. Melody stood at the threshold, hesitating, like she was a visitor in someone else's life.

Inside, Mrs. Thompson, the school counselor, looked up from her desk. She didn't stand when she saw them. There was no smile, no warm greeting—just a professional nod.

"Melody," Mrs. Thompson said flatly, her voice business-like, like she was dealing with any other student. "You're here to pick up your schoolwork."

Melody nodded, but didn't speak.

Charlotte didn't wait for the counselor to elaborate, her tone sharp as she crossed her arms. "Is that everything?"

Mrs. Thompson didn't seem to mind Charlotte's impatience. "Yes, that's all. Here," she said, pushing a thick folder across the desk to Melody without further explanation. "These are the assignments you need to make up. I'd suggest getting started on them as soon as possible. School will want you back on track quickly."

Melody hesitated, her fingers brushing the edge of the folder. She could feel the weight of it, but it wasn't just the paper that made it heavy. It was the weight of returning to a place that had never felt like home, a place that had only served as a reminder of everything that had gone wrong.

Charlotte didn't wait for Melody to react. She grabbed the folder from the desk and turned toward the door. "We're done here," she said curtly, without another word.

Melody didn't protest. She grabbed the folder and followed her mother out of the office, but the walk back to the car felt longer than it had any right to. The walls of the school seemed to close in on her, and every step away from the counselor's office was a step closer to something she couldn't escape.

When they reached the car, Charlotte was already in the driver's seat. Melody didn't get in right away. Instead, she just stood there, staring at the school for a moment longer.

It was the place where everything started to unravel.

It was the place where she had always felt like an outsider.

As the car pulled into the driveway, Melody's stomach sank. A police cruiser was parked in front of the house. An officer was leaning against it, his arms crossed, watching them as they pulled up.

"What's going on?" Melody asked, her voice quiet but edged with confusion.

Charlotte didn't answer immediately. Her hands gripped the steering wheel so tightly that her knuckles turned white. She stared straight ahead, the tension in her posture radiating through the car. After a long moment, she exhaled sharply and shifted the car into park, but she didn't move to get out.

"Mom?" Melody asked again, her voice rising slightly, trying to catch her mother's attention.

Charlotte's gaze flickered toward her for just a second before she opened the door, her movements stiff and deliberate. "Stay in the car," she snapped, her voice flat and tense.

Melody hesitated, her mind racing with questions. She watched her mom approach the officer, her posture still rigid, but now it was clear that something was off. She couldn't make out what they were saying, but Charlotte spoke with a low, controlled tone, glancing at Melody occasionally, her face hard to read.

Melody stayed in the car, her hands clenched in her lap as she watched her mom's interaction with the officer. It felt wrong, like there was something happening that she wasn't being told. Charlotte didn't seem herself—tense, almost like she was trying to keep something contained. The officer nodded, his expression serious as he stood there, his gaze occasionally flicking toward the car where Melody sat.

It wasn't long before Charlotte finished speaking with the officer. She turned toward Melody and gave her a sharp look. "Come inside," she said, her voice colder than usual. "Now."

Confused and still uneasy, Melody opened the door and stepped out of the car, glancing nervously at the officer, who was now following them up the porch steps. He didn't speak as he followed behind them, just walking in step with Charlotte, his eyes flickering between her and Melody, his face unreadable.

The door creaked as Charlotte pushed it open, stepping aside so that Melody could enter. The officer followed closely behind them, his footsteps heavier in the quiet house. The air felt thick, charged with something Melody couldn't quite grasp. The officer's presence made her even more uneasy, as though the house itself was holding its breath.

But before they went farther in, something small and familiar streaked across the hallway floor. Melody blinked—and then smiled weakly.

"Wednesday..." she whispered.

The black cat padded into view, meowing softly as she approached Melody with slow, cautious steps, tail upright and twitching. As soon as Melody knelt down, Wednesday pushed her head into her hands and purred, loud and urgent.

Melody's breath hitched, and she wrapped her arms around the cat, burying her face in the thick black fur. A tear slipped down her cheek.

"I missed you," she whispered into Wednesday's fur, her voice cracking. "I missed you so much."

Wednesday nuzzled against her chin and purred even louder, like she somehow knew something was wrong. In that small moment, kneeling on the tile floor with her cat in her arms,

Melody felt her heart clench. Everything else was falling apart, but Wednesday was still here.

The officer paused, watching them silently. Even Charlotte didn't say anything—just looked on, her arms folded tightly across her chest.

After a few moments, Melody slowly stood, still holding Wednesday close to her chest.

"I'm Officer Hayes," the man finally said, his voice calm and steady. "I just wanted to introduce myself before we sit down to talk. I know this might be a bit unsettling for you..." His tone was reassuring, his eyes kind, as if he were aware of how strange it all must feel for her.

Melody's heart was pounding in her chest, her palms slick with sweat. She couldn't help the feeling that something wasn't right. Her mind kept circling around Lucian—is the officer here because of him? What had happened? Why did a police officer need to speak to her about him?

"What's going on?" she asked, the question slipping out before she could stop it. Her voice wavered slightly, betraying the confusion and worry that knotted in her stomach.

Officer Hayes took a moment before answering, his expression soft but serious. He motioned for her to sit on the couch, and Charlotte took a seat across from her, arms crossed, looking anywhere but at her daughter. The officer settled into the chair next to Melody, not too close but close enough to show he was trying to offer some comfort.

"I understand this might be difficult to hear, Melody," Officer Hayes said, his voice gentle. "But we need to talk about Lucian Rodríguez."

Her breath caught in her throat, and for a moment, the room seemed to shrink around her. She opened her mouth, but no sound came out.

He continued, his voice steady. "There are concerns about your relationship with him, and I'd like to have a conversation about it. It's important that we understand everything that's been going on."

Melody felt a chill spread through her body, her mind scrambling to make sense of it. Lucian? What did they know? What had happened?

"What do you mean, 'concerns'?" she asked, her voice trembling as she finally found her words. "What's going on with him?"

Officer Hayes looked at her with empathy, his brow furrowed just slightly. "We're investigating some serious matters regarding Lucian's involvement with you. And we need to make sure you're safe. That's our priority right now, Melody."

Her mind raced, thoughts whirling in a dizzying spiral. Safe? What was he talking about? Safe from what? From Lucian?

Melody's hands clenched tightly in her lap, and she swallowed hard, trying to process the flood of emotions and confusion that rushed through her. "What are you investigating? What exactly do you think happened?"

"I can't get into too much detail just yet," Officer Hayes explained, his voice calm and soothing. "But we need to talk about everything that's been happening between you and him. Anything you can share will help us understand the situation."

For a moment, Melody didn't know what to say. She wanted to lash out, to demand answers, to scream at him that she didn't know what they were talking about. But deep down, something in her knew that she was the one who had to talk. If she kept quiet, everything might spiral further out of control.

"I—" She paused, her voice faltering. "I don't know what you're talking about. I... I don't know how to explain. We just talked, that's all. He was nice to me. He listened when no one else did."

Officer Hayes nodded, his eyes full of understanding. "I'm not here to judge, Melody. I'm just trying to understand. It's really important that we have this conversation. The more open you can be with me, the better I can help you."

The words didn't sink in right away, but Melody felt herself getting lost in them, feeling the weight of everything coming crashing down in a way she hadn't expected. Lucian—he wasn't just someone she'd trusted, someone who had been kind to her when no one else had. Now, he was at the center of all this confusion and suspicion.

The officer gave her a small, reassuring smile. "Take your time, Melody. We're here to listen. And when you're ready, we can talk more about what happened between you and Lucian."

CHAPTER TWENTY-THREE

Melody's hands were clammy as she sat in the living room, the weight of Officer Hayes's words settling heavily in her chest. His voice had been calm, but there was something about his demeanor—something about the way he was watching her—that made the room feel colder, more suffocating. The sound of her own heartbeat was louder than it had ever been before, pounding in her ears, as if her body was trying to warn her of something she couldn't quite grasp.

Charlotte sat across from her, arms crossed, her face unreadable. The silence between them felt thick and oppressive, like the walls were closing in. Melody's mind raced, bouncing between thoughts and questions she couldn't quite answer. *What had Lucian done? What did they know?* She couldn't make sense of it all, but her gut was screaming that something was wrong.

Officer Hayes shifted in his chair, his eyes never leaving Melody's. His gaze was gentle, but there was a determination there, too. He wasn't just here to ask questions, he was here for answers. And the more he stared at her, the more Melody wanted to curl up and disappear. She couldn't stand this.

She had to say something. *But what? What could she say?*

Her mouth felt dry, her tongue thick. Finally, she blurted out, "I don't know what you want me to say. I—I didn't do anything wrong."

Her voice wavered, betraying her, and she hated it. Hated how small she felt.

Officer Hayes leaned forward slightly, his voice still soft but insistent. "Melody, I'm not here to accuse you of anything. I just need to understand what happened, what kind of relationship you had with Lucian."

Her throat tightened, the words she wanted to say trapped somewhere deep inside her. *She trusted him,* she thought. *He listened when no one else did. He understood her.* But now, everything was turning upside down. Was Lucian really the person she thought he was? Had she been blind to something she didn't want to see?

Melody shook her head, trying to shake off the panic that was beginning to settle deep in her chest. *No. No, this couldn't be happening.*

The officer watched her carefully, waiting for a response, but the longer she stayed silent, the harder it became to breathe. She could feel the sweat pooling on her palms, and the tremor in her hands was undeniable.

"Please, Melody," Officer Hayes pressed gently, his voice just the slightest bit more insistent. "You don't have to be afraid to talk to me. I'm here to help you."

The words didn't bring comfort. Instead, they made her feel even more exposed, like a fish caught in a net. *What did he mean by 'help'?* She felt trapped, like she was sinking deeper into a quicksand of confusion and fear.

"I don't know what you want me to say," she repeated, her voice quieter this time, as if the words were somehow less real when she said them aloud. "I—I don't understand what's going on. What's wrong with me talking to him?"

Her eyes flicked to her mother, who had said nothing, just sat there with her arms tightly crossed. Charlotte was like a statue—distant, cold. Melody's stomach twisted painfully. It felt like Charlotte was keeping something from her, like there was something she wasn't saying. *Why wasn't she helping? Why wasn't she defending me?*

Officer Hayes gave a slight nod, and for a moment, the silence between them felt even heavier than before. "Melody, I understand this is difficult for you. But we need to be clear about what happened. Lucian isn't just anyone. He's under investigation for something very serious, and we need to hear your side. Whatever you can tell us will help."

The words felt like ice being poured down her spine. *Investigation. Serious. What did that even mean? What had Lucian done?*

She opened her mouth, but the words wouldn't come. Her breath caught in her throat. *What if this wasn't just about Lucian? What if this was about her?*

Her hands fisted in her lap, nails digging into her palms. She wasn't sure if she wanted to run, scream, or just vanish. The world around her felt as if it were spinning out of control, and she was stuck in the middle of it, trying desperately to hold on to something real, something that made sense.

"I—" She choked on the words, feeling heat rise in her chest as embarrassment flooded her veins. "We started out as friends. Just talking. He... he understood me. No one else really did." Melody's voice wavered. "He cared about me, and he told me I was special." She felt the weight of the confession, like a heavy stone lodged in her throat. She didn't want to admit it, not even to herself. But it felt too real, too undeniable now.

The officer leaned in, his eyes still steady but more focused, as if he could sense the tension tightening around Melody's chest. "Were you dating?" he asked, his tone matter-of-fact but gentle.

Melody's face flushed. The heat surged in her cheeks, and she looked down, ashamed. Her mind raced, but the answer felt so obvious, so painful. "Yes," she whispered, barely audible. "We were dating."

Officer Hayes nodded slowly, his eyes soft but searching. "I've seen the messages between you two," he said, his voice even and calm. "This is a very serious matter, Melody."

A cold shiver ran down Melody's spine, her heart hammering in her chest. *Which messages?* The weight of what he said landed like a heavy blow. She wanted to deny it, to say they were wrong, that they didn't know the whole story, but she knew it wouldn't help. The words were out there, beyond her control.

"Was there any communication outside of text messages?" Officer Hayes asked, his voice still calm, but the urgency in his words was palpable.

Melody hesitated, her hands shaking in her lap. She felt so small, so exposed. "We... we talked on the computer and had phone calls sometimes." She winced as the words left her mouth. It felt like a confession, even though she didn't know what it meant, what it implied. She wanted to protect him. She wanted to protect herself. But it felt like the more she said, the more she was digging herself into a hole.

Officer Hayes gave a small, understanding nod, but there was no mistaking the seriousness in his expression. "I need to know everything, Melody. How far did this relationship go?"

The question made her stomach flip. Her chest felt tight, her breath shallow. She wanted to lie, to say it was just innocent, just words. But that wasn't true. *How could she protect Lucian? How could she protect herself?*

She swallowed, her voice trembling as she spoke. "I—I don't know... It... it went too far, I guess." Her eyes fell to the floor, not able to meet anyone's gaze.

Officer Hayes's voice softened. "It's okay, Melody. You're not in trouble. I just need you to be honest with me."

But the words didn't comfort her. She wanted to scream, to tell him that Lucian had been kind to her, that he had cared when no one else did. But she was too ashamed, too embarrassed, to voice those things now.

Officer Hayes waited, his expression full of patience, but Melody felt her face burn with humiliation.

Finally, she whispered, "It... it became sexual."

Charlotte's reaction was immediate—she shot up from her seat, her face twisting in disbelief and outrage. "What?!" she snapped, her voice rising, sharp with anger and shock.

Melody's heart broke at the sound of her mother's voice, the hurt and shame laced into her tone. She could feel the tears building up, threatening to spill over.

Before she could respond, the dam broke, and tears streamed down her face. The emotions she had buried so deeply, the confusion, the guilt, and the shame, all spilled out in a rush, too much to hold back any longer. She couldn't stop herself.

Officer Hayes, still calm, turned to Charlotte. "Maybe it's best we take a break," he said quietly, his voice soft and kind, but firm. "Let her have a moment."

Charlotte stood frozen, her face twisted with anger, but she didn't say anything. She just turned and walked to the other side of the room, muttering to herself, as Melody's sobs filled the room.

The break didn't last long, but it was long enough for Melody to catch her breath, if only for a moment. She'd gotten a glass of water from the kitchen, her hands trembling as she tried to steady herself. The cold liquid didn't seem to help, and she could still feel the weight of Officer Hayes's questions pressing against her chest, suffocating her.

As she returned to the living room, Wednesday wove silently between her ankles. The soft brush of fur startled Melody at first, but she looked down and gave the cat a weak smile. She scooped Wednesday into her arms and held her tightly against her chest, feeling the soft rumble of purring begin beneath her fingers. It helped. Just a little.

Charlotte, meanwhile, had retreated to the far end of the room, trying to compose herself. Her back was to Melody, and her shoulders were shaking ever so slightly. Was she crying, too? Melody couldn't tell. Was it real? Or was this just another act— another performance in a life that was full of nothing but masks and pretenses?

The officer gave her a moment to regain some composure, but when he spoke again, it was clear they were not finished. His voice was still gentle, but there was a firmness in it now, a quiet determination that made Melody want to shrink further into herself.

"I know this is hard, Melody," Officer Hayes said, his voice steady and kind. "But I have to ask these questions. It's important we understand the full scope of the situation, okay? We need to keep going."

She nodded, her throat tight, barely able to respond. She was terrified, but she felt cornered, like there was nowhere left to hide. Her eyes flitted to Charlotte, who had stopped sobbing but was still wiping at her eyes, as though trying to pull herself together. Was she still angry? Was she really upset, or was this some twisted game she played? Melody couldn't tell anymore.

Wednesday shifted in her arms, curling into her lap as Melody sat back down. She ran her fingers absently through the cat's fur, grounding herself with the familiar rhythm.

The officer cleared his throat, bringing Melody's attention back to him. "You confirmed earlier that you had a sexual relationship with Lucian. I need to understand what you mean by that, specifically. We know he lives out of state, so what did this relationship look like?"

Melody's heart pounded painfully in her chest. Her mind was swirling with a thousand thoughts, all of them full of shame and guilt. *How could I explain this?* she thought. *How could I possibly say it out loud?*

Her hands were shaking so much that even petting Wednesday became difficult. She swallowed hard before speaking, her voice barely a whisper, "We would... we'd send each other pictures." Her cheeks burned, and she could feel the heat crawling up her neck. "Suggestive pictures," she added, barely audible.

The officer's expression softened, though his eyes never left her. He nodded slowly, and then, after a moment's pause, asked, "Did he send you pictures of his genitals?"

The shame that filled her chest felt like it was suffocating her, and she could feel her face burning with embarrassment. She wanted to say no, to deny it, but the truth was there, heavy and undeniable.

"Y-yes," she stammered, her voice small and trembling. "He sent me pictures... of his... of his genitals."

Charlotte gasped loudly, and the sound pierced through Melody. Melody's heart thudded painfully in her chest. Her mother stood abruptly, her hand pressed to her mouth, eyes wide with shock, and then she started crying.

Melody's mind couldn't process the tears fast enough. Was she really crying? Was she upset, or was this just another act? Melody's thoughts spiraled, unsure of what to believe anymore.

Wednesday jumped down from her lap with a soft thud, trotting to the far corner and curling up on a blanket with a flick of her tail, like she'd had enough of the tension in the room.

The officer's gaze never wavered from Melody. His tone remained calm and empathetic as he spoke, "Melody, I know this is difficult, but I need to ask you a few more questions. Did you send him pictures as well?"

Melody couldn't breathe, couldn't focus on anything except the crushing shame that clung to her. She wanted to say no, to take it all back, but the truth clawed its way out of her, and she couldn't stop herself.

"Yes," she whispered, her voice barely audible. "I... I sent him pictures."

Her stomach twisted with disgust, and the tears started falling again, hot and fast. What had she done? She couldn't take it back. She couldn't change what had already happened. How had it gone this far?

The officer nodded again, though his expression remained solemn. "Did you send these pictures of your own accord, or did Lucian ask you to send them?"

Melody's body trembled. The shame was unbearable, the guilt too much to carry. She clenched her fists in her lap, willing herself not to fall apart. But she knew she couldn't lie. Not now. Not when the truth was already laid out in front of her.

"He... he asked me to send them," Melody said quietly, her voice breaking on the words. She wanted to hide, wanted to crawl into a hole and never come out, but there was no escape now. No easy way to take back what she had done.

Hayes's voice was still soft, but steady. "Did he ask for any other kinds of pictures?"

"Yes," she said, barely above a whisper. "He... he asked me to send him pictures of me in the shower."

Officer Hayes's voice was quiet, gentle, but full of the gravity of the situation. "Melody, I know this is hard. But I need you to understand how serious this is. What you've told me... this is illegal. And Lucian, he's the one who took this too far. But I need to hear everything. You're doing the right thing by talking to me."

Melody's heart felt like it was breaking all over again, but she nodded. She wanted to believe that she was doing the right thing. She just wished the right thing didn't feel so awful.

Suddenly, Charlotte shot up from the couch, her voice sharp and defensive.

"There weren't any pictures like that on her phone," she snapped, pointing an accusing hand toward Melody. "Her father and I looked. We checked when she was in the facility."

Melody blinked, her throat tightening again. Her voice was barely a whisper. "I deleted them."

Charlotte turned toward Officer Hayes, her face twisted in confusion and fury. "Can you still find them? I mean, can the police get photos that have been deleted?"

Hayes nodded calmly. "Yes. Depending on the phone and how long ago it was, our forensics team can often recover deleted files."

Charlotte's face contorted with rage. "Then do it. That sick bastard is a predator. I want him arrested. I want him behind bars."

And that was the moment Melody broke.

"No!" she shouted, her voice ragged and desperate. "No, please! Don't arrest him! Please!"

Her body shook as the sobs came in waves, her fists clenched in helplessness.

Tears streamed down her cheeks as she tried to speak through the storm in her throat.

"It wasn't just him. It was me too! It's my fault—I let it happen!"

Hayes leaned forward, his voice low but firm. "Melody, no. I need you to hear me—this is not your fault. You are a child. He is an adult. The law is very clear about that."

She could hardly breathe. "But I loved him. I *love* him. I didn't want to hurt him. I never wanted any of this to happen. Please don't press charges. Please..."

Her eyes pleaded with his, full of devastation.

The officer's expression softened, but the weight in his voice didn't ease.

"Melody... the police in Lucian's town have already spoken to him."

Melody froze.

Hayes continued carefully, watching her reaction. "He admitted that he was in a relationship with you. He said you two were close, but he left out certain details. The ones you're telling me now."

She felt like she'd been stabbed in the chest.

Lucian talked to the police.

He told them about her, but not the truth. Not *all* of it.

And now she had.

The betrayal sank in, slow and cold. Her hands shook as she stared at the floor.

She had told. She had given him up. Even if she hadn't meant to.

And the guilt... it was unbearable.

"I didn't mean to betray him," she whispered, more to herself than to anyone else. "I just... I thought he loved me."

Her voice cracked again. "I thought he understood me."

"I didn't want this," Melody choked out. "I just wanted someone to care."

The room fell silent except for the sound of her shaky breathing. Charlotte sat frozen beside her, lips pressed into a tight line, her eyes unreadable.

Officer Hayes leaned forward, his tone still gentle, but firm. "Melody... I need you to know that none of this is your fault. But this situation is serious. The law exists to protect you from exactly this kind of relationship. It never should've happened."

Melody's eyes filled again, her voice raw. "Please... I'm not going to talk to him anymore. I swear. It's over. I won't ever speak to him again, just...please...don't press charges. Don't arrest him. I couldn't live with that. I just... I couldn't."

She looked at Officer Hayes with a desperate, pleading gaze that made her seem younger than she was. Despite everything, some part of her still wanted to protect Lucian. She still believed that love meant loyalty, even now.

Charlotte stood, arms crossed tightly. "So what happens now? After everything she just admitted?"

Officer Hayes looked between them both, then exhaled slowly. "This isn't easy. But Melody's been honest. She's cooperating. And right now, our focus needs to be on protecting her, not punishing her, or escalating this unless we have to."

Charlotte's jaw clenched. "So you're not pressing charges?"

"No," Officer Hayes said. "Not at this time. But I'm going to contact Lucian's local department. He *will* be told that he is not to contact Melody again. If he does, if he even tries, we will move forward with pressing charges. There will be no warnings. No second chances."

Charlotte nodded, reluctantly. "Good. He's a predator. He needs to be put in his place."

Melody broke then, her shoulders collapsing as she cried, a strange, confused mix of relief and heartbreak. She had protected him, but a piece of her knew it was the end.

"We're going to help you, Melody," Officer Hayes said gently, but firmly. "You deserve safety. You deserve to heal."

Charlotte didn't say anything as she sat back down beside Melody, her face pale and unreadable. The silence between them was thick—too many things unsaid, too many wounds suddenly exposed.

Officer Hayes stood, gathering his notepad and voice recorder, but his gaze remained on Melody. "You've been very brave today. I know it doesn't feel that way right now, but it will. One day. This was the first step."

Melody nodded faintly, but didn't speak. She felt emptied out, like something had been carved from her chest and left gaping.

"We'll be in touch," he added, glancing at Charlotte. "And if he reaches out in any way, you contact me immediately. No hesitation. Understand?"

Charlotte nodded. "I will."

The officer gave them both a last look—half reassurance, half warning, before stepping out of the room and quietly closing the door behind him.

Melody stared down at her hands, her fingers twisting in the fabric of her sleeves. Her chest ached with a kind of sorrow that had no shape—just heaviness. Shame. Confusion. A longing for something she wasn't even sure was real anymore.

Charlotte sat stiffly beside her. For a long time, neither of them spoke.

Finally, Charlotte let out a breath. "You should've told me."

Melody's throat tightened, her voice no more than a whisper. "Would you have listened?"

Silence again.

And then Charlotte, for once, didn't have anything to say.

CHAPTER TWENTY-FOUR

The soft flicker of candlelight painted trembling shadows across Melody's bedroom walls. The scent of lavender and vanilla hung heavy in the air—once comforting, now cloying, like sweetness gone stale.

Her journal lay open on the bed. The pages were soaked with tears, the words blurred and streaked like bruises. Ink stained her fingers, her palms, her wrists. Her handwriting grew more frantic with each entry—rambling, raw.

She'd been writing for hours, maybe more. The clock had lost all meaning. The thoughts wouldn't stop. They spilled out in loops and scribbles and dark, heavy words she barely recognized as her own.

Wednesday curled at her feet like a silent shadow. Her eyes glinted in the candlelight, half-lidded but watchful. Every so often, she stretched a paw toward her leg or blinked slowly, as if to remind her that she wasn't entirely alone. When her breath hitched or her pen trembled, she responded with a soft purr or a gentle nudge of her head, grounding her in the quietest way.

I don't know how to do this without him.
I feel like he's dead and I'm the one who killed him.
I keep going back and forth. Was it real? Was I just
something for him to play with? But then why did it
feel like the only thing that ever made sense?
I think I broke something inside me.
I feel disgusting.
I'm scared I'll always need him, even if it's killing me.
I hate myself for missing him.

The stereo played low from the corner of the room, her chosen painkiller, "Broken" by Seether feat Amy Lee starts to play.

Amy Lee's voice wept through the speakers, merging with Shaun Morgan's anguish.

Tears poured from Melody again. As if the song was slicing her from the inside out.

She clutched the pillow to her chest, rocking gently, her breath shuddering. The words carved into her, finding every hollow place he left behind.

I know what he did was wrong. I know what he
asked from me wasn't okay. But he made me feel like I
mattered. He made me feel like I was beautiful. Not
just my body...but me. All of me. No one else ever has.

A sob ripped out of her, harsh and guttural.

She stood abruptly, as if needing to run from the weight, from herself. But instead, her eyes landed on her vanity.

Her phone.

She hadn't even thought about it since that awful afternoon. She had assumed it had been confiscated, erased, destroyed. But there it was. Sitting quietly under the soft glow of the string lights. Waiting.

Almost without thinking, like she wasn't in her body, Melody stepped toward it. Her hand hovered over it for a moment. Then she picked it up and turned it on.

Dozens of notifications flashed across the lock screen. **Lucian.**

> Where are you??

> I'm getting really worried. Please answer.

> Melody? Please baby I'm freaking out.

> You didn't say goodnight.

> I can't sleep without hearing from you.

> Did something happen??

> Melody please I'm going crazy.

> I love you. Please don't do this.

> Baby doll???

> I'm scared.

She stared at the screen, the tears falling harder now. Her hand shook as she scrolled through message after message. The tone shifted—first worried, then pleading, then slightly panicked. But always loving. Always him.

Her breath hitched violently.

He didn't know the police had come. That she had told. That it was over.

And her parents—how had they not deleted this?

More notifications blinked in:

Jace:

> Mel, what's going on? You okay? Heard some
> stuff from your mom. Please answer.

Anna:

> Mel?? You okay?? Please just send me a
> thumbs up or something. I'm really worried.

Melody didn't open those. She couldn't. She couldn't take in love that was real right now. She only had space for the ghost that was still haunting her through glowing text bubbles.

She sat down slowly at the edge of her bed, still scrolling, still reading Lucian's texts.

> I don't want this to be the end.

> Please don't let this be the end.

> I can't breathe without you.

Melody's thumb hovered over the reply box. Her whole body trembled. Her breath quickened.

Don't do it, something whispered.

But she couldn't stop herself.

She typed fast, frantic.

> Please. I need to talk to you. Please don't shut
> me out.

She stared at the screen, heart pounding.

Nothing.

She typed again.

> Please Lucian. I'm losing it. I don't know what
> to do. Please just say something. Just tell me
> you're okay. Tell me you don't hate me for what
> happened.

Still nothing.

Her breathing grew more erratic.

PLEASE. I NEED YOU. I CAN'T DO THIS.

Still silence.

She sobbed as she typed again.

I love you. I still love you. Please don't let this be the end.

Then—dots. He was typing.

Her heart nearly stopped. She held her breath.

The dots disappeared.

Gone.

She let out a choked scream and threw the phone across the room.

Her whole body shook. She couldn't take it. Couldn't take the silence. The not knowing. The guilt. The shame. The ache that wouldn't let go.

Her eyes darted to her nightstand drawer. Her hands moved before her mind caught up. She opened it.

There, tucked underneath an old notebook, was the razor.

She pulled it out with trembling fingers. Her vision blurred with tears, her breath uneven, shallow. She didn't want to think. She just wanted the pain to quiet for a second. Just one second of stillness. Of silence.

"Don't," she whispered to herself. "Don't be this girl again."

But she already was.

Wednesday, startled by the noise, padded over to her side and rubbed against her leg. Melody hardly registered the soft weight of her against her skin, too lost in the chaos of her thoughts. Her presence was a distant comfort, a small reminder that she wasn't alone, even when it felt like she was falling apart.

She sat on the floor. Pressed the cold metal to her skin.

She tried to pause. Just for a second. But her hand moved anyway.

The sting came quick and sharp. The relief, like a rush of numbness washing through her veins.

Then again. Another line. Deeper. Her breathing shook as blood welled up, staining the edge of her sleeve.

Wednesday gave a soft mew, as if sensing her pain, her fur brushing against her arm. Melody barely noticed, her mind too tangled in the ache inside her chest. Wednesday nuzzled her, purring, curling against her side, but her focus was elsewhere, lost in the storm of her emotions.

"Why can't I stop?" she hissed, voice cracking. "What the hell is wrong with me?"

She looked down at her arm, her body, her hands—disgust and shame rising like bile. "Why do I keep doing this? Why do I always ruin everything?"

Her sobs turned silent, mouth open but no sound coming. Just tears. Just blood. Just music.

She dropped the razor. Her body folded in on itself. Her arms wrapped around her legs, rocking again, slower now. Spent.

Wednesday, undeterred, curled next to her and pressed against her side, her purring a steady comfort. Melody didn't know why, but her presence felt like a small anchor in the middle of the storm.

Her phone vibrated.

She crawled toward it like it was the only thing tethering her to life.

Three new messages.

Lucian.

We're not supposed to talk again. But I want
you to know something.

I love you. And it wasn't over.

It will never be over.

Melody stared at the screen.
She didn't see the blood on the screen.
Only his name. Still glowing.
"...It will never be over."

EPILOGUE

Dear Younger Me,

I see you.

You're sitting in the dark, phone in hand, waiting for a voice to tell you that you matter. And when it comes, it feels like warmth. Like someone finally *sees* you. You think maybe this is what love is supposed to feel like. But deep down, there's a tightness in your chest. Something doesn't feel quite right, even when your heart wants it to.

I want you to know:

It wasn't your fault.

You were never too much. Never too weird. Never too emotional or dramatic or difficult. You were a child craving love, safety, and understanding. He gave you attention, but it came with control. That wasn't love. It was manipulation wrapped in false intimacy.

But *you*—you were real.

Your laughter, your fears, your dreams, your need to be held without strings attached—that was all sacred. And none of that was ever too much.

I love you. I will keep fighting for you. I will speak your story into the world so that no one can ever silence you again.

You survived something that tried to swallow you whole. And now, you're rising. Not in spite of what happened, but with the strength you've built from it.

But I need to warn you.

There will come a time, maybe when things are quiet, or when life feels heavy again—where you'll feel that same pull toward what once felt like safety. You'll miss the way it made you feel seen. You'll wonder, *what if it wasn't all bad?*

Please remember this: ***longing isn't proof that something was good for you.***

Not everything we miss deserves to be let back in.

The healing you're searching for isn't behind you. It's within you.

One day, you will feel peace.

And until then, I'm here. I won't abandon you.

If you've made it this far, I want to extend my deepest gratitude for walking with Melody through some of the darkest and most painful moments of her life. Writing this book wasn't easy, and revisiting these emotions was at times even harder. But my hope in sharing this story is to give a voice to those who have felt manipulated, controlled, or lost in the depths of unhealthy relationships, particularly those who have experienced the dangers of grooming.

This story is not just Melody's—it's mine too, in many ways. I've experienced the confusion, the emotional manipulation, and the heartache of feeling torn between what's right and what you believe you need. In sharing Melody's journey, I want anyone reading this who has faced similar struggles to know that you are not alone, and that there is always a way to find your strength, even in the darkest of times. Healing, as difficult as it is, always begins with taking that first step.

This book is the product of my own healing process. It's my first book, and writing it has been both therapeutic and cathartic. An unexpected form of release for emotions I didn't fully understand until they were put into words. Through Melody, I've explored the deep complexity of attachment, the pain of toxic relationships, and the ongoing journey toward self-realization. But this story is not intended to glorify or romanticize the relationship between Melody and Lucian.

Lucian, much like others in real life who manipulate and control, is a complicated character. He is not a savior or a hero, he is a reflection of something darker. This isn't a love story in the way that we often romanticize unhealthy connections, and I want to make that clear. Melody's journey with Lucian is not one that should be admired or sought after. It's a story of struggle, of breaking free, of learning to reclaim one's own life, and ultimately, of realizing that some attachments must be severed for the sake of one's well-being.

Grooming, like the relationship between Melody and Lucian, is often subtle and can be incredibly difficult to recognize until it has gone too far. The dangers of grooming are real, and the emotional manipulation that comes with it can be devastating. If you or someone you know is experiencing manipulation or grooming, I encourage you to seek support. There is no shame in reaching out to those who care about your well-being. Please understand that you deserve relationships where you are treated with respect, kindness, and love—not control and manipulation.

The ending of this book doesn't close the door on Melody's story, but it also doesn't promise a perfect resolution. Her journey is far from over. And while the pull to Lucian is strong, it's important to remember that healing doesn't always follow a straight path—it's messy, it's painful, and it takes time. There is more to come, and in the next chapter of her life, Melody will have to face even harder truths about herself, Lucian, and the consequences of their choices.

Thank you for taking this journey with me. Please remember, you deserve to be in relationships that uplift and support you. No one should ever make you feel like you are less than, or that your worth is tied to someone else's validation. If you are in a place where you are struggling with unhealthy attachments, there are people who care and want to help. You are not alone.

And as for Melody and Lucian—well, their story isn't over. But be warned: it's not a story of love as we often think of it. It's a complicated and painful journey, one that still has much more to unravel. I hope you'll continue on with me, as we explore what comes next.

With love,
Courtney

ACKNOWLEDGMENTS

To the girl I used to be,

You carried so much without a map, only a heartbeat and hope.

This book is a love letter to your resilience,
to the voice you thought no one would ever hear.
Now they will.

To those who hold these pages,

Thank you for your open hands, your open heart.
You are witnessing a reclamation,
a slow burning back to self.
May you find reflections of your own courage here.

To my husband, Rob,

You have loved me through silence, storms, and unraveling.
Thank you for seeing me even when I couldn't look at myself.
For giving me the safety I never knew I was allowed to want.
For being my rock.

To my sons, Axel and Trent,

You are joy in its purest form.
You remind me that light can be born from shadow.
I hope you grow up knowing how to protect your tenderness and respect it in others.

To Jenn (my therapist),

You helped me walk through fire with bare feet and come out softer.

Not scorched.

Thank you for holding the pieces until I could hold them myself.

I would not have made it here without you.

To survivors,

Especially those who loved their abuser, who questioned their memories.

Who stayed quiet because no one ever asked them to speak...

This story is for you.

I will not name the past, but I will name the truth:

What happened to you was real.

And so is your healing.

Hi, I'm Courtney Young. I was born and raised in Pennsylvania, and I've always felt drawn to the parts of life that most people tend to avoid—grief, trauma, death, and the kind of beauty that lives in broken things. Writing has been a way for me to process all of it. I write to understand myself, to make sense of pain, and to hold space for the parts of us that don't usually get spoken aloud.

Where the Darkness Found Me is more than just my debut novel. It's a story I lived in pieces, a reflection of my past, and a way to give voice to the version of me that didn't know how to speak up back then. Melody came to me slowly, quietly, and over time, she became impossible to ignore. This book is her story—but it's mine, too.

Right now, I'm studying Mortuary Science and working in a funeral home. I've always believed that death deserves tenderness, and I feel honored to be learning how to care for people in their final moments with reverence and respect. Outside of that, I'm a lover of horror movies, true crime, Halloween, and anything a little eerie or strange.

I live with my husband Rob, who is my grounding force, our two sons Axel and Trent, and a house full of animals. When I'm not writing or studying, you can usually find me wrapped in a blanket, reading a book, lighting too many candles, and being a little witchy.

Thank you for holding this story in your hands. It means more than you know.

I'm currently writing the second installment of Melody's story, and what comes next is darker, deeper, and undeniably real. The shadows still have secrets left to tell.

Find me where the strange things bloom:

instagram.com/courtleayoung
tiktok.com/@graymourning
goodreads.com/graymourning